Declaration of Independence

Han stared into her com screen at Simon Hodah's worrie[illegible] reading the fear and fury in his eyes [illegible]n in hers. His mo[illegible]s voice was harsh[illegible]

"Captain Li, [illegible]s of War. You [illegible]d person at once, [illegible]ce Admiral Eric Hale. You will heav[illegible]ait my boarding party. Officers designated by myself will relieve you of command and place you under close arrest to await trial. This is a direct order, logged and taped. You may authenticate with Admiral Hale."

"Captain Hodah," Han said softly to her old friend, "I must respectfully refuse your order."

"You have no authority to refuse!" Even the rage in Hodah's voice couldn't hide the pleading under his fury. "Now cut your shields and get out of my way, Captain, or by the living God, I'll blow you apart!"

Han looked around her bridge crew. Every set of shoulders was tense, every face knotted with tension, but not a voice protested as she turned back to her superior officer. God, she was proud of them!

She raised her eyes once more to Simon's. She knew him so well. He *would* fire—indeed, she would leave him no option—and when *Enwright* and the superdreadnoughts fired, *Longbow* would die. No battle-cruiser ever built could survive that concentration of fire at this range.

She hadn't anticipated when she handpicked her crew that she had chosen them only to die with her.

Her face was calm as the death of her ship and crew looked back at her from Hodah's eyes. It was unfair. It was cruel. Yet in a sense, it was also the sublime completion of her life. She drew a deep breath, hoping no one would notice.

"Go to hell, sir," she said very gently.

BAEN BOOKS by DAVID WEBER

Honor Harrington:
On Basilisk Station
The Honor of the Queen
The Short Victorious War
Field of Dishonor
Flag in Exile
Honor Among Enemies
In Enemy Hands
Echoes of Honor
Ashes of Victory
War of Honor

edited by David Weber:
More than Honor
Worlds of Honor
Changer of Worlds
The Service of the Sword

Honorverse:
Crown of Slaves
(with Eric Flint)

Mutineers' Moon
The Armageddon
Inheritance
Heirs of Empire
Empire From the Ashes
(MegaBook)

Path of the Fury

The Apocalypse Troll

The Excalibur Alternative

Oath of Swords
The War God's Own
Wind Rider's Oath

with Steve White:
Insurrection
Crusade
In Death Ground
The Shiva Option

with John Ringo:
March Upcountry
March to the Sea
March to the Stars

with Eric Flint
1633

DAVID WEBER
STEVE WHITE

INSURRECTION

A Baen Books Original

Baen Publishing Enterprises
P.O. Box 1403
Riverdale, NY 10471
www.baen.com

ISBN: 0-671-72024-4

Cover art by Paul Alexander

First printing, November 1990
Seventh printing, June 2004

Distributed by Simon & Schuster
1230 Avenue of the Americas
New York, NY 10020

Printed in the United States of America

TABLE OF CONTENTS

"Politics is the womb in which war is developed."

"If this be treason, make the most of it!"

"A man can die but once; we owe God a death . . ."

"Courage above all things is the first quality of a warrior."

"War is fought by human beings."

"Thank God I have done my duty."

"Politics is the womb in which war is developed."

General Karl von Clausewitz,
On War

Gale Warning

Ladislaus Skjorning frowned at his watch and re-scanned the sparsely-peopled late-night ante-room of Federation Hall, but there was no sign of Greuner. It was unlike him to be late, and, from the code phrase, his news was urgent, so where *was* he?

Someone tapped him on the shoulder, and he turned slowly, one hand moving unobtrusively to the small slug thrower in the sleeve of his loose tunic of Beaufort seawool. A man faced him in the conservative informal dress of New Zurich's upper classes—but it wasn't Greuner. Greuner was a little man; this fellow rivaled Skjorning's own 202 centimeters, and, unlike many Corporate Worlders, he looked fit and mean. Ladislaus eyed him with hidden distaste, and the muzzle of the invisible slug gun settled on the newcomer's navel.

"Mister Skjorning?"

"Aye, I'm to be Skjorning." Ladislaus' deep voice sawed across the thin New Zurich accent like a doomwhale catcher through fog.

"Mister Greuner sends his regrets."

"Not to come?" Ladislaus asked slowly, broad face expressionless as scorn for his uncouth dialect flared in the Corporate Worlder's mocking eyes. He plowed on like an icebreaker, pandering to the man's contempt. "Would it chance he's to be sending a wording why not?"

"Illness, I believe." The Corporate Worlder's mouth was a thin slash of dislike as he eyed the bearded giant.

Skjorning was a Titan for any world—especially a heavy grav planet, even one whose chill temperatures favored large people—but the one huge hand he could see was a laborer's, thick-knuckled and scarred by a childhood with the nets and a young manhood with the purse seines and harpoons.

"Not to be serious, I'm hoping," Ladislaus said sadly.

"I'm afraid it may be. In fact, I believe he's decided to return to New Zurich for . . . treatment."

"I'm to see. Well, grateful I'm to be for your wording, Mister—?"

"Fouchet," the tall man said briefly .

"Aye, Fouchet. Remembered to me you'll be, Mister Fouchet." Skjorning turned away with a bovine nod, and Fouchet watched him enter a deserted washroom. He started to follow, then stopped and turned on a scornful heel. Whatever Greuner might have thought, that thick-witted prole was no danger.

The washroom door eased slowly open behind him, and one brilliant blue eye followed his retreating back. The slug gun eased back into its sleeve clip regretfully, and Skjorning stepped out of the washroom.

"Aye, Mister Fouchet," he said softly, barely a trace of accent coloring his voice, "I'll remember you."

Fionna MacTaggart looked away from her terminal and rubbed her eyes wearily, then glanced at the clock and allowed herself a crooked grin. Old Terran days were tiresomely short for someone reared to the thirty-two hour Beaufort day. The air was bothersomely thin, and the gravity was irksomely low, but one could grow used to anything, including feeling tired at such a ridiculously early hour. She rose and poured a cup of Terran coffee, one of the only two things about the motherworld she would truly miss when she finally returned to Beaufort for good.

A chime sounded, and she crooked a speculative eyebrow and pressed the admittance key. The door hissed open, and Ladislaus Skjorning towered on the threshold, his blue eyes bright with annoyance.

"Damn it, Chief!" Mister Fouchet would never have recognized his tone. "You're *still* not checking IDs!"

"No, I'm not," Fionna said coolly. "Not inside our own enclave, anyway. Nor am I meeting guests at the door with a laser in my hand." She shook her head with mock severity. "Sometimes I think all this security nonsense is going to your head, Lad."

"Do you, now?" Ladislaus sank into one of the recliners, his anger ebbing, and closed his eyes wearily. Fionna's face tightened with sudden concern. "I wish our friend Greuner shared your opinion."

"He didn't show?" Fionna knelt on the recliner next to him and massaged one taut shoulder.

"No," he said softly.

"They got to him, is it?" she asked, equally softly.

"Aye. Hustled him back to New Zurich—I hope. But there's little to be putting past a Corporate Worlder who smells gelt, Chief." She felt him relaxing as her strong fingers dug the tension from him, then frowned and stopped massaging, leaning her forearms on his massively muscled shoulder.

"You're right, Lad. I just wish I knew what he had for us!"

"I feel the same," Ladislaus rumbled, allowing himself a frown, "but let's be grateful for what he already gave us. He turned from his own to be helping us because he thought it right; now I've the thinking he's to be paying for it soon and late."

"I know, Lad. I know." She patted his shoulder, smiling contritely, and he felt a surge of guilt. It was hard enough heading a Fringe World delegation without your own people snapping at you. Besides, Fionna was right to worry. The one clue they had to Greuner's message was the phrase "Gale Warning," and that was the code he and the little man had arranged to indicate a major Corporate World offensive against the Fringe.

"I did pick up something a mite useful," he proffered as a peace offering. "The name of the new New Zurich bully boy, I'm to be thinking. Fouchet. A tall, mean son-of-a sand-leech with a face like boiled blubber."

"He's their new security chief?" Fionna asked, eyes narrowing.

"Chief, you know they're not to be using such titles! They're not so crude as that—he'll to be called Computerman's

Syndic or some such. But, aye, he's the one. And had he just a little more curiosity or a little less brain—mind, I'm not sure which it was—it's squeezing Greuner's information from him I'd be the now."

"Lad," Fionna said sternly, "I've *told* you we can't operate that way! They already call us 'barbarians'. What do you think they'll call us if you start acting like that?"

"Aye? I don't have the thinking it's to mind me the much," Ladislaus said, laying the accent with a trowel. "It's maybe 'Corporate Worlder' they're to call me if I have the doing of their own against them. And where's the difference to lie? Yon Corporate Worlder flays his whales with money, Chief; *I'm* only after the doing of it by hand."

Fionna started to reply tartly, then stopped. She and Ladislaus had grown up together on the cold and windy seas of Beaufort, and she knew it irked him to play the homespun fool for men like Fouchet—but she also knew he recognized the advantages of his role. During his time in the Federation's navy, Ladislaus had acquired a cosmopolitanism at odds with the Innerworld notion of a Fringer, though, like anyone, he tended to revert to the speech patterns of childhood under stress. The slow Beaufort accent had drawn attention even in the Fleet, where such idosyncrasies were far from rare, and Lad had learned the hard way to speak excellent Standard English. But his sense of humor had stood him in good stead, and he'd also learned to ape the stereotype so well few of his victims ever realized they were being hoodwinked. He found his hayseed persona useful as head of security for the Beaufort delegation, and he usually enjoyed it. Yet it seemed this latest episode had cracked his normal shield of humor. He'd evidently become closer to Greuner than she'd thought . . . and he was *right*, damn it! The little banker had jeopardized his career, certainly, and possibly his life, to help worlds he'd never even visited—and now he'd pay for it. She felt a sudden hot stinging behind her own eyes, and her hands squeezed his shoulder in silence until she felt the new tension run slowly out of them both once more. . . .

A low, murmuring rumble filled the chamber, and Fionna MacTaggart looked across from her console at the tall podium in the center of the vast hemispherical room. It stood over two hundred meters from her seat in the center of the Beaufort delegation, separated from the ranked tiers of delegates by a floor of ebon marble shot with white veins like tangled skeins of stars. After twenty-five years in the Assembly—twenty of them as head of her planet's delegation—Fionna had learned the bitter, sordid realities of the Federation's government, but the Chamber of Worlds still took her breath away. She wished she could have seen it when the Assembly had lived up to its promise, but not even the gangrenous present of partisanship and exploitation could diminish the grandeur of the ideal this chamber had been built to enshrine.

Her eyes swept over upward-soaring walls hung with the flags and banners of scores of planetary systems, all dominated by the space-black Federation banner with its golden sunburst and the blue planet and white moon of the homeworld. The air stirred coolly against her skin as she adjusted her hushphone headset over her red hair. Ladislaus was going to be late if he didn't get a move on.

A tiny light glowed on her panel as the Sergeant at Arms warned her a member of her delegation was on his way, and she looked up, hiding a smile as Skjorning lumbered down the aisle. Thank God none of their constituents ever visited Old Terra! They'd have a fit if they ever saw the role Ladislaus had assumed so well.

The big man sidled bashfully through the crowd in a state of perpetual embarrassment, then sank gratefully into the chair at Fionna's left hand and leaned forward to fumble clumsily with his hushphone.

"Any clues, Lad?" she asked softly.

"No, Chief." Ladislaus' lips barely moved. "Only the code, and it's a seaharrower's own luck *that* much got to us."

Fionna frowned and nodded in agreement. She started to say something more, but the echo of a soft chime cut her short.

The Legislative Assembly of the Terran Federation was in session.

Fionna fidgeted uneasily as the opening formalities filtered past her. She could see the Galloway's World delegation from where she sat, and Simon Taliaferro wasn't in his usual place. The New Zurich delegation was less than ten meters away, and she noted sinkingly that Oskar Dieter wasn't with his fellows, either. Whatever Greuner had tried to warn them of, those two would be at the heart of it. Her fingers flew over her information console, keying their names and punching up a cross index of the committees on which they sat, for she'd learned long since that it was in the closed committee meetings that the Corporate Worlds wove their webs.

The screen lit, confirming her memory. Both men were from populous worlds; combined with their personal seniority in the Assembly and the "representative membership" committee rules the Corporate Worlds had rammed through twelve years ago, that gave them membership on dozens of committees . . . including shared membership on Foreign Relations and Military Oversight. She frowned. Not only was each a member of both, but Taliaferro chaired Foreign Relations and Dieter chaired Military Oversight. It was an ominous combination.

The Clerk finished the formalities of the last session's minutes and stepped aside for David Haley. By long tradition, the Speaker of the Legislative Assembly was a citizen of Old Terra, and Fionna listened to his beautiful Standard English as he turned the Assembly to business, wishing his office still had the power it once had. Unlike most of his Heart World fellows, Haley had traveled to the Fringe; he knew the hostility and hatred for the Corporate Worlds festering on the Fringe Worlds—and what was happening under the false cordiality of the delegates' relations. Unfortunately, there was little he could do about it.

"Ladies and Gentlemen of the Assembly," Haley said, "the Chairman of the Foreign Relations Committee has requested a closed session of the Assembly sitting as a committee of the whole. Are there any objections?"

Fionna keyed her console and saw Haley glance down as her light pulsed on his panel. Then he looked out over the sea of faces to the Beaufort delegation, and his face vanished from the giant screen behind the podium, replaced by Fionna's, though his image continued to stare up from the small screen before each delegate.

"The Chair recognizes the Honorable Assemblywoman

for Beaufort," he said, and Fionna's headset beeped to indicate a live mike.

"Mister Speaker, this is highly irregular," she said quietly. "I would ask why the Chairman of the Foreign Relations Committee feels the need for a closed session? And why we were not informed in advance?"

The face on her console screen was clearly unhappy. Haley was too experienced to show his emotions openly, but the assemblymen were too experienced not to read him anyway.

"Ms. MacTaggart, I can only tell you that the Chairman of the Foreign Relations Committee and Minister of Foreign Affairs Assad jointly have requested the Assembly's attention to a matter of grave import. That is all the information I have. Do you wish to object to the request for closure?"

Fionna certainly did, but it would accomplish little, since she would know no more about Taliaferro's plans after blocking the secret session than she did now. Damn him! Despite the warning, he'd managed to keep her completely in the dark!

"No, Mister Speaker," she said softly. "I have no objection."

"Is there any debate?" Haley asked. There was none, and the Speaker gaveled the Assembly into secret session.

The chamber buzzed with side conversations as the Sergeant at Arms and his staff escorted the news people out. The great doors boomed softly shut, and sophisticated anti-snooping defenses were set in motion. There would be no way for the outside world to discover what was said or done here unless a delegate leaked the word. Such "accidental leaks" were far from uncommon these days, though they once had been. As the Fringer population base had slowly grown to challenge the Corporate Worlds' domination of the Assembly, the campaign of secret slander and counter-slander had taken on vicious overtones. Initially, the Outworlders had been at a considerable disadvantage, but Fionna was almost saddened by how well they'd learned to play the game since. Only this time, leaks wouldn't be enough. Greuner's disappearance proved that.

Two new figures appeared beside Haley. One was Oskar Dieter, though he was as careful as ever to stay in the background. The other was Simon Taliaferro, possibly the man the Fringers hated most of all.

Taliaferro could have been prime minister, but his position as head of his delegation was more useful, and he would have been forced to resign it to accept the premiership. On the other hand, he could never have been president, for that largely gelded office was still decided by direct election. As heir to one of the shipbuilding dynasties which had used political power to cement its stranglehold on the Outworlds' commerce, he could never have carried enough of the popular vote. Ninety percent of all Federation cargo moved in hulls owned by Corporate World shipping magnates, yet over sixty percent of the Federation's systems lay in the Fringe and Rim. Which was why Taliaferro was hated . . . and why he was prepared to embrace any expedient to stave off the rapidly-approaching day when the Fringe's delegates would be numerous enough to demand an accounting for two centuries of economic exploitation.

"Ladies and gentlemen," Haley said, "the Chair recognizes the Honorable Simon Taliaferro, Delegate for Galloway's World and Chairman of the Foreign Relations Committee. Mister Taliaferro."

"Thank you, Mister Speaker." Taliaferro's dark face was incongruously jovial on the huge screen, and Fionna's lips curled with dislike. It was like a badly crafted disguise, she thought. A threadbare mask for the ruthless brilliance under that jolly exterior—yet the rules of the game required one to pretend his bonhomie was real.

"Members of the Assembly," Taliaferro said, "I bring you great news! After months of negotiation, I can now tell you that perhaps the most momentous departure in the history of the Galaxy has been proposed. President Zhi and Prime Minister Minh have received a direct communication from the Khan of the Orions, borne by a fully empowered plenipotentiary." He paused for effect, knowing he'd gathered the eyes and ears of every delegate. "The Khan proposes nothing less than the amalgamation of the Terran Federation and the Khanate of Orion!"

His voice rose steadily through the last sentence, but it

was almost lost in the roar which burst forth at the word "amalgamation," and Fionna was on her feet, one fist clenched on the top of her console.

"*No!*" she shouted, but her voice was lost in the uproar. It was just as well, she realized a moment later. She was the leader of the Fringe Caucus. She must appear calm and reasonable. Above all, reasonable! Yet such a proposal would be intolerable to her constituents, and the Corporate Worlds knew it. In fact, only those fat-headed, liberal-minded, bureaucracy-worshiping Heart Worlders could be so blind as to think the Fringe *wouldn't* fight this!

Her eyes narrowed as she sank back into her seat. Of course the Corporate Worlds knew, and Taliaferro's obvious delight made cold, ugly sense. How was the huge population of the Khanate to fit into this new, amalgamated monster? Were the Orions suddenly to find themselves enfranchised to vote for the first time in their history? It had taken over a century of slow, painful population growth in the outworlds to earn the delegates to challenge the Corporate Worlds. With such a huge influx of votes, the Assembly would have no choice but to cut the representational basis . . . which would just coincidentally gerrymander the sparse Fringe population out of the representation it had finally gained.

Just who, she wondered, had proposed what to whom? Had the Orions conceived this on their own? Or had the Corporate Worlds suggested it to them? Or had they, perhaps, simply misled the Khan's ambassadors into thinking the proposal would be joyfully accepted throughout the Federation? There were too many possibilities and too few answers—yet.

She pressed her call button. Haley's panel must be bloody with scores of red attention lights, and she almost hoped Taliaferro would refuse to yield to her. But he would, if only to give her the opportunity to cut her own throat, and, in a way, it would be a relief to take a stand, whatever the outcome. She had no choice but to voice the Fringe's position . . . and it was time, part of her cried, to have done with careful maneuvering. It was time to speak from the heart.

"Mister Speaker," Taliaferro's amplified voice cut through

the uproar, "I yield temporarily to the Honorable Assemblywoman for Beaufort!"

The background noise died instantly as Fionna appeared on the giant screen, and her green eyes flashed fire.

"Mister Speaker," her voice was clear and strong, "I must tell the Honorable Assemblyman for Galloway's World that he has made a grievous error if he expects every Federation citizen to greet this proposal with loud hosannas! No one in the Federation has more respect for the Orions than we of the Fringe. We have fought against them and beside them. We admire their courage, their fortitude, and their spirit. They have their own claims to greatness: the first race to hypothesize the possibility of warp travel; the first to create a stellar empire; and the first to recognize the inevitable end result of blind militarism and turn away from it. But, Mister Speaker, they are *Orions*—and we here represent the *Terran* Federation! We represent a society forged, in part, in combat *against* the Orions, one which has made for itself a place second to none in the known Galaxy. And, Mister Speaker—" her long anger and frustration burned in her throat as she hurled the final words at Taliaferro "—the Fringe will *never* consent to this so-called amalgamation!"

She sat down abruptly, and the Chamber of Worlds went berserk.

Soft, somehow mournful music swirled like the sea as Fionna stood at the head of the receiving line, smiling and gracious despite her exhaustion. The last week had been a nightmare, and only the extravagance of her personal exertions had held the Fringe bloc together. It wasn't that any delegation favored the proposed amalgamation; the reverse was true—they were angry with her for not taking a more extreme position.

But if twenty-five years in the Assembly had taught her anything, it was that the Heart Worlds didn't understand the Fringe. The Corporate Worlders knew their outworld cousins and enemies far better than the motherworld and its oldest colonies did, though she suspected not even the Corporate Worlds fully realized the fulminating anger they were fanning. But the Heart Worlds were too far removed from their own frontier days. They'd forgotten what it was like to know that any outside attack must come through *their* systems to reach the heart of empire. As they'd forgotten—if they'd ever known—what it was to have their commerce, the lifeblood of their societies, manipulated and exploited by predatory merchants with a yen for power.

And because they had forgotten or did not know, they were a terrible danger to the Fringe. Fionna had seen the "new liberalism" of her Heart World colleagues. The Heart Worlds had it too good, she thought bitterly; they were too content, too ultracivilized. The Corporate Worlds could convince them the Fringe really was peopled by uncouth barbarians but little removed from outright savagery. Worse, they could be convinced to do what was "best" for the Fringe—even if it killed the object of their kindness!

Knowing that, she also knew it was imperative to convince the Heart Worlds of the Fringe's maturity . . . or at least open-mindedness. The position she'd taken was the strongest she could take. The firebrands who longed to denounce the Corporate Worlds openly, to point the accusing finger where it so richly deserved to be pointed, would play straight into Taliaferro's and Dieter's hands, but only one Fringer could convince them of that. Fionna MacTaggart wasn't a vain woman, yet she knew no one else among the Fringe delegates had the prestige and power base she'd built against this very day.

Of all the Fringe Worlds, Beaufort, perhaps, most despised Corporate Worlders. Beaufort's heavy gravity had not been kind to its colonizers, despite their selection for high pressure tolerance, yet there had been fierce competition for space on the colony ships. The rebels of the Corporate Worlds, those who could no longer tolerate their roles as cogs in the vast machines, had seen in Beaufort a world poor enough and distant enough to be secure from manipulation and control. They'd gone to Beaufort to escape, and many had died there—so many BuCol actually closed the planet to immigration for almost sixty years.

Fionna's parents and grandparents had spoken of those bitter years. The gene pool was small; the environment was harsh; and BuCol's Corporate World bureaucrats had not gone out of their way to help. Those six decades of isolation had produced the dialect the Innerworlders mocked—and left a burning hatred in the hearts of the people who spoke it.

But then the unsuspected pharmaceutical potential of the Beaufort doomwhale had rocked Terran medical science, and suddenly the Corporate Worlds and the Assembly were filled with concern for the colony they had ignored for so long. The Corporate World combines had moved in, and the Corporate World nightmare had come for the people of Beaufort once more.

Yet cold, hostile Beaufort had trained them well, and the planetary government moved quickly to regulate doomwhaling and exclude the Corporate Worlds, unmoved by threats of economic reprisal. There was little anyone could do which the Corporate Worlds hadn't already done, and, for the first time in over a century and a half, Corporate World plutocrats were forced to dance to the economic piping of a Fringe World.

They had hated it, and it was Beaufort's successful resistance to their penetration which gave her delegation such prestige. Beaufort had proved the Corporate Worlds could be stopped; now it was time to prove they could be pushed back, and Fionna MacTaggart had dedicated her professional life to that goal. Yet there was only one of her, and she was tired . . . so very, very tired. Beyond each confrontation, another loomed, and she faced each a little more diminished, a little more weary.

She shook herself mentally, banishing the dark thoughts. It had been a bad day—perhaps that was why she felt so somber. Or perhaps it was this reception. It had been scheduled before Taliaferro dropped his bomb, and canceling it now was out of the question, but it was a strain to be polite to the Corporate Worlders as they arrived. Still, she thought with a sudden flicker of amusement, it might be equally hard on them.

She glanced at her watch. Another ten minutes and she could find herself a drink and begin to circulate. That might help. It was always easier to deal with people in small, intimate groups rather than in formal, antagonistic public forums. Then she looked back up and bit off a curse as Oskar Dieter entered with his now-constant shadow, Fouchet.

She felt Ladislaus materialize by her side. Dear Lad! He

played the buffoon for the Innerworlders, but his fellow Beauforters knew his worth. Indeed, she sometimes wished she didn't know him quite so well. It would be nice to lose herself in an affair with someone with his strength and integrity, but any liaison with him would have felt incestuous.

Dieter paused at the head of the reception line, and his dark eyes glittered. Fionna didn't like Dieter; she never had, and she knew the feeling was mutual. Unlike Taliaferro, Dieter was a poor hand at hiding his emotions, and she'd flicked him on the raw often in debate. He resented that, and resented it all the more because she was a woman. The Constitution might outlaw sexual discrimination, but New Zurich's unwritten law enshrined it, and she suspected Dieter found her an insult to his prejudices as well as to his ambitions. Still, there were amenities to be observed, and she held out her hand with a smile.

"Mister Dieter."

"Ms. MacTaggart." He bowed slightly, ignoring her hand, and his voice was cold, his eyes scornful. Fionna's palm itched.

"A pleasure to see you, sir," she made herself lie. "I understand you will be taking a major role in tomorrow's debate?"

"Indeed," he said. "And so, I hear, will you. Playing your usual obstructionist role, I presume."

Conversation slackened, and Fionna felt Ladislaus tighten beside her. She touched his hand unobtrusively.

"I prefer, sir, to consider my role as that of a constructive advocate for the Fringe Worlds," she said, equally coldly. "We, too, have a right to present our point of view and to contend for our values and dreams."

"Values and dreams?! *Fringe garbage!*" Dieter flushed suddenly, his voice hissing, and Fionna's eyes widened. Good God, what ailed the man? One simply didn't say things like that at formal receptions!

"Yes, Mister Dieter," she heard herself say, "we, too, have our dreams and aspirations—or will the Corporate Worlds take even those from us?"

Ripples of silence raced outward. Fionna dared not turn to see the effect of the acid exchange, yet neither dared she retreat. It was one thing to appear reasonable; it was quite another to appear weak.

"We have no desire for them," Dieter sneered. "You speak very prettily in debate, for a *Fringe Worlder*, Madam, but the Assembly will not be blind to your barbarism and xenophobia forever. You and your kind have stood in the path of civilization too long!"

He almost spat the last words, and suddenly she smelled his breath. Reefgrubs! He was almost in orbit on New Athens *mizir!* How could he be so stupid as to meet her in this condition? But whatever madness possessed him wasn't her worry; responding to his attack was.

"We may be barbarians, sir," she said, and her voice rang clearly in the silence, "but at least we have the advantage of you in manners!"

Dieter's face twisted as the crowd murmured approval. Even through the haze of *mizir* fumes he could sense the incredible blunder he'd made. But recognizing it and retrieving it were two different things, and his fuddled brain was unequal to the task.

"*Slut!*" he hissed suddenly, thrusting his face close to hers. "You've aped your betters for too long! Get home to your stinking little ball of mud and make babies to play in the muck!"

Fionna and her guests froze. Enmity between political leaders was nothing new, but this—! No one could quite believe Dieter was so lost to self-control, yet his words hung in the supercharged air like a sub-critical mass of plutonium, and they waited breathlessly for the explosion.

It came. Ladislaus Skjorning's huge right hand lashed open-palmed across Dieter's face.

The New Zuricher rebounded from the blow, crashing into Fouchet, blood bursting from the corner of his mouth. He stared at Ladislaus for a moment of terror, then clawed himself upright, gobbling curses while Fouchet's hand darted inside his tunic. But Ladislaus wasn't yet done, and Fionna's world reeled about her as his quarterdeck rasp cut through Dieter's fury.

"You're to meet me for this," he grated.

Dieter's mouth snapped shut as a warning battered at the *mizir*. He was in the Beaufort enclave; the enclaves enjoyed extraterritoriality; and on Beaufort, dueling was an accepted fact of life. He stared at the giant before him, and for the first time he understood the difference between a patiently plodding ox and a charging bull.

"I—I—" He fought for words. "This is . . . is preposterous! Barbaric! You can't be—"

"Aye, we're to be called barbarians," Ladislaus agreed grimly, "but it's to meet me you'll be for all of that."

"I—I won't!" Dieter gasped desperately.

"No?" Ladislaus wrapped one hand in the New Zuricher's tunic, and muscles bred to a gravity a third again that of Old Terra's rippled as he lifted him from the floor. "You've the right to be calling barbarians, but not the guts to be facing one, have you? But it's on Beaufort soil you are the now! It's Beaufort law has the ruling of it here."

"Let him go, Skjorning!" It was Fouchet, his hand still inside his tunic, and Ladislaus' blue eyes moved coldly to the security man's tight face.

"Chief?" the big Fringer said softly.

"Mister Fouchet," Fionna's voice rang through the horrified room, "You are legally on the soil of Beaufort, and as chief of her delegation, I will thank you to remove your hand from your tunic—empty."

Fouchet eyed her contemptuously, then paled. Three grim-faced Assembly lictors stood behind her, stun batons in hand and a hard light in their eyes. He hadn't seen them appear, but he knew whose orders they would obey in this room.

His hand came out of his tunic—empty.

"Thank you," Fionna said icily, then touched Ladislaus lightly on the arm. "Put him down, Lad," she said quietly.

For a moment it seemed the towering blond giant might refuse, then he slammed Dieter back onto his feet, and the Corporate Worlder swayed. Fionna's eyes were emerald ice, but her voice was colder.

"Mister Dieter, you have been challenged to honorable combat by Ladislaus Skjorning. Do you accept the challenge?"

"I— *No!* Of course not! It's—"

"Be silent!" Fionna's voice whiplashed across his spluttering and shocked him into silence. "Very well. You have declined the challenge—as is your right. But as representative of Beaufort on Old Terra, it is my duty to inform you that you are no longer welcome on her soil. Leave. If you ever return, you will be forcibly ejected."

Dieter stared at her like a gaffed fish, the mottled red print of Ladislaus' hand the only color in his white face. He looked desperately around the circle of hostile faces, and he found no support. Not a man or woman present questioned Fionna's decision. He opened his mouth.

"One word, *Mister* Dieter," Fionna said softly, "and I will ask these lictors to escort you from the premises. Now leave!"

And Oskar Dieter turned to stumble away through the crowd.

Fionna couldn't fault Lad—except, perhaps, in that the challenge had rightfully been hers to give. Such behavior was not tolerated on Beaufort, nor most other Fringe Worlds. Sparse societies in alien environments tended to be armed, and insults carried a stiff price. Yet even if she couldn't question his act, she regretted the impact she expected it to have.

But the actual impact surprised her. The Corporate Worlds might have convinced the Heart Worlds the Fringe was uncouth, but not even they dared argue that a society's customs could be challenged with impunity. That sort of intolerance would have destroyed the Federation long since, and no Heart Worlder hesitated to condemn Dieter's behavior. Not even the excuse that he'd been drugging (acceptable on most Heart Worlds, though not in the Fringe) could mitigate his unforgivable boorishness. So far as the Heart Worlds were concerned, the whole focus of the Corporate-Fringe World debate had been shifted by a single instance of supremely bad manners.

The Fringers' reactions were even more startling. She'd expected a ground swell of anger she would never be able to control; instead, she got a tightening of ranks and an upwelling of ever stronger support. The hatred she'd expected was there, but it was controlled by respect for her and Ladislaus.

Dieter's stupidity had strengthened her prestige with Fringer and Heart Worlder alike, and the Corporate Worlds lost ground steadily in debate. The amalgamation issue was far from resolved, but under her leadership the Fringe had emerged as a moderate and reasonable entity, and as the days passed, she felt the pendulum swinging in her favor.

Simon Taliaferro's joviality was in abeyance, and his eyes were cold as Oskar Dieter and Francois Fouchet entered his office.

"You idiot!" he flared. "How could you *be* so stupid?!"

"I—I wasn't myself," Dieter muttered. "I was provoked!"

"Provoked, hell! You were glitter-dusted to the eyeballs, that's what you were! Look at *these*"—he slammed a fist on the sheaf of printouts on his desk—"and tell me it was worth it!"

"Mister Taliaferro," Fouchet's calm voice cut the superheated tension like an icicle, "we're prepared to stipulate an error was made, but fixing blame won't solve our difficulties. Clearly you have something to tell us; equally clearly it isn't something you much care for. Very well. Tell us, and let's see if we can't find a way to retrieve the situation."

Fouchet's coolness seemed to calm Taliaferro, and he drew a deep breath. Then he let it hiss out and squared his shoulders.

"You're right, Francois," he said finally. "I'll say no more about the . . . episode. But the consequences are out of all proportion, I assure you. These—" he thumped the printouts again "—tell it all. A week ago, we had them; today, they're rolling us up like a rug."

Dieter mopped his forehead with a tissue and said nothing. In one, terrible week he'd fallen from the Corporate Worlds' second most powerful leader into a sort of limbo. Every insider knew Fouchet spoke for New Zurich, and most expected Dieter to be recalled so Fouchet could replace him officially. He was ruined, and his eyes burned into Fouchet's back as he remembered who had encouraged him to glitter-dust that evening . . . and provided the drug that was so much more potent than he normally used.

Dieter knew *mizir* produced no delusions, that it couldn't make a man say what he didn't actually feel, yet his statements had shocked him even more, perhaps, than they had Fionna MacTaggart. They'd revealed a personal hatred he hadn't even known existed. But Fouchet had known. Fouchet had maneuvered him, yet accusing him would be worse than useless. If there was anything the Corporate Worlds had less use for than a fool, it was a dupe.

"Those projections are confirmed?" Fouchet asked, and Taliaferro nodded. "But, of course, they're based on certain givens, aren't they?"

"Any projection is, but there's not much room for change in the parameters. What it boils down to is that we've lost the high ground. In a straight debate over something as emotional as amalgamation, they'll probably beat us—even without the reapportionment issue. God! To think of a brainless lummox like Skjorning bumbling into the *only* thing that could hurt us this way!"

"I'm not so sure he *is* brainless," Dieter offered in a subdued voice.

"Of course you're not," Taliaferro sneered. "That'd make your little fiasco look better, wouldn't it?" Dieter wilted under the savage irony. "But he *is* a fool. He reacted with his muscles, the way he always does, and it just happened that this time it was the best thing he could do—or the worst, depending on your viewpoint!"

"But it comes down to Skjorning and MacTaggart, doesn't it?" Fouchet murmured thoughtfully, recapturing Taliaferro's attention.

"Eh? I suppose so—not that *he's* too important. It's MacTaggart. She's spent a quarter-century building a power base. She's got the best political brain in the whole Fringer crowd, and they know it—that's why they follow her lead—but her control was slipping. Another few days and I'd've moved the vote, and every projection said she'd lose the firebrands on the floor. Well, the hotheads are hotter than ever, but she's got more authority than ever. They'll never break with her now."

"No, I can see that," Fouchet said slowly, "but if there were some way to remove her from the equation?"

"Without MacTaggart, they'd attack us like wolves," Taliaferro said simply, "and that'd be just as good as their scattering like sheep. But we can't touch her. She can't be bought, she can't be blackmailed, she can't be intimidated, and she's headed the Fringe Caucus for fifteen years. After last week, she might as well be in God's hip pocket!"

"True," Fouchet said, his lips curving slowly, "but accidents do happen, don't they? And Granyork isn't like a colony world. Why, we're right in the middle of the Northeast Corridor Conurbation, and that's a sort of jungle Fringers aren't well equipped to deal with. . . ."

"What are you *saying?*" Dieter's horror cut the sudden silence like a saw. "You can't possibly suggest—"

"I didn't hear Mister Fouchet suggest a thing, Oskar," Taliaferro said coldly. "I only heard him speculating idly on matters totally beyond our control. And, of course, he's quite right. If Ms. MacTaggart were to suffer an . . . accident, it could only help us on the floor. Unless, of course, our enemies were able to . . . invent . . . a connection between her accident and us."

"Oh, of course," Fouchet agreed. "Of course."

Fionna MacTaggart considered the face in her mirror critically. It wasn't quite as young as she still liked to think of herself, and she'd never been—in her opinion—a beauty, but her image had nothing to apologize for. She nodded companionably to herself.

"Just you and me, girl," she said softly. "No one else has to know how hard we worked for that, do they?"

She chuckled and reached for her small evening bag. God, it felt good to be going somewhere besides to another floor fight! But the Corporate Worlds were on the defensive now. Now *they* were fighting to delay the vote, though she didn't really know what they hoped to achieve; delay only strengthened her hand at this point. No doubt they planned something devious, and equally no doubt Ladislaus or one of the others would figure it out if she didn't. But for now she felt younger than she had in weeks, and she looked forward eagerly to the night's entertainment. True, the thin Old Terran atmosphere detracted a bit from her enjoyment, but the strength of the performance more than compensated. Opera had been born on Old Terra, and in her opinion it still achieved its highest expression here.

She glanced into her bag at the snub-nosed and chunky two-millimeter needler and debated leaving it behind, for if it was small, it was still heavy. And it wasn't as if she were headed into the back islands. Granyork was the epicenter of the ultracivilized Heart Worlds. Still, she knew how Lad would react if she went unarmed. . . . She sighed and closed the bag.

She keyed her bedside terminal and the screen lit briefly with an attention pattern, then with Ladislaus' face.

"All set, Lad," she told him cheerfully. "Would you have the car sent around, please?"

"Aye . . . if you're not leaving your little toy behind," he said suspiciously.

"Me?" She laughed and clunked the bag solidly against the terminal. "See, Daddy?"

"Laugh if you will," he said with a slight grin, "but I rest easier knowing you're armed, Fi."

"I know, Lad." She was touched by his use of her name, for Ladislaus was always careful to call her "Chief" to avoid any impression of taking advantage of their lifelong friendship. "I may think you're a little paranoid, but you're the man I chose for security chief. If you want me in a combat zoot with a grenade launcher, that's how I'll go."

"I know you mean it for a joke, but it's happier I'd be for it," he said, only half-humorously. "Still, it's the offalbirds are on the rocks the now, it's to be seeming. So go—have a good time, Chief!"

"Why, thank you, Lad," she cooed, batting her eyes. "I certainly shall." She touched the button again, and the terminal blanked.

Twenty minutes later, Ladislaus' terminal hummed once more, and he looked up from his report with a frown, for he'd left orders not to disturb him. Then he looked again, and his brow furrowed. It was an outside call on his priority number, and his eyes widened as he touched the acceptance key and Oskar Dieter's sweating face filled the screen.

"Please excuse the intrusion, Mister Skjorning!" Dieter took advantage of his shock, speaking quickly to wedge a toe in the door. "I had to call you. I have . . . have vitally important information for you."

"Do you, now?" Ladislaus' voice was cold, but his mind raced. Under Beaufort's code, Dieter no longer existed as far as he was concerned, and he could imagine nothing they might have to discuss. Yet the Corporate Worlder had to know he would feel that way, so it followed that there *was* something important here—but what?

"Yes. I—I don't know who else to give it to," Dieter sounded desperate, and Ladislaus suddenly noted how low-pitched his voice was. Was he afraid of being overheard?

"And what's that information to be?"

"B—before I say any more, you have to promise to keep its source confidential," Dieter said feverishly, wiping his brow.

"I'm to be but a simple fellow. What's—"

"*Please*, Mister Skjorning! You may have convinced the others—indeed, you play the part very well—but must we continue to pretend?"

Ladislaus' eyes narrowed. So a Corporate Worlder had finally bothered to pierce his mask. Yet it seemed Dieter had little interest in sharing his deductions with his fellows . . . not if he was honestly seeking to impart some sort of sensitive information. . . .

"All right, Mister Dieter," he said. "You have my word."

"Thank you, Mister Skjorning!" Dieter drooped with relief, yet now that he had Ladislaus' promise, he seemed to find it difficult to go on. Ladislaus could almost feel the painful physical effort with which he screwed up his courage.

"Mister Skjorning, I—I made a fool of myself the other night. I know it and you know it, but I swear to God I had no idea where it would lead!"

"What are you talking about?" Ladislaus' brows knitted. Could the man be drugging even now?

"I wrecked a lot of plans," Dieter said in a fast, frantic monotone. "I'm sure you know what I mean. But I never realized just how . . . how *desperate* some of my colleagues have become! They're going to kill her, Mister Skjorning!"

Dieter seemed to sag, as if simply voicing the words lifted a great weight from his shoulders, but Ladislaus was totally at a loss for an instant. Then it penetrated.

"Are you serious? They're going to *assassinate* Assemblywoman MacTaggart!"

"Yes! That is—I think so." Dieter squirmed in fresh uncertainty. "All I really know is that there was a lot of talk. You know—hypothetical discussion about how 'convenient' it would be if something happened to her. I—I tried to oppose it, but I don't have the influence I had . . . ."

"Who's going to do it and when?" Ladislaus snapped.

"I'm not even positive they *are* going to do it," Dieter said anxiously. "I think . . . I think it's Francois Fouchet's project. I don't know when or how."

"Is that all you have for me?"

"Yes. Except . . . except Francois said something about how dangerous Granyork can be."

"My God!" Ladislaus paled and reached for the disconnect, then paused, his eyes on the wretched man before him. "Mister Dieter, I thank you. What was between us is no more." Dieter's miserable expression lightened slightly as he recognized the formal renunciation of challenge.

"Thank you," he whispered. "And for God's sake, don't let them kill her! I never dreamed—" He stopped and chopped his hand at the pickup. For a moment, he became the man he once had been. "Enough! Protect her, Mister Skjorning. And tell her . . . tell her I'm sorry."

"I will. Good night."

Ladislaus cut the circuit and immediately punched for another, staring at his watch. With any luck and normal Granyork traffic, Fionna had not yet reached the Met.

"Goodness, Chris, I don't believe we've ever made such good time," Fionna remarked as the ground car slowed.

"I think you're right, Chief," the young security man agreed, his eyes flickering over the smartly dressed crowd before the opera house.

"Good. I hate finding my seat after the house lights go down."

Chris Felderman opened her door and she stepped out, picking her way through the crowd towards the huge front doors behind him.

"Stop, thief!"

Fionna and Felderman swung to face the shout as a running man suddenly burst from the crowd and snatched at the purse of the wife of Hangchow's chief delegate. His course carried him close to Fionna, and she punched her bodyguard's shoulder sharply.

"Stop him, Chris! That's Madam Wu's purse!"

"Yes, ma'am!" Felderman lunged after the thief, his long legs gaining ground quickly, and Fionna watched for an instant, then felt something like a chill on the nape of her neck. She turned, and her eyes widened as she saw two men approaching her. She'd never seen them before, but something in their purposeful expressions woke a warning deep inside her. She felt an instant of helpless panic as a terrible premonition struck—replaced in an instant with icy calm.

She knew better than to turn and run. There was no time to resummon Chris. The thoughts flicked through her brain like lightning, yet her reactions were even faster. Her hand darted into her bag. Her fingers found the butt of the needler. She didn't try to draw the weapon; she simply raised the bag and pistol together.

The killers were from the world of Shiloh. They hadn't expected their target to be armed; still less had they allowed for the reaction speed a high-grav planet instills. But they could not mistake her movements, and they were the best money could buy.

The thunder of two compact machine pistols buried the high, shrill whine of the needler.

Fionna was lying on the sidewalk. It hurt—God, *how* it hurt!—and she whimpered a little at the terrible pain. She lay in a puddle of something hot, and she felt a gentle hand under her head, raising it to slip some sort of cushion behind it.

She opened her eyes. It was Chris Felderman leaning over her, she thought confusedly. But why was he crying?

"Chris?" The voice was hers, but she'd never heard herself sound so weak. Something dribbled down her chin, and she realized it was blood. She felt only a distant curiosity at the thought.

"D—Don't try to talk, Fionna. *Please*! The medics are coming."

"M—medics?" She blinked at him. A mist was rising from the pavement, obscuring her vision, and the temperature had fallen. Then she understood, and she managed a weak smile. "Don't think . . . it'll matter . . . much," she whispered.

"It will! *It will!*" Chris sobbed, as if saying it could make it so.

"May—maybe." She knew better, but it struck her oddly detached brain as needlessly cruel to tell him so. "What about—?"

"Dead!" he whispered fiercely. "You got 'em both, Chief!"

"G—good." The mist was much thicker, and she was much, much colder. Yet the darkness beyond the mist seemed suddenly warm and inviting. It wouldn't hurt so much there . . . but she had something left to say, didn't she? She cudgeled her fading brain, then her bloody mouth smiled up at Chris. Two police floaters screamed to a halt, but she ignored them as she gripped his hand.

"G—give . . . Lad . . . my love," she murmured. "And . . . tell him . . . tell him . . . I got them b—"

The light went out of her universe forever.

Ladislaus Skjorning sat in the Chamber of Worlds like a boulder of Beaufort granite, and the black-draped seat beside him was less empty than his soul.

He had failed. He'd failed his planet and himself, but, far worse, he had failed Fionna. Chris Felderman thought the failure was *his*, but Ladislaus knew. The entire surviving Beaufort delegation was in shock, but the others had managed somehow to keep going. Not Ladislaus.

He remembered their childhood on windy, purple seas under the orange Beaufort sun. Remembered sailing and fishing, the first time she stood for office as a seaforcer, the day she convinced him to seek the new Assembly seat. "I need someone to watch my back, Lad," she'd said, and for ten years he'd done just that— until he let her go out onto a street on the birthworld of Man to be gunned down in her blood like an animal.

His teeth ground together on the agony of memory, and suddenly a single, clear thought stabbed through his brain like an ice pick.

The Federation wasn't worth Fionna's life.

Four and a half centuries of human history had come down to this, he thought bitterly, looking at the banner-hung walls and marble floors. To this holodrama show-piece, this mausoleum dedicated to dead ideals and housing a government whose members connived at murder.

His broad face went grim. Fionna was gone, and with her went her dream. There would be no transition, no gradual change. Without her, the Fringe bloc was leaderless, headless, already splintering in rage as the local authorities sought uselessly to link the dead assassins to someone—*anyone*—but the tracks were well buried.

The killers had been Fringers, not Innerworlders, but the Outworlds knew who had hired them. Ladislaus had Dieter's confirmation, though his oath meant he couldn't use it. His fellows didn't need it, for the Fringe knew its enemies well. Yet there was no proof, and without proof, there was no guilt. Without guilt, there was no punishment; and without punishment, the Fringe would shatter in incoherent fury and be swept aside by the Corporate World machine. He saw it coming, and he was glad. *Glad*!

He rose and pressed his attention button, and there was a moment of silence as the delegate from Xanadu looked down from the giant screen and recognized who sought recognition.

"Mister Speaker," the delegate said slowly, "I yield to the Honorable Assemblyman for Beaufort."

Ladislaus Skjorning's grim face appeared on the master screen, and the chamber fell silent. In ten years, he had never sought the floor.

"Mister Speaker!" His voice was harsh, with little trace of his habitual accent, and he felt a stir around him as he put aside his mask at last. "I would like clarification on a point of law, Mister Speaker."

"Certainly, Mister Skjorning," Haley said, his face compassionate.

"Mister Speaker, am I not correct in believing that many years ago—in 2357—Winston Ortler of Galloway's World was accused of murdering his Old Terran mistress?" A silent gasp rippled through the Assembly, and Simon Taliaferro's face twisted in fury while Haley stared at Ladislaus in shock.

"Am I not *correct*, Mister Speaker?"

"Yes . . . yes, you are. But no formal charges were ever filed—"

"Precisely, Mister Speaker." Ladislaus' face was bleak. "No formal charges were filed—just as no formal charges have been filed over the death—the *assassination*—of Fionna MacTaggart. But in the earlier case, I believe, there was substantial evidence of guilt, was there not? Is it not true that his colleagues ruled that, as an assemblyman, he was immune from prosecution for *any* crime under the Constitution?"

"Yes, Mister Skjorning," Haley said softly. "I am very much afraid that was the case." He drew a deep breath and gripped the dilemma by its horns. "May I ask the purpose of your questions, sir?"

"You may." Ladislaus drew himself up to his full height, towering over the other assemblymen like an angry Titan. "It is only this, sir; just as there was no prosecution then, there will be none now. Because the men who murdered Fionna MacTaggart *are in this very chamber!*"

The Chamber of Worlds exploded as the words were spoken at last. The Speaker's gavel pounded, but Ladislaus grabbed the volume control on his console and wrenched it to full gain. His mighty bass roared through the tumult, battering the delegates' ears.

"Fionna MacTaggart was murdered by the political machine headed by Simon Taliaferro!" Confused shouts of outrage and approval echoed from the floor, but Ladislaus thundered on. "Fringe World fingers pulled those triggers, but Corporate World money bought them! It may never be 'proved,' but Francois Fouchet planned her murder because she stood in the Taliaferro machine's way!"

His savage words shocked the Assembly into silence at last, but for a handful of shouted denials from the Corporate World seats, and Ladislaus slowly turned down the volume.

"But let it pass," he said very softly, his amplified voice echoing in the silence. "We of the Fringe have learned our lessons well. We cannot turn to this Assembly for justice; the Assembly is the tool which *took* our rights. But let that pass, too. Let all of it pass. It doesn't really matter any more, because when you killed Fionna—" his eyes burned across at the New Galloway delegation "—and when these other Innerworlders *let* you kill her, and demanded no accounting, you also killed this Assembly. You're dead men's shadows in a hall of ghosts, and you will wake one morning to find that you are all alone here . . . ."

His voice trailed off, and an icy hush hovered as he started to turn away. But then he paused. His fists clenched at his sides, and when he turned back to the pickup the muscles in his cheeks stood out like lumps of iron in a face reduced to elemental hatred by loss and rage.

"But happen to be one last service this putrid Constitution have the doing of for Fionna," he said thickly. "Happen to be a Fringe Worlder can claim a Corporate Worlder's protection!"

They were still staring at him in confusion as he vaulted the low railing of his delegation's box. Members surged to their feet as his long legs flew over ten meters of marble to the New Zurich box.

Fouchet saw him coming and lunged up, his hand snaking into his coat, but Ladislaus was too fast. Muscles trained in a gravity thirty percent greater than Old Terra's—almost forty percent greater than New Zurich's—hurled him into the New Zurich delegation, and his right hand locked on Fouchet's wrist. His fingers closed like a vise, twisting, and Fouchet screamed as his wrist shattered like crushed gravel.

Ladislaus jerked the moaning Corporate Worlder to the front of the box, his left hand scything a New Zurich aide contemptuously aside, and his bull voice roared through the tumult.

"Happen to be"— he shouted, tears streaming down his bearded cheeks—"even a Fringe Worlder can find justice if he make it for himself!" His left hand gripped the back of Fouchet's neck while the entire Assembly rose to its feet in disbelief. Two lictors raced towards the box, but they were a lifetime too late. Fouchet shrieked as steely fingers tightened, but Ladislaus' bull-throated roar battered through all opposition. "Happen to be your stinking Constitution give *me* immunity for *this!*"

And he snapped Fouchet's neck like a stick.

Council of War

"My friends!" Simon Taliaferro raised his glass and beamed at the men and women seated around the conference table. "I give you victory!"

Agreement rumbled as glasses were lifted and drained, but Oskar Dieter left his on the table and felt dull, smoldering anger burn in the pit of his belly. His eyes were narrowed to knife-hard sharpness as they sought to strip away the false joviality which always shrouded Taliaferro's inner thoughts. How had he worked so long with him without realizing exactly what he was?

"Yes, my friends," Taliaferro continued, "much as I regret the death of Francois Fouchet, his murder—his *martyrdom*—has assured our victory. I received the latest projections this morning." He beamed at them like a fond uncle. "Within two months—three at the outside—our majority will be sufficient to assure approval of the Amalgamation!"

The rumble of approval was even louder, and Dieter felt a chill breeze whistle around the corners of his soul. The Amalgamation was but the first step of the plan he and Taliaferro had worked out years before, but Dieter had always regarded it as a theoretical exercise, a sort of "what if" in case the opportune moment ever arrived. He'd never really believed that they would succeed. Nor would they have . . . without murder.

He stared into his glass. The media, with its customary voracity for sensationalism, had arrived even before the medical examiner, and Dieter's heart chilled as he recalled the pathetic figure lying almost neatly in the wide, dark pool of blood. The assassins hadn't bled as much as she; men who die instantly bleed very little.

Dieter had watched those news shots with a sort of self-flagellating fascination. He'd tried to prevent it, but his efforts had been too little too late, and for all that he'd striven to stop it, it was also his unforgivable stupidity which had made the act inevitable . . . and stripped him of the power to forbid it.

He looked up from his glass with a bitter half-smile. Fouchet's death had restored him, however temporarily, to the ranks of the Corporate World autocrats on Old Terra. He lacked the power and prestige which had once been his, but there was no one else to speak for New Zurich, so his fellows had been forced to accept him once more, at least until the New Zurich oligarchs replaced him. Yet he was an outcast, now; more so even than they realized. He understood the dreadful attraction he held for them—the near hypnotic fascination of a tainted man whose career lay in wreckage. But they seemed unaware how deep the taint truly went.

"Of course, we all regret the terrible events which led to this," Taliaferro was saying smoothly, "but one cannot deny that the entire crisis is tailor-made for our needs."

"Maybe," Hector Waldeck rumbled. The chief delegate from Christophon was a choleric man, and his face flushed as he spoke. "No doubt the Amalgamation will pass, Simon, but what about Skjorning? The bastard's a damned savage! He ought to pay for what he did, by God!"

Dieter's mouth twisted behind his hand as others murmured agreement. They were all so sanctimonious about Skjorning's act—what about what *they* had done? They knew the truth about Fionna's death, yet Waldeck was so smugly self-righteous he could demand punishment for Skjorning!

His sighed, anger tempered by shame as he realized that once he would have shouted as loudly as any. He glanced around the angry, self-important faces, seeing them as they were now that he was no longer part of them, and it was like looking into a terrible mirror. They were no more truly "evil" than he himself. Like him, they played by the only rules they knew, and they played the "game" well. That was the problem. For them, it was *only* a game, a vastly exciting contest for the wealth of a galaxy.

They were manipulators and users because it had never occurred to them to be anything else. The Legislative Assembly was no government; it was a tremendous, fascinating toy, a machine whose buttons and levers disgorged ever more wealth, ever more power, and ever more intoxicating triumphs.

Sorrow filled him. The Corporate Worlds had spent trillions of credits and decades of political effort to master that machine, and when the growing Fringe population threatened their control, they'd moved ruthlessly to crush the opposition—all as part of "the game." For all the time and effort they spent plotting and planning, they were even blinder than the insulated Heart Worlders, for they saw Fringers only as obstacles, not as people, and certainly not as fellow citizens. They saw them as pawns, dupes—cartoon caricatures cruelly drawn by habitual contempt and denigration.

"No, Hector," Taliaferro said firmly. "We don't want to punish him—though I certainly share your outrage!" He managed to sound quite sincere, Dieter thought bitterly, and revised his earlier estimate. Some of these people *were* evil, however you defined the term. "But despite what we feel, we must remember that Skjorning's accusations can be made to work for us rather than against us. We need to use him, not indict him."

"Crap," Waldeck said harshly. "I want that murderous bastard stood up against a wall and shot! We need to teach these barbarians a lesson—especially the Beauforters!"

Dieter saw a few sardonic smiles. Christophon's medicinal combines had tried hard to move in on the doomwhaling industry, and Beaufort's government had slapped them down with a sort of savage delight. Waldeck's fellow oligarchs hadn't taken that well, nor had they cared for the loss of prestige they'd suffered.

"No, Hector," Taliaferro repeated more forcefully. "In fact, I intend to oppose any effort to try him on civil charges. We need him gone, true, but we can arrange that without a civil trial—and we damned well better after the insane charges he made in the Chamber! If we come down as hard as he deserves, his supporters will scream that it's part of a cover-up, and some of the Heart Worlders might believe it. Besides, if we can send him home in disgrace, it'll undermine the Fringe far more effectively, not to mention the approval our forbearance will win from the liberals."

"But—"

"Listen to me, Hector," Taliaferro said sharply. "All our projections say that as soon as Skjorning's gone, scores of Fringer delegates will resign in protest. They'll take *themselves* out of the picture and give us an absolute majority. But if we make him a martyr the Fringe'll close ranks to 'avenge' him. It'll be as bad as having MacTaggart back!"

"I don't like it," Waldeck grumbled.

"Nor do I, but the Amalgamation is what matters."

"Is it?" Dieter was more surprised than any of the others to hear himself speak. Eyes swiveled to him, filled with a sort of cold curiosity, but Taliaferro's eyes weren't cold. They were fiery with contempt.

"Of course it is, Oskar," the Gallowayan said, sweet reason sugarcoating the disdain in his voice. "You worked as hard as anyone else to arrange it." His tone added the unspoken qualifier "before you lost your touch," and Dieter flushed. But his chin lifted, and he looked around with a sort of calm defiance which was new to him.

"I did," he said quietly. "Before I saw what it's going to cost."

"What are you talking about?" Amanda Sydon's harsh-voweled New Detroit accent grated on Dieter's ears, and he eyed her with distaste. Sydon was a cobra, every bit Taliaferro's equal. And then he remembered his drugged insult to Fionna. Was his damned prejudice speaking again? But, no, there was no comparison between Fionna and Amanda Sydon. They both happened to be women, but Fionna had also happened to be human.

"You know what I'm talking about, if you'd care to accept the truth, Amanda," he said quietly.

"The truth," she sneered, "is that the Fringe won't even know what hit it for at least ten years—if they manage to figure it out then! With our majority, *we'll* control the post-amalgamation reapportionment. We'll gut them, and they'll stay gutted for fifty years!"

"Fifty?" Dieter allowed himself a chuckle. "Amanda, you obviously don't know as much about the demographics as you think." He felt spines stiffen as he threw his challenge into her teeth, filled with a courage based for a change on conviction rather than convenience. "It won't be fifty years, dear; if the Fringe population curves hold steady and the borders continue to expand, it'll be more like a *hundred* and fifty years."

He glanced at Taliaferro amid a hiss of indrawn breaths as the others heard the true figures for the first time, and the fury burning behind the fixed joviality amused him. So Simon hadn't wanted his minions to know the full extent of his ambition? Was he afraid even they might see the result?

"Dear me, Amanda—didn't Simon mention that?" Dieter's voice was harsh in the semi-silence. "He should have, because the Fringers have waited two hundred years for their representation to match ours; they'll certainly run a worst-case projection and realize they're facing at least another century of powerlessness. How do you think they'll react to that?"

"How *can* they react?" Taliaferro scoffed. "They won't have the votes to stop it."

"Precisely," Dieter said flatly. He drew a deep breath and rose, his gaze burning over the faces around him. Guilt over Fionna's death and over the part he had played—intentionally and unintentionally—in bringing the Federation to this pass supported him. It wasn't enough that he'd only played the game. Games were for children; adulthood carried the duties of adulthood. Angry self-loathing gave him a sort of visionary strength, and he suddenly knew how Cassandra must have felt, yet he had to try, if only to prove to himself that once he'd had the right to sit in the same chamber as Fionna MacTaggart.

"Listen to me, all of you," he said softly. "We can do it. We can use Skjorning to break the Fringe and then ram reapportionment through whatever opposition is left, but are you all too blind to see what will happen then?"

"Tell us, Oskar, since you seem so prescient," Taliaferro sneered, no longer hiding his contempt.

"I'll tell you, Simon," Dieter said, his voice sad. "War."

"War!" Taliaferro's laugh was harsh. "With whom, Oskar? That penniless bunch of ragged-assed barbarians? Hell, man, the Taliaferro Yards alone can build more hulls than all the Fringe Worlds put together! Not even Fringers could be stupid enough to buck that much firepower!"

"Can't they? Simon, I chair Military Oversight. I know what I'm talking about. They can fight, and they *will*. They'll be ready enough if you only railroad Skjorning out of the Assembly—" he saw frowns of distaste at his deliberately honest choice of verb "—but that isn't all you'll be doing. This amalgamation is an antimatter warhead, man! The mere *threat* of enfranchising the Orions will drive them berserk. And it won't be 'barbarian xenophobia,' whatever you tell the Heart Worlds. It'll be a cold sober appreciation of what adding that many non-Terran voters will do to their representation."

"So what?" Taliaferro shot back. "Let some of them try to secede! We'll squash them like bugs, and it'll *prove* they're barbarians! The Heart Worlds'll be as eager as we are to expel them from the Assembly—for good!"

Cold shock knifed through Dieter. Not surprise, really; perhaps he'd guessed Taliaferro's real intent all along and simply chosen not to face it.

"My God," he said softly. "You *want* a war."

"Nonsense!" The denial was just a bit too quick, a touch too offhand. Some of the others were clearly shaken by Dieter's charge, and Taliaferro made himself smile. "It won't come to a war, no matter what you think. The absolute worst may be a police action or two, and we've had those before, haven't we, Hector?" He winked at the Christophon delegate, and the reminder of the food riots on Christophon, three hundred years past, woke a rumble of nervous laughter. "But nobody's left the Federation after a police action," Taliaferro went on persuasively, "and that's all it can be. The Fringers don't have a fleet *or* the means to build one; *we* have both. All I'm saying is that if they're that stupid, it'll only strengthen our position in the long run."

Dieter saw Taliaferro's words sink home. They were the

words his allies wanted to hear, the ones that told them everything was fine, that they still controlled "the game." He'd jolted them, but not enough to break Taliaferro's hold. They would follow him despite anything a political has-been said, and Dieter swallowed an angry rebuttal.

"You're wrong, Simon," he said. "Even assuming all we get is a 'police action or two,' the damage will be done. You've all forgotten that the Federation exists only because its citizens *want* it to exist. When enough of them stop wanting it to live, it will die." He shook his head, feeling their disbelief and rejection.

"No doubt you'll all do exactly as you wish," he said heavily, "but I warn you now—I'll oppose you, both here and on the floor."

The tension in the room suddenly doubled.

"Go ahead!" Taliaferro snarled, his face dark with rage. "If not for your stupidity, we'd already have carried the amalgamation vote! So go on, damn you! We'll still be here when you're a memory—and you know it!"

"Perhaps so, Simon," Dieter said sadly across the immense breach between them. "And you're probably right about whether or not I can stop you. But when you turn the Federation into armed camps which can never live in peace again—" his eyes were live coals as they swept the silent room "—remember I told you it would happen. And when it does, I'll be able to say I tried to stop it. . . What will *you* be able to say?"

"You're almost as eloquent as Skjorning," Taliaferro sneered.

"No, Simon," Dieter's quiet voice sliced back through the silence, "I'm nowhere near as eloquent as he is—but I'm just as accurate."

Taliaferro made a contemptuous gesture, but even under his anger there might have been just a trace of uncertainty. Dieter didn't know, but if Taliaferro did feel any lack of confidence, it wasn't enough. Dieter looked at the stony faces and knew he'd failed. He'd tried to convince them, but they refused to hear; now he could only fight them.

He closed his briefcase, the sound loud in the breathless hush, and walked to the door through the silence, and hostile eyes burned his back. He knew he'd just sealed his political fate, but what mattered was that he would make his fight on the Assembly floor . . . and lose.

He closed the door gently behind him, and the corridor was as empty as his future as he walked slowly to the elevators. He felt the approaching defeat in his bones, but he'd forfeited his career the night he insulted Fionna and discovered he was not the man he'd thought himself to be, and the floor fight would be his Gethsemane. His self-destruction could never expiate his guilt, but perhaps it would let him face Fionna's memory with a sense of having done his best. With a sense of having stood up on his hind legs and said "I am a man—with a man's duties and a man's right to destroy myself for what I know is right."

Oskar Dieter stepped out into the night of Old Terra under a blanket of stars—a man who held his chin high again at last.

Change of Orders

Captain Li Han, commanding officer of TFNS *Longbow,* shrugged as her tunic's seams slid back off the points of her shoulders and the dragonhead flash of her planet dipped low. She should have stood over that tailor with a club! He wasn't used to dealing with officers who massed less than forty kilos, and it showed.

The intraship car slowed and Han banished her frown, squaring her cap on her sleek black hair. The trick, they'd explained at the Academy, was never to notice that anything was wrong. If *you* didn't, *they* didn't. Assuming, of course, that the Protocol Procedures profs were correct.

The door hissed open on the boatbay, and Han watched the side party snap to attention beside her cutter as the electronic bosun's pipe shrilled. There were few non-Oriental faces in *Longbow*; she was homeported on the Fringe World of Hangchow and her crew reflected her ethnicity, and even those few were from other Fringe Worlds. There was not a single Innerworlder in *Longbow*'s complement, and Han sometimes wondered if any of her personnel ever guessed just how and why that had come to pass.

She hoped not. She hoped they would never have to know.

She shook herself mentally and stepped from the car. Hangchow ran to about ten percent more gravity than the one standard G all TFN ships maintained—enough to make the one-gravity field restful—and Han moved with a dancer's grace, hiding a familiar wry smile as she passed through the side party. The top of her cap was below shoulder level on the sideboys, and she wondered if they found her small size amusing? Probably. Han's diminutive size dogged her career like a shadow. She'd probably always be remembered as the smallest midshipman ever to enter the Academy, rather than as the woman who graduated with the honor sword by her side, but the fact that she stood just under 107 centimeters hadn't kept her from showing the whole pack her heels, she thought cheerfully. And captain's rank in Battle Fleet at thirty-seven was no mean accomplishment, either.

She returned the salutes, and the cutter's hatch slid shut as she dropped into the cushioned chair. And so, she thought, off to another scintillating courtesy call . . . but this one might be more important than most.

The cutter idled clear of *Longbow*, and Han allowed herself a moment of pride as she studied her command through the port. The huge, ungainly bulk of Skywatch Three, the orbital headquarters of Galloway's World System Defense Command, made a perfect foil for the battlecruiser's elegance. Light from the system's G4 primary glittered on *Longbow*'s graceful flanks and turned her recessed weapons bays into sooty ovals of shadow, hiding the deadly devices crouching within. Even the clutter of external ordnance hardpoints and the massive housings of her drive pods seemed graceful and balanced. Other ships carried heavier armaments, or more defense, but none matched the speed, maneuverability, and power blended in *Longbow*'s sinister beauty.

Han sighed and looked away. Beautiful, yes, but still a killing machine. A weapon of war to engage and destroy humanity's enemies. It passed belief that Navy personnel might someday have to decide just which *humans* were enemies.

Air screamed past the cutter's hull as it skipped into Galloway's World's atmosphere, and the little boat banked gently as it headed for the Yard's landing pads. Han watched the Jamieson Archipelago grow, amused as always by the anomaly which left the Fleet's fourth largest shipyard the only Navy base in existence without a name. It was just "the Yard," as it had been since the First Interstellar War, when Galloway's World was *the* navy yard for the Federation —just as the sprawling kilometers of dependent housing around it were simply "the Reservation." There were larger bases now, Zephrain for one, but no other planet rivaled the sheer numbers of hulls which emerged from the military and civilian building slips of Galloway's World.

The cutter swooped over the innocent weather domes that hid the Yard's missile silos and projector pits. As a rule, the TFN preferred to defend inhabited planets with orbital forts, sparing civilians the incidental destruction attendant upon modern combat, but there was no point pretending about the Jamieson Archipelago. The Yard alone made the island chain a priority target for any enemy, and the Yard wasn't alone. It crowded shoulder-to-shoulder with the Taliaferro Yard; the Kreuger Space Works; Vickers-Mitsubishi–Galloway's World; General Dynamics of Terra; and a dozen other major building centers. Coupled with the orbital facilities where the ground-built components were assembled, the Archipelago represented the largest concentration of industrial might in the known galaxy.

The cutter dropped quickly for its landing circle, and Han watched the ground rush up to meet them, but her thoughts were on her meeting with the Port Admiral. She drew a deep breath, concentrating on the mental discipline that calmed the pulse, and glanced at her watch. Right on the tick. Good.

"Good afternoon, Captain Li." The yeoman in the outer office smiled respectfully as the tiny captain entered. "Please have a seat. Admiral Rutgers' last appointment is running a little over."

Han settled in a comfortable chair and checked her watch again, hoping Admiral Rutgers wasn't going to be tied up long. She was due to ship out for Christophon in two hours, and there were always last-minute details to crowd a departure time. It was well known that Port Admirals' whims had much the same force as direct decrees from God, but that never seemed to help when the admiral at the other end wanted to know where you'd spent that extra hour or two.

The door slid open and Han glanced up—then came

quickly to her feet at the sight of a vice admiral's sleeve braid. The tall, dark-faced man with the neat beard nodded to her.

"Captain."

"Admiral Trevayne."

"Another penitent here to see the Admiral, Captain Li?"

"No, sir." Han hid a smile. "Just a courtesy call before departure."

"Ah!" Trevayne nodded and turned away.

Li Han regarded his broad shoulders thoughtfully. Now what did that "Ah!" mean? There was something hidden behind it; she could almost taste it. Did he know something she didn't? Possibly. Quite possibly. Trevayne was a marked man in the service: the youngest man ever to command a monitor battlegroup, and no question that he was headed for CNO and possibly even Sky Marshal before he was done. If there was any loose information floating around, it would have come to his ears long since. Rumor credited the man with an uncanny ability to read the future. Was he reading it now?

Han didn't know him well enough to be certain, though she knew his son quite well. It was always easier to know one's juniors than one's seniors, but even if it hadn't been, Lieutenant Commander Colin Trevayne of the scout cruiser *Ashanti* was a highly . . . visible personality within the Fleet. Centuries of tradition decreed that the Federation's widely-diverse military people *must* be nonpartisan. In a sense, accepting a TFN commission was to take a vow of political celibacy—or so it had been until very recently—and Ian Trevayne honored that tradition. Colin, however, was as fiery as his father was calm and controlled. His outspoken sympathy for the Fringe put him firmly in the "Young Turk" camp, and Han wondered if rumor exaggerated the rift between father and son.

The yeoman's panel beeped gently, and he spoke into his hushphone, then listened briefly.

"Admiral Trevayne, Captain Li; Admiral Rutgers would like to see you both, if you please," he said, and Han felt her eyebrows rise. There *was* something in the wind! She waited courteously for Trevayne to lead the way into the inner sanctum, and her nerves were strung to fever pitch.

Fleet Admiral William Rutgers was a bulky man of indeterminate ancestry, and Han smiled warmly as a paw like an Old Terran bear's enveloped her tiny hand in greeting. Rutgers, once her father's chief of staff, had been her own fifth-year tactical instructor almost fifteen years ago.

"Thank you both for being patient," he said, sitting back down and waving them to chairs. Han waited until Trevayne sat before she followed suit. It was just a little awkward to be so junior to the only other two people present . . . especially after coming straight from her own ship, where she was mistress after God and even that precedence was a bit blurred.

"Patient, Bill?" Trevayne chuckled. "Junior officers are always patient—or they bloody well better learn to pretend they are!"

"Except for the ones like you, Ian," Rutgers said, shaking his head in mock sadness.

Trevayne laughed easily. His elegant frame—no problems with *his* tailoring—was seated casually, almost carelessly, right ankle on left knee. To sit like that in the presence of an admiral, you had to *be* an admiral. But Trevayne had something else, something beyond even his membership in one of the "dynasties" of the Federation's Navy. His rapid rise wasn't due solely to birth or brilliance. Han's father had been an admiral before his retirement, and his father before him, yet she lacked that not-quite-arrogant "something else." Charisma, perhaps?

But from what source? He was a man who valued style and flair, and one who carried it off with ease, yet that wasn't explanation enough. It came to her suddenly that Trevayne had been reared to lead even as she had, but in a society which openly acknowledged and accepted such expectations. He *expected* to be a leader, and because he expected it of himself, others expected it of him, as well. His undoubted brilliance simply confirmed the wisdom of those mutual expectations.

"Well, today I have good reason for being in a hurry," he said. "Tomorrow is Courtenay's birthday, and I haven't picked out a present yet. And your godson is shipping out tomorrow on *Ashanti*." His jaw clenched for an instant, as if with sudden hurt. "I'm supposed to have lunch with him . . .

lunch and—" he added, looking straight at Rutgers "—a much-needed talk."

Han carefully did not take note of the pain in her senior's dark face.

"I'm sorry, Ian," Rutgers said, suddenly serious. "You'd better delegate the shopping to Natalya. As for Colin . . . I know things are touchy just now, and I'll try to leave you time for lunch, but I may not be able to. Your leave's been canceled."

Han sat straighter and felt her face become masklike. Vice admirals' leaves were not cut short on whims.

"I see." Trevayne's face was very calm as he studied the Port Admiral. Too calm. It was a mask, too, Han realized sadly; everyone wore masks these days, even in the Fleet. "And might one ask why, Admiral?"

"One might," Rutgers said grimly. He glanced over at Han for a moment. "I asked you two to come in together to save a little time; what I have to say will affect you both. On the other hand, I trust that I don't have to remind you both that what's said here *stays* here. Clear?"

Both his juniors nodded.

"All right. As you know, the Assembly's been in a furor ever since the MacTaggart assassination. And it didn't help a bit when Skjorning murdered Fouchet! I—" He broke off and glanced at Han, then smiled unwillingly and shook his head.

"Captain, I seem to recall a certain midshipman's expression which generally indicated disagreement. Why am I seeing it now?"

"Disagreement, Admiral?" Han shook her head. "Not disagreement. It's just that I find it difficult to condemn Assemblyman Skjorning."

"Who said I condemned him? I only said it didn't help, which it didn't. Mind, I'm not saying the same thing wouldn't have happened if he'd held his hand; I think it would have, in fact. But it's happened now, and it's up to us to pick up the pieces."

"Yes, sir."

"What 'pieces' d'you mean, Bill?" Trevayne asked, his eyes narrowing.

"I wish I knew," Rutgers sighed, running a hand over his hair. "I take it you're both reasonably informed on events on Old Terra?" They nodded, and he continued. "Well, things are coming to a head. The Assembly has decided to impeach Skjorning."

"It's not as if they really have a choice, Bill," Trevayne pointed out, "but it doesn't automatically follow that the impeachment will be sustained."

"Oh, you're so right, Ian," Rutgers said softly, and pulled out a classified binder. He slapped it down on his blotter and pressed his thumb to the lock. Scanners considered for a moment, then released the latch, and he pulled out a sheaf of yellow security paper.

"This," he said, "is an ONI evaluation of the situation as of three weeks ago. It arrived today . . . by courier drone."

Han's inner tension clicked higher. Galloway's World was a Corporate World, tied into the communications net the Corporate Worlders had used to deadly effect against the Fringe for decades. No com beam could be driven through a warp point, but it was quite possible to build deep-space relay stations within star systems. All messages had to be physically carried through warp points aboard ships or small, unmanned courier drones, but once through, they could be transcribed and transmitted to the next warp point. Yet such systems took time to emplace, and they were incredibly expensive, both to build and maintain.

The Corporate Worlds had capitalized upon that. In the spirit of "generosity," their delegates had declared that it was only proper that each system should be responsible for its own relay networks rather than making them a charge upon any other system, and, since they controlled the Assembly, the Assembly had agreed. But the Fringe Worlds, of course, were too poor to build and extend the relay nets to *their* worlds. *All* of their messages must travel by ship or drone, which—just coincidentally—meant that it was far, far easier for Corporate World politicos to confer with their homeworlds. They could send a message and get a response in days; the same process took months for a Fringer delegation, and that explained a great deal about the smoothly-oiled precision of the Taliaferro Machine.

But if ONI had sent this data by drone, it meant whoever had sent it didn't trust the relays. It wasn't all that unusual for classified data to be sent physically rather than risk interception, but Admiral Rutgers' tone and expression told her *this* drone was more important than most.

"Indications are that the Taliaferro crowd doesn't plan to challenge the Ortler precedent," the burly admiral continued grimly. "Rather than push for Skjorning's civil trial on Old Terra, they're going to expel him from the Assembly and send him back to the Kontravian Cluster under Lictor escort. As Taliaferro puts it—" he thumbed through the Naval Intelligence report for the passage he sought, and his voice was harsh as he read aloud "—'Let us send the barbarians among us back to the Fringe where they belong!' "

Han felt her face blanch. No wonder Trevayne's leave had been canceled! When the Fringe heard about *this*—!

Rutgers watched her calmly, and she returned his gaze levelly. He shook his head.

"Han, someday you may be able to keep me from guessing what you're thinking. Until that day comes, I wouldn't waste the effort, if I were you."

"Sir?"

"You know precisely what I mean. This—" he tapped the piece of paper "—is probably the stupidest brilliant political maneuver in human history. And, my dear, you know it as well as I do."

"As the Admiral says," she said in a colorless voice.

"One day, Han," Rutgers mused, "you'll try the China doll trick once too often." Despite her concern, Han's lips twitched, and he grinned at her. Then he sobered.

"This is also—" he said slowly, tapping the paper again "—going to make a bad situation much, much worse. Amalgamation and reapportionment would be terribly hard for the Fringe to swallow under any circumstances, but when you add the MacTaggart assassination and what they're going to see as a calculated and contemptuous rejection of justice. . . ."

"I should bloody well think so!" Trevayne said. "Talk about a cat among the pigeons!"

"I know, Ian. I know. But ONI thinks it's going to happen."

"But it hasn't happened yet, has it?"

"No, but it will, Ian. It's only a matter of time, and what matters to us right this minute are the Fleet orders which came in the same drone. They're the reason your leave's been canceled, and why you, Captain, aren't going to Christophon after all."

He pinched his nose wearily. "In all my days in the TFN, I have never received orders quite like these," he said soberly. "As of now, the Fleet's primary mission has been changed 'for the duration of the current political crisis,' as our instructions so neatly phrase it. Our new mission is to play fireman across the width and breadth of the Federation when this gets out."

"Good God, Bill," Trevayne said mildly. "They have to be out of their minds. They *do* realize the Federation is over fourteen hundred light-years across, don't they? How do they expect us to be everywhere we'll have to be?"

"They don't. Intelligence has identified a dozen critical systems and clusters with an exceptional potential for disaster. Our immediate concern is to place a battlegroup or two to cover each of them as a show of force."

"Against our own people, sir?" Han asked softly.

"Against *anyone*, Captain," Rutgers said heavily.

"If you'll pardon my saying so, Bill," Trevayne said quietly, "that's an excellent recipe for disaster if something does go wrong. Since you're talking to us, I assume you mean Battle Fleet units, not Frontier Fleet."

"I do," Rutgers said. "Frontier Fleet's spread too thin as it is—Frontier Fleet is *always* spread too thin." And, Han thought sadly, too many of Frontier Fleet's officers were too sympathetic to "their" sectors' needs to be "reliable." "So we're dispersing some of Battle Fleet to the trouble spots; a little less than half our active units, to be precise."

"And if the balloon goes up, we won't have concentration of force anywhere," Trevayne pointed out.

"I know that. You know that. Probably the Joint Chiefs know that. The Assembly, unfortunately, doesn't know it and doesn't *want* to know it. And we, as you may recall, work for the civilians."

"Yes, sir."

"Thank you. Now, Ian, your battlegroup is headed for Osterman's Star. I want you to ship out before nineteen hundred zulu today."

"Yes, sir."

"You, Captain Li, will sign for this binder. You will

personally deliver it to Fleet Admiral Forsythe and attach your ship to his command. He'll give you further orders at that time."

"Yes, sir."

"All right." Rutgers rubbed the binder and drew a deep breath. "I'm going to say something I really shouldn't say. I'm going to tell you that I think the Assembly's lost its mind and that when—not if—the shit hits the fan, it's going to be up to us to scrape it off our faces and salvage something from the wreck. We're the Federation Navy, and the Federation Navy has never fired on Terran civilians. I'd like to keep it that way. But if it comes to it—" his eyes burned into Han's and then swiveled slowly to Trevayne "—remember that we are the *Federation* Navy."

There was a moment of silence, and Han felt something like guilt as she returned her old teacher's regard.

"Very well." Rutgers rose to signal the end of the interview and held out his hand again. "My yeoman has your orders. Pick them up and carry them out. And may God have mercy on us all."

Li Han reclined in lotus position in the center of her cabin carpet. By planet-side standards, her cabin was small and cramped; by Navy standards, it was luxuriously large; and by anyone's standards, a proud Hangchow government had furnished it with elegant taste. Her eyes drifted to the priceless fifth-century lacquered screen hiding her safe, and the thought of what lay within it undermined her ability to find tranquillity.

She sighed and rolled out of the lotus. There was no point pretending, and it was a bad habit to pretend to relax. She flowed to her feet and considered more stringent exercises, but activity wasn't the anodyne she needed now. Her doubts demanded resolution.

Yet there was nowhere for a captain to turn when troubled by doubt. Junior officers could discuss their fears; enlisted people could do the same. Even admirals could talk with other admirals, or at least their flag captains. But captains' absolute authority during their months-long voyages robbed them of that luxury. God was the only person to whom a wise skipper admitted her doubts. Infallibility.

Her lips quirked at the thought. That was what a captain must radiate. Absolute confidence.

Han had never made any secret of her own apolitical loyalty to her homeworld, and though, like most Fringers, she'd studied politics closely, she wasn't a political person. Or, at least, she hadn't *been* a political person. Like every child of Hangchow, she'd learned at an early age that the Corporate Worlds controlled her people's economic destiny, yet she had always believed the Legislative Assembly would somehow safeguard their political rights . . . until she'd gained her fourth ring and become privy to the inner workings of the policies the Fleet sometimes enforced. Her first deployment as captain had based her ship on New Detroit, and, for the first time, she had realized how totally the Corporate Worlds controlled the Assembly.

Even then, she'd believed time and demographics were on the side of the Fringe; now it seemed the Corporate Worlds were determined to turn back the clock and disenfranchise her people. They even had a precedent, for the Reapportionments of 2184 and 2240 had done exactly the same thing.

Han had not been a political person, but she had been and still was a direct one. She never lied to herself. When the first doubt appeared, she'd dragged it ruthlessly into the open, examining it pitilessly.

To her surprise, the light of day did not kill it. Indeed, it thrived in the sunlight, and her suspicion-sharpened eyes saw things she'd never noticed before. And as a direct person who accepted the Fleet's admonition to be prepared, Han had begun to consider what she—Li Han the woman, as well as Li Han the captain—would do if the unthinkable happened. What was her duty? Where did her loyalty lie if the madmen on either side pushed the Federation beyond its strength? Her conclusions had shocked her, but she was what she was. She could be no other; and being what she was, she had acted.

Captian Li Han, TFN, woke frequently these nights—woke praying that the Federation she loved and served would survive the storm lashing across it. But if the day came when the Federation toppled under the hurricane, she also knew what she would do . . . what she would have to do.

* * *

"Challenge from the flagship, sir."

Han glanced at her executive officer and then at the plot displaying the might of Task Force Seventeen. Eight monitors, eight superdreadnoughts, six assault carriers, two fleet carriers, ten battle-cruisers, dozens of cruisers, and scores of destroyers, Marine transports, repair ships, colliers . . . It made an imposing sight on the tactical display. More firepower than the TFN had committed to most campaigns of the Fourth Interstellar War—certainly more than had ever been deployed in a single battle. And all this panoply of war, she thought sadly, was to overawe the citizens of the Federation, not to defeat their enemies in battle.

"Standard acknowledgment, Chang," she said.

"Yes, sir."

The message reached out across the emptiness to the task force. There was a communications lag of over two minutes at this range, even as *Longbow* loped towards Task Force Seventeen at ten percent of light speed.

"Reply from Flag, sir. We are to take position in company with *Flintlock*. Captain to report aboard *Anderson* as soon as convenient. One query: do we have dispatches on board?"

"Reply affirmative, Exec." She pressed a stud on her command chair arm console. "Boatbay," she said.

"Boatbay, aye," a voice replied in her mastoid battlephone.

"Chief Ling, this is the Captain. I need my cutter in twenty minutes."

"Yes, sir. She'll be ready to flit."

"Thank you, Chief." She killed the circuit and returned her attention to the plot, watching the tiny blips blink from the red-ringed circles of unidentified ships to the green-ringed dots of known units as *Longbow*'s computers sorted out their transponders. One dot was circled in gold—TFNS *Howard Anderson*, the monitor flagship—and it swung to the center of the plot as *Longbow* headed straight for her. Han studied it a moment, then punched up identities on the others, looking for familiar faces among their commanders.

Anderson's skipper she knew: Captain Willis Enwright, Fleet Admiral Forsythe's handpicked flag captain and one of the most brilliant of the many Fringe World officers in the Fleet. Nor was he the first such in his family—*Anderson's* sistership, the *Lawrence Enwright*, was named for one of his ancestors. Captain Simon Hodah had her, Han remembered with a warm smile. Simon was ten years her senior, but they'd been close friends since Han's middie cruise as his assistant astrogator. There were other names and faces out here to be remembered. Vice Admiral Traynor in command of one of the superdreadnought battlegroups; Vice Admiral Eric Hale, commanding the other. Vice Admiral Analiese Ashigara, a Fringe Worlder from Hokkaido, flying her lights aboard the assault carrier *Basilisk*. Vice Admiral Singh, Forsythe's second in command, flying his lights aboard Hodah's ship.

Meetings between this many Fleet units were rare, and it felt good to see the light codes, to remember the men and women in the tight knit Navy community. They were professionals one and all; brothers and sisters of the sword, dedicated to the pure service of the Federation's ideals.

Or that was the idea. That was the Navy's credo, even if its members were merely human and often fell short of the ideal. Han's smile faded as she weighed herself against the standards of the Fleet, and she wondered how many of those others she knew were doing the same thing over there behind the weapons and armor, behind the armor of their eyes?

She shook her head and rose.

"You have the con, Exec," she said formally. "I'm going to my quarters for a quick shower before I report to the Admiral."

"Yes, sir."

Commander Tsing Chang took the command chair as the captain left the bridge. His eyes flicked over the readouts as the intraship car's doors hissed quietly shut. Only then did he allow himself a glance at the blank doors which had hidden his tiny captain. Did she really think no one else on board had guessed what she was thinking? He returned his attention to the tactical plot, his face expressionless, his mind busy behind his dark eyes.

"Greetings, Captain Li." Fleet Admiral Stepan Forsythe held out his hand, and Han could not help comparing his dry, frail grip with the firm, hairy clasp of the last fleet admiral she'd met. Stepan Forsythe was William Rutgers' physical opposite in every way, she thought. He was slender, stoop-shouldered, showing his advanced age in his lined face and thinning hair. Forsythe was a living link with the days of the Fourth Interstellar War, and Han knew he was due for retirement soon. His body was old and frail, for he was one of the rare individuals who responded poorly to the anti-aging therapies, but keen intelligence and will power glinted behind his gray eyes.

"Thank you, sir," she said, returning the clasp.

"You made a fast passage," Forsythe continued, waving her to a chair and touching the security binder on his desk as if to restrain a venomous serpent.

"We tried, sir."

"Yes. Well, would you like a drink while I glance through this?"

"No, sir. Thank you."

"Very well. If you'll excuse me?"

Han arranged her cap very precisely on her knees and sat quietly as the old admiral opened the binder and extracted the sheets of closely printed material. He read slowly, carefully, but no change of expression betrayed his thoughts. Perhaps the contents were less of a shock to him than they'd been to her. Perhaps he'd gone even further than she in analyzing the crisis, or perhaps he simply had access to more information than a mere captain.

Forsythe sighed and turned the final page at last, then jogged the sheets neatly back into order. He returned them to the binder and pressed a stud on his console, glancing into the screen as it lit.

"Willis? Would you come to my quarters, please?"

"Yes, sir."

Forsythe cut the circuit and smiled tautly at Han. "I realize you probably don't know any more than is contained in these documents, Captain Li, but I'd appreciate it if you'd give Captain Enwright and myself the benefit of your firsthand impressions. We're rather isolated out here, and neither of us has had any personal contact with the Innerworlds in almost a year."

"Of course, sir," Han said, hiding her discomfort.

"Thank you. We— ah! Here's the captain."

Han rose quickly as Willis Enwright entered the cabin with a hurried stride. That was one of the things she associated with Enwright—quickness, speed, almost haste. It was as if he resented the dawdling pace of time and wrestled with every second for the maximum utility he could wring from it. It made for a thorny personality, but it also made him a superb captain and would someday make him an equally outstanding admiral.

"Han!" He squeezed her hand warmly. "Good to see you again. How are your parents?"

"Mother is as beautiful as ever; Father is as handsome." Han smiled. "What else is there to say?"

"I suppose that does just about cover it," Enwright agreed with a grin. He dropped sloppily into a chair, and Han seated herself again, glancing at Forsythe for his reaction to Enwright's informality. The old admiral only smiled at his flag captain. Then his expression tightened.

"Willis, Captain Li has brought us some disturbing information." He slid the binder across the desk. "Want a look?"

"Why?" Enwright shrugged. "No doubt the Assembly's done something else foolish. They've specialized in that for years, or we wouldn't be out here, sir."

"Foolish or not, they're still the duly constituted government," Forsythe said, the slight edge in his voice suggesting that this wasn't the first time he and Enwright had struck sparks on the subject. "However—" Forsythe shook his head "—I have to agree that this time they really have been foolish. Look at this." He opened the binder and handed Enwright the top sheet, and the captain's face tightened.

"Foolish isn't the word, sir," he said quietly, his humor vanished. "My God, if this goes through the whole Fringe will go up in smoke . . . and I don't know as how I'll blame them, either." He read further, then whistled. "Jesus! If they *do* expel Lad Skjorning, the shit will really fly, Admiral!"

"Precisely," Forsythe said frostily. "And if, as you so quaintly put it, the shit *does* fly, whose job is it to quiet the situation back down?"

"Ours," Enwright said, his voice troubled.

"Ours, indeed, Captain." Forsythe turned back to Han.

"Captain Li, is it your impression this evaluation is essentially accurate?"

"Well, sir," Han said carefully, "Admiral Rutgers certainly seemed to think so when he spoke to me." She shrugged. "But you probably know more about it from his dispatch."

"His dispatch, like many things these days, is written on many levels." For just an instant, Forsythe showed every year of his advanced age. "It seems we're afraid to be totally open even in secure communications."

"It's because no one wants to face it, Stepan," Enwright said. "But we have to. The Federation is on the verge of civil war."

It was the first time someone had come right out and said it in Han's presence—trust Willis to be the first. She watched Forsythe, but the old admiral had his expression well in hand.

"On the verge is not the same thing as actively at war, Willis," he said quietly. "It's our job to see it doesn't go that far."

"Agreed," Enwright nodded. "But what if it's a job we can't do, sir?"

"There *is* no job the Fleet can't do!"

"Sir, Fringers aren't Arachnids—or even Tangri or Orions. Dealing with aliens may come down to a matter of firepower more often than we like, but it doesn't bother the Fleet much—that's our job, after all. But firing on our own people?" Enwright shook his head sadly. "With all due respect, I'm not sure the crews could do it."

"It won't come to that," Forsythe said. "We'll warp out immediately for routine maneuvers in Kontravian space. Not even the Beauforters are crazy enough to start something with a task force this size overhead."

"Probably not," Enwright said softly. "But what if it's already started, sir? I've served with Lad Skjorning. He's no hothead, but once he makes up his mind, not God nor the devil can change it."

"Skjorning is only one man, Willis."

"But if they send him home, he'll be the most important 'one man' in the entire Kontravian Cluster, sir. He's inherited all of Fionna MacTaggart's prestige, as well as his own, which was already pretty considerable."

"Admiral," Han said diffidently, "Captain Enwright has a point. I don't know if you realize just how critical Skjorning has become. If the Assembly expels him, hundreds of Fringer delegates will resign in protest."

"Then they're fools!" Forsythe snorted. "They should stay and fight!"

"That's easy for us to say, sir," Enwright pointed out gently. "We've been safely isolated here in the Fleet. We're more like one of the old monastic fighting orders than a representative segment of our society, and we certainly haven't personally faced the Corporate World political machine. Its manipulation of the Assembly has become so blatant no Fringer delegate had any doubts left even before MacTaggart was murdered. Now the writing's on the wall, as far as they're concerned. They're tired of fighting within a system that won't let them win, sir."

"But if they persist in this madness they'll force an open break! They're playing right into the hands of this sort of manipulation." Forsythe tapped the binder. "Don't they *see* that?"

"With respect, Admiral," Han said, "they're too angry to care."

"And do you share their anger, Captain Li?" Forsythe asked softly.

"Yes, sir, I do." It was the first time a superior had asked her that, and Han found it almost a relief to answer openly.

"Stepan," Enwright's quiet voice drew the admiral's eyes away from her, "most of the Outworlders in the Fleet share Captain Li's feelings. You're not a Fringer, so maybe you don't see it that way, but the Fringers *do*. That's why I'm so concerned about this 'show of force' business. If it comes to a real confrontation, there's no telling how the Fleet will react. More than sixty percent of our personnel *are* Fringers, Stepan."

"They are also sworn members of the Federation's armed forces," Forsythe said levelly. "If the time comes, they'll remember that." He waved a hand briskly, as if to dispel the tension which had sprung up. "But we're going to the Kontravian Cluster to make certain it never comes to that."

"Yes, sir," Enwright said, leaning forward in his chair,

"and with the admiral's permission, I'd like to make a suggestion."

"Of course." Forsythe watched Enwright thoughtfully.

"You're absolutely right on at least one point, sir; the best way to make sure nothing happens is to create a Fleet presence in Kontravian space before any explosion. I suggest that we detach Admiral Ashigara's carrier group and the battle-cruisers and send them on ahead. They're fifty percent faster than the monitors. At flank speed, they could reach the Kontravian Cluster almost three months before the rest of the task force. That'd give us that much more time before the Kontravians can do anything rash."

Forsythe swiveled his chair slowly back and forth, considering, and Han watched him closely. Willis was right. The sooner they got warships into the cluster, the better. Even the most fervent Fringe sympathizer in the Fleet would be willing to nip trouble in the bud *before* it reached shooting proportions.

"No, Willis," Forsythe said finally. Enwright looked prepared to argue, but Forsythe waved a hand gently. "I'm glad you're thinking in terms of prevention, but if we send a detachment ahead the whole idea of a routine visit goes out the airlock. And I think you overestimate the depth of feeling in the Cluster. I don't question your reading of the Fringe leadership, but there's a deep reservoir of loyalty to Old Terra among the population. We'll get there before their leaders push them into anything truly rash."

"Stepan," Enwright said, "please don't equate loyalty to the motherworld with loyalty to the Assembly! Fringers see them as two separate entities."

"Perhaps," Forsythe said testily, "but there's enough overlap to offset any rashness, I think. And the last thing we can afford is to look as if we *expect* a break. No, Willis. We'll do it my way."

Han held her breath and wondered if Enwright would push it. She glanced at the captain, reading the worry in his face, but he held his tongue.

"That's settled, then," Forsythe said with the same finality. He glanced at his desk chronometer. "I see it's just about time for dinner, Captain Li. Will you dine with us?"

"I'd be honored, Admiral," she said, accepting the change of subject, and rose to follow her superiors from the cabin, glancing back at the sealed security binder on the desk as they left.

A cold breeze blew through her bones as she passed the Marine guard and the cabin hatch closed behind them. Admiral Forsythe was a good man, a loyal man—one who cared about *all* the Federation's citizens. Yet she had a premonition that a terrible mistake had just been made.

Homecoming

The wrenching stress of warp transit echoed in every inner ear aboard the starship *Capricorn*, though liners never transited warp points at the same speed as warships lest their delicate (and paying) passengers lose their breakfasts. The moment of indescribable tension passed into memory as *Capricorn*'s momentarily addled electronic systems recovered, and her deck plates trembled gently as her powerful drive sang back up to maximum, for *Capricorn* was a fast ship, with a reputation to maintain.

Ladislaus Skjorning stepped out of his cabin into the carpeted passages of first class. After months of travel, he no longer bothered to glance over his shoulder at the calm, expressionless face of the Assembly lictor gliding a pace behind him. In all the long, dreary days of shipboard existence, Ladislaus had not even learned the man's name, not that it mattered. One lictor was very like another, he'd found; none permitted mere humanity to hamper the discharge of their duty.

He frowned at his own derisive thought, for he knew it was unfair. From the Lictor General down to the rawest first-year recruit, the lictors had no planetary loyalties and ground no partisan axes. They were servants of the Assembly, with Federation-wide citizenship so no single world could challenge their devotion to it. But fair or not, Ladislaus could see his anonymous shadow only as an extension of the Assembly.

A familiar throb of rage touched him as he recalled the

farce the Assembly had called an "impeachment." He'd never attempted to deny his guilt; indeed, Wu Liang, Hangchow's chief delegate and Ladislaus' advocate, had based his entire defense on the Ortler Decision, claiming the same immunity for his client, and so underlined the defiant Fringe insistence that his act had been neither more nor less than an execution and thrown the Corporate Worlds' hypocrisy back into their teeth.

Ladislaus had known how thin a thread his life hung upon, but hatred had supported him, feeding on the vituperation the Corporate Worlds heaped upon him and stoked by his cold appreciation of the skill with which the Taliaferro Machine used the Fringe's own fury to destroy it. The decision to expel him like a pariah—to send him back to the Fringe as if that were the one proper dumping ground for "barbarians"—had cut like the flick of a whip, and it had driven the Fringe berserk. Delegate after delegate had risen to denounce the Corporate Worlds, and the Heart Worlds had heard only their incoherent fury. They had not chosen to recognize the manipulation which spawned that rage, and Ladislaus had watched the Innerworld delegations recoil from the Fringers' passion, accepting the damning Corporate World caricature as truth.

He'd seen it sound the death knell of compromise, and he had felt only a grim eagerness to go back out among the sane worlds of the distant stars and begin what must be begun.

Yet he'd felt a sort of admiration for the handful of moderates who had fought to stem the furious tide of history. It had been overshadowed by his own impatience, his own awareness that the dream they sought to preserve had already died, but it had been real. And he'd admired no one more than he had Oskar Dieter.

How many other delegates had felt his own astonishment when the slim New Zuricher begged for moderation and reason? When he, as head of Fouchet's own delegation, moved to drop all charges against Fouchet's killer? When he met Simon Taliaferro headlong in the furious debate, fighting with every ounce of parliamentary skill to save both Ladislaus and the Assembly? It had been a doomed battle, but he'd refused to surrender and a few—a tattered remnant—of the erstwhile moderates had rallied to his banner, as if they, like Ladislaus, recognized the true stakes. . . .

He shook free of the past and made his way into the lonely first-class lounge. He was *Capricorn's* last first-class passenger, for Beaufort was the end of her run—the last, ultimate end point of the Federation, in a sense. Many worlds lay still further out, but Beaufort was the end of the warp lines into the Kontravian Cluster, a lonely world, ignored by the magnates who moved and shook the Federation until the doomwhale had suddenly beckoned profit.

Ladislaus parked himself in a lounger under one of the magnifying screens as the ship swept towards the planet of his birth. Already he could make out the orbit port, tiny with distance as it waited with shuttles and cargo. Ships like *Capricorn* were creatures of the void, fated never to taste atmosphere, and before the days of doomwhaling there had been no orbit port at Beaufort. Only the tramp freighters, adapted for atmospheric travel, had come here then, gleaning a fragile profit in waters too shallow to attract the huge combines like the Taliaferro Line or even the chartered mail packets of the Mobius Corporation.

Beyond the orbit port loomed the vast, purple bulk of Beaufort, and he stared at it with hungry eyes. He could almost taste the iodine-rich wind, almost feel the heavy pull of gravity. Huge clouds covered half the visible planet, and he smiled. There was heavy weather in the Hellbore, and heavy weather on Beaufort was like heavy weather nowhere else in the Galaxy. Most of the planetary surface was water, the deep, purple, surging water of home. Except for the small southern continent of Grendelsbane, the limited habitable land masses were found only in the loose necklaces of islands threaded around the watery sphere. Some of the islands were huge, by Terran standards, but they were still islands, the peaks and plateaus of sunken mountains rearing sheer and indomitable from the cold, cold seas. Man had shaped those islands into homes for himself and his children, but Beaufort had shaped Man, too. The granite of its stony archipelagoes was in the Beaufort soul, and Ladislaus longed to touch the surface of his world, longed to draw the strength of that bedrock presence within himself once more.

Yet first he must face his failure. He had gone to Old

Terra as Chief of Security; he returned a broken man, derelict in his duty and expelled from the Assembly. The people of Beaufort were compassionate and understanding in ways which far outreached the Innerworlders on their safe, tamed planets, but Beauforters did their jobs. On a world where gravity, pressure, and the sea all conspired against the human intruder, there was only one fully acceptable excuse, and that was death. Ladislaus understood that side of his people, for it made them what they were even as it had made him what he was, and he dreaded their silent disapproval almost as much as he dreaded his own sense of failure.

He sat motionless for long hours as the orbit port grew and grew. They passed the bulk of Beaufort Skywatch, spartan and pure in the black and white blazonry of Fortress Command, and he watched a light cruiser slide past *Capricorn*, her white hull and blue Frontier Fleet markings gleaming under the distant light of Beaufort's sun. The stylized galactic lens of her service glistened like silver on her forward hull as she altered course and slashed away with all the arrogance of her greyhound breed, and Ladislaus wondered what so heavy a Fleet unit was doing here.

Beaufort's massive moon cleared the edge of the planet, looming huge and lovely in the sun's reflected light, for Beaufort's Bowditch was bigger than Old Terra's neighbor Mars, with a .5 G gravity and nearly enough atmosphere to support life. It was one of the universe's more bitter jokes that Beaufort—a planet almost too massive for Man—should possess a moon not quite massive enough for him. Ladislaus could still recall his initial shock upon seeing Old Terra's Luna and realizing what a miserable lump of rock had given birth to the white moon on the Federation's banners. And as for the ridiculous little ripples Old Terra called "tides"—!

Then *Capricorn*'s drive died at last. The tractors of the orbit port reached out, and the liner shivered as they snubbed away her last motion and rolled her, aligning her with the huge, flexible docking tubes. Within minutes, she would be secured, her cargo and personnel ports open, and Ladislaus rose slowly. He turned and left the lounge, the lictor like an expressionless ghost behind him.

* * *

The shuttle dropped away from Beaufort Orbit Port like a seashrike striking at nearcod, and Ladislaus sat silently, watching out a port. The shuttle's wings configured back, their leading edges glowing as the pilot skimmed atmosphere to dump orbital velocity. He watched them extend slowly as the shuttle's speed dropped, the orange glow fading as the heat bled away into Beaufort's cold air and their speed dropped still further, until the engines took over, pushing them the last few hundred kilometers to the Beowulf Archipelago . . . and home.

The sprawling island of Kraki came into sight, the modest space port dead center in its star-shaped mass. It was a small port, by Innerworld standards, and few attempts had been made to gloss over the gaunt functionalism of early days. Beaufort wanted its spaceport grim and cold.

The shuttle touched down, and Ladislaus felt an icy pang of dread as he looked out at the unexpected throng awaiting him. They ringed the shuttle pad, coats and clothing whipped by the bitter wind of Beaufort's spring, hair flying in the near gale. The shuttle rocked uneasily until the grapples engaged, holding her against the wind, and only then did Ladislaus rise and walk towards the opening hatch. Cold air invaded the shuttle, and he shrugged into his seawool coat as the familiar wind whined beyond the hull.

The lictor followed, and Ladislaus eyed him curiously. He'd been guard and protector in one, his simple presence extending the protection of the Assembly over Ladislaus to shield him from arrest and extradition, but his had been a silent presence. No word of welcome, no word of condemnation or approval, had ever passed his lips, and Ladislaus wondered if he meant to change that now that his duty was discharged. But he merely followed Ladislaus silently to the hatch and stopped. From the moment Ladislaus' foot touched Beaufort soil, he would need no protection, and the lictor watched calmly, silently, as Ladislaus stepped through the hatch without a backward glance.

The damp cold of Beaufort's dense atmosphere slapped his bearded cheeks, and the heavy hand of gravity dragged at his bones. He hadn't been home in five years, and almost he had forgotten how it felt to be his proper weight. He walked down the gangway, moving carefully until muscles and reflexes could adjust to the thirty percent jump over *Capricorn*'s artificial gravity, and the crowd pressed closer around the foot of the ramp. He saw his father and brother looming above the forest of heads like giants, and then his foot touched the soil of his homeworld, and for just an instant the shock of homecoming vibrated through him like an icicle of relief.

He turned towards his father and stopped. A slender woman stood before him, the colorful plaid of the Beaufort-circling MacTaggart Clan's chieftain blowing from her shoulders. Age had not dulled the flying red of Dame Penelope MacTaggart's hair, yet she looked frail and slight as the eternal Beaufort wind sang about her. She stood with all the dignity and strength of her authority, and Ladislaus stopped before her, feeling suddenly gross and huge as he confronted the calm, emerald eyes in which pride and composure glistened over a sea of sorrow.

"Dame Penelope," he said softly, his deep voice frayed by the wind.

"Lad," she said quietly.

"I—" He broke off and swallowed, feeling the familiar burning behind his eyes once more. "It's sorry I'm to be, Dame Penelope," he said humbly. "Warned I was, but too late. Gone she was, before I was knowing, but it's to be my fault. I owe a life."

His head bent and he felt the crowd stiffen as he spoke the formal acknowledgment of blood guilt. In a Beaufort court, such an admission was tantamount to accepting sentence of death. This was not a court of law, but Ladislaus had still given his life into Dame Penelope's hands, to do with as she willed. He sensed the shock of the crowd, yet even that admission was too little to express the depth of his guilt.

"Ladislaus Skjorning, I am hearing you," Dame Penelope's voice rang through the wind in formal response, and Ladislaus raised his eyes to her face, its graceful planes so like Fionna's. "But to be telling me this, Ladislaus Skjorning—was it not that both the killers died by her hand? And was it not that you it was caused her to be armed? Was it not that you had warned her? Was it not that you protected her for ten long years before they had the killing of her?" Ladislaus' face was grim as her questions underscored his ultimate, unforgivable failure, but he nodded.

"Then, Ladislaus Skjorning, do not be telling me you owe a life!" Dame Penelope's voice cut the tension like a knife. "It's proud we're to be—proud of my daughter, who did not go alone to death, and of you, the man who made it so! There's to be no blood debt between you and the MacTaggarts, Ladislaus Skjorning, for it's one of our own you're to be, my son!"

Ladislaus' head came up, and tears tracked his bearded cheeks as Dame Penelope's strong arms reached around his waist and she laid her proud head on his massive chest, her last words burning in his heart like new hope. They were the formal words of adoption, and the foster tie she offered meant almost more than blood on cold, harsh Beaufort. His hands fluttered helplessly over her slight shoulders, feeling the strength of Beaufort in them, and he bent his head, his blond beard mingling with the wind-blown red of the MacTaggarts.

"It's a daughter you've lost, Mother Penny," he said softly, his great voice choked, "a debt no man can pay. But it's a mother you're to be to me, and I a son to—" His voice broke before he could complete the formal phrase, and Dame Penelope drew his face down against her shoulder, tears cutting her own cheeks before the crowd of her neighbors.

"Ah, Lad, my Lad," she murmured in his ear, stroking his heaving shoulders, "it's always a son you've been to me—did you not know it?" And she led him to his father's side.

Seapine burned on the huge hearth. The dried, tree-like kelp glowed with a clear, blue flame, and Ladislaus was grateful for the rolling heat, for his blood was thin by Beaufort standards, and he was still shaken by the emotional catharsis he'd endured. Firelight flickered across the metal and stonework with which the people of Beaufort brightened their homes, and the dancing light rippled like sun off water. His father sat across the hearth, his craggy face, sculpted by sea and wind into a cliff of character, gilded by the fire. His brother Stanislaus sat behind him, even taller and broader than he in the seawool tunic with the crossed-harpoons shoulder badge of the master doomwhaler, and Dame Penelope sat beside Sven Skjorning.

Ladislaus let his eyes rest on her and remembered his own mother, Ireena Skjorning, thirty years dead, and her unborn daughter with her. Even with the best of medical science—which Beauforters had not been offered before the doomwhale brought them wealth—Beaufort's high gravity and hostile environment exacted a high price of its women. Beaufort weeded its people mercilessly; only the strong survived its unyielding harshness.

"It's to be good to be having you home, Lad. I was feared they were to have your life, as well." Sven Skjorning's voice was even deeper than his son's, and bitter with hate. He had given a son to the Federation already, dead in the destruction of his heavy cruiser.

"I had the same thinking for long," Ladislaus agreed soberly, "but it's too smart they're to be for that, Father, and they're to place their harpoons with care. They *let* me go, because it's to suit their purpose to paint us as barbarians and themselves as 'civilized" men!' " His face twisted, and he felt the same fury simmering in his audience.

"Sven," Dame Penelope said into the silence, "it's too long we've been waiting." Her voice was cold as the Beaufort sea. "Too many have had the giving of too much, and what's it to be bringing us? Shame and oppression, Sven Skjorning!"

Ladislaus nodded unconsciously, watching his father with burning eyes. Sven Skjorning stared into the heart of the fire, and his face was hard.

"Aye," he said slowly, "you've the right of it, Penny—as always. Thirty years past I gave Ireena my word, but if she'd lived, it's to agree with you she'd be, I think." Ladislaus straightened in his chair. His father stood high in Beaufort's sparse community, but for thirty-three years he'd honored his promise to his dying wife, throttling the hatred which had burned in his heart since the death of his eldest son. The heavy cruiser *Fearless* had died for one reason only: a Corporate World merchant prince had possessed the political power to demand her service as an escort for a "vital" cargo during the height of a Tangri raid.

"It's our children they're to be taking," he rumbled like

slow-flowing magma. "Our wealth they cannot touch, our rights they've had the taking of long since—but no more of our children will they be having!" He looked up from the fire, and his eyes were as bright and blue as the flames. "A son from me, a daughter from you—enough! It's to be ending!" His fist slammed the thick arm of his chair, and the expensive wood cracked under the blow.

"I've the same thinking, Father," Ladislaus said softly, "but it's to be careful we must. The Federation's arm is long, and it's the Corporate Worlds have the owning of that arm the now."

"And we're to do nothing?" Sven Skjorning demanded dangerously.

"No, Father. But it's to speak to others before the government I must. It's to be taking time, and when we strike, it's to be with care."

"You're to be talking treason," Stanislaus said softly.

"Aye," Ladislaus replied levelly, "and past time for it, too."

"No argument from me," Stanislaus said, "but to be thinking what it's to mean to Beaufort if you fail, Lad."

"I have," Ladislaus said bleakly. "Stanislaus, it's to be better to die than accept some things. There's no stomaching more—I'm not to be standing by any longer. Can you be seeing that?"

"Aye, Lad, of course," Stanislaus said simply, gripping his brother's shoulder, "but it's to be sure *you* do before you have the starting of a war upon your head. For you're to see it's *you* must have the doing of it here."

"I know," Ladislaus said softly. "God help me, I know."

The planetary government of Beaufort was not the sprawling bureaucracy that was the Federation, or, for that matter, any of the Innerworld governments. There were less than six million people on the planet, and the Beaufort Assembly reflected the sparseness of its population base. There were only fifty-six members, all told, and for the most part they were the elders of the great clans which had formed in the Years of Abandonment. The social and survival requirements of an environment humanity was never bred to face had created a paternalistic order, a semi-feudalism, that carried over into its political processes, as well.

Yet Ladislaus had never felt more nervous in the Chamber of Worlds. The conference room didn't even hold the full Assembly—only its leaders sat around the rectangular table, their eyes calm and dispassionate upon him.

Three weeks of cautious, private conversations had brought him here. Despite his care not to involve the government in his discussions, it seemed the government had decided to involve itself. Now he gazed at the people in the room—President Bjorn Thessen, President Pro Tem Knute Halversen, crucial committee chairmen—and waited for the inquisition to begin.

"Ladislaus," President Thessen said finally, "you've been meeting with influential people in the short time you've been home. We're wondering why you haven't asked to meet with us."

Ladislaus tightened inwardly at Thessen's Standard English. Since the days of the Abandonment, the dialect of Beaufort had become a badge its people wore consciously. It was their declaration of defiance to the worlds which had ignored them in their hour of need, and while almost any Beauforter could speak barely accented Standard English, most would see themselves damned and in Hell before they would . . . except in official settings, where the planetary government's members felt they somehow stood in the presence of their Old Terran ancestors. So if Thessen chose to speak Standard English, it meant he spoke as President of the Beaufort Assembly . . . an officer charged to preserve and maintain the Federation.

"Forgive me, President Thessen," he said softly. "I wanted to sample public opinion before I spoke to you officially."

"And why was that?" Thessen wondered slowly. "Could you be thinking of seizing power from us, Ladislaus?"

"No!" Genuine horror sharpened his voice. "It was only—"

"Enough," Thessen said with a headshake. "Excuse our doubts, but we're a suspicious lot these days. Blame it on the times. At any rate," he added with a wintry smile, "we chose you for the Assembly because you've a quick mind and strong will, like your father. We can't very well complain because you act accordingly. But now that you're here . . ."

Thessen straightened, an age-spotted hand touching a document before him.

"You probably won't be surprised by this, Lad." He handed the single sheet over, and Ladislaus ran his eyes down it, then raised them to Thessen's face with renewed respect. As delegation security chief, he'd thought he knew all their avenues of information, but their intelligence network obviously reached further than he'd believed possible. What he held was a memo signed by Simon Taliaferro himself.

"It's no surprise, no," he said quietly.

"We've read your reports—and Fionna's. Is this memo accurate? Will the Amalgamation pass, do you think?"

"Like a doomwhale through nearcod," Ladislaus said flatly.

"Aye, I had the fearing of that." Thessen's Standard English lapsed briefly, then he shook himself.

"You should know, young Lad, that *Capricorn* brought a writ of extradition from Old Terra. I sent it back marked 'opened by mistake'—" a mutter of laughter filled the room "—but you're right; Fionna's murder is but the beginning. I've viewed the chips of that 'impeachment.' " The old man's face wrinkled with disgust. "It's clear there's no reasoning with them. Except, perhaps, this man Dieter, of all people. How say you, Lad?"

"Dieter?" Ladislaus frowned. "I'm thinking he's a good enough man . . . but he's only one man. Aye, he insulted Fionna, but he was drugging, and . . . in a way, that may have been the making of him. But whether he's to be surviving . . ." He broke off with a shrug.

"So no matter what he feels, there's little he can do, eh?"

"Aye. It's Taliaferro has them in his grip the now, and it's a mad seashrike with a mouthful of blood that man's to be. There's to be no stopping him!" He stopped, a little abashed by his own vehemence.

"Then, young Ladislaus," Thessen asked slowly, "what's to be done? Fionna spent twenty-five years seeking our rights. Was it all for naught?"

"Not for lack of trying," Ladislaus said grimly. "No one

ever fought harder than Fionna. You know—you *all* know—she wanted no more than justice, no more than a transition. If even *one* Corporate World had reached out a hand to her—!"

"But fail we have?" Thessen pressed quietly.

"Aye, Mister President," Ladislaus said heavily. "We have."

"And it's that message you've been sharing with others, is it?" Thessen's old eyes were keen.

"Aye." Ladislaus looked up almost defiantly. "It's not to make any difference what wording I share, Mister President. You're to know that. And even if you're not to—" he drew a deep breath and committed himself "—it's to tell them I must."

"I see." Thessen's voice was very level. He glanced at his colleagues, and Ladislaus felt the tension. What he'd said was treason.

"Young Lad," Thessen said finally, "it's not quite fair we've been with you. This group—" he gestured around the table "—is more than just the leadership of the government. This—" he tapped the memo "—is no more than a part of what we've done. Are you, then, prepared to tell *us* the Federation is doomed? Is it to defy all of us you are? Knowing we're to have information even you are not to know?"

"Aye, Mister President. If so I must, then it's to defy you I will be doing! Fionna had the giving of her life for her dream, but her dream had no life of its own. I'm not to be seeing more! It's to be enough of our blood they've had the taking of! It's to be war they're waging, a war of 'laws' and 'writs' and 'reapportionments.' Well, to *give* them their war!" He was on his feet, blue eyes flashing, and his voice was rolling thunder in the chamber. "To give them a bellyfull of war—and not with words!"

He choked himself off abruptly. Whatever he felt, whatever he thought, these were the leaders of his people. It was not proper to raise his voice to them, and his temerity shamed him. Yet he was resentful, too; resentful of their slowness, resentful that age and high position blinded them to what he saw so clearly.

He sank back into his chair, watching Thessen glance once more around the gathered faces. Here and there a head nodded slowly, wordlessly, and Ladislaus felt his heart sink at the slow confirmations.

"Ladislaus Skjorning," Thessen's voice was deeper and more powerful, his old face flushed, "it's to be too long you've had the living amongst Innerworlders!" The Beaufort dialect penetrated, and Ladislaus raised his head. He stared at Thessen's bearded face, and the old man smiled slowly. "Did you have the thinking it's to be only you to know these things, Lad?" The president shook his head. "We've had the thinking of such thoughts for long now, and we've had the preparing for it, as well. You're to make no rebellion against *us*, Lad Skjorning, for we're to be before you. Aye, young Lad—if it's to make war they are, then it's to make war *we* are, as well!"

Ladislaus gaped at the old man, and the pieces suddenly fell together. The copy of the memo, the channels of information, the persistent questioning—he'd come into this chamber convinced he alone saw what must be done, only to find they'd already seen it!

"We've had the making of our plans for long," Thessen said slowly, "yet we're to be old, Ladislaus. We're to be worn and tired—we're not to have the strength and youth for this. But it's to see *you* do. So to tell us, young Lad—will it be you who has the leading of us?"

"Aye," Ladislaus said softly. There was no hesitation in him, only the grim, cold certainty that it was for this moment he had been born and trained, and he looked around the circle of old faces, seeing the same bitter determination in the wise eyes and lined faces looking back at him. He nodded his head slowly, and when he spoke again, it was to swear an oath.

"Aye," he repeated. "It will be that!"

"If this be treason, make the most of it!"

William Patrick Henry,
Before the Virginia
House of Burgesses

Secession

Fleet Admiral Stepan Forsythe looked up from his paperwork as his communicator lit with the face of his staff communications officer.

"Yes, Mister Qwan?"

"Sir," Lieutenant Doris Qwan said carefully "we're picking up something from a Mobius Corp mail packet. A transmission, not a courier drone."

Forsythe cocked an eyebrow. A transmission meant they were in the same system as the packet, but why transmit at all? This system was uninhabited and far outside the Innerworld relay nets; logically there was no one to hear the message, except for the unmanned recorders in the warp point nav beacons.

"What sort of message, Lieutenant?"

"I . . . don't really know, sir. May I play it off for you?"

Forsythe nodded, and his screen flickered abruptly, then steadied with the image of a lean, uniformed man. The twisted-loop collar insignia of his firm was overlaid by the crossed starships of a Federation mail carrier's captain, and his dark, strong face was tense, almost frightened.

"This is Captain Donald Stiegman, Federation mail packet *Rising Moon*, TFMP-11329. The following information *must* reach government authorities as quickly as possible. Stand by to receive coded data; this is a Class One Priority signal." Forsythe stiffened. Class One Priority was assigned only to threats to the very existence of the Federation, and his finger stabbed the emergency buzzer on his desk as the screen dissolved into a blur of static. The image danced insanely for perhaps ten seconds, then cleared, replaced by Captain Stiegman's worried face. "Reverse course immediately. Do not enter the Kontravian Cluster. Get that message out. Stiegman, message ends."

Forsythe's cabin door opened as Captain Enwright and Commodore Samsonov hurried in past an astonished Marine sentry. They slid to a halt, faces anxious, but Forsythe motioned them to silence. He watched the screen blank briefly before the message repeated itself, then gestured both men to chairs and punched the override to recall Lieutenant Qwan.

"It's a loop, right, Lieutenant?"

"Yes, sir, with an 'all ships' header. We've been in-system over an hour without hearing a thing, so I think we caught his first transmission. I'd guess he came through from Bantu and started transmitting the moment he hit normal space."

"I see. Anything on that coded sequence?"

"No, sir. I'm afraid the computers haven't broken the scramble yet, much less the code. I think he's using mail service protocols, sir."

"Very well. Keep on it and do what you can." Forsythe felt little hope. Mail service codes were at least as good as the Fleet's codes.

"Yes, sir. Any response?"

"Not yet. I'll get back to you."

Forsythe turned to his juniors. Enwright's expression was thoughtful and waiting; only someone who knew him well would recognize the questions burning in his hazel eyes, but the curiosity in Gregor Samsonov's wrinkled forehead and hooded brown eyes was more evident. Forsythe smiled a wintry smile as he nodded to his flag captain and his chief of staff.

"Gentlemen, it seems we have a mystery."

"Mystery, sir?" Trust Willis to ask the first question.

"You know as much as I do, Willis. You heard the message. Reactions?"

Enwright sat very erect. "A few points seem obvious, sir."

"Indeed?" Forsythe cocked his head. "Enumerate, please."

"Yes, sir. First, he doesn't have any drones or he'd've sent the message direct to a Fleet base. Secondly, whatever the message is, it's both urgent and hot. If it wasn't urgent, he wouldn't be transmitting; if it wasn't hot, he'd transmit in clear. Third, he's worried about pursuit. He's not in range of our scanners, so we sure as hell aren't in range of his. That means he's transmitting blind and hoping someone hears. Couple that with his injunction to clear out fast—" He shrugged. "He must be afraid there're bandits on his tail, and he's warning any unarmed civil ship to stay clear of them.

"And those three points, sir," he finished levelly, "lead to a fourth: he's absolutely right to declare a Priority One emergency."

Forsythe drummed gently on his desk. It was a mark of Enwright's true stature, he thought, that there wasn't even a trace of 'I told you so' in his voice. He glanced at his chief of staff.

"Gregor?"

"I'm afraid I have to agree, sir," Samsonov said unhappily.

Forsythe sighed heavily, feeling the full weight of his years, then nodded and managed a bleak smile. "Well, I'm afraid I agree, too. It seems you gentlemen were right to urge me to split the task force." It was a bitter admission, but he made it calmly, then turned to his communicator and punched up the flag deck. The screen lit with Lieutenant Qwan's face, and he could just see his operations officer behind her. He smiled to himself. Commander Rivera must have heard about his summons to Samsonov and Enwright.

"Lieutenant. Commander." His voice was as gravely courteous as ever. "Task Force orders, Commander. We will increase to flank and close the Bantu warp point. Detach the battle-cruisers and Admiral Ashigara's carriers—send them ahead of the battle line."

"Yes, sir," Rivera said crisply.

"Lieutenant Qwan, inform Admiral Ashigara of the situation and see to it she gets a copy of *Rising Moon*'s message. Then I want a message transmitted to *Rising Moon* immediately. Message begins: Fleet Admiral Forsythe, CO TF 17, to Captain Donald Stiegman, master, TFMP *Rising Moon*. Message received—give him the time,

Doris. My force headed to meet you at max. Estimate rendezvous with my advanced screen in—" he raised an eyebrow at Enwright.

"Call it nineteen hours, sir."

"In approximately nineteen standard hours, Lieutenant," Forsythe continued to Qwan. "Courier drone with your transmission dispatched. Good luck. Message ends. Got it?"

"Yes, sir. It's on the tape."

"Good. Send it standard civil service code, no scramble."

"Yes, sir."

"Thank you, Doris." Forsythe switched off the communicator and turned back to Enwright and Samsonov. "And now, gentlemen, let us give some thought to our circumstances." He smiled his bleak smile again. "Somehow I feel certain even my delicate touch will not suffice to make them any worse."

Vice Admiral Analiese Ashigara, slim and severe in her black and silver uniform, sat on the flag bridge of TFNS *Basilisk* and watched the bright dot of the mail packet on her display. She glanced at a com rating.

"Anything from the patrols, Ashworth?"

"No, sir. They're 150 light-seconds out, and they report nothing detectable in scanner range."

"Thank you." She glanced at her operations officer. If the recon fighters' exquisitely sensitive instruments weren't picking up anything, then there was nothing to pick up. "Recall them, Commander Dancing."

"Aye, aye, sir."

"Communications, raise *Rising Moon*."

"Aye, aye, sir."

There was silence on the bridge—the silence of a professional team aware of the dangers of unnecessary chatter—as Admiral Ashigara leaned back in her command chair and waited. Suddenly the main screen filled with the image of a dark, lean face wreathed in a huge smile of relief.

"Captain Stiegman, I am Vice Admiral Analiese Ashigara. I assume you have a reason for declaring a Priority One message condition?"

"I wish to hell I didn't," Stiegman said in a rich New

Antwerp accent. "All hell's broken loose out here, ma'am, and no mistake. If you don't mind my asking, where's Admiral Forsythe?"

"He is following with the battle-line, Captain," Ashigara said. "I expect him in approximately six hours."

"*Battle-line?!* Thank God!" Stiegman seemed to sag towards the pickup. "You don't know what's going on out here, Admiral! They're crazy! They—"

"Captain Stiegman," Ashigara cut him off, "I appreciate the strain you are obviously under. I would request, however, that you say nothing more over an open channel. I will, with your permission, send my cutter for you so that you can deliver your message to me in person. And confidentially."

"Yes." Stiegman inhaled deeply. "Certainly, Admiral. Send your cutter at once. The sooner I can tell someone else, the better, by God!"

"Well, Captain Stiegman," Admiral Forsythe said as he handed the man a drink. "I have the essentials of your story from Admiral Ashigara." He sounded too calm. The Galaxy was collapsing around his ears, and he sounded too calm about it all. "I don't yet have all the details, however, and I'd appreciate it if you'd summarize for my staff, as well."

"Summarize, Admiral?" Stiegman drained half the glass in a single gulp. "Gladly. In fact, I'll be delighted to let someone else worry about it for a while." His slowly easing tension wasn't lost on his listeners, and they hunched closer to him as he began.

"It started about a month ago," he said slowly. "I put into Bigelow with a mail consignment—they break it down on Hasdruble for transshipment to the rest of the cluster—and they told me my departure clearance and return cargo would be delayed a day or two." He shrugged. "Two days is a long layover, but I've had longer, so I didn't think much about it.

"But a few hours later, the port master called me up again—something about a viral infection and they couldn't find one of the people who'd been exposed. He agreed the odds were against their plague carrier being on board, but SOP required a search of the ship. Well, I wasn't too pleased, but nobody wants to chance another plague outbreak, so I agreed."

He paused and stared down into his drink. When he looked back up, his eyes were hot.

"But it wasn't any damned medical inspection party they sent aboard my ship," he grated. "It was an entire platoon of Marines—or they wore Marine combat zoots, anyway." He relaxed his muscles with a visible effort. "But they were already aboard, and no one in his right mind argues with a platoon of zoots, whoever's inside 'em." He shook his head slowly, remembering.

"They were polite as hell—I'll give the bastards that! But they posted two men in each drive room and two more on the bridge, and they told me—*me*, the skipper of a Federation mail packet, damn 'em!—that they had to 'detain' me." His lips twisted. "Wouldn't say why or for how long. Wouldn't say *anything* else. Just stood there and waited for their reliefs."

He growled something under his breath and finished his drink. Forsythe personally refilled the glass, to his obvious relief, and he sipped again, more slowly.

"Anyway, they had us. I tried getting a message out when I saw a Frontier Fleet cruiser on my screens, but they were on top of me in seconds. No nastiness, you understand—just another guard suddenly appeared in the com section and they stripped off our drones in case I got any smart ideas about using *them*.

"At first, I thought it was some kind of mistake, but then I figured out the whole orbit port was in on it—whatever 'it' was. And at least some of those 'Marines' really *were* Marines. I'm sure of it. I considered piracy, a real medical emergency—hell, even a port-wide outbreak of mass insanity! But I never once considered what was really happening."

"And that was, Captain?" Willis Enwright prompted when Stiegman paused once more.

"Treason, Captain," the mail packet captain said harshly. "Goddamned, old-fashioned, dyed-in-the-fucking-wool treason! The whole damned system's decided to 'secede' from the Federation!"

The blood drained from Lieutenant Qwan's face. Enwright's features only tightened slowly, but Samsonov looked as if he'd been punched in the stomach and Rivera looked murderous. Only Forsythe seemed unaffected—but, then, only he had seen Admiral Ashigara's scrambled transmission.

"I see, Captain Stiegman," he said quietly. "And their objective, obviously, was to keep *Rising Moon* from letting the cat out of the bag?"

"Exactly. Took us a while to put it together, Admiral, but there had to be some contact between my tech crews and the port service personnel.

"Near as we can figure it, it all began a month or so after Ladislaus Skjorning got home. Nobody's sure whether it was his idea or whether it was his whole damned planet's notion, but Beaufort's where it started, and whoever planned it must've had one hell of an organization! Given the way the warp lines run, Beaufort's at the bottom of a sack; all the rest of the cluster sort of drains down to 'em. They knew what that meant, too, because they didn't start *on* Beaufort; they started *from* Beaufort."

" 'From Beaufort'?" Enwright repeated.

"They sent out 'emissaries,' Captain. God only knows what kind of underground's been cooking away out here, but they sure as hell knew who to talk to where, and they sent out people like Stanislaus Skjorning and Dame MacTaggart. Hell, no wonder people listened! I'm a Fringer myself; I know how hot tempers are running out here since the MacTaggart murder. But goddamn it to hell, there's no excuse for a full-scale civil war!"

"A war, Captain?" Rivera did not—quite—sniff. "What do they plan to use for a navy?"

"Damned if I know," Stiegman said frankly, "but it's going to take a fleet—and I mean a *fleet*—to change their minds."

"How so, Captain?" Samsonov asked.

"Because they're not stupid, however crazy they are. They stage-managed it perfectly. Just one day everything is peaceful and fine; the next, Killiman Skywatch is in mutinous hands."

"*Killiman Skywatch?*" Rivera half-rose. "Good God, man, do you know what you're *saying?*"

"Damn right I do." Stiegman seemed almost gloomily satisfied by Rivera's reaction. "I don't know how they did it, but I know they had Killiman, and I'm pretty sure they had Beaufort. Don't know about Bigelow—they were playing it mighty close to their chests in Bigelow, which could mean they didn't have Bigelow Skywatch—but Bigelow's the only way into the cluster, so it could just mean they were being careful in case of visitors."

"Even if they have Skywatch," Samsonov said, thinking out loud, "there's still the Frontier Fleet orbital base. No armament to speak of, but there's a Bigelow-based cruiser squadron. They might not want—"

"Exactly, Gregor," Forsythe cut in, and Samsonov broke off as he remembered a civilian was present. "Captain Stiegman," the admiral went on, "did you at any time monitor . . . unusual, shall we say, com traffic between the orbit port and Skywatch or the Fleet base?"

"Never," Stiegman said flatly, "and we kept a good listening watch."

"I see. And how did you finally come to escape, Captain?"

"We were lucky—or maybe they got careless. My engineer contacted a buddy in the orbit port and suggested most of the Fringers in our crew were on their side and ready to mutiny against me with a little help from their 'Marines'. Stiegman shrugged. "They went for it. Guess I'm a better actor than I thought. At least, the 'fight' between me and a half dozen others and the 'rebels' in the crew seemed to convince 'em. Fair amount of shooting to tear up the bulkheads, chief engineer stopping me at gunpoint just before I wrecked the drive—that sort of thing. Nobody hurt, thank God!"

"Very neat," Forsythe congratulated him. "And after the 'mutiny'?"

"Locked me up in my own brig," Stiegman said cheerfully, "and then *Rising Moon* was a good rebel ship. Took 'em a few days to feel sure of it, then they pulled the Marines off. Needed 'em elsewhere, I gather."

"I see. And then?"

"We waited another few days, behaving like perfect little rebels till we were pretty sure they believed it. Then we powered the drive real slow—told 'em it was an equipment test—and ran for it."

"You ran for it," Samsonov repeated. "Why didn't you contact Bigelow Skywatch or the Fleet base?"

"Because if either of 'em *were* rebel controlled, stopping in com range'd be a real good way to get our ass shot off. Besides, there were Frontier Fleet units in-system. If they were loyal, well and good—but if they weren't? *Rising Moon*'s fast, but not that fast. If we were going to have light cruisers on our tail, I wanted all the start I could get!" Stiegman grinned wearily. "We made transit so fast nobody's eaten since, and our backup astrogation computer's *still* pitching fits!"

"I see. And then you headed for Innerworld space?"

"Not directly. Actually, I was headed for Heidi's World. Figured to check in with the Frontier Fleet base and come back loaded for bear. Never figured on meeting half the Navy this far out!"

"I understand, Captain." Forsythe forced the warmth of approval through the winter of failure in his voice. "But I'll take care of that with a courier drone. I'm afraid I'm going to have to commandeer your vessel."

"Why not?" Stiegman grinned wryly. "I'm getting used to it by now."

"Then I want you to head for the Fleet base at Cimmaron to carry my dispatches and your own account directly to Vice Admiral Pritzcowitski. He'll know what to do from there."

"Glad to." Stiegman finished his drink and set it aside, his face thoughtful. "And may I ask what *you* plan to do, Admiral?"

"You may," Forsythe said with a wry smile, "but I'm afraid I haven't really decided, yet."

"I see." Stiegman rose. "In that case, I'll get back to my ship, with your permission. But, Admiral—" he met Forsythe's eyes levelly "—I'd recommend some caution. You haven't talked to these people; I have. They're serious, mighty serious." He shrugged uncomfortably. "I haven't seen your intelligence reports, but this is my normal run. I've felt the tension growing out here for months, and I can tell you this—the Fringe is a nuke about to go off, Admiral."

"I know, Captain Stiegman. I know."

There was a brief silence after Stiegman's departure. Forsythe and his juniors stared down at the carpet, wrapped in thought. Finally the old man raised his head.

"Captain Stiegman," he said, "is a most resourceful man."

"Yes, and he's got guts," Enwright's voice was tighter than usual, "but I can't help thinking he was a little too lucky, sir."

"In what way, Willis?"

"He got away with it," Enwright said bluntly. "No one fired on him and no one chased him. If they had, they'd've caught him. A packet's fast, but so is a light cruiser—and a cruiser's armed."

"True. But if they haven't taken the Fleet base or Skywatch, the rebels couldn't have fired on him—assuming they had anything to fire with—without alerting those installations."

"No, sir. But why didn't either of those bases ask *Rising Moon* where she was going and why? Don't tell me she had departure clearance!"

"A point. You're suggesting, then, that the rebels control everything? The entire cluster, fortifications and all?"

"We can't know that, sir. I'd say they hold Bigelow, but the rest of the cluster?" Enwright shrugged. "Still, it seems probable. *Rising Moon* may have jumped the gun on them, but they let her go. And since Bigelow's only six transits from Heidi's World, that must mean they figure they're about ready anyway."

"I see. But assuming you're correct, where do we go from here? Gregor?"

"I don't know, sir," Samsonov said frankly. "I'm no Fringer—I don't pretend to know how these people are thinking. But even if Willis is right, they couldn't have known TF Seventeen was coming. They must figure on at least another three months before anyone can turn up; and if they're expecting a relief from Heidi's World, they're only expecting Frontier Fleet units—not monitors and assault carriers."

"Gregor's probably right, sir," Enwright said, "but remember our discussion with Captain Li. Everything I said then still holds true."

"I know you think it does, Willis," Enwright said. "You may even be right. God knows I don't want to go down in history as the first Navy commander to fire on other Terrans! But I don't see that we have any choice. If Bigelow

Skywatch *isn't* in rebel hands, it's going to need all the help it can get, and the same is true of the Fleet base, the repair yards in Killiman—the entire cluster, for that matter."

"Admiral, please," Enwright's voice was urgent, "send in a few destroyers first. Find out what's happening before we barge in in force. The cans will have the entire task force behind them—and they can say so. That should stop any itchy trigger fingers long enough for a parley."

"With respect, Admiral," Rivera said harshly, "I think that would be a mistake. If Bigelow Skywatch is still loyal, it could touch off the very incident Captain Enwright wants to avoid. Take the entire task force. *Show* them the odds, and they'll cave in."

"Don't delude yourself, Commander," Enwright said coldly. "If these people've gone this far, they're ready to go further. The actual presence of the task force won't achieve anything except to up the stakes for everyone!"

"Perhaps," Forsythe said softly, "but if the entire task force is there, we can be certain anything that happens is over quickly, Willis." His heart ached at his flag captain's look of desolation. "Face it, Willis," he said gently. "We can't afford delays. There's no way to keep this quiet—we can't even try to; we need to warn the other Fleet bases, warn the government, warn *everyone*—and the word is bound to leak. We need to be certain a *resolution* follows the news as quickly as possible, or other Fringe Worlds will be tempted to follow suit. You know that as well as I do."

Enwright looked away from the thin, troubled face with the wise old eyes. Yes, he thought, some of the other Outworlds will follow suit if the Kontravians aren't stopped. But this is the wrong way to do it. He knew it was the wrong way. Or did he? Was that the TFN officer in him, or was it the Fringer? His intellect, or the confusion of his loyalties? He looked back.

"Please, sir. Talk to them first."

"I'll talk to them, Willis." Steel showed through Forsythe's compassionate tone. "But from the flag bridge of this ship with the task force behind me." He rose, terminating the meeting. "Gentlemen, check your departments.

I want a complete status report in one hour. We will then formulate our precise plans."

His staff saluted and left. Willis Enwright walked slowly to the hatch and paused, then turned back to his admiral, his face older than his years.

"Sir, what if they don't surrender? What will you do if they fight?"

"Do, Willis?" Forsythe felt the cold of interstellar space blow down his spine. "I'll honor my oath to defend and preserve the Constitution—any way I must."

"You'll open fire, then," Enwright said almost inaudibly.

"If I must," Forsythe said steadily. "I don't want to. I'll tell them I don't want to. But I have orders to execute and four centuries of history to defend. Unlike them, I have no room to make personal choices, do I?"

"I suppose not, sir," Enwright said quietly. "But consider this, I beg of you. What you see as a personal choice may not seem like one to others." He seemed to be trying to tell Forsythe something, but the old admiral was too worried and heartsick to hunt for the meaning.

"I understand that, but I don't have an option. No one can ask more of any man than that he do his duty as he sees it." He shook his head sadly. "No matter how painful it is."

"Yes, sir. I hope we *all* remember that," Enwright said quietly. Then he drew himself up and gave Forsythe the sharpest salute the admiral had ever seen from him. He stepped through the hatch, and it closed behind him.

DUTY

"Captain Enwright and Admiral Forsythe are both *dead!*" The gasping words came hoarse over the com channel, but the screens were blank with electronic hash. Commander Windrider didn't recognize the distorted, faceless voice. Who was it? Had they ever met?

"They're *all* dead on flag bridge!" the voice went on desperately. "There's fighting everywhere . . . crew quarters . . . officer country . . . power rooms. . . We need *help*, for God's sake! We—"

The snarl of a laser pistol slashed across the words and the voice went silent. The blinking light codes on Windrider's fire control screens chilled his blood, and his hands clenched on the gunnery console of the monitor *Enwright* as the flagship fell away, the first mutiny in the Federation Navy's history raging on her command bridges and in her drive rooms.

Jason Bluefield Windrider couldn't believe it. No, he told himself grimly, he could believe it; he just didn't want to. Mutiny was an obscenity to a man like him, but he understood the mutineers. Not long ago, some of them would have been guests in his quarters, discussing the crisis, wondering where their true duty lay. It seemed they'd decided aboard *Anderson*.

He looked into the strained faces of his control team. They knew what was happening aboard the flagship—but what could they do about it? For that matter, what could *he* do? He and his ratings sat at the very core of a tremendous hull, 285,000 tonnes of alloy and armor wrapped around their fragile bodies and sensitive instruments. They were *Enwright*'s fighting brain, controlling the power to vaporize a planetoid or sterilize a world, and soon they might have to perform actions which would scar their souls. He didn't know what the men and women of his crew would decide. He was certain of only one thing; he himself was about to face a moment of truth he did not believe he could endure.

The communicators muttered, ghostly voices blurring in his battlephone implant as frantic commanders conferred, afraid to expose their inner convictions, yet compelled by duty and training to act decisively.

And that was their true curse, Windrider thought savagely. Navy training and their own inclinations forced them to *act*. They weren't politicians (the word was a vicious epithet in his thoughts) who could confer and debate and duck responsibility. When you put on Navy black and silver, you put your judgment on the spot. "An imperfect response *now* is a thousand times better than recognizing the perfect response too late." That was what the Academy taught—but there were *only* imperfect responses to this!

Windrider shook his head angrily. The universe was crumbling before his eyes and he was *philosophizing*? Yet what else could he do? He, too, had "reacted" long since, but his had been a hypothetical decision, one he'd hoped never to face. One he'd *believed* he would never face, because he had dared not believe anything else. But now its hungry breath was in his face, hot and stinking as a pseudopuma's.

It wasn't *fair!* Hadn't the bureaucrats *known*? Were they so blind to human needs and loyalties they hadn't even *considered* what might happen out here?

But of course they had. That was why the Marine contingents aboard the transports consisted almost entirely of Innerworlders.

Yet the politicos had miscalculated, he thought grimly. They'd guessed at the hatred they were about to unleash, but not how quickly the flames would erupt. Their planned show of force was supposed to nip rebellion in the bud, on the ground. They'd never dreamed the Kontravians might seize their local orbital defenses and Frontier Fleet squadrons or have the guts to defy TF 17's might after they did. Besides, the Navy's monumental dependability was the bedrock of the Federation; it had never occurred to them that the Fringers in the Fleet might be as conscious of planetary loyalties as any Corporate Worlder. So they hadn't "sanitized" the Fleet as they had the ground forces.

Perhaps they couldn't have, really, given the high proportion of Outworlders in the Fleet. Only a few ships had "reliable" Innerworld crews. Most had heavy Fringe contingents; some were completely Fringer-crewed. Now their officers were caught between their oaths and the dreadful prospect of turning their weapons on fellow Fringers, and it was intolerable. Faced with the unfaceable, Enwright had acted, Forsythe had reacted, and laser fire had gutted *Anderson's* flag deck. But they were only the first casualties; Windrider could already taste the blood to come, and it sickened him.

"Captain! Admiral Singh is coming up on the all-ships channel!"

"Throw it on the big screen, Mister Sung." Li Han held her face calm and her voice level as she waited for the screen to light, but she felt her bridge crew's tension. Even her imperturbable executive officer showed the signs; Tsing Chang's breathing was harshly audible.

Thomas Singh had always struck Han as belonging to an earlier age. The neatly-trimmed beard in fashion among the Fleet's male officers somehow contrived to look fierce and predatory on Singh, and never more so than now. His dark eyes flashed, and the lips under his hooked nose were tight. When he spoke, his voice was harsh and cold.

"Ladies and gentlemen, I will be brief. Captain Willis Enwright and others aboard the flagship have mutinied against the lawful orders of their superior officers and against their oaths as officers and enlisted personnel of the Federation Navy. I will not permit this to spread! I believe Admiral Forsythe to be dead, and I hereby assume command. All Marine detachments will report to the armories and draw full combat equipment." Han tensed, and a soft sigh ran around her bridge. "Marines from the transport group will board *Anderson*. Any individual participating in this disgraceful violation of the Fleet's trust will be arrested to await tr—"

"No!"

Despite her iron control, Han jerked as the single word cut across Singh's cold voice. She thought it had come from one of her own people . . . until Singh whipped around to stare behind him. Then he was flinging himself aside, dropping towards the deck, and a laser bolt slashed across the pickup. His command console flared—plastics burning, metals melting—and the snarl of lasers continued for a fractional second before someone's fire incinerated the entire command station.

Han's eyes jerked to her tactical display, and her heart froze as data codes began to blink and change. Mutiny flashed through the task force like a nuclear blast as Fringer after Fringer realized what loosing Corporate World Marines on their fellow Outworlders meant. The sleek carrier group flagship *Basilisk* slid to one side, drive faltering as she convulsed internally. Her flight group was entirely Fringer, and now the pilots joined the Outworlders of the ship's company against their fellow crewmen. Ever since the Theban War officers and senior ratings went to action stations with side arms; now those weapons created holocaust within her compartments and passages . . . and she was but one ship among many.

"Captain?" Tsing's normally passionless voice questioned, and Han felt his eyes, felt the burning questions in the minds of her bridge personnel. It was against this cataclysmic instant of ruin that she had prepared for all these months; against this decision that she'd selected her crew, trading ruthlessly on past debts and owed favors. Now her handpicked personnel looked to her, tense and straining as attack dogs, their fear and confusion checked only by their trust in her.

And how strong was that trust? They were Federation officers, trained and sworn, yet they were also Fringers. How could she—how could *anyone*—hold them in a moment like this? For an instant, she felt as small and frail as her appearance suggested, but her finger touched a stud on her chair arm, and she heard Tsing's breath hiss as her com panel lit with the face of Captain Wang Chung-hui, commander of *Longbow*'s Marine detachment.

Wang's cheeks quivered under her level regard, but there was no strain in *her* face, he thought almost resentfully. What was she about to demand of him? He knew his duty . . . but he, too, was a Hangchowese.

"Major Wang," Han's voice was cool, and Wang felt a stab of near hysterical mirth. There could be only one "captain" aboard a warship, yet it was typical of Li Han to remember a point of etiquette and give him his courtesy promotion at a time like this. She was the smallest person in *Longbow's* complement; she was also the largest.

"Yes, sir?" he said hoarsely, and his heart sank as he realized that when she ordered it he and his men would don their combat zoots and board *Anderson*, blasting down anything in their path. Not because of duty or Admiral Singh, but because Captain Li had ordered them to.

"You heard Admiral Singh, Major," Han said softly.

"Yes, sir."

"Report to the armory, Major." Wang's heart plummeted. "Draw combat gear for your men, then post guards on the boatbay and all auxiliary hatches. Nobody leaves this ship. Is that clear?"

"Sir?" Wang blinked. Guard the boatbay and hatches? *Seal* them? Then she wasn't . . . "Yes, *sir!*" Wang barked, and the salute he threw her would have done credit to the commandant of the Corps.

"Thank you, Major." Han broke the circuit, her face still calm, despite the sweat beading her hairline. She continued to ignore her bridge crew, forcing herself to remain oblivious of the holstered lasers riding at every hip as she touched another stud.

"This is the Captain," she said, ignoring the normal preambles of an all-hands announcement, and speakers throughout the ship rattled with her measured voice. "You know what's happening." She drew a deep breath. "Now I'll tell you what's going to happen in *Longbow*. We are not going to obey Admiral Singh's orders." She felt her bridge crew twitch in near convulsive reaction. "I am your commander. As a sworn officer of the Federation Navy, I have no choice but to obey my lawful superiors, just as you have none but to obey me. Yet some orders cannot be obeyed, and Admiral Singh's are such orders. I cannot order you to mutiny"—she used the word deliberately—

"but understand this: the only way *Longbow* will assist in suppressing the outbreak aboard *Anderson* is by mutinying against *me*."

She paused, tasting the shock and confusion in some of her officers, the burning determination in others. She felt weak and shaken, as if her body were a hollow shell filled with air, and wanted desperately to lick her lips, but she didn't.

"I intend," she went on, her voice clear and strong, "to place this vessel at the service of the Kontravian Cluster. Any who disagree with that decision are free to leave. Report to Major Wang at the boatbay—without weapons. That is all."

She released the stud and turned her chair slowly, meeting Commander Tsing's eyes squarely before she let her gaze sweep her other officers. Every holster was sealed. No one spoke in encouragement or condemnation. That wasn't the Hangchow way, she thought almost whimsically. But there was a way to gauge their true feelings.

"Lieutenant Chu?"

"Yes, sir?" Her navigator sounded breathless, but there was snap in his voice.

"Lay off a course to place us between *Anderson* and the rest of the task force, Lieutenant Chu."

"Aye, aye, sir."

And that was all there was to it.

Commander Windrider watched *Basilisk* peel off the edge of the formation—and she was only the first. The monitor *Prescott* slid drunkenly aside as fighting wracked her command deck and navigation spaces before the drive could be cut. The destroyers and cruisers of the screen went berserk as their complements turned on one another, and garbled scraps of chatter told him the fighting had become general aboard *Enwright*, as well. Only one ship was under complete command. He watched his display as a single battle-cruiser shot out of the scrambling formation to hover between *Anderson* and her consorts. The data codes gave her identity, and her shields were up, her weapons on line.

"Alert! Alert!" A computer voice wailed, then choked off, replaced by Captain Hodah's voice, and Windrider smiled bitterly. There was no taped message for this madness.

"This is the Captain! All persons resisting their lawful superiors will cease immediately or face summary courts martial for mutiny! Marines will lay aft to the boatbay and prepare to board *Anderson* pursuant to the orders of Admiral Thomas Singh. Any person resisting execution of this order will be *stopped*. Marine officers are instructed to use weapons immediately in any case of resistance. This is a direct order—and your final warning!"

Windrider blanched. Hodah was a calm, humane man; for him to turn the Marines against his own people with a virtual license to kill—and to announce it for all to hear—must mean he felt the situation could get no worse. And what the hell had happened to Admiral Singh? Why wasn't *he* on the com?

A strident buzzer shrilled, and his eyes widened. The passages outside fire control were depressurizing . . . and that could happen only if someone deliberately spilled atmosphere! God! The blast doors and armored bulkheads were slamming shut, sealing fire control even more tightly. With zero pressure beyond and atmosphere within, it would be impossible to open those doors from outside—and blasting them open would take hours . . . or a nuke. Had Hodah done it to keep mutineers away? Or had the mutineers done it to isolate fire control from the loyalists? But the deck plates still pulsed to the rhythm of the drives, so Hodah had secured the power plants, or slaved their controls to the bridge. Was the power gang alive, or breathing space? What was *happening* out there? Who controlled what in the lunatic asylum which had once been a capital ship?

One of his ratings jerked on his gauntlets and reached for his helmet, and Windrider stabbed him with an angry stare.

"Where do you think *you're* going, Bearclaw?"

"B—but, sir! Those are our *friends* out there! We've got to do *something!*" The missile tech was a product of Windrider's own world, an Amerind from Topaz, and his words tore at Windrider's soul. He felt sweat under the tooled leather band at his temples and remembered the scent of the evergreen *tomash* trees above his home.

"What you're going to do, Bearclaw," he said harshly, "is stand away from that hatch and sit down."

Bearclaw sat slowly, and his crewmates looked away in confusion. What was Windrider doing? Where did their own officer stand? The click of plastic and metal jerked their eyes back as he laid his laser on the console.

"No one enters or leaves this compartment without my permission," he grated. "*No one.* Is that understood?"

He met each of his subordinate's eyes in turn, pinning them with a brown, bitter glare until they nodded. Then he turned back to the targeting screens, sick at heart at what he'd just said, and sicker still at what he might yet have to do.

Red lights flared on status boards as whole computer sectors fell out of circuit. Shot out or cut, it made no difference to his own command station. They could cut the drives, they could cut the data net, they could blow the bridge to atoms; as long as *Enwright* had power, *he* controlled her weapons.

But what of it? He asked himself that with all the pent up bitterness and helplessness—and fear—which filled him. It had seemed so simple in the bull sessions. Nothing violent. Just a refusal to fire if the time came. Passive resistance. Not this! Never this mindless murder of fellow Navy men and women who were only doing their duty as best they understood it!

His battlephone beeped a priority code, and he punched a console key, shifting to a secure intraship battle channel. It was Hodah.

"Commander." The captain sounded harassed, but his voice was still crisp. "These damned mutineers must have planned this ahead of time. They've taken the armory and most of the Marines' quarters—we can't even get to the combat zoots, much less the boatbay! We still control the drive, and I think we still hold the power rooms, but I don't dare release the remotes to find out. I've confirmed the loss of auxiliary fire control and CIC, and all contact with flag bridge went out five minutes ago. We had a shoot-out in plotting, too, and there was a godawful explosion in datalink control right after we lost touch with flag bridge. I hold the command deck, and I've got armed Marines on the bridge elevators, but all I've got left up here for battle control is the auxiliary nav tank. Have you got all that?"

"Yes, sir." Windrider felt sweat matting his eyebrows.

"All right. It comes down to this, Commander," Hodah grated. "I can still move this ship, but that's *all* I can do. *You're* the only man who can target and fire her weapons. So tell me, Commander Windrider—are you prepared to do your duty?"

"My duty, Captain?" Windrider hesitated, his face ashen, then answered firmly. "Yes, sir. I'm prepared to do my duty."

"Then understand this, Commander," Hodah said softly. "Admiral Forsythe is dead, and Admiral Singh was apparently killed when they took out our flag bridge. Admiral Traynor may be dead; we've lost all contact with *Vesuvius*, so I have to assume she's either dead or a prisoner. I've got contact with Admiral Hale, but the mutineers have all the engineering spaces in *El Chichon*; he can't even maneuver. Admiral Ashigara apparently went over to the mutineers aboard *Basilisk*, so as near as I can figure it, Hale's the senior man left, and he's given me orders to terminate the fighting aboard *Anderson*—fast. Maybe we can bring the whole task force back to its senses if we get some Marines in there quickly. But Captain Li and *Longbow* are in the way, and they've threatened to destroy the first boat launched against *Anderson*. I've got two superdreadnoughts from Admiral Hale's group, and one attack transport is prepared to go in, but they can't launch until *Longbow's* neutralized . . . one way or the other." Windrider heard the pain in his voice and remembered the evening Captain Li had dined aboard as his guest. "I'm going to give Li one last chance to move aside," Hodah said quietly. "If she refuses . . . Then, Commander, it's all up to you and your team."

"I—understand the situation, sir," Windrider whispered.

"Good. Switch to the intership channels, Commander. I want Captain Li to hear us if I have to pass you orders."

"Yes, sir." Windrider shifted channels and ran his fingers over the cool plastic console, feeling the latent destruction and understanding Hodah's pain too well, for Windrider, too, knew Li Han's reputation.

* * *

Han stared into her com screen at Simon Hodah's worried, angry face, reading the fear and fury in his eyes and wondering if he saw the pain in hers. His mouth was a slashed wound and his voice was harsh.

"Captain Li, you are in violation of the Articles of War. You will surrender your command and person at once, pursuant to the orders of Vice Admiral Eric Hale. You will heave to and await my boarding party. Officers designated by myself will relieve you of command and place you under close arrest to await trial. This is a direct order, logged and taped. You may authenticate with Admiral Hale."

"Captain Hodah," Han said softly to her old friend, "I must respectfully refuse your order."

"You have no authority to refuse!" Even the rage in Hodah's voice couldn't hide the pleading under his fury. "Now cut your shields and get out of my way, Captain, or by the living God, I'll blow you apart!"

Han looked around her bridge crew. Every set of shoulders was tense, every face knotted with tension, but not a voice protested as she turned back to her superior officer. God, she was proud of them! Yet her heart ached at matching their courage against their own fellows. It was such a waste—such a tragic, stupid waste—yet all of them were caught in the conflicting webs of duty, loyalty, and trust. Did her people suspect how much strength she drew from them? Or did they think they drew theirs from her?

She glanced down at her plot almost idly, watching data codes flash as weapons and tracking systems came alive aboard the trio of capital ships, and the deadly threat of those weapons was her reality. Her mind flickered over her life, remembering the things she'd done, recalling those she'd meant to do. How would her father react to this? What of the children she'd always known she would someday bear?

She raised her eyes once more to Simon's. She knew him so well. He *would* fire—indeed, she would leave him no option—and when *Enwright* and the superdreadnoughts fired, *Longbow* would die. No battle-cruiser ever built could survive that concentration of fire at this range.

She hadn't anticipated when she handpicked her crew

that she had chosen them only to die with her, yet Hodah's margin for error was razor thin. *Longbow*'s destruction would clear the path to *Anderson*, but it was a deadly expedient which might well recoil upon him, for it would give every mutineer his options, spell out the full, deadly consequences of resistance. It might awe them into surrender, but she thought not.

Her face was calm as the death of her ship and crew looked back at her from Hodah's eyes. It was unfair. It was cruel. Yet in a sense, it was also the sublime completion of her life. She drew a deep breath, hoping no one would notice.

"Go to hell, sir," she said very gently.

The deck shivered as *Enwright* moved deliberately towards the slim, defiant *Longbow*, and the Corporate World-crewed superdreadnoughts *Nanda Devi* and *Pentelikon* moved in beside her, shields glowing. The transport *Chief Joseph* slid in behind them, but she was unimportant in the confrontation of Goliaths, and Windrider's fingers flew over his own console even as his mind tried to reject the firing setup he was creating. Horror froze his subordinates into shocked, speechless immobility as the target codes appeared on their monitors, and he heard Han's reply and waited in a private hell for the words he knew must come.

"Fire Control!" Hodah's voice pounded in his brain.

"Yes, sir?" He was astounded he could sound so calm.

"Lock on all weapons. Prepare to fire at my command."

"Aye, aye, sir. Locking on now."

His fingers pressed the commit keys, and red lights glowed as weapon bays opened. Massive beam projectors snouted out and missiles slid into their launchers, backup rounds dropping silently into the loading trays. The ranked missiles riding the external racks woke to malevolent life, and sweat burned his eyes. He was sealed in a cage of ice and fire, for he was both a Fringer and a Federation officer. What *was* his duty? It mattered, and his uncertainty was agony as his hands hovered above the firing keys.

"Captain Li, this is your last chance!" Hodah snapped.

"Go ahead, Simon!" Li Han's voice was harsh at last,

almost as if she were deliberately goading her old friend. "Fire and be damned!"

"Very well, Captain." Hodah's voice was as cold as space. "You leave me no choice. Fire Control, you have your orders. Open fire—*now!*"

Windrider's hands trembled on the deadly snakes of his firing keys and he blinked his eyes, fighting to focus. *Longbow* and the superdreadnoughts were virtually shield-to-shield, floating in his targeting screens at suicidal range, the battle-cruiser small and alone, frail despite her weight of armor and weapons. Visions and sounds filled his mind. Memories of his homeworld. The final parade at the Academy. Men and women he knew in the ships on his control screen. Men and women waiting to die when he touched those keys. All of them flashed through his mind, and his hands were paralyzed. He couldn't do it. God help him, he couldn't *do* it!

"Damn it, Windrider! Open fire!" Hodah roared, his own grief flogging his fury. "Do your duty, man!" The word "duty" flared in Windrider's mind like a bomb, and he jerked spastically.

"Aye, aye, sir," he said very softly, and his eyes flicked over the targeting codes, a professional double-checking his work even in his anguish. Then his fingers tensed, and *Enwright*'s weapons spoke.

The world of the com channels shattered around him, battered by the roar of a hundred furious, denouncing voices and as many more that bellowed with triumph. A tide of destruction ripped from *Enwright* in a fury of beams and the impassioned streaks of missiles, and devastation rocked the vacuum as her weapons found their targets—Windrider's targets. Shields flared and died. Plating split, ruptured, disintegrated, vaporized. Atmosphere fumed from a gutted hull, and Jason Windrider clung to his sanity with bleeding fingernails while tears streamed down his cheeks and TFNS *Nanda Devi* died under his fire.

THE MARK OF CAIN

Naomi Hezikiah felt out of place in *Pommern*'s command chair, for a heavy cruiser was not normally a lieutenant commander's billet, and even the thin Bible in the breast of her vac suit was scant comfort as she contemplated what was about to happen.

She punched up communications, and a painfully young ensign answered her. Yet another sign of the times; it should have been at least a full lieutenant.

"Anything from the flagship, Harvey?"

"No, sir." The young black man shook his head in mild surprise. "Standing orders are to maintain com silence, sir," he reminded respectfully.

"I know." Naomi probed the ensign's face for any uncertainty and started to say more, but she'd set her hand to the plow, as Elder Haberman would say. To everything there was a season . . . even to this, she supposed drearily. So she made herself smile, instead. "Carry on, Ensign."

"Aye, aye, sir," the com officer said, and the screen blanked.

Naomi leaned back and closed her eyes. All she wanted was to be back on cold, bleak New Covenant. But she couldn't be there—and after what had already happened . . . after what was *about* to happen . . . not even New Covenant would want her back. She remembered Abraham and prayed silently for God to send another ram before the blade fell. But he wouldn't.

Her mind went back over the past, terrible two weeks

that had started so wonderfully. She and Earnest had had the medic's official report; they'd actually been discussing ways to finagle their assignments so she could take her maternity leave at home on New Covenant when the scrambled transmission came over the relay net. An entire Battle Fleet task force—not just a battlegroup, a *task force*—taken by its own personnel. Casualties had been heavy, and the few ships which remained loyal had been hunted down and captured or destroyed before they got far. But not before they got their courier drones away.

Commodore Prien had been a fool. Naomi's eyes stung as she remembered the kindly old man, a Heart Worlder who couldn't believe his own squadron might follow suit. He'd actually broadcast his decision to return to base immediately . . . and why. He should have known what would happen—and it had happened within hours. Desperate men and women had met, and the Fringers among his crews had risen against him.

But not all of them. No, not all of them. The meetings had been too clandestine, too hurried. Everything had been improvised by isolated groups, trusting no one outside their own little band. Not until the first mutineer drew his weapon could anyone know who stood where outside whatever tiny group *they'd* discussed it with, and the loyalists had fought back furiously. The carnage had been more savage than she would have believed possible; there were laser scars on the bulkheads around her, and the victorious mutineers had barely half the personnel they theoretically needed.

And when the fighting ended, Naomi found Earnest sprawled over his fire control panel, laser in hand, and two dead mutineers before him.

She had barely been able to read the funeral service through her tears. Had he known they were on different sides? Would he have fought beside her if he'd known? Or would his stubborn sense of duty, the courage she loved so much, still have ranged them against one another?

She didn't know. She couldn't know, for Earnest had died, and she had inherited command of a heavy cruiser . . . and even Elder Haberman would never be able to convince her that God could forgive her.

Not that the Elder would have the chance, she thought

mordantly, glancing at the nav tank. She would have the opportunity to plead her case before the Lord herself all too soon, for the pulsing pattern of the nav beacons was clear in the tank, and her astrogator turned to her.

"Thirty seconds to warp, Captain," he said quietly.

"Very well," Naomi nodded curtly. "Carry on."

"Aye, aye, sir."

And so it was official. Toshiba wasn't going to relent.

"We have no choice," Captain Victor Toshiba had told his "captains." "We're too deep in Innerworld space. We'd never make it to the Fringe if we just ran, and we've burned all our other bridges. We all know why we did it, but that doesn't matter. We're all of us—every one of us—mutineers."

He'd scanned his subordinates' faces, reading their despair, but his eyes were determined as he went grimly on.

"We're walking dead, ladies and gentlemen. Face it. Accept it and use it, because we're just as dead whether we spend our lives profitably or not. There is one, and only one, thing we can do for the Fringe now." His finger had stabbed the crazy quilt of warp lines in his nav tank. "Galloway's World. *That's* what we can give the Fringe . . . by taking it away from the Federation!"

Naomi had stared at him in horror, yet she was his senior "captain."

"But, sir," she'd said softly, "we don't begin to have the strength to seize Galloway's World. Surely you're not suggesting . . . ?"

"That's precisely what I *am* suggesting," Toshiba had said coldly. "We can gut the shipyards if we get in unchallenged. It's gone too far to stop now. It's war, Commander, war between the Fringe and the Innerworlds, and we both know who holds the industrial trumps. Can we stand by while the Corporate Worlds beat our people to death? No! We're going to hurt them—hurt them *now* and hurt them *badly*. We're going to buy time for our people, the one way we can." He'd paused, as if steeling his own nerve. "The only way: a nuclear strike on Galloway's World."

Naomi had wanted to vomit. They were the TFN, sworn to *defend* humanity against mass murder! And yet, wrong as he was, he might also be right. They *were* doomed, and they owed their people a chance. She remembered the winter wind howling around the dome on New Covenant and knew she could kill to defend the civilians of her world—but could she kill *other* civilians for them? She'd looked up and her lips had parted, but Toshiba's voice had marched on ruthlessly, forestalling her objections.

"I know there are bound to be heavy casualties—civilian casualties. The Jamieson Archipelago is the most densely populated area of the whole planet. Only an idiot could think you can nuke a target like that and *not* kill civilians; only a liar would tell you you could.

"But I also know what we're defending—and so do you! Our own homes, our own societies . . . the kind of societies that let humans be *people*, not just well-fed, two-legged domestic animals producing for Corporate World masters!"

His vehemence had shaken them all, and Naomi had felt her resistance waver. Then he'd paused and looked at them sadly. When he resumed, his voice was very soft.

"I know what you're thinking. Do we have the right to do this, even in self-defense? I don't know how you'll answer that, but I know how *I* will. They say a flower will grow toward sunlight through ceramacrete, and perhaps they're right. But . . . what if *everything* is covered with ceramacrete? What if the flower finally breaks through, but there's no one left who can recognize a flower when he sees one?"

Naomi had bent over her hands, feeling his eyes on the crown of her head as his will beat against her, and realized how pivotal her own decision was. They'd endured one mutiny—perhaps they had another in them yet. But the first had cost her too much. Whatever God demanded of her, it couldn't be another spasm of the bloodshed which had taken Earnest. Her head remained bent, her eyes locked on her fingers, and the moment for rebellion passed.

"We've got a good chance of pulling it off," Toshiba had said softly as Naomi silently withdrew her opposition. "No one knows we've mutinied. We can put into Galloway's World for new orders, carry out the strike, and run. It's even possible—" he'd tried to sound as if he meant it —"some of us may get home. We're fast and well-armed;

we may be able to split up and avoid action. But"— his voice had grown somber once more— "that's not what's important. Whether we can get away or not, we *have* to do it."

And every rebellious officer in his cabin had nodded silently.

"Warp in five seconds," Astrogation said softly. "Four . . . Three . . . Two . . . One . . . Warp!"

Naomi flinched as the indescribable surge of warp transit gripped her. She knew it was impossible, but in that instant she thought she felt the child within her. Thank God Doc Sevridge had understood. Losing her command would have left her a mere spectator, and no matter what her private purgatory, she had to *do* something. So he'd wiped the pregnancy report from the data banks with a tired smile.

"Might's well carry mutiny to its logical conclusion," he'd said. . . .

"I have a challenge, Captain!" The voice in Naomi's implant jerked her back to the present. "Standard query for ID and purpose."

"Stand by, Gunnery," she said through dry lips, watching the warp point forts on her tactical display. "Commodore Toshiba will roll the tape any minute now. Then we'll know." Her anxious eyes moved to a secondary screen as the carefully crafted composite of Prien's recorded messages went out over the com channels. It was good, she thought distantly. The electronics boys had done a bang-up job. But was it good enough?

" . . . so after the fighting," the dead commodore said from the screen, "we patched up our damage and headed here. Commodore Jacob Prien, Tenth Cruiser Squadron, Frontier Fleet, awaiting orders."

"Good report, Commodore. Excellent!" The florid-faced admiral in the reception screen had a strong Fisk accent. "We had some trouble here, too, when the news first hit, but the local reservists turned the trick. We've got our heel on the scum now, and we're keeping it there! Shape your course for Skywatch Three. They'll have new orders cut by the time you get there."

"Aye, aye, sir," the recorded composite said. "Commodore Prien out."

"And thank God for that," someone muttered as the admiral disappeared. Naomi heard but didn't respond. If God were truly kind, that fathead would have been suspicious. They would have had to fight or flee well clear of the planet. She knew she could die happily in a ship-to-ship action, and she found that she'd been secretly hoping for just that.

She watched the plot as *Kongo* led the squadron in-system. *Revenge* and *Oslabya* fell in astern, followed by Naomi's own ship and then the two DDs. It all looked harmlessly normal, but *Pommern*'s battle board glowed a steady scarlet. All but the shields. They still blinked green and amber, for to raise them would raise questions, as well.

The hours dragged endlessly past, Galloway's World looming slowly before them, and Naomi considered the bitter irony which brought *Pommern* back to the yards which had birthed her in a terrible act of matricide. No one down there would spare a thought for the holocaust lurking in the belly of her ship, she thought bitterly. Fleet missiles were to protect them, not kill them.

And then, finally, Skywatch Three loomed close aboard of them, and she gritted her teeth, watching her board, waiting for what she knew must come.

It came. Command codes flashed over the data net from *Kongo*. The squadron's shields slammed up. Hetlasers swiveled in their bays. As one ship, drives and engines slaved to the flagship, they charged the orbiting fortress, minnows against its bulk. The external ordnance racks belched their deadly loads, joined by the internal launchers, and Naomi Hezikiah was a spectator as the Tenth Cruiser Squadron, TFN, blew Skywatch Three to half-vaporized rubble in less than thirty seconds.

The com channels went wild as incredulous loyalists realized what was happening. Naomi's battlephone hummed and whined as hastily-tuned jammers came on line, fighting to shatter the squadron's datalink, but the cruisers drove onward, drives howling at max as they arrowed towards the planet.

The first defensive missiles lanced out to meet them,

and Naomi watched her display as point defense stations spewed counter missiles against them and space burned with detonating warheads. They were fast on their feet, those gunners, but where were the beams?

"Communications seizure attempt!" her com officer shouted, and her battlephone shrieked into her mastoid for a fraction of a second before the filters damped the sound.

"Data net jammed," the ensign snapped.

"Independent targeting," Naomi ordered, feeling her shock frame tighten about her. *You should be my husband*, her brain screamed at the gunnery officer, but she strangled the thought as she scanned the battle plot. "Take those destroyers ahead of us. We have to hold them off the flag."

"Aye, aye, sir!"

Naomi found it easier to cling to her sanity as her ship's weapons moved independently at last, reaching out to rake the oncoming ships with hetlasers and missiles. *Kongo*'s own ECM must be jamming the tincans' data net, for their point defense was late, and *Pommern*'s fire tore the lead ship apart.

But missiles were getting through among the squadron as their own point defense stations went to independent control. She winced as a direct hit smashed at *Pommern*'s outer shields. *Kongo* was taking hits, too, and so was *Oslabya*, but no so many as *Revenge*. Naomi watched the second cruiser shudder in torment as her shields went down and the first warhead ripped at her drive field and mangled her armor.

"Shields one through three down," Gunnery reported. "Incoming missiles tracking *Kongo* from astern, sir. There's somebody on our ass. Somebody *big*. Those are capital missiles."

"Understood," Naomi said coldly, and under her crisp surface, a little girl recited ancient words. "*Yea, though I walk through the valley of the shadow of death . . .*" She shook free of the thoughts. She'd wanted a ship-to-ship action; perhaps she had one.

"New course!" she snapped. "Bring us around on a reciprocal. Let the commodore deal with those cans—we've got bigger fish to fry!"

Pommern snarled around in a tight turn. Even through the drive field, she felt the lateral motion as her ship fought inertia and momentum. "Communications!" she barked. "Advise the commodore of our heading and intent." They steadied on course, and the author of the capital missile fire was before her.

"Battle-cruiser at eleven light seconds!" Gunnery yelped. "Computer reads her as the *Kris*."

Naomi knew her well. She'd served on her as a lieutenant —an eternity ago. Homeported on the Yard, and no doubt as fanatically Corporate World as her own madmen were Fringer.

"Gunnery," she said softly, "there's your target. Maneuvering, I want a random evasion course and I want it now. We're up against some heavy metal; let's be where it isn't!"

The acknowledgments came, and she watched her missiles going out as the range closed. More capital missiles scorched in, but they were no longer targeted on *Kongo*. *Kris* had accepted *Pommern*'s frail challenge.

"*Kongo*'s opened fire on the planet, sir! Track looks good for the Taliaferro Yard!"

Naomi shut it out. She no longer wanted to think of the two cities clustered tight against the Taliaferro Yard, of the civilians with seconds to live. She no longer wanted to think of the mark of Cain she wore. She pressed one palm over the Bible in her vac suit and sealed her helmet as they entered laser range, and *Pommern* shook and quivered to the fury of missiles and counter-missiles bursting around her hull.

"Missiles away from *Oslabya*, sir! Tracking for the Yard!" But Naomi's attention was riveted to her gunnery officer.

"Laser range!" he announced, and here it came. The deadly energy sleeted from the battle-cruiser and howled around *Pommern*'s hull.

"Second strike off from *Kongo! Revenge* launching now!" Naomi wasn't listening. She was watching her screens as her own lasers raved defiance at *Kris*. *Pommern*'s gunnery had always been good, she thought sadly as armor vaporized on the battle-cruiser. Better than any capital ship's in the Fleet, Earnest had always said.

"*Oslabya*: Code Omega!" communications reported. So

Lieutenant Jolson's first command was no more. Well, he'd soon have company.

"Oh, dear God!" Naomi's eyes jerked toward her white-faced scanner rating. "*Oslabya*'s missiles must've been under shipboard control, sir! They're going to a standard dispersion pattern!"

Naomi's heart chilled as she stabbed a quick look at Battle Two. It was true. With her computers out of the circuit, *Oslabya*'s missiles were spreading to cover the target with maximum devastation, and what was supposed to be a precision strike had become an atrocity. They were only tactical nukes, but they'd land all over the Reservation and dependent housing. . . .

"Good hits on target." Gunnery's almost droning report jerked her eyes away from the horror unfolding on Battle Two. "She's streaming air, sir!"

And then *Kris* found the range.

Pommern screamed as the lasers raped her. Naomi had always known ships had souls—she felt it now, in her own soul, as the cruiser's armor puffed to vapor and vanished under the radiant energy.

"Forward launchers gone!" Gunnery's professional calm had disappeared. "Laser One destroyed!"

Naomi turned towards him, but she never completed her order. *Kris* found them again, her hetlasers knifing through armor and plating and flesh. Naomi gasped involuntarily as air screamed from the holed compartment and her suit puffed tight, and *Pommern* lurched as a drive room died, and then another. She was toothless and naked, but *Kris* was badly hurt herself, and the Jamieson Archipelago was a forest of poisonous mushrooms as Toshiba blasted the shipyards and her crew's homes and families burned.

Naomi looked away from her looming executioner, her own eyes burning as *Oslabya*'s missiles laid their artificial suns across the Navy base. How many were dying down there? How many whose husbands and wives and fathers and mothers wore the same uniform as she? Yet they were only a few more deaths against the civilians dying around the other yards. How many would there be? A million? Two million? Three? Against that kind of devastation, what could a few thousand Navy dependents matter?

Kris slid alongside at point-blank range, and Naomi watched almost incuriously in an outside screen as the battle-cruiser's surviving hetlasers swiveled across her ship. *Kris* poured fire into the gutted, mutinous cruiser.

Naomi had a tiny fraction of a second to see the end of her bridge explode into vaporized steel. Only a fraction of a second before the fury came for her—but long enough to feel the mark of Cain in her soul again and know that death would be sweet. . . .

DISASTER

"Mister Speaker," Simon Taliaferro said somberly, "I take little pleasure in being vindicated in such fashion." He looked around the Chamber of Worlds and shook his head sadly. "We should have known it would come, I suppose, when so many Fringe World delegates resigned their seats to protest the 'severity' of a decision far more merciful than just. Barbarism, Mister Speaker—the acts of little, frightened minds which must not be allowed to destroy all the Terran Federation stands for."

Oskar Dieter sat quietly, listening to the beautifully trained voice, wishing he possessed some of the same histrionic ability. But he didn't; all he could do was tell the truth, and where was the appeal of truth when lies were so convincingly presented?

"I ask you, Ladies and Gentlemen of the Assembly," Taliaferro went on, "where is the reason in *this*?" He waved his hard copy of the report which had originated this secret session. "Even if, as I do not for an instant believe, amalgamation is an unmeant threat to the Fringe Worlds' representation, is *this* the way to contest it? Where are the Fringe World delegates, ladies and gentlemen? Where are the petitions? We see none of them. Instead we see *this*!" He crumpled the sheet of paper contemptuously, and Dieter winced as the theatrical gesture evoked a spatter of applause.

It was sadly scattered applause, for the Chamber of Worlds was sparsely populated, the blocks of assemblymen and women separated by the empty delegation boxes of Fringe Worlds no longer represented here.

The Fringer delegations had been small, but there were many Outworlds, and their absence cut great swathes through the larger, less numerous Innerworld delegations. And it was Simon Taliaferro and others like him who created this absence, Dieter reminded himself, staring at the heavy-set Gallowayan with a hatred it no longer shocked him to feel.

"They have made no effort to oppose amalgamation," Taliaferro went on. "They have not even bothered to discover whether or not it has in fact been ratified! They have fastened upon it—fastened upon it as a cheat and a pretext for *treason*, and let us not delude ourselves, my friends! The act of the Kontravian Cluster *is* treason, and when Admiral Forsythe has brought these traitors to their knees, we must show them that the Federation is not prepared to brook such criminality."

Here it came, Dieter thought grimly. Taliaferro had spent forty years maneuvering for exactly this slash at the Fringe's jugular.

"My friends," Taliaferro said soberly, "we must face unpleasant facts. The Kontravian rebels are not the only treasonously inclined members of the Fringe. If we falter, if we show weakness or hesitation, the Federation will vanish into the ash heap of history. Only strength impresses the immature political mind. Only strength and the proven will to use it! We must demonstrate our will power, whatever it may cost us in anguish and grief. We must punish ruthlessly, so that a few salutary lessons will prevent the wholesale bloodshed which must assuredly follow weakness. I therefore move, ladies and gentlemen, that we draft special instructions to Fleet Admiral Forsythe and all other commanders, instructing them to declare martial law and empowering them to convene military courts to try and punish the authors of this treason. And, ladies and gentlemen, I move that we inform our commanders that the sentences of their courts martial *stand approved in advance*!"

Dieter was on his feet in a heartbeat, fists clenched in shocked outrage. He'd known Taliaferro was ruthless, prepared to provoke civil war to gain his own ends—but *this* was simple judicial murder!

His fury turned icy as the full implications registered. If one could only be as conscienceless as Taliaferro himself it was almost admirable. Killing the Beaufort "ringleaders" would, at one stroke, remove the Fringe leaders best able to oppose him, inflame the extremists on both sides, and stain the hands of the Assemblymen with blood. Even if their ardor cooled, even if they later realized Taliaferro had used them, they would be his captives. They would share his guilt, and so would perforce becomes his accomplices in future crimes, as well.

Dieter forced himself to use his anger, burning the fury from his system and replacing it with frozen calm. He must speak out, must inject an element of opposition and carry at least a minority with him, so that when the fit passed there would be someone free of Taliaferro's blood guilt.

He drew a deep breath and touched his attention button as David Haley opened debate on Taliaferro's motion.

"The Chair recognizes the Honorable Assemblyman for New Zurich," Haley said, and Dieter heard the relief in his voice.

"Thank you, Mister Speaker." Dieter's huge face stared out over the delegates, showing no sign of his inner turmoil. How should he address them? With fury, denouncing Taliaferro as a madman? Or would that merely brand him another hothead? Should he, then, try cold logic? Or would that stand a chance against the hysteria Taliaferro had been fanning for so many months? Derision, perhaps? Would mockery achieve what head-on opposition could not? He shook his thoughts aside, knowing he must play it by feel.

"Ladies and Gentlemen of the Assembly," he heard his own stiffness and prayed no one else did. "Mister Taliaferro proposes to recognize the depth of this crisis by enacting extraordinary legislation. He argues—and rightly so—that this is a moment to show strength. The Federation has withstood many external threats, yet today we face an *internal* threat to our very existence. Indeed, Mister Taliaferro may well be too optimistic, for he overlooks the composition of our military. As chairman of the Military

Oversight Committee, I can assure you there are enough Fringe Worlders in the military to make the ultimate loyalty of our own armed forces far from assured."

He felt the surprise as he admitted even a part of the Gallowayan's arguments. The Dieter-Taliaferro enmity had been a lively topic of Assembly gossip for months, and he knew the wagers in the ante-rooms were heavily against him. But they'd reckoned without the years of favors he'd desperately called in among the hierarchy of his homeworld. And without the recorder his briefcase had concealed during his final, parting-of-the-ways meeting with the Taliaferro Machine's leadership. He'd hung on, emerging as Taliaferro's only real opposition, and though his Assembly membership still hung by a thread, that thread grew steadily stronger as his warning penetrated deeper into the fundamentally conservative minds of the bankers who owned New Zurich.

His secretly made recording had helped immensely, for he knew some of the New Zurich syndics shared his private opinion that Taliaferro was no longer sane. They were willing to keep him on as a counterweight—at least until they knew whether the Gllowayan would succeed. And if Taliaferro did, Dieter knew, he would be the sacrificial lamb offered by the New Zurich leaders as they sought rapprochement with Galloway's World.

He shook such thoughts aside and forced his mind back to the present. His increasingly frequent woolgathering mental side-trips worried him.

"Yes, ladies and gentlemen, Mister Taliaferro is quite correct—and he is also entirely *wrong*. He would have you believe the only strong reaction is to crush the rebels, that the only strength is the iron fist of repression. Ladies and gentleman, there are more strengths than the whip hand! Let us acknowledge that this is an unprecedented crisis. Let us admit that what we face is *mass* treason—treason not of a single person, or a single clique, or even a single world, but of an entire cluster! Let us ask ourselves *why* eight star systems and eleven inhabited worlds and moons would *simultaneously* take such a drastic step! Has some mysterious madness gripped them all? Or is it, perhaps, much as we would hate to admit it, *we* who have driven them to it?"

He paused, feeling the hovering resentment like smoke. Some would hate him for opposing their carefully laid plans, and others for saying what they themselves had thought without admitting. Only a tragically small few would understand and support him. But it had to be enough. It must be.

"Ladies and Gentlemen of the Assembly, I oppose this motion. I oppose the creation of kangaroo courts whose only possible verdict can be death. I oppose the institutionalization of the fracture lines splitting our polity at this critical moment. Let us demonstrate that we are strong enough to be reasonable and wise enough to be rational. Let us show the Fringe that we are willing to listen to grievances and, for a change, to act upon them. It is time for compromise, ladies and gentlemen, not for judicial murder."

He sat down abruptly, feeling his last two words ringing in a sudden silence that proved some, at least, had heard. But not enough, he thought grimly. Not enough.

Indeed, he was surprised only by the extent of his support, for as delegate after delegate rose to speak, almost a third supported him. He would have wagered on less than a quarter, and he was gratified to see so much sanity, even as he recognized his failure to stop Taliaferro.

The motion passed by slightly less than a two-thirds majority, and a license to kill was dispatched to the Federation's far-flung commanders.

Dieter prayed they would have the moral courage to ignore it.

"Chief! Mister Dieter! Wake *up* sir! *Please* wake up!"

The grip on Dieter's shoulder wrenched him awake, and his hand darted under the pillow to the pistol butt which had become so unhappily familiar in the past fourteen months. The weapon was out, safety catch released, before his sleep-dazed mind recognized Heinz von Rathenau, his security chief.

Rathenau stepped back quickly, and Dieter lowered the needler with a twisted grin and a shrug of apology. Since the first attempt on his life, he'd found himself uncomfortable without a weapon to hand.

"Yes, Heinz," he said. "What is it?" He glanced at the

clock and winced. Four A.M. He'd been asleep less than two hours.

"A priority message, sir." Rathenau looked desperately unhappy in the light of the bedside lamp. "From the Lictor General's office."

"The Lictor General?" Dieter rose quickly, shrugging into a robe even as he headed barefooted for the door. "What priority?"

"Priority One, sir."

"Oh, God! Not again!" Dieter bit off further comment as he walked quickly down the hall beside Rathenau. The armed New Zurich Peaceforcers at the elevators snapped to attention as Dieter passed, and Rathenau noticed that his normally affable superior didn't even acknowledge the courtesy.

They reached the communications room, and Rathenau stopped outside as Dieter stepped through the heavy security door. His predecessor would have walked through at Dieter's elbow with a calm assurance of his right to be there, but Rathenau felt no desire to appear even remotely akin to Francois Fouchet. Fouchet had mistaken Dieter's trustfulness for weakness . . . and paid for it, Rathenau thought with grim satisfaction. For himself, he would follow Oskar Dieter back to New Zurich without a murmur when the axe fell. It wasn't often a Corporate World security man found himself serving a chief worthy of personal loyalty.

Dieter shut the door without sparing Rathenau a thought. He had eyes only for the flashing red light on the panel, and his blood ran cold. The last time he'd seen that light had been three months ago to receive news of the Kontravian secession.

He presented his eye to the retinal scanners, automatically suppressing the blink reflex. It took thirty seconds to satisfy the brilliant lights; when he finally read the message, he wished it had taken thirty years.

He stared at the screen, his mind encased in ice. God, he thought. Please, God. Why are You letting this happen?

But there was no answer. There would be none.

He rose finally, like an old, old man, switching off the communicators and wishing he could switch off his mind as easily. He opened the door and saw young Rathenau's face tighten at his own expression.

"Chief?"

"Heinz—" Dieter's hands moved for a moment, as if trying to recapture something that was irretrievably shattered.

"What is it, Chief?" Rathenau's voice was much softer, almost gentle.

"Wake the others, Heinz." Dieter drew a deep breath, but the oxygen was little help. "Get everyone assembled in conference room one in—" he glanced at his watch "—twenty minutes. Tell them to forget dressing."

"Yes, sir. May I ask why, sir?"

"I'm afraid you'll have to wait for the briefing. There'll be an emergency session at 0600 hours, and I have calls to make."

"Yes, sir."

Rathenau watched Oskar Dieter move brokenly down the corridor, and his heart was cold within him.

The Chamber of Worlds was hushed, wrapped in a silence it had not known in decades—if ever. Dieter looked around the shocked faces and wondered if even the Battle of VX-134 had produced such an effect. Howard Anderson's battle had been Man's first with a rival stellar empire; this news was worse.

He glanced up as Taliaferro walked briskly to his seat. He wanted nothing else in the Galaxy so much as to see Taliaferro's expression, to read the emotions in the dark, arrogant face of the man who'd orchestrated this disaster. The man whom he, God help him, had *helped* create this catastrophe.

Taliaferro dropped into his chair almost as the chime struck, and Dieter understood. He'd timed his late arrival to preclude any buttonholing, but how would he deal with it? How would he manage *this* session?

"Ladies and Gentlemen." David Haley's voice sounded as if it had been pulverized and glued unskillfully back together. "Ladies and Gentlemen of the Assembly, the Legislative Assembly is in session." He paused and cleared his throat, his face pale in the vast screen.

"I am certain all of you have been apprised of the reason

for this emergency session. However . . . however, for those of you who may not be fully informed, I will summarize." His hands trembled visibly as he adjusted his terminal, but Dieter was certain he didn't really need any notes. Like himself, he no doubt found the information burned into his quivering brain.

"On February 12, 2439, Terran Standard Reckoning," Haley said slowly, as if seeking protection in the formality of his phrasing, "Task Force Seventeen of the Terran Federation Navy Battle Fleet entered the system of Bigelow in the Kontravian Cluster for the purpose of suppressing the secessionist elements therein. It was hoped—" his voice broke, then steadied. "It was hoped this force was strong enough to overawe the rebels. It was not. The Kontravians refused to surrender, and, after the failure of lengthy negotiations, Fleet Admiral Forsythe moved against them."

He drew a deep breath, and a strange strength seemed to possess him, the strength which comes only to those who have faced the worst disaster they can conceive. When he continued, his voice was cold and clear.

"Task Force Seventeen," he said quietly, "no longer exists. Apparently—the message is not entirely clear, ladies and gentlemen—but apparently mutiny first broke out aboard the flagship. It spread. Within a very short space, virtually every ship was involved. Most—" he drew another breath "—went over to the Kontravians."

They'd known, but the shock which ran through his audience as the words were finally said was actually visible. Dieter looked away from Haley, fixing his gaze on Taliaferro, willing the man to show some reaction, but the Gallowayan had himself under inhuman control.

"There was some fighting between loyal and mutinous elements," Haley continued. "Our only information comes from a courier drone from the superdreadnought *Pentelikon.* The drone carried an Omega message." The chamber was utterly still; Code Omega was used only for the final communication from a doomed ship.

"As nearly as we can determine," Haley said into the hushed silence, "the entire task force—minus those units destroyed in the fighting—went over to the Kontravians or was subsequently captured. As of the time *Pentelikon*'s drone was dispatched, the count of survivors was approximately as follows: eight monitors, six superdreadnoughts, seven carriers, eleven battle-cruisers, twenty-one heavy and light cruisers, forty-one destroyers and escort destroyers, and virtually the entire fleet train. At least six destroyers, three light and heavy cruisers, one carrier, and two superdreadnoughts were destroyed in the fighting.

"Ladies and Gentlemen," the Speaker said very quietly, "this means, in effect, that there are *no* loyal survivors from the entire task force."

The silence grew, if possible, even more complete. Most of the delegates were staring at Haley's image in horror. Very few seemed capable of coherent thought—and that, Dieter thought, was what was desperately needed now.

He was reaching for his own attention button when the sound of another bell cut the air. An edge of uncontrollable bitterness crossed the Speaker's face, but when he spoke, his voice was as impersonal as ever.

"The Chair recognizes the Honorable Assemblyman for Galloway's World."

Dieter leaned back as Taliaferro appeared on the screen. His face was taut, but any sense of guilt was well hidden as he looked out over the depleted delegations for a long second, then spoke.

"Ladies and Gentlemen of the Assembly," he said sadly, "this is the most horrible, damnable news ever to come before this Assembly. Not only have the traitors not been suppressed, but the madness has infected even our own Navy! The Terran Federation Navy, the most loyal, the most courageously dedicated fighting force in the history of Man, has been touched by the insanity of treason!" He shook his head in eloquent disbelief.

"But we must not allow shock and shame to paralyze us. However terrible the news, it is our responsibility to act and act promptly. Consider, my friends—the Kontravian traitors have acquired the equivalent of their own navy out of this. The ships of Task Force Seventeen will be turned against us, the legitimate government of the Federation. Threats of force and force itself may be used against us by these damnable traitors! Our defenses are strong; it is unlikely any rebel attack will penetrate Innerworld space, and our loyal commanders will surely move quickly to prevent the spread of this insidious rot, but we must accept that some additional fraction of the Fleet may join this contemptible attack upon us. I have said before—and this Assembly has agreed with me—that this is a time for strength, and so it is. Our only option, ladies and gentlemen, is to show our steel, our determination that this criminal conspiracy shall not succeed! We must mobilize the rest of Battle Fleet. We must call in every loyal ship, every loyal military man and woman. We must crush the heart out of the Fringe World conspiracy! We must show these barbarians that *we*—not *they*—are the representatives of civilized humanity! And with God's help, we *will* show them that! We will defeat them, and we will hunt down and execute every traitor who has dared to raise his hand against the might and dignity and justice of the Terran Federation!"

A roaring ovation sealed his words, and Dieter shuddered. Damn the man! Damn him to *hell*! This disaster demonstrated the fundamental, destructive insanity of his entire self-serving policy. It should have stunned him. Instead, with a few brief words and a simplistic appeal to patriotism and pride, he had the Assembly eating out of his hand! Bile rose in Dieter's throat and, for the first time, he allowed himself to wonder if such an Assembly was even worth saving.

He bowed over his hands in defeat. He'd tried. As God was his witness, he'd *tried*. But he'd failed, and the Taliaferros and Waldecks and Sydons had inherited the Federation . . . or whatever smoking ruins would be left. He felt hot tears behind his eyes and turned in his chair. He would have no more of it. He would resign his seat, leave them to their madness. . . .

A hand touched his shoulder, and the concern and desperate faith in Heinz von Rathenau's eyes stopped him. Of all the New Zurich delegation, Heinz saw most clearly. He *understood*, and as Dieter saw the faith in those green eyes, he could not leave it unanswered. He owed it to Heinz, to the Federation, and most of all—God help him—to Fionna MacTaggart.

"Chief?" Rathenau asked softly. "Are you all right?"

"Yes, Heinz." Dieter rested his hand on the fingers

gripping his shoulder and squeezed gently. "Yes, I'm all right now. Thank You."

He saw Rathenau's confusion and hoped the young man would never realize just what that "thank you" meant. But whether young Heinz ever did or not, all that mattered now was the battle which must be fought. And as he thought of Heinz, as he thought of Fionna and Taliaferro's greed, anger returned. He was not like Taliaferro, but for today, just for this morning, it was time to take a page from Taliaferro's book. His hand stabbed the button, and the attention bell chimed softly.

"The Chair," David Haley's amplified voice cut through the hum of excited conversation, "recognizes the Honorable Assemblyman for New Zurich."

Dieter stood in the ringing silence and knew the Chamber of Worlds was agog with curiosity. How would he respond? How could he possibly continue to oppose Taliaferro now that they faced a life and death struggle for survival itself? But he let his bitter eyes sweep over them for long, long seconds before he finally spoke, and when he did, his voice was a whip.

"You *fools*," he said coldly, and the Assembly recoiled, for no one spoke to them in that flat, bitingly contemptuous tone! Dieter felt their anger and let it feed his own as he leaned into the pickup.

"Can't you see what this *means*? Are you all so blind you can't recognize reality just because it happens to clash with your comfortable image of yourselves as the last bright hope of humanity? By God, you don't *deserve* to survive! Think of the *date*, you idiots! Task Force Seventeen mutinied *five months ago!* Who knows what's happened since?"

His words shattered the rising anger like a lightning bolt. They'd lived with the reality of the Fringe's slow communications all their lives, had learned to use their faster communications for ruthless advantage, yet until he threw the date in their faces, they hadn't even considered the time element. But now the implications were before them, and their palms were suddenly slick with fear.

"Yes," Dieter sneered. "It takes a long time for courier drones to come that far—and who knows where other drones were sent? *We* have one from a single unit of the task force. Do you seriously think that was the only drone launched? Do you seriously think other Fleet units haven't heard by now? Sixty percent of the Fleet is Fringer. *Sixty percent*. Can none of you understand what that means? *We* don't have the numerical advantage in the civil war you've provoked—*they do*!"

His words unleashed the ugly, snarling pandemonium of terror. For over a year, he'd hammered away, warning them, pleading with them, and all but a minority had ignored him. *They* controlled the Fleet. *They* spoke with their every word backed by the suppressive might of the Federation's military. And now, suddenly, they saw the nightmare at last, and the man who'd warned them, who'd earned their contempt for his weakness, had been right all along.

Dieter's voice thundered above the tumult.

"*Yes!* Yes flog the Fringe! Ignore their legitimate complaints! Call them barbarians because they're more honest, more desperate than you are! And now see what you've created! God help me, I helped you do it—now I must bear the same guilt as you, and the thought makes me *sick*."

"But what are we going to do?" someone yelled. "My God, what are we going to *do*?"

"Do?" Dieter sneered down at him. "What do you *think* we're going to do? We're going to fight. We're going to fight to save what we can, because we have no choice, because the only alternative is the utter destruction of the Federation—that's what we're going to *do*. But understand this, all of you! The days of contempt for the Fringe are over. Fight them, yes. But never, *never* call them 'barbarians' again! Because, ladies and gentlemen, if they really *are* barbarians, we're doomed."

His words plunged them back into silence. A fearful, lingering silence.

"We're doomed because they have Task Force Seventeen, ladies and gentlemen, and by now they have other ships. By the time we can get our own courier drones to the Fringe, they may have all of Frontier Fleet—perhaps even the Zephrain Fleet base." He felt the sudden whiplash of terror that thought woke in the delegates who knew what it meant, but he hammered the point mercilessly home. "I know what that means, and so should you. Weapons research in the data base of Zephrain Research and Development Station. Research on weapons which may outclass anything this galaxy has ever seen—and it lies in the *Fringe*, ladies and gentlemen, not in the Innerworlds." He glared at them, and his voice was cold.

"And if they act as what you've called them—if they truly are barbarians and choose to seek vengeance rather than relief—they will not use those ships and weapons in self-defense. Oh, no, ladies and gentlemen! If the Fringers are barbarians, you will find those ships *here*, striking the Innerwords, and you will find those weapons turning your precious planets into cinders." He hissed the last word, and its chill ran through his audience like a wind.

"So get down on your knees," he finished. "Get down on your knees and pray you were wrong."

He cut the connection with a contemptuous flick. Silence roared about him, and he was heartsick and frightened, yet he could almost feel Fionna at his shoulder, and knew he had finally paid the first installment on his debt.

A bell chimed.

Dieter looked up and saw what he'd known he would. Simon Taliaferro was pressing for recognition, his shoulders hunched, his face bitter. He had no choice but to respond, and Dieter knew that if his security showed the tiniest chink, he himself was a dead man.

"The Chair," Haley said, "recognizes the Assemblyman from Galloway's World."

Taliaferro appeared on the screen, and his face shocked Dieter. The compelling strength had waned, and the arrogance was mixed with desperation. It struck him suddenly that Taliaferro had actually never considered this possibility. That he, too, had missed the significance of the drone's date. That he'd brushed aside Dieter's warnings about the Fleet simply because his blind, overweening confidence had never considered the chance of failure.

But though Dieter might hate him, Simon Taliaferro had cut his way to power with courage as well as conspiracy, and he gathered his shaken will to respond.

"Ladies and Gentlemen of the Assembly," he began, his formal courtesy somehow pathetic after Dieter's contempt. "My friends. The Assemblyman for New Zurich—" he drew a deep breath. "The Assemblyman for New Zurich may be right. Perhaps we have lost more Fleet units since the . . . mutiny. But it changes nothing. *Nothing!*" He shouted the last word, and suddenly he seemed to find fresh strength. Dieter recognized the signs. Like himself, Taliaferro was unleashing his anger, letting fury sustain him.

"We are still the Federation, and they are still barbarians! Even if they have every ship in Frontier Fleet, even if they have every dispersed unit of Battle Fleet—even if they have the Zephrain Fleet base itself!—what of it? Before they can injure us, they must come to us, ladies and gentlemen! They must fight their way through Fortress Command. They must deal with the remaining strength of Battle Fleet. They must deal with the Reserve, ladies and gentlemen. Fifty percent of Battle Fleet—*fifty percent* —is in mothballs! How will they deal with that when we mobilize it? Even if they have Zephrain, surely the base personnel—personnel rigorously screened for loyalty and integrity—destroyed the facilities before they could be taken! And what will they use for shipyards? They have only a few, scattered repair bases and small civilian yards. *We* hold the Fleet shipyards! *We* hold the major construction facilities!"

Dieter felt the shaken Assembly take courage from Taliaferro's words. Couldn't they recognize the counsel of despair when they heard it?!

"Let them come against us, ladies and gentlemen! It will prove that I was right—that *we* were right—when we called them barbarians! Driven to it? *Poppycock!* This is a coldly calculated act of treason. This is—*must* be—the end product of a long and careful conspiracy! We have driven them to nothing—but we *will* drive them. We will drive them to destruction and retribution! Our worlds are safe behind our fortifications; their worlds will lie open to our attack when the Fleet is fully mobilized! Let us teach them the true meaning of war, my friends! Let us cauterize this cancer of conspiracy in the only way they understand—with the flames of war and iron determination!"

It took all Dieter's strength to keep his dismay from his face. He'd shaken Taliaferro, but the Gallowayan was rallying his forces, and without the Outworlds not even a unified bloc of Heart Worlds and the few Corporate World moderates could fight the political steamroller Taliaferro controlled.

"And if it is a long war, what of it?" Taliaferro demanded hotly. "We have fought long wars before and come back to victory. We will do it again! We have the strength to crush these traitors—it is only a matter of mobilizing that strength! My friends! As chief of delegation for Galloway's World, I place the combined building capacity of the Jamieson Archipelago—the greatest concentration of industrial might in the Galaxy—unreservedly at the service of the Terran Federation! Let us see how the rebels like *that!*"

A roar greeted his words—the desperate roar of a panicked crowd which suddenly sees salvation. Dieter hammered his call button, but Taliaferro ignored him as he ignored Speaker Haley's urgent, amplified pleas for calm, smiling fiercely out at the shouting, clapping delegates. He'd done it. He'd salvaged victory and his career from the very teeth of disaster.

And in that moment of heady political triumph, the sealed doors flew open and the Sergeant at Arms raced down the aisle, followed by the red cloak of the Lictor General. A shockwave of quiet fanned out from them, and Taliaferro's fierce grin faded as he saw them.

The two men hurled themselves up the steps to Haley's side, and only later did Dieter come to recognize the blind providence—or the brilliance of David Haley—which had left the Speaker's mike open. Every ear in the Chamber of Worlds heard the message the Lictor General gasped into Haley's ear.

"A message from Galloway's World, sir! It-it's terrible! Skywatch HQ is gone! A dozen destroyers blown apart! And the Jamieson Archipelago!"

"What about the Archipelago?" Haley's question was sharp.

"Gone, sir! The yards, the Fleet base, half the Reservation—just . . . gone, sir. It was a nuclear strike. . . ."

The Lictor General's voice trailed off as he realized the microphone at his elbow was live, but no one noticed. Every eye was on Simon Taliaferro as he swayed, his swarthy face pale, his eyes blank, and stumbled silently away.

Atrocity

The furrows stretched out behind Fedor Kazin's lurching tractor—miles and miles of furrows, hungry for Terran wheat, waiting for spikeweed sprigs. The one to feed Innerworld bellies, he thought sourly, and the other to liven their dreams, and which did they value more, eh?

Yet whatever they paid him, it wouldn't be enough . . . again. Not with the shipping fees those Corporate World *vlasti* extorted from the Fringe. For thirty years he'd harvested his wheat and spikebalm, and *still* he was perpetually in debt to the shipping lines.

He glanced up at the clouds. His grandfather had always claimed Novaya Rodina's steppes were almost as beautiful as Old Russia's, but for the color of the sky. Fedor wouldn't know; he'd seen only recordings from the motherworld, and he'd always suspected they touched the things up a little—surely no sky could be *that* blue!—but he knew his own sky well. He only hoped he finished his plowing before the storm struck.

Thoughts of the weather turned his mind to the storm ripping through the entire Federation. He couldn't believe the tales coming out of Novaya Petrograd! Did those madmen think they were all back in the days of the tsar? That the Federation was run by Rasputin? And who were *they*, these men who called themselves 'Kadets' once more? Kerensky? Trotsky? Fedor had no more love for the Corporate Worlds than the next man, but the Federation was the *Federation!* It had risen from the flames of Old Terra's

Great Eastern War and reached out to the stars, protecting its people as it placed them on worlds light-years from their birthworld. It was the Federation of Howard Anderson and Ivan Antonov. Four centuries it had stood—what were a hundred years or so of mistakes against that? And Novaya Rodinans were Russians: they knew a thing or two about endurance.

But these crazy Kadets—! Madness! Even if they succeeded, where would his wheat go? There had to be *some* form of foreign exchange—and who in the Fringe needed foodstuffs? What Fringe farming world could sell Novaya Rodina the manufactured goods she needed?

So Fedor plowed and sowed, for the day would come when the crazy men realized they couldn't succeed. It might be necessary to chastise them a little first, but in the end the Federation would take them back. And when it did, Fedor Kazin would have a crop ready, by God!

He looked up as thunder muttered and the squall line in the east swept closer. He wasn't going to finish today after all: best to stop at the end of this furrow and head home. 'Tasha would have supper waiting.

Pieter Tsuchevsky looked around the quiet room at his fellow Kadets. So this was how it felt to be a rebel. He'd never really wanted to be one. He doubted any of the others had. But it was inevitable for those who controlled the old government to call their opponents "rebels." He'd known that from the start, just as he'd known where his first public expressions of discontent might lead.

They'd led here—to the men and women who had declared themselves the new Duma of Novaya Rodina and stated their determination to withdraw from the Federation . . . not without fear and trembling. There was something almost holy about the Federation, but a government was only a government, and surely its function must be to make the lives of its people better, not worse. The purpose of an elective assembly *couldn't* be to murder its own members!

Pieter had never met Fionna MacTaggart, but he'd corresponded with her over the light-years, and even from her recorded messages he'd felt the intelligence and determination which had made her the Fringe's leader. Had she done her job too well? Was murder the fate small minds always reserved for great minds they could not silence? He didn't know, but from the morning the news arrived, he'd known the Federation was doomed. Anything that rotten at its core deserved to die, and die it would.

If only communications were less chaotic! Novaya Rodina had never had a relay system, and courier drones had become notoriously unreliable since the Kontravian Mutiny. No doubt many nav beacons had been shut down or destroyed, but it went further than that. The Corporate Worlds handled a tremendous percentage of the total drone traffic, just as they monopolized the freight lanes. Almost certainly they were tampering with the drones to keep the "rebels" disorganized.

Well, if he were in their position, he would probably do the same. But in the meantime, it left him with the devil of a problem! He cleared his throat, and the eyes around the table returned to his face.

"So there you have it, comrades," he said slowly. "The Federation has declared martial law and suspended *habeas corpus* . . . among other rights. And we—you and I, my friends—we are all rebels." He shrugged. "For myself, I realized this must come, but possibly some of you did not. So it is only fair that we reconsider what we have done, I think. We have made our gesture, voiced our protest. Is that all we wish to do? If so, we had best dispatch a courier drone with apologies and renewed protestations of loyalty at once! But if we do not, if we continue as we have begun to follow the lead of the Kontravians, God alone knows where we shall end."

"Pieter," Magda Petrovna stroked her prematurely silvering hair, "you say you knew this would come. Do you think we were all fools, Pieter Petrovich?" She smiled in gentle mockery. "How noble of you to give us a choice! But tell us—what will *you* do when we all run crying home to *babushka* Terra?"

A soft laugh ran around the table, and Pieter smiled unwillingly; but he also shook his head.

"This is no laughing matter, Magda. This is life and death. Oh, we hold the cities and universities, but the farmers and ranchers think we're mad. They won't raise a hand if it comes to a fight—and we've little chance of defeating the Federation if they would!"

"Mega shit!" The tart remark could come only from one man, and Pieter's eyes twinkled as he turned to Semyon Jakov, the single *megaovis* rancher in their Duma. The old man's blue eyes were fiery as he puffed his walrus mustache, looking as fierce as one of his huge, vaguely sheep-like herdbeasts. "No way we could beat the Federation, no," he snapped, "but we won't be fighting the Federation—only an Innerworld rump, and well you know it, Pieter Petrovich Tsuchevsky! And they won't even have the full Navy. Damnation, man, the Kontravians took a task force—a *task force*—in one snap! D'you honestly think they haven't lost *more* ships? I wouldn't be surprised to hear they've lost half the Fleet by now, Pieter!"

"True, Semyon, but Novaya Rodina is no Navy base. There were no ships for *us* to seize; it was pure luck Skywatch supported us. They could've blown our leaky old tubs out of space—and those are still the best ships we can scare up. No, Semyon Illyich, whatever the Kontravians may have taken, *we* can't fight what the Federation can send here."

"But why send anything?" Tatiana Illushina asked plaintively. "We're not exactly the richest of the Fringe Worlds!"

"No, Tatiana," Magda said gently, "but we *are* what the Fleet manuals call a 'choke point.'" The others listened carefully. Semyon Jakov had been a Marine for fifteen years, but Magda had reached the rank of captain in Frontier Fleet before resigning in protest.

"A choke point?" Tatiana asked.

"An especially valuable warp nexus," Magda explained. "The way the warp lines lie, some systems control access to several others. The Corporate Worlds are mostly on early choke points of the Federation. That's why they're so powerful; every ship to the Heart Worlds has to go through choke points they control." Tatiana nodded. When it came to the *economic* implications of the Corporate Worlds' galactic position, every Fringe schoolchild understood.

"Well, the same thing makes choke points militarily important," Magda said. "If Novaya Rodina goes over to the Kontravians, we'll block a whole section of the Fringe off from the Federation; they'll have to take this system before they can attack the others. But if we remain loyal to the Federation, the Fleet will have several possible avenues of attack into Fringe space to choose from, you see?"

"But . . . but in that case, they're *certain* to come here—aren't they?" Tatiana asked very quietly.

"They are," Pieter told her gently, "and soon, I think. They wouldn't have sent this—" he waved the official message form gently "—if they didn't mean to back it up. There's some pretty stiff language in here; if they planned on talking us back into the Federation, they'd've taken a more flexible initial position."

"I agree," Semyon said harshly. "and I say—fuck 'em! Let them come! There's twenty million people on this planet. It'd take half the Corps to hold us down!"

"Except that only eight million or so of them are actively on our side," Pieter begun, but Magda interrupted.

"It doesn't matter anyway, Semyon Illyich," she said with an affectionate smile. "Just because you grunts spend *your* time crawling around in the mud doesn't mean the Fleet does! They don't care about planets, only warp points and the normal space between them."

"So? They still need someplace to base ships!"

"Certainly," Magda nodded, "but what if a monitor drops into orbit and zeros a few missiles on Novaya Petrograd? Or Novaya Smolensk? You think we shouldn't surrender to keep them from firing?"

"Well . . . "

"Exactly, you old cossack!" Magda punched the old man's arm lightly.

"Are you saying we should just give up?" Jakov demanded incredulously.

"Did I say that? Certainly not! We've already sent off our own drones, so the rest of the Fringe knows what's happening. I'm only saying that if it comes down to ultimatums, we'd better decide what we'll do ahead of time. I don't want to believe a TFN commander would fire on civilians; it goes against all we've been taught. But he might. And I want us to know *now* what we're going to say to him to keep any itchy finger off the button."

"So what you're saying, Magda," Pieter cut in pacifically, "is that we should continue as we have, possibly even to fighting in space, but that if it's a choice between bombardment and surrender, we should surrender?"

"Exactly." Magda's face was unusually grim. "I don't like it any more than you do, Pieter—or you Semyon. But what alternative do we have?"

"But what'll happen to us if we surrender?" Tatiana asked. "I don't mean the rest of our people, I mean *us*, right here in this room?"

"Hard to say," Magda said with a shrug. "There's never been a case like this, and it's not as if we're the only planet to secede. I'd think the government would have to follow a fairly lenient policy—especially with any of us 'rebels' who surrender—if they have any hope of ever healing the break. Unfortunately, we can't depend on that."

"They might execute us?" Tatiana asked faintly.

"They might," Magda agreed calmly. "Of course, even under martial law, any death sentence has to be confirmed by the civilian authorities. I'd think that confirmation would be unlikely."

"All right," Pieter said suddenly. "I propose a vote. All those in favor of declaring our immediate surrender?" There was no response, although several uneasy glances were exchanged. "All those in favor of continuing as we have but surrendering to avoid bombardment?" A chorus of affirmatives ran round the table. "Very well, the ayes have it."

Fedor Kazin watched the fields soak. Another day, at least, before he could resume plowing. Well, there were advantages to bad weather. Such as sitting with 'Tasha on a Spring morning instead of bouncing around in his poorly sprung tractor. If only it weren't for those crazies in Novaya Petrograd! He had half a mind to go talk to them himself.

He frowned and glanced over at his wife. Maybe he should. After all, here he was cursing their stupidity, but had he done anything to change their minds? They might just not realize how others felt. And old Semyon Jakov was one of them . . . and Andrei Petrov's girl Magda. They were good people. Maybe he could make them see reason?

Of course, 'Tasha would have a fit if he took himself off to the city and left her and the boys alone with the planting. On the other hand, if this madness wasn't settled, there wouldn't be a market come harvest, now would there? He filled his pipe with Orion tobacco (his one true luxury), and the pungent smoke curled up around his ears.

Yes, the idea of going to Novaya Petrograd to confront the Duma . . . it definitely bore thinking on. . . .

Admiral Jason Waldeck, of the Chartiphon Waldecks, regarded his subordinates so coldly they shifted uneasily under his glare.

"I don't want to hear any more crap about poor misunderstood Fringers!" he snapped. "They're mutineers and traitors—and that's all! That bastard Skjorning should've been shot. Might've nipped the whole damned thing in the bud!"

His officers remained prudently silent. Admiral Waldeck had never been a good man to cross, and it was far more dangerous now. News of the Kontravian Mutiny was still threading its way through the Fleet, but one consequence of it was already clear: moderation was not in great demand among TFN commanders. Indeed, any "softness" might well be construed as treason by the angry (and frightened) cliques of "reliable" Innerworld admirals.

"I don't give a good goddamn why they're doing what they're doing," he grated. "We've got to stop them, and Fleet's shorthanded as hell after the mutinies, especially in capital units and carriers. Hell, we've lost so many pilots there won't even be fighter cover for most operations! So it's up to *us*—understood?"

"Yes, sir," his juniors murmured.

"Good. Now, I don't expect these hayseeds to put up much resistance, but if they try, I want some examples made."

" 'Examples', sir?" one officer asked carefully.

"Yes, Captain Sherman—examples. If anyone wants to fight, let 'em. Don't give them a chance to surrender till you've burned a few bastards down."

"But, sir . . . why?"

"Because these traitors have to learn the hard way," Waldeck said grimly. "The Assembly's finally gotten its head out of its ass, and we're under military law now; that means *my* law. I'm going to teach these proles a little lesson in obedience. Is that *clear*, gentlemen?"

It was clear. They might not much like it, but it was clear.

"All right, then, Commodore Hunter, here's your first objective." The cursor in the chart tank settled on a warp nexus, and Commodore Hunter squinted at the tiny letters. "Novaya Rodina," they said.

"It's confirmed, Commodore. From the drive strengths, they have to be warships."

"I see." Magda Petrovna nodded as calmly as she could. They'd hoped someone would turn up from the Kontravians or one of the other Fringe systems before this, but Asteroid Four watched the warp point to Redwing, and Redwing was part of The Line, one of the fortified Terran-Orion border systems whose mighty orbital forts had remained loyal to the Assembly. She looked around her crowded bridge wryly. It only remained to see what strength the Fleet had scraped up. Her collection of armed freighters might—possibly—hold its own against light units, and Novaya Rodina's Provisional Government had short-stopped two mutinous light cruisers headed for the depths of the Fringe. But that was all she had; that and Skywatch.

She sighed. Unless the mutinies had hit really hard, there was no point even hoping. A single fleet carrier—even a light carrier—would eat her entire force for breakfast, and she hated to think what a few battle-cruisers might do! But the worst of it was that she didn't *know*. Except for Skywatch, none of her units had long range scanners; without those, she could form only a vague impression of what was headed for her.

"Query Asteroid Four for exact drive strengths," she said suddenly.

"Sir," the commander of her cruiser flagship said as they awaited an answer, "those miners don't have the equipment for precision work—and an hour-long transmission lag doesn't help. Why not take *Jintsu* and *Atlanta* out and see for ourselves?"

"I appreciate your spirit, Captain," Magda said, peculiar though it felt to call a mere lieutenant "Captain" onboard a light cruiser, "but we can't take our only cruisers into scanner range all by themselves . . . and if we took the freighters with us, we couldn't run if we had to."

"Yes, sir." Lieutenant Howard blushed as he realized his commodore had just tactfully advised him to let her tend to her own knitting.

"Asteroid Four says they *think* they're all strength twelve or less, Commodore," her com officer finally said dubiously.

"Thank you. Any incoming messages from them?"

"No, sir. Nothing."

That was bad, Magda thought. No surrender demands? Did that mean they were unaware they were being scanned? Or that they had a pretty good notion of what she had and figured she meant to fight no matter what they said? And did she intend to fight? Exactly what had they sent against her?

Well, now, if they *were* strength twelve or less, then almost certainly there was nothing out there larger than a cruiser. If only Asteroid Four could relay the information directly onto *Jintsu*'s cramped battle plot!

"We've got an amplification from Asteroid Four, Commodore. They make it three at strength eight to twelve and three strength six or below. They sound confident, too."

All right, Magda—think, girl! Strength six drives were destroyers. Strength twelves *could* be light carriers, but she doubted it. Too many fighter jocks were Fringers. Assume they were all cruisers . . . a heavy and two lights? They might make it a standard light battlegroup, if the CA were a *Goeben*. . . .

"Ask Asteroid Four if—"

"Commodore," her com officer's voice was very quiet, "they just went off the air in midsentence."

Magda closed her eyes. No messages, and they just casually polished off an unarmed listening post *en passant*. That sounded more like Orions than the TFN, but it resolved her dilemma. They'd drawn first blood; if she had any chance at all, she'd fight.

She thought furiously. Against command datalink, her own forces were at a severe disadvantage. The enemy ships would think, move, and fight as a single, finely-meshed unit; her ships were not only more lightly armed, but they'd have to fight as individuals. On the other hand, she had over a dozen armed freighters, and her two light cruisers formed a datagroup with Skywatch, as long as they were in range—and Skywatch was a lot bigger than any CA, especially a *Goeben* with all that armament sacrificed in favor of data net equipment. Of course, if it *was* a *Goeben*, she'd also mount jammers to take out Magda's own datalink at close range.

All right, Just suppose she had them figured right—what did she do with them? They'd be in missile range of the planet in eleven hours, or she could go out to meet them. If she went out, she lost Skywatch; if she stayed, she lost maneuvering room. Decisions, decisions.

She drew a deep, unobtrusive breath and nodded to Lieutenant Howard.

"Captain Howard, the flotilla will assume Formation Baker. We'll wait for them here."

"Yes, sir," Howard's voice wasn't especially enthusiastic, and she felt a twinge of sympathy. Light cruiser captains were imbued with the notion of maneuver and fire—they hated positional battles.

"If I'm right," Magda said slowly, "there's a *Goeben* out there, Captain. I want maximum firepower laid on her as soon as we can range on her. If we can break their data group—and keep their ECM from breaking *ours*—we'll have a good chance. They'll outclass us ship for ship, but we've got the numbers. If we don't break them—" She shrugged.

"Yes, sir." He sounded more enthusiastic as he digested her plan. God, what she wouldn't give for a properly trained staff! But in another sense, she wouldn't trade these people for anything. They might be mutineers and traitors, but they'd put their lives on the line just to get here. There would never be any reason to question their devotion, and maybe enough of that could make up for their rough edges.

"Skywatch has them on scanners, Commodore!"

Magda jerked awake in her command chair as her chief scanner rating's voice burned into her dozing ears.

"Coming up from data base now, sir . . . Flagship's definitely a *Goeben*. She's *Invincible*, sir, and she's the only heavy! The other cruisers are strength nines—light cruisers! They're . . . *Ajax* and *Sendai*, sir!"

Thank God! They had a chance, but their losses were still going to be awful. She turned to Howard.

"Captain Howard, tune in your datalink. If those bastards don't say something soon, Operation Borodino is about to begin."

"Aye, aye, *sir*!"

The hours of waiting were suddenly minutes, flitting past like raindrops. Magda watched her plot, almost praying for a surrender demand. But there was nothing, and the range continued to drop.

"Enemy force launching missiles," her fire control officer said suddenly. So there it was. They didn't even *want* to negotiate.

"Stand by point defense," Magda said coolly. "Targets?"

"Tracks look like Skywatch, sir."

"Very well. Lay our own missiles on *Invincible*."

"Aye, aye, sir."

"Open fire!"

Jintsu quivered as her external ordnance let fly, and Magda's plot was suddenly speckled with flecks of light as *Atlanta* and Skywatch flushed their external racks at the oncoming cruiser, as well. She felt her lips thin over her teeth. Even command point defense was going to have trouble with *that* lot, and she wondered if the loyalist commander knew Skywatch had taken delivery of antimatter warheads just before the mutinies? If he didn't, he'd be finding out shortly.

But incoming missiles were sleeting in at Skywatch, and there were a lot of them. Point defense crews aboard the cruisers and fortress tracked the incoming fire while battle comp sorted out the clean misses from the salvo, but there weren't many; orbital forts weren't very elusive targets. Then the small laser clusters trained onto the probable hits. Counter missiles zipped out, and for seconds space was wracked with brilliant flares of detonating warheads.

"Hits on *Invincible!*" Gunnery screamed. "One . . . three . . . *five* of them, sir! She's streaming air!"

But Skywatch's blip was pulsing, too, as missiles slipped through to impact on the big fort's powerful shields. Magda gripped her lower lip between her teeth, waiting as the brilliant dot flickered and flashed. Then the report came in.

"Eight hits on Skywatch, sir—all standard nukes. Took out most of her shields, but she's still in business!"

"Good!" Magda ignored the informality of the elated report. "Captain Howard, *Jintsu* and *Atlanta* will engage *Invincible* at close range. Captain Malenkov will come with us. The remainder will engage targets of opportunity among the enemy formation."

"Aye, aye, sir!"

The rebels lurched into motion. Only Malenkov's three big freighters could even hope to stay with a warship . . . the others were much too slow, and Magda had no choice but to turn the engagement into one huge melee and hope.

The two forces closed to energy weapon range, and the TFN loyalists were taken aback by the rebels' reckless courage. Those lumbering freighters were sitting ducks . . . but they were so goddamn *big!* They soaked up force beams and hetlasers as they bumbled into range for their own light armaments, and what they lacked in datalink they made up in determination and sheer volume of fire.

Commodore Hunter realized Admiral Waldeck had made a serious error in assuming they would face only local yokels. There *had* to be Fleet regulars or reservists over there! Well, the hell with standing orders! His own orders went out: break through and get free, then stand off with missiles where his datalink would do him the most good.

But as his ship merged with the milling freighters, Magda's careful briefings took effect. No one tried to *destroy* his vessels; instead they concentrated on battering down shields and armor just far enough to get at the datalink. As soon as a ship fell out of the link, fire shifted to someone else.

Commodore Hunter cursed as the first ship dropped out of his net. They were stripping away his coordination, and if his outnumbered units had to fight as individuals among that many enemies, they wouldn't stand a chance! But he didn't have much choice, because two light cruisers were lunging straight for him.

He watched in something very like awe as the rebel ships soaked up the fire from his own lights, homing on his wounded flagship. He saw hits going home all over them

. . . both of them were streaming atmosphere . . . and *still* they came on. One suddenly staggered and yawed aside as she took a direct hit on a drive pod, but she hauled back on course and kept coming. He barked an order, and *Invincible* tried to turn away, but her crippled drive faltered. He looked back into his plot and swallowed as *Sendai* blew in half and the rebel cruisers closed to half a light-second, energy weapons aflame.

"Abandon ship!" he screamed—but he was too late. *Jintsu*'s hetlasers zeroed in on his command deck with uncanny accuracy, and a burst of finely-focused X rays tore him and his staff apart.

The battle collapsed into a mad, whirling ball of snapping ships. *Atlanta* exploded in a massive fireball, followed by *Ajax*. The surviving loyalists began a limping withdrawal, and a dozen gutted freighters drifted helplessly in their wake, glowing from the hits they'd taken . . . but there was a dead destroyer to keep them company. Skywatch streamed air through a dozen huge rents, but her energy weapons were still in action—some of them—and her missiles pursued the two retreating destroyers.

"Break off the engagement, Captain Howard," Magda Petrovna said wearily. He looked at her in surprise. *Jintsu* was hard hit, but half her weapons were still in action. "If we chase them and we're dead unlucky, we might catch them, Captain. Just us. We're the only ship that could."

Howard's face lit with understanding. "Yes, sir," he said.

"And send a message down to the planet," Magda said, looking at her battle plot. Better than half her "fleet" had been destroyed in the short, savage action, and all the rest were damaged. "Tell them we won—I think."

"And you mean to tell me," Admiral Waldeck said icily, "that a handful of armed freighters shot an entire light battlegroup to hell?"

The white-faced lieutenant commander across his desk stared straight ahead. Spots of color burned on his cheeks, but his voice was controlled.

"Not precisely, sir. There were also two Fleet cruisers and a class three fort, if you'll remember. With antimatter warheads."

Waldeck flushed with fury. His lips worked, and the commander thought he'd gone too far. But the admiral gradually regained control.

"All right, Commander, the point is well taken," he said coldly. "But the fact remains that in the first engagement against rebel forces, we lost virtually an entire flotilla. Your ship will be out of action for months, and I doubt *Cougar* will ever fight again."

"Yes, sir."

"*We* were supposed to teach *them* a lesson!"

"Yes, sir."

"Well, by God, we *will* teach them one!" Waldeck punched up a com link to his flag captain. "Captain M'tana, the task force will move out in one hour. We're going to Novaya Rodina!"

"Yes, sir."

"And you, Commander," Waldeck returned his attention to the unfortunate in front of his desk, "are going to come along and see what three battle-cruisers do to your precious rebels!"

"Well, Pieter Petrovich, that's that." Magda raised her glass of vodka in a tired toast. "After all the repairs we can make out of local resources, the 'Novaya Rodina Fleet' consists of one crippled light cruiser, one crippled OWP, and four crippled freighters. We *might* be able to hold this system against a troop of Young Pioneers."

"I see." Tsuchevsky's face was lined and tired. He was appalled by their losses; only Magda and Semyon had really had any concept of what a fleet action was like. "What do you think the chances are that the Kontravians will get here first?"

"Poor," Magda said grimly, refilling her empty glass carefully. "The Rump was surprised by the mutinies, but it still has an intact command structure and better communications. What do we rebels have? A handful of planets that are partially organized and tied together only by courier drones; it'll be a while yet before we can get beyond that point and start throwing task forces around."

"So all those people died for nothing," Pieter said sadly.

"Maybe, maybe not. You can't run your life on Russian melancholy and the second sight, Pieter Petrovich, and we know what would have happened if we *hadn't* fought. Still, I'll be surprised if we have time to do much of anything else before the next TFN force arrives, and this time it'll be a battlegroup worth the name." She shrugged, but her voice was softer when she went on. "We did our best, my Pieter. Maybe we should have surrendered if they'd given us a chance, but they just opened fire."

"I know." He swiveled his chair to look out the window at the bright spring morning. "Well," he said heavily, "if they come back in force, we have no option but to surrender. Agreed?"

"Agreed," she sighed. "Those are good people up there, Pieter. I don't want to see them die uselessly."

"All right. Will you see to the communication arrangements, Magda?"

"I already did," she said with a tired smile. "After all, that's why I'm commodore of our magnificent fleet, isn't it?"

"Hush, Magda." Pieter grinned slowly. "Now *you're* being maudlin! Drink your vodka and cheer up. Things could be worse."

"What do you mean, going to Novaya Petrograd?" Natasha Kazina put her hands on her hips and glared at her husband. "Who do you think you are? Vladimir Lenin? You're maybe going to bore from within like a mole and topple the government?"

" 'Tasha, you *know* why I'm going—me and Vlad Kosygin and Georgi—we need to be sure those people understand what they're doing to us."

"Really?" Her voice dripped sarcasm. "And you think they don't already? Idiots! Firing on a Terran Fleet! Next thing you know, there'll be missiles on the cities, and there you'll be, playing *Menshevik* in the middle of it!"

"Hush, 'Tasha! You know I agree with you—but maybe they aren't all idiots, no? There are good people mixed up in this, *our* people. Let me go see them. Let me try to convince them they're wrong."

"Argue with the rain! It pays more attention!"

"Natasha, I'm going, and that's an end to it. Sure the Federation has problems, but this isn't the right answer! If

I don't try to tell the Kadets that, I won't be able to sleep nights."

"Ahhh! Men—you're all idiots!" Natasha exclaimed, throwing up her hands in disgust. "But go! Go! Leave me and the boys to see to the planting! Just don't come crying to me when they don't listen!"

"Thank You, 'Tasha," Fedor murmured, kissing her cheek gently. "I knew you'd understand."

"Get out of my sight!" she told him, but her eyes twinkled as he backed off the porch. "And don't forget to bring home some new dress material!" she admonished in a parting shot as he climbed into Kosygin's chopper and it chirruped aloft.

Alarms whooped as the ships emerged from warp, and Magda watched her display in silence. At least they'd been able to mount proper instrumentation out there: no helpless miners to be vaporized this time! But the story her scanners told was heartbreaking. Ship after ship slid out of the Redwing warp point; three battle-cruisers, two heavy cruisers, five light cruisers, and *fifteen* destroyers. God, it was an armada, she thought wearily, and tuned her communicator to Tsuchevsky's priority channel.

"Yes, Magda?" His eyes were puffy. She'd waked him up, she thought. Waked him from a sound sleep to face a nightmare.

"They're coming, Pieter," she said sadly.

"How bad is it?"

"If I order a shot fired, it will be as good as executing every man and woman in my fleet."

"All right, Magda," he said softly. "I understand. Patch me through to their commander, if you can. I'll handle it from here."

"I'm sorry, Pieter Petrovich," she said very quietly

"You did your best, Magda. Time was against us, that's all."

"I know," she said heavily, and turned to her com officer.

Pieter Tsuchevsky stared into the screen at Admiral Jason Waldeck, TFN. The admiral's cheek muscles were bunched, and Pieter shivered as he realized the man had *wanted* a fight.

"Admiral, I am Pieter Petrovich Tsuchevsky of the Provisional Gov—"

"You, sir," Waldeck cut in coldly, "are a traitor, and that is *all* you are!" Pieter fell silent, staring at him, and the admiral went on implacably. "I understand the purpose of this communication is to arrange your surrender. Very well. All ships in space will land immediately at Novaya Petrograd Spaceport. Any armed vessel incapable of atmospheric flight will lower its shields and await boarding by one of my prize crews. The same applies to what's left of Skywatch. Is that clear?"

"Yes." It took all of Pieter's strength to get out the strangled word, and Waldeck made no effort to hide his own savage satisfaction.

"As for your so-called 'Provisional Government,' " he sneered, "you will surrender yourselves to me as soon as my ships planet. There will be no exceptions. Anyone who resists will be shot. Is *that* clear?"

"Yes," Pieter managed once more.

"It had better be. I will see you aboard my flagship in three hours." Waldeck cut communications curtly, and Pieter stared at the blank screen for long seconds as he tasted the ashes of defeat.

"Look at that!" Fedor Kazin gasped as the chopper swooped past the spaceport after a ten-hour flight. The others turned and looked—and looked again. Novaya Petrograd Spaceport had never seen such a concentration of shipping. Fedor's index finger moved slowly from ship to ship as he counted.

". . . twenty-three . . . twenty-four . . . twenty-five . . . Twenty-five! And those big ones—are they battle-cruisers, Georgi?"

"Yes." Georgi Zelinsky grunted. "My God, it's all over! There wouldn't be any grounded battle-cruisers if it weren't. They're about the biggest warship that can enter atmosphere at all, and they have to take it mighty easy when they do. No commander lands them any place he might have to get out of in a hurry."

"Look!" Fedor said excitedly. "All the hatches are open—see? And over there! Look at all the *people!*"

"Yeah," Vlad said, squinting into his teleview. "All in

uniform, too. Looks like they must've stripped the crews off the ships."

"They wouldn't do that," Georgi disagreed. "Not all of them. There has to be a power room watch on board."

"Yeah? Well *look* at 'em! They didn't leave many on board."

"You're right there." Georgi tapped his teeth, his mind going back over the decades to his own five-year hitch in the Navy. "Looks like they've mustered all hands for some reason. And over there—what's that?"

"That" was a long snake of civilians winding its way out from the city. Vlad swooped low over their heads. There were thousands of them.

"What do you think is going on?" he asked.

"Damned if I know," Fedor said slowly, "but I think better we should land and find out, no?"

"I think yes," Vlad agreed.

The helicopter landed quickly, and as the three farmers hurried over to the edge of the crowd something nibbled at Fedor's awareness. They were already merging into the front ranks of the long snake when he realized what it was.

"Look—no guns!" he whispered.

"Of course not," Georgi said after a minute. "They must've declared martial law while we were in the air. Martial law means no civilian guns."

"Well what about *us?*" Vlad whispered, tapping the heavy magnum automatic at his hip. It was a clumsy weapon, but Vlad was old-fashioned; he preferred a big noisy gun that relied on mass and relatively low velocities.

"I recommend," Georgi said, unbuttoning his coat and shoving his laser pistol inside, "that we get them out of sight—fast!"

Fedor tucked his own pistol (a three-millimeter Ruger needler with a ninety-round magazine) under his coat, then turned to the nearest townsman.

"What's happening, *tovarich?*" he asked softly.

"You don't know?" the townie looked at him with shock-hazed eyes.

"I just landed, *tovarich*. Came all the way from Novaya Siberia to talk to this Provisional Government."

"*Shhhhh*! Want to get yourself arrested, you fool?!"

"Arrested? For *talking* to someone?" Fedor blinked in astonishment.

"The whole bunch of 'em are under arrest," the city man said heavily. "We're occupied."

"Well, what're you all doing out here, then?"

"Orders," the townie shrugged. "I don't know. They landed two hours ago and went on the city data channels. Somebody named Waldeck—he says he's the new military governor. He ordered the head of every household in the city to be out here by seventeen hundred . . . he didn't say why."

"*Every* head of household?" Fedor blinked again at the thought.

"Right. So here we are."

Fedor looked up as the long column shuffled to a halt and began to spread. Anxious-faced Marines in undress uniform, armed with autorifles and laser carbines, dressed the crowd, but something was wrong here. Those men looked worried, almost frightened—but they'd *won!*

"*Hsst!* Look at those shoulder flashes!" It was Georgi, whispering right in his ear. "Not a Fringer among 'em!"

There was a great sigh from the crowd, almost a groan, and he looked to one side. More Marines were herding a group of fifty or sixty men and women into an open space between two of the battle-cruisers. The newcomers were manacled, and when he looked more closely he recognized Magda Petrovna and Semyon Jakov among them.

"The Provisional Government!" someone whispered. "All of them—and the defense force officers!"

Fedor shook his head, trying to understand, and wiggled his way into the very front rank, staring over at the prisoners. He knew Magda well—he'd danced at her parents' wedding, too many years ago—and it angered him to see her chained like an animal. All right, so she'd broken the law! But she'd been provoked. It might have been wrong of her, but she'd only been doing what she believed she must!

There was another stir as the Marines drew back from the prisoners and formed a line between them and the crowd. They faced the prisoners vigilantly while the Navy personnel formed two huge blocks, separated by about ten meters, and a party of officers strode briskly down the open lane.

Fedor was no military man, but even he could figure out the tall man with all the sleeve braid was an admiral. But he wondered who the other officer—the black one arguing with the admiral—was? Whoever it was, they were going at it hammer and tongs. Finally the admiral gave a curt headshake and said something loud and angry, but Fedor was too far away to hear. . . .

"Admiral, you can't do this!" Captain Rupert M'tana said yet again. "It's illegal! It violates all their civil rights!"

"Captain," Waldeck said savagely, "I will remind you—for the last time—that this planet is under martial law. And no one—I repeat, *no one*—rebels against the government, kills Navy personnel and gets away with it on my watch! Especially not ignorant, backworld Fringe scum!"

"For God's sake, Admiral!" M'tana said. "You—"

"*Silence!*" Waldeck whirled on the dark-skinned officer, and his eyes snapped fire. "You will go to your quarters and place yourself under close arrest, Captain M'tana! I'll deal with you later!"

"I'm your flag captain," M'tana began angrily, "and it's my duty to—"

"Major," Waldeck turned coldly to a Marine officer. "You will escort the captain to his quarters!"

"Yes, sir!" The major had a thick DuPont accent, and his eyes were very bright. He saluted sharply, then jerked his head at M'tana as the admiral turned on his heel. M'tana could almost taste the Navy crews' confusion, but the Marine major tapped the butt of his laser meaningfully, and the flag captain knew it was hopeless. Sagging with defeat, he allowed the major to lead him away.

Waldeck mounted an improvised platform and turned to face the crowd of murmuring civilians. He gripped a microphone, his eyes bitter as he stared at them. The only way to avoid more bloodshed was to rub these stupid proles' noses in what happened when they rebelled. He looked at his own massed crewmen. Yes, and show *them*, too. Let them see what awaited those who defied them. He raised the mike.

"People of Novaya Rodina!" Fedor's head snapped around as the massively amplified voice roared. "You have rebelled against Federation law. You have harbored and abetted mutinous members of the armed services. Such actions are treasonous."

Fedor flinched from the harshness of the admiral's voice. Treasonous? Well, maybe technically—but a man could stand only so much. . . .

"By the authority of the Legislative Assembly, all civil law on this planet is hereby suspended. Martial law is declared. All public gatherings are banned until further notice. I now announce a curfew, to take effect at 1900 hours. Violators will be shot."

Fedor blanched. *Shot!* For walking the street?

"Before you stand the leaders of your rebellion against legitimate authority," Waldeck went on coldly. "As military governor of this planet, it is my responsibility to deal with these ringleaders." He paused and glanced contemptuously at the prisoners. "The Federation is just," he said. "It extends its protection and support to those who obey our laws and justly deserved punishment to those who defy them.

"Now, therefore, as military governor of Novaya Rodina, I, Admiral Jason Waldeck, Terran Federation Navy, do hereby sentence these traitors to death!" A great silence gripped the crowd. "Sentence—" Waldeck finished harshly "—to be carried out immediately!"

Fedor couldn't believe his ears. This couldn't happen! Not in the Federation! It was a nightmare! It was . . . it was an *atrocity!*

He stared at the scene before him, unable to comprehend, as two Marine privates took Pieter Tsuchevsky by the arms. He moved slowly, as if in shock, but held his head high. As he and his guards moved away from the group, two more privates singled out Tatiana Illyushina. The slender young woman drooped in their hands as she realized she would be next, yet she fought for control and tried to stand erect.

Paralysis gripped Fedor. He was suspended in disbelief, unable to think, barely able to breathe. He watched numbly as Tsuchevsky was turned to face the crowd. Six Marines with autorifles marched smartly out and took position before him, weapons at port arms.

"Firing squad!" a Marine officer shouted. "Present arms!"

Weapons clattered.

"Take aim!"

Butt plates pressed uniformed shoulders. Fedor felt something boiling in him against the ice, but still he could not move.

"Ready!"

The pressure building in his throat strangled him.

"Fire!"

Six shots rang out on semi-automatic.

It all happened in slow motion. Fedor saw Tsuchevsky's shirt ripple, saw great, red blotches blossom hideously as the slugs tore through his body, and Pieter Petrovich Tsuchevsky, Chief of the Duma, President of the Provisional Government of Novaya Rodina, jerked at the impact, then toppled like a falling tree.

And as he hit the ground, the pressure in Fedor Kazin burst. His sustaining faith in the Federation died in an agony of disillusionment, and his hand flashed into his coat.

"*Noooooo!*" he screamed, and the heavy needler came free.

For one instant he faced them all alone, one man with a pistol in his hand and rage in his heart. Then the pistol rose. It lined on the burly admiral as he turned angrily towards the single voice raised in protest.

He never completed his turn. The needler screamed, and Admiral Jason Waldeck's uniform smoked under its hyper-velocity darts. He pitched to the ground seconds behind Tsuchevsky, and the crowd went mad.

Fedor never knew who struck the first Marine, but the guards never had a chance as the screaming, kicking mob went over them. Here and there an autorifle spoke, a laser carbine snarled. The Marines didn't die easily, and they didn't die alone—but they died.

Fedor wasn't watching. He was racing across the open space, needler in hand, dashing for the guards who were already training their weapons on the helpless prisoners. He slid to a halt, bracing the needler with both hands as a laser bolt whipped past him, thermal bloom scorching his hair. A guard saw him and turned, his jaw dropping, but too late. A stream of needles spat from the weapon, and the guards went down like autumn wheat before Fedor's reaper.

Screams and shouts were everywhere. Weapons fired. Men and women beat Marines to death with fists and feet. Navy personnel scattered—only senior ratings and officers were armed, and they were outnumbered by hundreds to one. They fought desperately to bring their weapons into play, but they hadn't known what Waldeck intended, and they were just as shocked as the civilians. Their minds needed time to clear and adjust, and there was no time.

Fedor ran to the manacled prisoners.

"Are you all right?" he bellowed as Magda Petrovna picked herself up off the ground. She stared at him for a moment with burning eyes, then nodded sharply and snatched up a dead Marine's laser with her chained hands. Her voice rang out over the tumult.

"*The ships!*" she screamed. "*Take the ships!*"

Some of the crowd heard. They seized the weapons of their fallen enemies and fell in behind her, and their discordant yells coalesced into a single phrase, thundering above the bedlam.

"*The ships!*" they roared, and foamed forward in an unstoppable human wave behind a mutinous ex-captain and a farmer who had wanted only justice.

Irony of Power

Oskar Dieter blinked wearily and fingered the advance. The strains of a New Zurich waltz filled his office, but the soft music was at grim variance with the data on his screen, and he sighed and leaned back, pinching his nose and trying to shake himself back to a semblance of freshness.

It was hard. Catastrophe had followed disaster with monotonous regularity for months, and in his nightmares endless trains of courier drones whizzed towards Sol, packed with tidings of fresh calamity.

What was happening in the Fringe was bad enough, but affairs on Old Terra were little better. The Assembly had been stunned by the Taliaferro suicide, but not Dieter. His fellow Gallowayans might put it down to grief over the Jamieson Archipelago—which *was* a tragedy of staggering proportions—but Dieter knew better. Understanding, the terrible realization that the "game" had become real, had driven Simon's hand. Dieter almost pitied him . . . but only almost, and his face hardened as he wondered yet again how many others would die before the madness ended.

Yet Taliaferro's death only compounded the Federation's plight. His had been the dominating presence behind the Corporate World bloc for over thirty years, and now that superbly engineered machine was flailing itself to destruction . . . and threatening to take the Federation with it. The desperate survivors were haunted by guilt they could not admit even to themselves and terrified of its consequences. The succession battle was the most vicious Dieter had ever seen, yet whoever finally won would inherit only a corpse.

It wouldn't be very much longer before the ground swell of public opinion rolled over the politicos. Already the first combers were crashing through the Chamber of Worlds; a few more disasters, and it would become impossible for them to cling to power, and—

His communicator chimed, and he reached automatically for the button, eyes narrowing as he recognized the neatly groomed face of Oliver Fuchs, President Zhi's executive secretary.

"Good morning, Mister Dieter," Fuchs said politely. "Would it be convenient for you to meet with the President in his office this evening? At 1800 perhaps?"

"Why, of course, Mister Fuchs," Dieter replied slowly, and his thoughts raced. "Ah, might I ask what the President desires?"

"I'm sorry, sir, but he wishes to explain that to you himself," Fuchs said with a pleasantly diffident smile.

"I see," Dieter said even more slowly. "Very well, Mister Fuchs. I'll look forward to asking him in person."

"Thank you, sir. I'll tell him to expect you," Fuchs said, and the screen blanked.

Dieter sat and stared at it for a long, long time, and his mind was busy.

Fuchs was waiting in the Anderson House foyer when Dieter arrived at the presidential residence at 17:45. He whisked the visitor into an elevator with the skill of a veteran *maitre d'* and filled the short ascent with utterly inconsequential small talk, but Dieter noted a strange intensity in the secretary's eyes. Curiosity, or evaluation, perhaps. Whatever it was, it only added to the tension hovering within him.

The elevator deposited them outside Zhi's office, and Fuchs opened the old-fashioned manual doors and stood aside, waving him through, then closed them quietly behind him.

The office was a large room—huge, by Innerworld standards—furnished with all the sumptuous luxury due the Federation's head of state. To be sure, the power of the man who occupied it had waned over the decades, but the trappings of authority remained. And they weren't entirely a facade, Dieter reminded himself. Prime ministers came and went, but the president provided the state's stability, and he still represented the popular choice of the majority of the Federation's myriad citizens.

But Dieter had been here before, and his attention was not on the rich carpets and indirect lighting. It was drawn inevitably to the cluster of people sitting around the President's desk.

Zhi himself was a small man, shorter even than Dieter, though more sturdily built. He rose as Dieter approached, and his handclasp was firm, but his face bore the stigmata of strain.

"Mister Dieter," he said. "Thank you for coming."

"Mister President," Dieter returned noncommittally, glancing at the others, and Zhi smiled wryly.

"I believe you know most of these people, Mister Dieter," he murmured, and Dieter nodded, then bowed slightly to the group, his mind whirring with speculation.

Sky Marshal Lech Witcinski, commander-in-chief of the Terran military, responded with a curt nod, half-raising his burly body from his chair. His uniform was immaculate, and his blunt, hard features showed surprisingly little sign of the tremendous strain focused upon him.

Not so the man seated beside him. David Haley had aged appreciably in the past weeks, but his smile of welcome was far warmer than it once had been.

Dieter returned it in kind, then raised an eyebrow at the sharp-eyed man at the Speaker's left. Kevin Sanders, he thought musingly. Admiral Kevin Sanders, retired, one-time head of the Office of Naval Intelligence. Now wasn't *he* an interesting addition to this gathering? Even seated, Sanders managed to exude a sense of mingled composure and agility, like a lean, gray tomcat, and his amused eyes gleamed as if he could read Dieter's mind. And perhaps he could. Far more esoteric powers had been ascribed to him during his career.

The single person Dieter didn't know wore the space-black and silver of a vice admiral, and he felt a stir of admiration as he looked at her. Long, platinum hair rippled over her shoulders, and her eyes were a deep, almost indigo blue. She was certainly the most attractive flag officer he'd ever seen, he thought wryly, and held out his hand to her.

"Good evening, Admiral—?"

"Krupskaya, Mister Dieter," she said in a soft, clear voice. "Susan Krupskaya."

"Enchanted," he murmured, raising her hand briefly to his lips, and her own lips quivered in an amused smile.

"Well, then," Zhi said briskly, reclaiming Dieter's attention and waving him to a chair, "to business."

"Of course, Mister President. My time is yours," Dieter said, seating himself, and Zhi's sardonic smile surprised him.

"In more ways than you may suspect, Mister Dieter," he said softly, and Dieter's eyebrows crooked politely.

"I beg your pardon?" he said, but Zhi didn't respond directly. Instead he nodded to David Haley.

"Mister Dieter—Oskar—" the Speaker said, "I'm afraid we have you at a bit of a disadvantage. You see, the Minh Government has resigned."

Dieter managed to hide his surprise—barely. The government had fallen? Why hadn't he already heard? And how in the Galaxy had they kept the press from finding out?

"It won't be announced at once," Haley continued, "because, under the circumstances, it seems vital to follow the news with the immediate announcement of the formation of a new govenment." Dieter nodded. The last thing they needed was a prolonged ministerial crisis.

"Which brings us to you, Mister Dieter." President Zhi took over once more. "You see, when I asked Prime Minister Minh and Speaker Haley to recommend a successor to form a new government, they both suggested the same man: you."

This time Dieter's surprise was too great. His jaw dropped, and he stared at Zhi in disbelief. *Him?* He was a pariah, repudiated by his own long-time allies! They couldn't be serious!

"Mister President," he said finally. "I-I don't know what to say. I'm honored, but—"

"Indulge me a moment, Mister Dieter," Zhi said quietly. "Officially, I am not supposed to have opinions in these matters, but, to speak frankly, there are no other choices. You, more than most, are aware that the Minh Government has been totally discredited. Indeed, the situation is worse even than you know, but the critical point—politically speaking—is that anyone else is unacceptable. To put it bluntly, Simon Taliaferro's associates are all tainted by their support of his policies, yet they remain a very potent force in the Chamber of Worlds. If we are to find an alternative to one of them, it must be someone who can gather support from both the Assembly moderates *and* the public. Someone like you."

"But, Mister President! I—"

"Oskar," Haley cut back in, "think a moment. You're a Corporate Worlder, yet you openly opposed Taliaferro's excesses. The Corporate World moderates will follow your lead, and so will the Heart World liberals. That gives you a power base, and the Taliaferro crowd can't very well oppose you without refocusing attention on their own mistakes."

"And, Mister Dieter," Witcinski put in, "you enjoy the support of the military." Dieter looked at him in astonishment, and the sky marshal shrugged. "I know. That's not supposed to be a factor, but we all know it will be. Your position on the Military Oversight Committee gives you a background knowledge which may be invaluable. And, if I may speak completely candidly, the Fleet views you as a moderate. As prime minister, you would be tremendously reassuring to the bulk of the officer corps."

"*But*," Zhi said warningly, "that same reputation is a two-edged sword. You *are* a moderate, and we need moderates, but we have a war on our hands. If you accept this office, you'll have to demonstrate that you're a war leader, as well."

"And how would I be expected to do that?" Dieter asked, eyes narrowing.

"By forming an all-parties cabinet," Haley said quietly, and Dieter nodded slowly.

Of course. Minh's government was associated solely with the extreme Corporate World interests, which was why it had to go. But its replacement must command broad support, and the only way to do that would be to combine all elements. Part of him quailed at the thought of exerting mastery over such a disparate gathering of interests, but he understood. And he was beginning to see why Zhi had turned to him.

"Mister President," he said finally, "why did the government resign at this particular moment? May I assume Admiral Sanders' presence has some bearing on that point?"

"You may," Zhi said heavily. He tugged at an earlobe and frowned. "I have asked Admiral Sanders to return from retirement and reassume direction of the Office of Naval Intelligence."

Dieter nodded mentally; he'd suspected as much. Whatever the immediate cause of the secession, the speed with which the Fringe had closed ranks behind the Kontravians spoke volumes for the degree of clandestine communication which must have been established long since among the Outworld governments. Yet no whisper of any of it had reached the Assembly, which pointed to a massive intelligence failure.

"I see." He regarded Sanders thoughtfully. "In that case, with your permission, Mister President, I'd like to ask Admiral Sanders a few questions before I give you my decision."

"I assumed you would. That's why I arranged to have the military represented," Zhi said dryly, waving a hand to proceed.

"Thank you. Admiral, I suspect the situation is even worse than most of my colleagues realize. Am I correct?"

"That depends, Mister Dieter," Sanders said carefully, "on just how bad they think it is. Off the cuff, however, I would have to say yes."

"Enlighten me, if you please."

"All right." Sanders eyed him measuringly. "Sky Marshal Witcinski could probably give you better figures on precise Fleet losses, but ONI estimates that in addition to TF Seventeen, at least fifteen percent of Battle Fleet has gone over to the rebels. Additional units in Innerworld space have mutinied and attempted to join them, but we've been able to stop most of them. The cost in loyal units—" he met Dieter's eyes levelly, and Dieter felt an inner chill "—has been high.

"At the same time," he went on even more dispassionately, "we don't really know what's happened to Frontier Fleet. No drones are getting through to us from any of our bases in the Fringe, which, since the rebels control the intervening warp points and Fleet relays, may or may not mean they've changed sides. On a worst-case basis, we're estimating the loss of at least ninety percent of Frontier Fleet."

Dieter was staggered, though he tried to hide it.

"Fortunately," Sanders continued, "our large Innerworld bases have remained loyal and the rebels have to set up their command structure from scratch, which gives us time to activate the Reserve while they get themselves organized. On the whole, and given the greater mass of Battle Fleet's capital units, the tonnage balance probably favors the rebels by as much as thirty percent, but the ratio of firepower is a bit in our favor when Fortress Command is allowed for."

"I see. And Zephrain RDS?"

"Unknown, Mister Dieter," Sanders admitted. "The only hopeful news is that one of our Battle Fleet battlegroups *may* have gotten through to it."

"May?" Dieter asked sharply.

"May. Vice Admiral Trevayne's BG Thirty-Two was cut off at Osterman's Star when the mutinies began, and we've received an official Orion complaint of a TFN border violation at Sulzan, about four transits from there. In all probability, that was Trevayne, and if it was, and *if* he managed to avoid internment, and *if* the Orion district governor at Rehfrak was willing to let a force that powerful pass through his bailiwick, then he *may* have reached Zephrain. Unfortunately, the Orions have since closed their borders completely. Any sort of confirmation from them will be a long time coming."

Sanders shrugged, and Dieter nodded again. He'd met Ian Trevayne exactly once, when he appeared before the Oversight Committee, but the incisive man he remembered just might have taken a chance on violating Orion space . . . and he would have known exactly how important Zephrain was.

"But that's only the present situation," Witcinski said, breaking the brief silence. "It doesn't address the future."

"No," Sanders agreed, "and that's really Susan's area."

He nodded to Krupskaya, and her dark blue eyes met Dieter's as she took her cue.

"As you know," she said, "the Innerworlds have a tremendous industrial advantage over the Fringe, but more than seventy percent of all our warships came from Galloway's World." Dieter felt his nerves tighten. He'd known this was coming, but that made it no more palatable.

"The Jamieson Archipelago attack may have been a mistake, politically speaking," Krupskaya continued, "since its 'barbarism' has generated such widespread shock and repugnance among the Innerworlds, but militarily it was brilliant. They knocked out more than ninety percent of the civilian yards as well as the Yard and all Reserve units mothballed there. We estimate that it would take two or three years for the rebels to set up any substantial yard capacity of their own, but *we* need time to rebuild Galloway's World. We can put the facilities there back into service faster than we could build new yards and their infrastructure on other planets, but it will be at least eighteen months—more probably two years—before we can even begin laying down new ships there.

"Which means, Mister Dieter, that—assuming the rebels *have* seized most of our bases in the Fringe—our current building capacity gives us no more than a twenty percent advantage over them. We believe we can expand existing yards faster than they can build new ones, but for the foreseeable future we are going to have to be very, very careful about risking losses, particularly, in light of their long construction times, among our heavy units."

"I see," Dieter said again, and another silence fell. God, it was even worse than he'd feared.

"But you asked why the government resigned," Zhi said finally. "Beyond the obvious erosion of its majority—of which, I am sure, you are aware—and general military situation, we have suffered yet another reverse."

Dieter wondered if he really wanted to hear any more bad news, but he nodded for Zhi to continue. Yet it was Witcinski who took over again.

"This morning, we received a message from Admiral Pritzcowitski at Cimmaron," he said. "He and Admiral Waldeck had initiated local operations to suppress the rebellion in the immediate vicinity. Unfortunately, their first effort, directed against Novaya Rodina with light units, was badly defeated by some sort of jury-rigged defensive force. Admiral Waldeck proceeded at once with his entire task force to retrieve the situation. As of the time Admiral Pritzcowitzki's message was dispatched, Admiral Waldeck's next scheduled report was seventy-two hours overdue."

Dieter closed his eyes. It got worse and worse. No wonder Minh had resigned! When the Assembly learned all that he'd just learned, Minh would be lucky to escape impeachment.

"So that's the situation, Oskar," Haley said quietly. "We've had our differences, but I hope you know how much I've admired you in the past few months—and that I hate to ask this of you. But we need you."

Dieter didn't even open his eyes, and behind his lids he saw every agonizing step which had led him and the Federation to this pass. The military position was grimmer than even he had feared, and he knew how the Assembly would react when they discovered the truth. The existing fury over the "sneak attack" and "massacre" at Galloway's World would mix with panic. The war fervor which already gripped the Innerworlds would intensify rather than ease as they drew together in the face of danger—and so would the extremity of the Federation's war aims.

If he accepted Zhi's request and formed a government, it would be a war government. It could be nothing else, and he would have to prove his own determination to achieve victory or go the way Minh had already gone. It would be the final, bitter irony of the political odyssey he'd begun when he broke with Simon. He, who had thrown away his career in an effort to preserve the peace, would be elevated to the highest office of the Assembly and charged with fighting the very war he'd tried to prevent!

"I realize we are asking you to make bricks with a very limited supply of straw, Mister Dieter," Zhi said, even more quietly than Haley, "but Speaker Haley is right. We *need* you. The Federation needs you—as the one man who may be able to form a stable government and as the one prime minister who may be able to control the extremism already rampant in the Assembly."

Dieter winced, for that was the argument he'd most feared to face. Zhi's violation of the president's traditional neutrality in such matters only underscored the point; if any of Taliaferro's old associates took the premiership, any chance for moderation would vanish . . . and he still had not paid his debt to Fionna.

He drew a deep breath. His wildest dreams had never included becoming prime minister—and certainly never like this! And yet, ironic as it was, he had no choice. He opened his eyes and looked at President Zhi.

"Very well, Mister President," he sighed. "I'll try."

DECLARATION

"Novaya Rodina, eh?" Ladislaus Skjorning watched the blue and white planet as the crew of the TFNS *Howard Anderson* brought their ship into orbit. "I take it you're finding this a strange spot for a convention of traitors, Admiral Ashigara?"

His eyes touched briefly upon the empty right cuff of the woman standing beside him. Analiese Ashigara was every bit as taciturn and unyielding as her severe exterior and precise Standard English suggested, but he felt a strange kinship for the hawk-faced woman with the almond eyes and white-streaked hair who'd given a hand for her beliefs.

"I would have expected the convention to convene on Beaufort," she said calmly. "Beaufort is, after all, the home of the rebellion." It was like her, Ladislaus thought wryly, that she never resorted to euphemisms.

"Aye, I can see why you might be thinking that, but Beaufort is too far from the frontiers. We've no command structure at all the now, and until we've had the creating of one, we're to need the shortest courier drone routes we can be finding. Novaya Rodina's well located for that."

"Yes, I can see that. But I think perhaps there is more to it than that, Mister Skjorning."

" Aye, there is. As you've said, Beaufort's to be a logical place—if it were a Kontravian rebellion we're after having. But we're after making this a Fringe-wide movement, so holding our convention somewhere else should be helping along a sense of unity, you see. I've the thinking it's Beaufort's to be the capitol of whatever it is we're to have the building of, but it's not the place to be declaring what we are."

"That seems sensible," Ashigara said, nodding slowly.

"Aye. But there's to be another reason. Have you had the hearing of the term 'bloody shirt,' Admiral Ashigara?"

" 'Bloody Shirt'? No, Mister Skjorning, I cannot say that I have."

"It's to be an old Terran political term, Admiral, and what it's to mean is appealing to emotions on the basis of lost lives and hatred." Ladislaus' face was grim. "It's not a tactic I'm proud to be using, but it works; and Novaya Rodina's after being the best place to be doing it."

Analiese Ashigara shook her head slowly. "I am more happy than ever to be a simple Fleet commander, Mister Skjorning. My mind does not work the way this business of creating a government appears to require."

"Don't be feeling any loss over it," Ladislaus said very quietly. "It's not to be something I ever thought to have the doing of, either."

He fell silent, watching the planet a moment longer, then left the bridge, and Admiral Ashigara turned her attention to the final approach maneuvers of her undermanned task force. No, she thought. She did not envy Ladislaus Skjorning at all.

The horde of delegates crowded the huge auditorium, their rumbling voices filling it like a solid presence, and the surviving Duma stood behind Ladislaus on the stage, surveying their visitors with slightly dazed eyes.

Magda Petrovna stood at his elbow, her mobile face quite still. Only Ladislaus knew she intended to resign from the Duma to accept a commission in whatever they were going to call their navy, and only Magda sensed how much he envied her freedom to do just that. But it wasn't freedom for her; it was flight.

She knew her own strengths: a flair for organization, level-headedness, moral courage, and compassion. But she also knew her weaknesses: blunt-spokenness, a tendency towards autocracy with those unable to keep up with her thoughts, and a well-developed capacity for hatred, and she felt that hate within her now, though few of her friends saw it or recognized it as the inevitable by-product of her compassion.

She'd been able to accept her own sentence of death, but not the brutality of Pieter's murder. Not the cruelty which had nearly snapped Tatiana Illyushina's sanity. That had been too much, yet as long as she'd believed that only Waldeck's madness was responsible, she'd maintained a degree of detachment.

But then the provisional government had found the special instructions from the Assembly in his safe.

Waldeck need not have acted on them, but giving men like him such an option was like giving a vicious child a charged laser, and she would never forget that the Assembly had done so. She would never be able to flush the hatred from her mind if ever she must deal with that government. Besides—she felt herself smile affectionately—there was a better choice to head the Duma now. Well, two, perhaps, but Fedor would kill himself first! No, only one person had emerged from the day of the riots as Pieter's true successor, and that person was Tatiana Illyushina.

Magda glanced at the slim young woman. Daughter of one of Novaya Rodina's very few wealthy families, Tatiana had never faced the hard side of life before the rebellion. Then the earthquake shocks had come hard and fast, but Tatiana, to her own unending surprise, had met them all. Her oval face was still as beautiful, she looked as much like a teen-aged child as ever, but there was flint behind those blue eyes now. Flint and something else, something almost like Magda's own compassion, but not quite.

But now, as acting Duma President, Magda had been granted a unique moment in history, and she stepped up to the lectern at Ladislaus' tiny nod. She drew a deep breath, and her gavel cracked on the wooden rest under the microphone. The sound echoed through the auditorium.

"The first session of this convention of the provisional governments of the Fringe will come to order," she said.

"Well, Ladislaus, what do you think?" Magda refilled their vodka glasses and hid a smile as he picked his up cautiously. "Will it work?"

"Aye, I'm thinking it will." Ladislaus sipped his second

glass far more slowly as Magda threw back her own in approved Novaya Rodinan fashion. "It's not as if any of us have the thinking we can go back again." He looked meaningfully around the small gathering of the Convention's crucial leaders.

"But it doesn't necessarily follow we can act together," Tatiana said. "Agreeing to hate the Corporate Worlds, yes." She smiled tightly. "But we're all so different! What else do we have in common?"

"Don't be underestimating the strength of hate, Ms Illyushina." Ladislaus' answering smile was bleak. "But that's not all we're to be having. I'm thinking we're to have a better understanding of what the Federation is supposed to be than the Rump has. We're agreed in that."

"True." Magda's cold voice raised eyebrows, but she leashed her rage and leaned back. Then she laughed. "Has it occurred to anyone else that *we're* not the radicals? We're the conservatives—*they're* the ones who've played fast and loose with the Constitution for over a century!"

"Aye, so Fionna had the saying, often enough," Ladislaus nodded. "And we've no hope of building something really new—not in the time we're to have. So it's something old we must be building on."

"So *that's* why you brought this along," Li Kai-lun mused, tapping the sheet of facsimile on the table and nodding slowly. His reaction pleased Ladislaus. Hangchow's diminutive chief convention delegate was not only her planetary president but a retired admiral, as well. His support—political and military—would be literally priceless in the weeks ahead.

"Aye." Ladislaus ran a fingertip over the ancient lettering. "It's a federal system we're needing, Kai-lun. Centralization was the Corporate Worlds real error. It's to give the government the most power, but it's to concentrate too much authority in one place—and even with relays, slow communications are to make it clumsy in responding to crises . . . or people."

"Agreed," Li said, then smiled. "And at least *this* constitution's got a good track record. If I remember my history, the United States did quite well for itself before the Great Eastern War."

* * *

" . . . and if fight we must, let it be under a common standard! I move to appoint a committee to select a suitable device for our battle flags."

The stocky delegate from Lancelot swirled the brilliant cloak of his hereditary rank and sat, and Magda sighed. She found the barons and earls of Durandel rather wearing, but he might have a point—even if he was inclined towards purple prose.

"Very well. It has been moved that we appoint a committee to design a flag for our new star nation," she said. "Is there a second?"

"I second the motion, Ms Chairman." Magda blinked as Li Kai-lun spoke up. Now why was *he* supporting a motion which could only waste precious time and energy? She shrugged mentally. Undoubtedly he had a reason.

"Very well. It has been moved and seconded that we appoint a committee to design a flag. All those in favor?" A rumble of "Ayes" answered. "Opposed?" There was not a sound. "The motion is carried. Mister Li, would you be so kind as to take charge of the matter?"

"Of course, Ms Chairman."

"Good. Now, to return to our agenda. . . ."

"But why, Ladislaus?" Tatiana demanded. "We have so many other things to do, why waste time designing a *flag*, of all things?"

"Well," Ladislaus rumbled, "you might be noticing who Kai-lun had the recruiting of for his committee."

"What? Who?" Tatiana asked, but Magda laughed suddenly.

"*Now* I understand! Very neat, Lad! And how did you put Baron de Bertholet up to it?"

"Jean de Bertholet isn't after being the worst sort, Magda. It's on our side he is, and he understands entirely."

"Well *I* don't," Tatiana said.

"You would if you'd seen the membership of that committee," Magda chuckled. "Between them, Lad and Kai-lun have shunted most of the 'noblemen' in the Convention off to a harmless flag-designing mission."

"Aye," Ladislaus nodded. "Not that I really think they're after creating a new hereditary aristocracy for us all, but it's not to be hurting a thing to be certain of it when the constitution's debated, now is it?"

"Ladislaus," Tatiana said sternly, "you're an underhanded, devious man."

"Aye," Ladislaus agreed calmly. "That I am."

"Ladislaus," Magda said, "I'd like you to meet Rupert M'tana."

Ladislaus looked up from his paperwork and frowned at the dark-skinned officer. M'tana returned an equally measuring look, and Ladislaus propped one elbow on a chair arm.

"Captain M'tana," he rumbled thoughtfully, "you're to be the senior prisoner, I'm thinking?"

"Yes, sir. I was Admiral Waldeck's flag captain."

"I see." Ladislaus' lips twisted in distaste despite himself.

"Just a moment, Lad," Magda said quietly. "I think, perhaps, you don't entirely understand. At the time of Pieter's execution, Waldeck had placed Captain M'tana under close arrest."

"Aye?" Ladislaus' blue eyes returned to M'tana's face, even more thoughtful now. "And why might that have been, Captain?"

"I . . . disagreed with his decision, Mister Skjorning."

"I see," Ladislaus said in an entirely different tone. He waved at two chairs and M'tana and Magda sank into them. "I've memory enough of my time in the Fleet to be understanding how far you must have pushed him, Captain. But, if I may have the asking, what's to be bringing you here?"

"The captain has a suggestion, Lad—a good one, I think," Magda said. "He approached me with it because we're both Navy or ex-Navy and we've come to know one another pretty well."

"Ah?" Ladislaus cocked a bushy eyebrow. "And just what is it you and the captain are after cooking up here, Magda?"

"It's like this, Lad. Like Beaufort, we had a number of . . . friends in various places in the Innerworlds. We spent years cultivating that network, but now that actual fighting's begun, we're cut off from it."

"Aye," Ladislaus nodded. "We're to have the same problem at Beaufort."

"Right. Well, Captain M'tana may have come up with a way to put part of our network back on line."

"Have you, now?" Ladislaus bent a hard look on M'tana. The captain shifted slightly in his chair but met it unflinchingly.

"Yes, sir. Understand something, Mister Skjorning. I'm an Innerworlder—a Heart Worlder—but when my people settled Xhosa, they didn't exactly do so completely voluntarily. I think we knew something about oppression, then, but we've forgotten since. We should have remembered, and that means we have a responsibility here. I don't want to see the Federation torn apart; in that respect, at least, you and I will never agree. But what I want and what's going to happen are two different things. There's no way to paper over the cracks this time—too much blood's already been shed.

"So as I see it, I can either join my fellow prisoners in refusing to give you any aid while we wait hopefully for repatriation and—with luck—another chance to contribute to the killing, or I can help you people. Not because I love your rebellion—I don't—but because the sooner the Federation realizes it can't win even if it defeats you militarily, the better."

"I see." Ladislaus grinned slowly. "Captain, I've the thinking I'm to like you—and I'm betting that's not to matter a solitary damn to you. But you've the right. It has gone too far for healing. So how is it you're to be helping?"

"What Captain M'tana suggested to me," Magda said, "ties in with our plans to allow correspondence between prisoners and their families. We'll give him the codes and address of our contact on Xhosa and his 'letters home' will reopen our best conduit."

Ladislaus studied M'tana's face, seeking some sign of treachery, any intent to betray. He saw exactly nothing.

"You're to have the knowing, Captain," he said quietly, "of the penalty if the Federation is ever to be finding out about this?"

"I do," M'tana said flatly. "But I know—now—what the Assembly's done to you people, and my oath is to the Federation, not just its government. If I can help shorten the war and reduce the killing, I have to do it. Besides—" he looked uncomfortable "—I don't enjoy killing Terrans, Mister Skjorning, not even ones who are technically traitors."

"I see," Ladislaus said yet again. Then he added slowly. "Let's have the discussing of the details, then, Captain. . . ."

"Well, Chang?" Commodore Li Han tipped back her chair in *Longbow's* briefing room as she regarded her chief of staff. Commander Robert Tomanaga, her new battlegroup operations officer, sat beside Tsing, and the pair of them were flanked by Lieutenant Commander Esther Kane and Lieutenant David Reznick, Han's staff astrogator and electronics officer.

"Commander Tomanaga and I have gone over the Fleet ops plan, sir," Tsing replied. "We'll know better after we run it on the tac simulator, but for now, it looks solid."

"You agree, Commander?" Han turned her eyes to Tomanaga.

"Yes, sir. Oh, we could use more weight of metal, but quality counts more than quantity." He grinned, and Han frowned mentally, bothered by his brashness and wondering if her worry was justified. Tomanaga was certainly qualified on paper; but *all* of her staff officers were qualified "on paper," with no real experience in their new positions. Nor did *she* have any, and with an inexperienced staff under a commodore who was herself as green as grass . . . She hid a shudder and nodded calmly.

"Run it down for us, Commander," she said.

"Yes, sir. First, I'd like to put our own operation in perspective to the overall situation. Our operational problems are complicated enough, but we *think* the Rump's are worse. So far, about seventy percent of Frontier Fleet has come over or been taken by our units, and it looks like we've got about twenty percent of Battle Fleet, too, but our forces are scattered all over the Fringe. With only drones for communication, concentrating them for operations is going to take time and, for the immediate future, our units here at Novaya Rodina constitute Admiral Ashigara's full disposable strength."

Han stifled an urge to hurry him up. There was time,

and it was better to be sure her entire staff understood Fleet HQ's viewpoint.

"Admiral Ashigara's intelligence people estimate that the Rump has suffered losses we don't know about, and that fighter losses have probably been *extremely* high because so many fighter jocks were Fringers. That's a bit speculative, sir, but it matches our own experience. At any rate, the Rump is undoubtedly strapped for striking forces, but has the advantage of an intact command, better communications, and the interior position; they can move what they have from point to point faster than we can shift around the periphery.

"Our own immediate strategic need is to secure our frontiers before the Rump begins to recover, for which purpose Fleet plans a series of attacks on choke points. Our own operation against Cimmaron will cut off four separate Rump axes of attack,"

He touched his panel, and the briefing room lights died. A hologram appeared over the table, and light from the tangled warp lines glittered briefly in his eyes as he picked up a pointer.

"Here's Cimmaron," he touched a tiny light dot. "Only two transits away via Redwing, but Redwing's covered by The Line. The forts are cut off now, but Fleet prefers to isolate them rather than attack them." Han felt a mental nod circle the table. No one wanted to tangle with *those* forts.

"So," Tomanaga went on, "we'll go from Novaya Rodina to Donwaltz—" his pointer hopped from star to star as he spoke "—to MXL-23 to Lassa to Aklumar to Cimmaron—a much longer route, but one we own as far as Aklumar. Because of its length, we're going in with only carriers, battle-cruisers, and light units, since battle-line units would slow us by thirty percent. On the other hand, there are no fortifications at Aklumar—thanks to the Treaty of Tycho—and they won't know we're coming, so we ought to retain the advantage of surprise until the moment we hit Cimmaron."

He laid the pointer aside and brought the light back up.

"Our best analysis of the defense is a guess," he admitted, showing an edge of concern at last. "The Fleet base's fixed defenses are negligible, but Cimmaron Skywatch is quite heavy: eleven type-four orbital forts, three covering the Aklumar warp point. Before the mutinies, there was also a strong OWP-based fighter force, and despite Fleet's estimate, there's no guarantee they haven't brought their fighter strength back up. They must be as aware of Cimmaron's strategic value as we are, so the system undoubtedly has priority for reinforcements."

He paused to let the numbers sink in, then went on.

"What *we* have, after essential detachments, is two battlecruiser groups (ours and Commodore Petrovna's) and four carrier groups with approximately three hundred fighters embarked, plus escorts. The balance of force should be with us, but our edge is slim and we don't have any superdreadnoughts or monitors. Without them, the battlecruisers will have to keep Skywatch occupied until the carriers can stabilize their catapults and launch."

All of them knew what that meant. Type-four OWPs were big and powerful, stronger than most superdreadnoughts. It was statistically certain some of the battlecruisers wouldn't be around to see the fighters launch.

"That's the bare bones of the plan," Tomanaga continued after a moment. "We're transporting several hundred crated fighters to hold the system once we have it, because half the carriers will have to pull out for Bonaparte and the Zephrain operation while the rest move on Gastenhowe. Other attacks should clear up additional choke points at the same time, but Cimmaron and Zephrain are the really critical ones. We need more depth to protect Novaya Rodina, and Fleet wants to deal with the research station as soon as possible."

"Thank you Commander," Han said quietly as he finished, then looked around once more, evaluating reactions.

Captain Tsing looked merely thoughtful, but he was a bulky, impassive man, virtually incapable of revealing much emotion. He was always simply Tsing—unreadable, phlegmatic, and utterly reliable.

Tomanaga looked confident. It was, after all, an ops officer's job to exude confidence, and certainly one could not dispute the neatness of the plan . . . assuming one could subordinate one's own survival to the other objectives. It seemed Tomanaga could do that—which could be a flaw in an ops officer. Best to keep an eye on him.

Lieutenant Commander Kane's eyes were intent, her lips pursed as she toyed with a lock of short-cut chestnut hair.

Han had watched her jotting notes as Tomanaga spoke; now her stylus ran down the pad, underscoring or striking through as she rechecked them. Han put a mental question mark beside Kane's name, but she was inclined to approve.

She turned finally to Lieutenant (junior grade) David Reznick, by far the youngest member of her staff, and perhaps the most brilliant of them all. At the moment, he was frowning.

"You have found a difficulty, Lieutenant?"

"Excuse me?" Reznick looked up and blinked, then flushed. "Could you repeat the question please, Commodore?"

Han hid a smile. It was difficult not to feel maternal towards the young man. "I asked if you'd found a difficulty,"

"Not with the ops plan, no, sir, but I'm a little worried about the electronics."

"Ah?" She regarded him thoughtfully.

"Er, yes, sir. *Longbow* wasn't designed as a command ship. We squeezed everything in by pulling those two heavy launchers, but the whole datalink setup is jury-rigged. It's put together with spit, prayers, and a lot of civilian components, sir, and we're spilling out of the electronics section. If we have to slam the pressure doors, we'll lose peripherals right and left."

"But the system does work?"

"Uh, well, yes, sir. Works fine. The thing is, if we start taking hits the whole shebang could go straight to shi—ummm, that is, the system could go down, sir. " Han couldn't quite hide her smile, and Reznick flamed brick red before his sense of humor rescued him. Then he grinned back, and Han's last real concern vanished as a chuckle ran around the table. The chemistry was good.

"Very well, David." She drew a pad and stylus toward her. "Give me a worst-case estimate and let's come up with ways around it."

"Yes, sir." He opened a thick ring binder and flipped pages. "First of all Commodore . . ."

"But, Lad, you got *your* Constitution adopted, and we're adopting *your* Declaration," Li Kai-lun said reproachfully. "The least you can do is endorse the flag you asked me to design for you!"

Ladislaus looked sourly at the sinuous, blood-red form coiled about the ebon banner's golden starburst. Except for the star—and the wings on the snake-like doomwhale—it looked remarkably like the Beaufort planetary flag.

"I'm thinking it won't be so very popular with the others," he rumbled.

"You round-eyes are always seeing difficulties," Kai-lun teased. "It's really childish of you. Why not just learn to accept your karma?"

"Because my 'karma's' probably to be a short rope when they see this, you old racist!"

"No, no!" Kai-lun disagreed. "It's only right that the symbol of Beaufort should adorn our banner, Ladislaus—the committee was unanimous on that. And for those who need a little symbolism, we've added the star and wings to indicate the sweep and power of our new star nation. You see?"

"Were you ever being a used-skimmer salesman?" Ladislaus asked his small ally suspiciously.

"Never."

"Ah. I had the wondering." He thought for a moment, then grinned. "All right. It's glad I'll be to be seeing the old doomwhale, anyway."

"Good." Kai-lun rose and headed for the door, then stopped to smile over his shoulder. "Actually, you know, that—" he waved at the banner "—is a symbol of good fortune."

"Eh? I've never had the hearing of the doomwhale being *that!*"

"Ah, but when you put wings on it, it's *not* a doomwhale."

"No?" Ladislaus' suspicions surged afresh. "What's it to be, then?"

"Any child of Hangchow knows that, Lad." Kai-lun smiled. "It's a dragon, of course."

Commodore Petrovna looked very calm in her new uniform, but she knew every officer of the new Republican Navy could see her on the all-ships hookup, and her warm voice was hushed with a sense of history.

"Ladies and Gentlemen of the Fleet, I introduce to you the President of the Republic of Free Terrans, Ladislaus Skjorning."

She vanished, and Ladislaus Skjorning appeared on the screen. His face was composed, but his blue eyes were bright—and hard. He sat behind a plain desk, and the crossed flags of the newborn Terran Republic covered the wall behind him.

"Ladies and gentlemen," his deep voice was measured, his famed Beaufort accent in complete abeyance, "fourteen years ago, I, too, was a serving officer in the Fleet of the Terran Federation. As one who once wore that uniform, I know what it has cost each of you to stand where you now stand, and I share your anguish. But I also share your determination and outrage. We have not come here lightly, but we have taken our stand, and we cannot and shall not retreat from it."

He paused, picturing the officers and ratings watching his image, hearing his voice, and for just a moment it seemed that he stood or sat beside each and every one of them. It was a moment of empathic awareness such as he had never imagined, and it showed in his voice when he continued.

"Ladies and gentlemen, it is you who will fight for our new nation; many of you will die for it. It is not necessary for me to say more on that head, for whatever else history may say of you, it will record that you were men and women who understood the concept of duty and served that concept to the very best of your ability. However, since it is you who will bear the shock of combat, it is only just that you know and understand exactly why we are fighting and what we are fighting for. It is for this reason I asked Admiral Ashigara for this all-ships hookup tonight.

"I am about to record our first official message to the Federation's Assembly, and I wish you to witness this communication as it is recorded. I suppose—" he permitted himself a bleak smile "—that this is an historic moment, but that is not why I wish to share it with you. I wish to share it because of who you are and what you will shortly be called upon to do.

"We represent many worlds and many ways of life. We spring from a single planet, but the diversity among us is great. We do not even agree upon the nature of God or the ultimate ends of our ongoing evolution. Yet we agree upon this: what has been done to us is intolerable, the systematic looting and manipulation of our economies and ways of life by others is not to be endured, and *no* government has the right to abuse its citizens as the government of the Federation has abused us. And if that agreement is all we share, it is enough. It is more than enough—as your presence in your ships, as your willingness to wear the uniform you wear, demonstrates. We may not share the same view of God, but before whatever God there is, I am proud to speak these words for you, and humbled by the commitment you and your worlds have made to support them."

He looked down at the concealed terminal built into his desk—not that he needed it; what he was to say was written in his heart and mind as surely as in the memory of his computer—then glanced up once more.

"Some of you will recognize the source of these words. Many may not, but, I think, no one has ever said it better—and their use may help the Federation's citizens to understand our motives despite their present government's self-serving misrepresentation."

He drew a deep breath and faced the pickup squarely, forcing his shoulders to relax. When he spoke once more, he appeared completely calm. Only those who knew him well saw the anguish which possessed him.

"To the Legislative Assembly of the Terran Federation," he began calmly, "from Ladislaus Skjorning, President of the Republic of Free Terrans, for and in the name of the Congress of the Republic of Free Terrans.

"When in the course of human events, it becomes necessary for one people to dissolve the political bands which have connected them with another, and to assume among the powers of the Galaxy the separate and equal station to which the laws of nature and the usages of justice entitle them, a decent respect for the opinion of all races requires that they should declare the causes which impel them to the separation."

He drew another deep breath, his voice rumbling up out of his chest, powerful and proud and defiant, yet somehow reverent as he spoke the fierce old words, newly adapted to changing circumstances.

"We hold these truths to be self-evident: that all sentient beings are created equal, that they are endowed with certain unalienable rights, that among these are life, liberty and the pursuit of happiness. . . ."

The survivors of the coming battles might see that recording many times in the course of their lives, yet never again would they see and hear it as it was made. They were joined with Ladislaus Skjorning, floating in the heart of a crystal moment, temporarily outside the bounds of space and time. Never before had so many men and women so intimately charged with the defense of a cause been joined in the moment of its annunciation; perhaps it would never happen again. Yet for all that they shared it as it happened, few could ever recall hearing the exact words Ladislaus spoke. What they remembered was the strength of his deep voice, the emotional communion as he forged words to hold their anger and frustration and their inarticulate love for the government they could no longer obey. The heard the list of abuses not with their ears, but with their souls—and they knew, knew now in their very bones, that the breach was forever. They could not return to what they had been, and in that instant of unbearable loss and political birth, the Terran Republic's Navy was forged on the anvil of history as few military organizations have ever been.

". . . We must, therefore," Ladislaus went on, drawing to the close of his message, "acquiesce in the necessity which denounces our separation, and hold you, as we hold the whole of the sentient races of the Galaxy, enemies in war, in peace friends.

"Now, therefore, the representatives of the Republic of Free Terrans, in general congress assembled, appealing to the Supreme Judge of the Universe for the rectitude of our intentions, do, in the name and authority of the good people of these worlds, solemnly publish and declare that these united worlds are, and of right ought to be, a free and independent nation; that they are absolved from all allegiance to the Legislative Assembly of the Terran Federation, and that all political connection between them and the Terran Federation is and ought to be totally dissolved; and that as a free and independent state, they have full power to levy war, conclude peace, contract alliances, establish commerce, and do all other acts and things which independent states may of right do."

He stared into the pickup, his face carved from stone, and behind his eyes he saw the crumpled body of Fionna MacTaggart—the final, unforgivable indignity to which the Fringe Worlds had been subjected—and the closing words rumbled and crashed from his thick throat like denouncing thunder.

"And for the support of this declaration, with a firm reliance on the protection of divine Providence, we mutually pledge to each other our lives, our fortunes, and our sacred honor."

"A man can die but once; we owe God a death . . ."

William Shakespeare,
Henry IV, Part II

OFFENSIVE

TRNS *Longbow* was five hours out of Novaya Rodina orbit as Commodore Li Han stood beside Captain Tsing Chang in the intraship car, her face tranquil, and worried over what she was about to discover about her crew.

The new Republican Navy was desperately short of veterans. Of the sixty percent of the Fleet which had been Fringer, roughly ninety percent had favored mutiny, but the furious fighting had produced casualties so severe the Republican Navy found itself with less than half the trained personnel to man its captured ships.

Figures were even worse among the senior officers. Admiral Ashigara was, so far at least, the most senior officer to come over to the Republic. Others might have joined her, but the carnage on most of the flag decks had been so extreme none of them had survived. Which explained Han's indecently rapid promotion . . . and also why she found herself wearing two hats. She might be a commodore, but experienced Battle Fleet skippers were at such a premium that she had to double as CO of the *Longbow*—not that she minded that!

Fortunately, they'd picked up a few unexpected bonuses, as well, such as Commodore Magda Petrovna. Han didn't know her as well as she would have liked, for Petrovna had been indecently busy on Novaya Rodina, splitting her time between the Convention and her new command, but the prematurely graying woman had certainly proved herself at the Battle of Novaya Rodina. Her choice of Jason

Windrider as her chief of staff only strengthened Han's respect for her. She felt no qualms about going into action with Commodore Petrovna on her flank.

The car stopped on the command bridge, and the officer of the deck stood as they stepped out. The other watch-keepers stayed seated as per her standing orders. Some captains preferred for their bridge crews to indulge in all the ceremonial rituals whenever they came on the bridge; Han preferred for them to get on with their jobs.

"Good afternoon, Exec," she said to Commander Sung.

"Good afternoon, sir. Commodore Tsing."

Han shook her head mentally at the titles. She was commodore of BG 12, but also *Longbow's* captain. For squadron purposes, she was properly addressed as "Commodore," but when acting as *Longbow*'s CO, she was properly addressed as "Captain." Just to complicate matter further, Tsing was now a captain—but there could be only one "Captain" aboard a warship, so Tsing was properly addressed as "Commodore," since courtesy promotions were, by definition, upward. Thus there were occasions on which they would both properly be addressed as "Commodore," but only Han would ever be addressed as "Captain," which meant that from time to time a "captain" outranked a "commodore" aboard *Longbow*. Not surprisingly, Sung, like most of her crew, took the easy out and addressed her only as "Sir" unless there was absolutely no alternative or it was completely clear which hat she was wearing.

"I have the con, Exec," she told Sung, sliding into the command chair.

"Aye, aye, sir." The short, slender commander stepped quickly back behind the chair, waiting.

"Mister Chu, how long to warp?"

"Approximately forty-three standard hours, sir."

"Very good." She swung her chair toward the exec. "Commander Sung."

"Yes, sir?" He looked nervous. That was a good sign.

"It's been a while since our last comprehensive drills," she said calmly. "Don't you think we might spend a few hours brushing the rust off?"

Sung Chung-hui had dreaded this moment. *Longbow's* casualties had been the lowest of any ship in TF 17, but the new Republican Admiralty had raided her ruthlessly for experienced cadre. He'd managed to hang onto barely half of her original bridge crew, and losses below decks had been worse. He'd done his best to fit the many replacements into his team, but all too many were on "makee-learnee," and he shuddered to think of the next few days.

He glanced at Tsing, but the former exec seemed thoroughly fascinated by the display on the main plot. No help there. He drew a deep breath.

"Whenever you wish, sir."

"Then sound general quarters, Exec," Han said, and Sung breathed a silent prayer as he pressed the button.

The word, Han thought as she worked up lather, was "horrible." She raised her face to the shower spray and the water dragged at her long hair. It really wasn't all that bad, considering, but war left no room for "considering." With nukes flying around your ears, there were only adequate crews—or dead ones. She remembered the fine-tuned instrument she and Tsing had made of *Longbow* before the mutiny and shook her head, but the present arthritic uncertainty wasn't Sung's fault. He hadn't had time to work up the new drafts, and he'd actually done quite well in the time he'd been given.

She finished rinsing and reached for a towel.

She and Sung were going to be unpopular over the next few days. At least she'd managed to hang on to most of her point defense crews—that was about the only department which had performed with a flourish—but damage control was terrible and engineering was no better. She couldn't fault Sung's initial concentration on gunnery and maneuvering, but gunners and coxswains alone couldn't make *Longbow* an effective fighting machine.

She wrapped the towel around herself sarong fashion and sat before her terminal. It was Sung's job to bring the crew up to her standards. Under the iron-bound traditions of the service, her ability, even her right, to interfere with his handling of the problem was limited. But she was also the captain. The ultimate responsibility was hers, and she and Sung both knew how new to his duties he was. She could stretch the point a bit, she decided, without convincing him he'd lost her trust.

She punched up the intraship memo system slowly, considering how to begin. Her fingers poised over the keys, then moved.

To: CDR Sung C.
From: CMDR Li H., CO TRNS LONGBOW
RE: Exercises conducted this date

Drills conducted by all departments indicate only point defense and maneuvering personnel fully competent in assigned duties. Engineering performance was far below acceptable standards, and general crew performance leaves much to be desired. I therefore suggest:

(a) series of intensive exercises of all hands in . . .

The words appeared with machine-like speed as *Longbow's* drive pushed the ship ever closer to battle, and Commodore Li Han, wet hair plastered to her bare shoulders, felt her mind reaching out to meet the test to come.

Han sniffed at Tsing's pipe smoke. Few spacers smoked, and she hated cigarette smoke, but though she would never admit it, she rather liked the smell of Tsing's pipe blend. Not that liking it kept her from scolding him over the filthy habit in private.

She glanced across the small table at Lieutenant Reznick and Commander Sung, noting the wariness in Sung's eyes. The past weeks had been a foretaste of hell for him, but he'd done well. *Longbow's* newcomers had slotted smoothly into place and even the abandon-ship drill had gone quite well, though she hadn't seen fit to tell Sung so. It wasn't nice, but it had inspired him to maximum effort.

"Well, Chang," she said finally, "could this crew zip its own shoes without supervision?"

"Just about, sir." Tsing blew a beautiful smoke ring and glanced at Sung, "Just about."

Sung's face fell, and Han shook her head reproachfully at Tsing.

"Actually, Exec," she said, "I think you've done very

well. There are still a few rough spots, but all in all, we've got one of the most efficient ship's companies I've seen."

"Thank you, sir!" Sung's face lit with pleasure.

"And just in time, too," she went on. She touched a button and a hologram of the local warp lines appeared above the table.

"We'll make transit to Lassa in about an hour, gentlemen," she said calmly. "Eighty-one hours after that, we'll be ready to fire probes through into Aklumar for a last minute report."

"Yes, sir." Tsing passed the stem of his pipe through the warp line between Lassa and Aklumar. "That ought to be an interesting trip."

"Not as 'interesting' as the one to Cimmaron," Han reminded him. "It had better not be, anyway!" She tapped the table gently, then turned a calm face to Sung. "Chung-hui, I asked you to join us because I'm going to depend heavily on you and Chang. I'll have to coordinate the battlegroup and fight *Longbow*, as well, and I can't do it unless you both understand exactly what I plan. You'll both have to exercise a lot of discretion in what you report to me and what you act upon yourselves, so I want us to have a very clear mutual understanding of the operation. Fair enough?"

"Yes, sir."

"Good. Then here's the first point; we're going into Cimmaron before Commodore Petrovna because the Rump data base won't list us as a command ship." Sung nodded; *Longbow* hadn't *been* a command ship the last time the Rump saw her. "On the other hand, our datalink has cost us two capital missile launchers, so we'll hold back our external ordnance when the others launch. We'll use the racks to hide our lack of internal launchers, because if they realize we're the command ship they'll go for us with everything they've got."

"Yes, sir. I understand."

"Good. Second, I want everything on line when we warp into Aklumar, no matter what the probes show. I hope we won't find anything to worry about—we *don't* need a Second Battle of Aklumar." This time both Sung and Tsing nodded. Aklumar had witnessed the climactic engagement of the First Interstellar War, but the last thing they wanted was a clash to alert Cimmaron.

"*But*," she went on, "if I were commanding Cimmaron there'd be at least a picket at Aklumar to watch for exactly what we hope to do. And if there is—" she brought up a schematic of the Aklumar warp junction "—he'll be right here." She touched the image. "Placed to dash down the warp line as soon as we enter scanner range. So we have to make sure we don't enter scanner range until we've dealt with him."

"Sir?" Sung sounded uncertain.

"If the admiral agrees, we'll go in cloaked," Han explained. "We'll close with him and—hopefully—pick him off before he knows we're there."

"But, sir, the battlegroup doesn't have cloaking ECM."

"No, but we do, and so do scout cruisers. We'll form a three-ship data group with two of them and clear the way for the rest of the task force."

"Unless," Tsing observed with the mild air of a man who'd made the same point before, "they've posted a light carrier, sir. A couple of long-range recon fighters on patrol, and we'll never get close enough."

"We've been over that, Chang, and I still don't expect it, not with so much of Frontier Fleet coming over. They'd never risk a fleet or assault carrier on picket duty, and all the lights were in Frontier Fleet. They can't have many of them left."

"You're probably right, sir, but it's my job to point out problems. And here's another: they might use a scout cruiser of their own."

"If they go by The Book, that's exactly what they'll do," Han agreed, "but they can't have many of them, either. If they do, the whole ops plan goes out the lock anyway. If they're cloaking, the probes won't spot them and they'll have just as good a chance to hide from us as we have to hide from them. Which gives them the advantage, of course, since their whole job is to run away while we try to locate and destroy them. But there's only one way to find out, isn't there?"

"You might ask Admiral Ashigara to send in a squadron of fighters to check it, sir," Sung suggested hesitantly.

"I might," Han agreed dryly, "if fighters carried *any* ECM."

"Sorry, sir. I should have thought of that." Sung sounded abashed.

"Don't worry about it." Han smiled. "But we're going to have to deal with this ourselves, so be certain plotting and gunnery are ready. We'll have to be quick to stop them from launching a courier drone."

"Yes, sir."

"All right. Now—" she switched to a schematic of Cimmaron "—this is where we're *supposed* to run into trouble. Commodore Tsing, Commander Tomanaga, and I have spent quite a while discussing how to handle this, Exec, and I want you to understand what we're up to. SOP would bring us in last to protect the command ship from the opening salvos, but the Rump knows The Book, too. Commander Tomanaga suggests we come in first, since that's the last place they'll expect the flagship, but I've decided to come in third. Lieutenant Reznick here tells me our datalink won't stand much pounding, so I don't want us out too early, just as I don't want us in the standard flag slot. We'll rely on the shell game approach—they'll know we have a command ship, but not which one it is . . . I hope. If we can force them to disperse their fire looking for us, we may survive until BG 11 comes through and offers so many targets they *have* to divide their fire. Understand?"

"Yes, sir."

"Good. And instead of a tight, traditional globe, we're coming in in line abreast for the same reasons— *everything* will be directed towards keeping them guessing."

"Yes, sir."

"And there's another point, one which relates to our datalink." Han turned to Reznick, who flushed slightly under her calm regard; it was amazing how readily he colored up. "Because we may lose our command data net so quickly, I want alternate standard datalinks set up between our units as a priority. If we lose the command net, I don't want any delays in dropping into smaller groups, Lieutenant."

"Yes, sir."

"All right. Now, here's the final point for you, Exec—

you won't be on the command deck when we enter Cimmaron."

"Sir?" Sung blinked. "But that's my duty station! I—"

"It is normally," Han cut him off calmly, "but this isn't normal. We don't have a flag bridge, and I have to be able to see battle plot. That means the flag will be on the command deck. If a single hit takes out me, Commodore Tsing, *and* you—" she shrugged.

"I see." Sung still sounded unhappy, and Han found it hard to blame him. "But where *will* I be, sir? Auxiliary fire control?"

"No, Commander Tomanaga will be there. I want you with Mister Reznick in command datalink." She caught him with a level stare. "Understand this, Commander. If the command deck buys it, you're suddenly going to inherit an entire battlegroup, because yours will be the only ship with command datalink capability. Hopefully Commander Tomanaga will still be around to advise you, but I can't even promise you that."

"I see, sir." Sung licked his lips, then nodded firmly. "I see."

"I'm glad you do, Chung-hui." She glanced at her watch. "All right—let's get back to the bridge." She killed the holograph and tucked her cap under her arm, facing them as they rose. "But remember, gentlemen, up to now, it's been a matter of seizing choke points where we happened to have mutinying units and cleaning up undefended systems. That's over now. We're going to fight for everything we get from here on out, and I want the Republican Navy to be just as dedicated and just as professional as the *Federation* Navy. This is a civil war, and passions are running high on both sides, but there had better not be any Jason Waldecks under *my* command. These aren't Arachnids we're fighting—they're Terrans. I expect you to act accordingly."

Then she turned, and they followed her silently from the briefing room.

"Good afternoon, Commodore Li." Admiral Ashigara regarded Han from her com screen, and Han watched her left hand play with her empty right cuff in the nervous gesture she'd developed since Bigelow. "We have the data from the Aklumar recon probes. It would seem—" the admiral permitted herself a thin smile "—your concerns were well founded. The probes report a single unit, probably a heavy cruiser, guarding the Aklumar-Cimmaron warp point."

"I see," Han said. "But there's not one on the Lassa-Aklumar point?"

"No," Ashigara said softly, and Han knew her admiral had considered the same point she had. It would have made a calculating sort of sense to post a second picket. The nearer watchdog would have virtually no chance of surviving any attack from Lassa, but her very destruction would insure a warning for the defenders of Cimmaron.

"I have decided to approve your plan, Commodore," Ashigara went on after a moment. "I will detach *Ashanti* and *Scythian* to accompany *Longbow*, and your force will make transit in two hours. The rest of the task force will follow eight hours later, in standard formation at half speed. We will remain beyond scanner range until you engage, but once you do, we are committed. Either you will destroy him before he dispatches a warning, or you will not. In either case, therefore, the task force will assume Formation Alpha and transit to Cimmaron immediately, without reconnaissance. There would be little time to evaluate the results of a probe recon even if we could send probes through without giving the warning we desire to prevent the picket from sending, so there is no point in delaying the inevitable."

"I understand, sir," Han said, hoping she sounded equally calm.

"Very well, Commodore. *Ashanti* and *Scythian* will report to you shortly. Good hunting."

"Thank you, sir," Han said, and the screen went blank.

"All stations report closed up, Captain." Lieutenant Chu was clearly more nervous over filling in for Sung than he was over the prospect of being blown to atoms, Han noted wryly.

"Thank you, Lieutenant." She glanced at a side screen which held the faces of Sung and Reznick. "Are you ready, gentlemen?"

"Yes, sir," Sung said. "Data net is operational and ECM is active."

"Very well. Let's go, Mister Chu."

"Aye, aye, sir!"

Longbow quivered as her drive engaged, and Han felt a familiar queasiness as the grav-damping drive field warred briefly with the artificial shipboard gravity. There had to be a better way to do such things, she told herself absently, but her attention was on Battle One.

The battle-cruiser nosed into the warp point to Aklumar, and her entire hull writhed as the tidal stress of transit twisted her. It was a brief sensation, but one which could be neither forgotten nor described to anyone who hadn't felt it, and Han gritted her teeth against the sudden surge of nausea. Some people claimed not to mind warp transit, or even to enjoy it. Some people, she thought, were liars.

The tactical display shimmered as delicate, shielded equipment hiccupped to the warp stress. Then the image steadied as the computers stabilized, and she was staring at a blank screen. Within the range of *Longbow*'s scanners, space was empty.

She felt herself relax as the emptiness registered. She'd expected it, but the confirmation was still a vast relief. Now all she had to do was sneak up on the ship watching the Cimmaron junction.

"All right," she said softly, leaning back. "I want a *sharp* watch. We should come into scanner range in—" she glanced at the chronometer "—sixty-four hours and ten minutes, but if he's decided to move, we may meet him much sooner and where we don't expect it. So stay on your toes."

He bridge crew made no reply, and she nodded in satisfaction. So far, she told herself, toying with the seal of her vac suit, so good.

"There she is, sir," Lieutenant Chu said, and Han nodded as courteously as if she hadn't already seen the small, red dot. A moment passed; then small, precise data codes flashed under the blip and it turned orange, indicating a cruiser class vessel. The red band of an enemy identification continued to pulse around it, but *Longbow*'s computers knew her now, and a quick search of the database provided her name, as well.

"She's the *Swiftsure*, sir," a scanner rating announced.

"Thank you, de Smit," Han said calmly, and watched the blip creep slowly across the display as her small squadron slid stealthily closer. She glanced at Battle Two, checking her own formation. Even *Longbow*'s scanners couldn't have located *Ashanti* and *Scythian* with certainty if they hadn't known exactly where to look. Now it remained to be seen whether or not *Swiftsure*'s scanners would detect them as they closed to missile range. The odds against it were astronomical, but it was possible. . . .

"Commodore, we're coming into extreme range." It was Lieutenant Kan, her gunnery officer. "I have a good setup."

"Stand by, Mister Kan." Han watched the tactical display unblinkingly, her expressionless face hiding her flashing thoughts as she considered. The range was long, but all three of her ships carried external loads of capital missiles, so she could fire now, banking on the fact that the motionless *Swiftsure* was an ideal, non-evading target. But the scout cruisers lacked *Longbow*'s more sophisticated fire control, so their accuracy would be poorer, and missiles were sublight weapons. Firing at longer ranges meant longer flight times and gave *Swiftsure* a better chance to detect their approach in time to get a drone off. On the other hand, the closer her ships came, the more likely *Swiftsure* was to detect *them*, which made deciding exactly when to fire a nice problem in balanced imperatives.

Han felt herself tightening internally, but her bridge crew saw no sign of it. She made herself lean back in her command chair. Ten light-seconds. That was the range at which detection became almost inevitable. She glanced at the tactical display. Eleven light-seconds. . . .

"Open fire, Mister Kan," she said quietly, and *Longbow* twitched as she flushed her external ordnance racks. The missiles lifted away, drives howling as they slammed across the vacuum between Han's squadron and her victim at sixty percent of light speed. She watched the speckled lights on her display as the missiles arrowed towards their target, and her brain concentrated on *Swiftsure*'s blip, watching like a hawk, hoping the doomed cruiser would die unknowing. But another part of her hummed with a sort of elated grief.

The missiles bore down on *Swiftsure*, and Han heard a murmur of excitement around her. Clearly their enemy had never suspected their proximity—even her point defense was late and firing wide. Only three missiles were stopped by her desperate, close-in defenses; the others went home eighteen seconds after launch in a cataclysmic detonation brighter than the star of Aklumar.

The dreadful fireball died, sucked away by the greedy emptiness, and Han stared at her display, her heart as cold as the void around her ship. There was nothing left. No courier drones—no escape pods. Just . . . nothing.

She stared at Battle One for perhaps five seconds, and somewhere deep within her was a horrified little girl. She was a warrior. This wasn't the first time she'd participated in the death of another ship and its crew. But it was the first time she'd struck down fellow Terrans from the shadows like an assassin. She'd given them only warning enough to know death had come for them. Only enough to feel the terror. . . .

She knew her success would save hundreds of her comrades when the Battle of Cimmaron began, but knowing did nothing to still her shame or the shocked sickness of triumph crawling down her nerves.

She turned her command chair to face Lieutenant Chu. "Take position two light-seconds from the warp point on the task force approach vector, Mister Chu, then get the XO racks rearmed." Her face was serene. "We'll wait here for further orders."

"Aye, aye, sir," Lieutenant Chu said. He hesitated a moment, but his enthusiasm was too great to resist. "That was beautiful, sir. Beautiful!"

"Thank you, Lieutenant," Han said coolly, and her eyes met Tsing's. He regarded her steadily, his face unreadable as he reached for the pipe lying on his console. He stuffed it slowly, and Han looked away.

"Battlegroup formed up for warp, sir."

"Thank you, Commodore Tsing." Han drew a deep, unobtrusive breath, tasting the oxygen in her lungs like wine, and felt *Longbow* gathering her strength about her.

Her beautiful, deadly *Longbow*, ready to plunge through the maelstrom of warp, eager to engage her foes. And suddenly Han, too, was eager—eager to confront her enemies openly. She allowed herself a last glance at the long, gleaming line of dots stretched out astern of her battlegroup, then touched a stud.

"Flagship." The voice in the implant behind her ear was brisk and professional, but she heard the tension blurring its edges.

"Commodore Li," she identified herself. "BG 12 ready to proceed."

"Very well, Commodore." Han recognized the harsh voice of her admiral. "Execute your orders."

"Aye, aye, sir. Commodore Li, out." She turned her head slightly, glancing at Commander Tomanaga and Lieutenant Reznick on her com screen. "You heard the lady, gentlemen. Full military power, Commander Tomanaga."

"Aye, aye, sir!" Tomanaga's face split in a sparkling grin of mingled tension and anticipation. His fingers flew over his command panel, and program codes flashed from his terminal to the datalink equipment sprawled across the electronics section. Reznick watched them flicker across his monitor, ready to reenter them if any of his delicate circuitry suddenly died, and Commander Sung sat beside him, feeling unutterably useless away from his station on the bridge.

Battlegroup Twelve awoke. The individuality of its ships vanished into the vast, composite entity of their data net. Drives snarled, snatched awake by signals flowing from Tomanaga's computer, harnessed and channeled to Han's will, and the battlegroup hurled itself at the warp point.

Han held her breath as the line of ships flashed towards the small, invisible portal—the tiny flaw in space which would hurl them almost two hundred light-years in a fleeting instant spent somewhere else. Only one ship at a time would enter that magic gateway; death was the penalty for ships which transited a warp point too close together. Two ships could emerge from warp in the same instant, in the same volume of normal space—but only for the briefest interval. Then there would be a single, very violent explosion, and neither ship would ever be seen again.

Now BG 12 led the Terran Republican Navy's first offensive, and the battle-cruisers struck at the warp point like a steel serpent. TRNS *Bardiche* vanished into the whirlpool of gravitic stress like a fiery dart, followed by *Bayonet*, and then it was *Longbow*'s turn. Han drew one last breath, her mind focused down into a tight, icy knot of concentration, and *Longbow* leapt instantly from the calm of Aklumar into the blazing nightmare of Cimmaron.

"Incoming Fire!" Kan snapped. "Missiles tracking port and starboard."

Damn, those gunners had been fast off the mark! Their missiles must have been launched even before they'd seen *Longbow*—launched on the probability that someone would be coming through from Aklumar to meet them. Thank God *Swiftsure* had been less alert! If the forts had been granted any more warning . . . if they'd had their energy weapons on line. . . .

More missiles flashed towards her ships. She ignored them. There was nothing she could do about them. They were Kan's responsibility, his and the point defense crews'; she had responsibilities of her own, and through the blur of battle chatter and the soft beeping of priority warning signals she heard Tsing hammering his keyboard as he and Tomanaga and Reznick fought to restabilize the net and feed her the data she needed.

There! The display cleared suddenly, the dots of her battlegroup clear and sharp, and they were all there! Dwarfed by the massive, crimson dots of the forts they might be, but they had all survived, and suddenly the data net had them. Missiles flashed away as their XO racks flushed. Brilliant detonations wracked the space around the fortresses, hammering their shields like Titans, and Han heard Kan's whoop of triumph. Their missile crews had been far more alert than their point defense gunners, she thought grimly. The first massive salvo went in virtually unopposed, and one of the forts was suddenly streaming atmosphere through shattered armor and plating.

But missiles were still screaming towards BG 12, and Han saw the dots of her ships flash crazily as Skywatch's warheads crashed among them. *Longbow*'s datalink took control of BG 12's point defense systems, dragooning them into a tight-woven network in defense of the entire battlegroup, and Han caught a brief impression of her two escort destroyers as their missile defenses flared like volcanoes against the incoming tide of destruction.

But not all of it could be stopped.

"Signal from *Bardiche*, Commodore! Code Omega!"

Han's eyes darted to her lead ship, the one in the spot Tomanaga had wanted for *Longbow*. The ancient, inverted horseshoe—symbol of death for the ships of Terra—flashed across her blip, brilliant precursor of her doom. Then her dot vanished, and Li Han no longer commanded four battle-cruisers.

"Close the range, Commodore Tsing. Missiles to sprint mode. Stand by to engage with hetlasers."

"Good hits on target two, sir!" Lieutenant Kan's voice rang in Han's ears. He had precious little time for reports, for it was his panel, feeding through the datalink, which controlled the gunnery of the entire battlegroup, but he was right. Target two was an air-streaming ruin, its remaining weapons no longer synchronized with its fellows.

"Two's datalink is gone, Gunnery," she said, amazed at the calm sound of her own voice. "Drop it. Concentrate on one and three."

"Aye, sir. Fire shifting now!"

"*Falchion*'s out of the net, sir!" Tsing reported sharply.

"Tell her to withdraw," Han said, not even looking up from Battle One. Without the protection of synchronized point defense, *Falchion* was helpless before the hurricane of missiles slashing in upon her. Her only hope was to break off. If she could. If the forts would let her go.

Time had stopped. Han's ship lunged around her, squirming desperately through the fortresses' fire. Half her battle-cruisers gone already, and the engagement had only begun! She heard her voice, cold as ice, belonging to a stranger as it rapped out orders, fighting for her ships' survival with every skill she had been taught, every intuition she had been given by God. And it wasn't enough.

She knew it wasn't enough. *Longbow* lurched as another missile slammed into her shields—and another. Where was Petrovna? Where was the rest of the task force? Surely she and her people had been fighting alone for *hours!*

"*Falchion*—Code Omega," Communications reported flatly.

"Scanners report enemy fighters launching, sir! ETA of first strike ninety seconds!"

"Abort standard missile engagement," she heard herself say. "Stand by AFHAWKs. Take the forts with beams, Chang."

"Aye, aye, sir."

Longbow lurched indescribably, and Han's teeth snapped together through her tongue. She tasted blood, and dust motes hovered in the air.

"Direct hit, sir! Laser Two's gone! Heavy casualties in Drive Three!"

"Initiate damage control. Tracking, anything on BG 11?"

"*Battleaxe* is emerging now, sir!"

Thank God! Help was coming. If she could just hold on—

Longbow twisted, writhing as force beams pummeled her. The shields were down, and armor and plating shattered under the assault. Han felt her ship's pain in her own flesh as the shock frame hammered her, bruising her savagely through her vac suit. The bridge lighting flickered and flashed back up, and she heard the deadly hiss of escaping air.

"Vac suits!" She snapped down the faceplate of her own helmet. It was too much. The price they were paying was too high.

"Here come the fighters!"

Han saw them on Battle One, sweeping in from port in a wave. They were too tight, showing their inexperience in the massed target they gave her gunners—but there were so *many* of them!

"Engage with AFHAWKs," she said coldly.

David Reznick no longer watched his monitor. He was too busy with his servos, fighting the mounting destruction of his jury-rigged equipment. Repair robots scuttled through forests of cables like metal beetles, bridging broken circuits, fighting the steady collapse. He was dimly aware that Commander Sung had taken over the backup monitor as he himself strove desperately against the inevitable. The vibration was even worse than he'd feared, yet somehow he kept the net on line despite the terrible pounding.

Then it happened. He was never certain, afterwards, exactly what it felt like. One moment he was crouched over his remotes, directing his army of mechanical henchmen—the next a wall of fire exploded through the compartment. He heard the screams of his datalink crew, and the air was suddenly thick with the stench of burning flesh.

He slammed down his visor in blind reflex, choking and gasping as his suit scrubbers attacked the smoke, and blinked furiously against the tears, fighting to see through the flames. He got only a glimpse of his monitors, but it was enough. There was no hope of restoring the net, and the heel of his hand slammed down on the secondary datalink. There was no response. The system was dead, and *Longbow* was on her own.

He whirled to another console, jerking a red lever, and his suit whuffed out as blast doors slammed and emergency hatches blew. The fire died instantly, smoke, oxygen, and fuel alike snatched away by vacuum, and only then did he wonder why he'd been left to throw the switch. That was Commander Sung's job—

He looked down and retched into his helmet. Less than half Sung's body lay there, and the fragment which remained was shriveled into something less than human. Reznick sobbed and dragged himself away, nostrils full of the smell of his own vomit as he crawled across the gutted compartment through the shattered circuitry and molten cables. Surely *someone* was still alive?

"Datalink gone, sir! Point Defense One no longer responds! Main Fire Control's out of the circuit! Heavy casualties in Auxiliary Fire Control!"

Han merely nodded as the litany of disaster crashed over her. *Longbow* was dying—only a miracle could save her ship now. She glanced at the plot, frozen in the instant her scanners went out. One fort was gone and one was badly damaged, but the third remained. Magda Petrovna was here, furiously engaging the remaining fortifications, and it looked as if all her ships were intact. And Kellerman's carriers were launching; she'd seen the tiny dots of strikefighters going out even as her display locked. But

BG 12 was gutted. *Bardiche* and *Falchion* were gone, and *Longbow* was savagely mauled. She had a vague memory of an Omega report on *Yellowjacket*, and it horrified her to realize she couldn't remember when the escort destroyer had died.

"Withdraw, Mister Chu," she said harshly. "There's nothing more we can do."

Longbow turned to limp brokenly away.

Han's shock frame broke as a massive concussion threw her from her chair. She turned in midair like a cat, landing in a perfect roll and bouncing back onto her feet in an instant. Lieutenant Chu was draped over his console—it took only a glance at his shattered helmet and grotesquely twisted spine to know she could do nothing for him. Lieutenant Kan heaved himself out of the ruin of his fire control panel, one hand slamming a patch over a hissing hole in his vac suit sleeve. Tsing was there, and five ratings. The rest of her bridge crew was dead.

She was still turning towards Tsing when the drive field died. There was no way to pass damage reports to what remained of her bridge, but she needed no reports now; the loss of the field meant the next warhead would vaporize her ship. There was no time for fear or pain or loss. Not now. Her chin thrust down on the helmet switch, and her voice reached every living ear remaining aboard her ship.

"Condition Omega! Abandon ship! Abandon ship!" she said, her voice almost as calm and dispassionate as when the action began. "Aban—"

Longbow's fractured hull screamed as another force beam ripped across her command section, shattering plating and flesh. The shock picked Han up and hurled her against a bulkhead, and darkness smashed her under.

Han's vision cleared. She felt hands on her arms and looked around dazedly. Tsing held her left arm, Kan her right, and the thunder of their suit packs came to her through their bodies as they fought for their lives and hers. She tried to reach her own pack controls, but she was weak, numb, washed out. They were risking their lives for her, and she wanted to order them to save themselves, but she had nothing left to give. She could only stare back at the gutted, shattered ruin of her splendid ship, her beautiful ship, her tremendous, vital, living *Longbow*, dying behind her. Point Defense Two was still in action, its Marine crew ignoring her bailout order as they fought to delay the moment of destruction—to give their fellows time to clear the lethal zone of the impending fireball, and tears clouded her eyes as she watched their hopeless battle. She should be with them. She should be there with her people. And how many of her other people lay dead within her beautiful, broken ship? How many of her family had she left behind?

The question was still driving through her as the missile struck. It took *Longbow* amidships—not that it mattered to the defenseless hulk. Han had a brief impression of fury and brilliance and light before her helmet polarized and cut off her vision. Then the fireball reached out to claim her, and there was only darkness.

CASUALTY

Li Han woke unwillingly. There was something horrible, she thought in drowsy terror. Something waiting—

She opened her eyes to a pastel ceiling and brilliant sun patterns, dancing and leaping as the window curtains fluttered, and relief filled her.

It had been a bad dream. She raised a hand to her forehead. A nightmare. If it had been real, she'd be dead. And she wasn't even . . .

Her hand slid over her forehead, and her eyes widened in horror, for she had no eyebrows. Her hand moved higher, trembling with the tactile memory of long, sleek hair . . . but there was no hair.

The discovery slashed away her drowsiness, and ivory-knuckled fists clenched. It had happened, and tears burned as her broken heart railed at a universe cruel enough to spare her from her beautiful *Longbow*'s destruction.

But long years of mental discipline chided the extravagance of her grief. The universe moved as it would; it was neither kind nor cruel, and all it asked of her was that she play her own part against its vast impartiality. Her pale lips murmured mind-focusing mnemonics, channeling grief in a technique which had served her well over the years, but this time it took over an hour to approach calm.

Yet calm came at last, and her eyes opened once more. She was in a hospital, she thought, turning to the window. On a planet with a small, warm sun that could be neither planetless Aklumar nor cool, barren Lassa and so must be

Cimmaron. Which meant that the Republic had won . . . or lost. She smiled with a ghost of real humor as she pondered the question. Was she a victorious hero in a conquered hospital? Or a miserable POW, doctored by her captors? There was only one way to find out, and she reached for the call button, dismayed by the languid, weary weakness of her muscles.

Her door opened within seconds, and she turned her naked head slowly, blinking against tears and light dazzle, as a woman in nursing whites entered. It took endless seconds to clear her eyes enough to read the tiny letters etched across the nurse's medical branch caduceus. "TRN," they said.

So they'd won; no Rump commander would permit POWs to wear the Republic's insignia, and her eyes closed again as relief ate at her frail reserves. Then she felt cool fingers in the ages-old, feathery touch as her pulse was checked and forced her eyes back open, staring up into a plain, serene face.

"How—" Her throat was dry and she felt a sudden surge of nausea, but she tried again, grimly. "How long?" she husked, and the rusty croak which had replaced her soprano appalled her.

"A little over a week, Commodore," the nurse said calmly, and offered her a tumbler of half-melted ice. She held the plastic straw to Han's cracked lips, and Han sucked avidly, coughing as the water ran down her desiccated throat. It was only when the nurse finally removed the straw, gently disengaging Han's weak fingers from their almost petulant, childlike grip, that her words penetrated.

A week! Impossible! And yet . . .

"A week?" she repeated, cursing the haziness of her thoughts.

"Yes, Commodore," the nurse said serenely, and touched a switch. The bed rose under Han's shoulders, and she clutched suddenly at the side rails, eyes rounding in pure astonishment as vertigo flashed through her.

"Too much?" The nurse released the button quickly, but Han shook her head almost viciously. She was a naval officer, and no hospital bed was going to make *her* whoop her cookies! The nurse watched her a moment, then shrugged and held the button down until Han sat bolt upright, wondering dizzily if her pride was worth such physical distress.

But the vertigo slowly diminished. The bed still seemed to curtsy gently and nausea still rippled, but it was better. Perhaps if she told herself that often enough she would even believe it. She focused with some difficulty on the nurse's nameplate.

"Lieutenant Tinnamou—"

"Yes, Commodore?"

"Mirror?" Han husked. The lieutenant's eyes remained serene, but Han saw the doubt and forced her hurtful lips into a smile. "I—can handle it."

"All right." The nurse produced a small mirror. It seemed to weigh fifty kilos, but Han managed to raise it and peer at the stranger it held.

Her eyes were huge holes in a thin, gray-green face, sores covered her lips, and dark mottled patches disfigured her complexion. Her hairless skull seemed obscene and tiny on the bony column of her neck, and her collarbone was a sharp ridge at the neck of her hospital gown.

Rad poisoning. She'd seen it before, but, her detached, dizzy mind decided calmly, she'd never seen anyone look worse and live. Her brain went back to that final nightmare instant of consciousness, seeing her helmet polarize again. Close, she thought. Her impression of the fireball reaching out for her was all too close to the truth.

"Captain Tsing?" she asked hoarsely. "Lieutenant Kan?"

"Both alive, Commodore," Lieutenant Tinnamou said briskly, reclaiming the mirror. But she laid it conveniently on the bedside table, and Han felt pathetically grateful. The gesture seemed to imply confidence in her ability to endure what it had shown her.

"H-how bad?" She gestured weakly at herself.

"Not good, sir, but you'll make it. I'd rather let your doctor give you the whole picture."

"When?"

"He's on his way now," the lieutenant said. "I expect—ah!"

The door hissed open and a small, cherub-faced man bounced in, smiling so hugely she wondered whether she was more amused by his antics or resentful of his abundant energy.

"Good morning, Commodore Li!" he said briskly, and her eyes widened at the harsh, sharp-edged vowels of his New Detroit accent. They dropped almost involuntarily to his uniform insignia.

"Yes," he grinned wryly, "I'm one of those damned loyalists, Commodore. But then—" his smile turned gently mocking "— uniforms don't matter much to us kindly healers. I can find you a good, honest rebel if you like, but I'm really quite a good doctor." His ironic tone touched something inside her, and her cracked lips quivered.

"Much better!" he chuckled, crossing his arms and looking down at her. "I'm Captain Llewellyn, by the way. Pleased to meet you at last. I've been in and out for the last week or so, but you've only been out."

"How bad?" Han asked hoarsely.

"Could be worse," he said frankly, "but not a lot. It was all touch and near-as-damn-it-go, actually. At the moment, you weigh about twenty-eight kilos." She flinched, but her eyes were steady, and he nodded approval.

"You were lucky it was only a nice, clean fighter missile," he went on. "On the other hand, you'd already have checked out of our little hotel if you'd had the shielding of an escape pod. I understand the bridge pods were buckled and your crew got you out just in time, as it were."

"H-how many?" she husked.

"From the bridge?" He looked at her compassionately. "Five—counting you." She winced, and he went on quickly. "But overall, you did much better. Over half your crew got out safely." Her lips twisted. He was right, of course; fifty percent was a miraculous figure. But if over half had survived, almost half had not.

"As for you, you got an awful dose, but your chief of staff seems to have unusual rad tolerance. He got you and your lieutenant picked up and hooked to blood exchangers in time, but even so, it was a rough forty-eight hours. We've managed to scrub you out pretty well, and the cell count looks okay, but it was tight, ma'am. Really, really tight."

"Don't look much like I made it anyway," Han rasped.

"Ah." Llewellyn nodded. "You *are* a bit the worst for

wear, Commodore. We doctors should, after all, be honest. But you'll improve quickly now we can get you off the IV's and put a little weight back on you." He examined her face critically and rose briskly. "But for now, I want you to go back to sleep. I know, I know—" he waved aside her half-voiced protests "—you just got here. Well, the planet isn't going anywhere, and neither are you. We've got you scrubbed out, but you have seven broken ribs, a cracked cheekbone, a fractured femur, and a skull fracture—just for starters. I'm afraid you're going to take a while healing up from *that*."

Han blinked at him, wondering where the pain was. They must have her loaded to the gills with painkillers, she decided, which helped explain her wooziness. His last words seemed to echo around a vast, dark cavern, and she realized dimly that the cavern was her own skull. She blinked again and let herself sink into the lightheadedness. The sun patterns on the ceiling danced above her, weaving the pattern of her dreams. . . .

The next few days were bad. Han was sick and dizzy, and she hated her surrounding forest of scrubbers and monitors. The instruments were silent, but she knew they were there—probing and peering for the first sign of uncorrected damage. They were part of the technology which kept her alive, and she hated them because they were part of what confined her to her bed.

It took long, hard effort to attain her normal calm, and it slipped away abruptly, without warning. She hated her loss of control almost as much as she did her weakness, and that loss showed when Lieutenant Tinnamou refused to let her visit Tsing Chang.

Han tried reason. It didn't work, so she pulled rank, only to find that medicos are remarkably impervious to intimidation. And finally, she resorted to a hell-raising tantrum which would have shocked anyone who knew her and, in fact, shocked her—but not as much as the flood of tears which followed.

That stopped her dead. She fell back on her pillows, exhausted by the expenditure of emotion, and her emaciated form shook with the force of her sobs. She turned her face away from the nurse's compassionate eyes, and the lieutenant frowned down at her for a moment, then stepped out into the hall.

Han heard the door close with gratitude, for her reactions both shamed and frightened her. How could she exercise command over others if she could no longer command herself?

But then the door opened again and someone cleared his throat. Her head snapped back over, and Captain Llewellyn looked down at her, his cherub's face incongruously stern.

"I suppose, Commodore, that we could call this 'conduct unbecoming an officer'—but I'm old-fashioned. Let's just call it childish."

"I know," she husked and turned her head away again. "I'm sorry. Just—just go away. I-I'll be all right. . . ."

"Will you, now?" His voice was sternly compassionate. "I think not. Not, at least, until you accept that you're merely human and entitled as such to moments of weakness."

"It's not that," she protested, scrubbing her eyes with balled fists like a child. "I . . . I mean . . ."

"Yes, it is," he said gently. "I've checked your record, Commodore. Sword of honor. Youngest captain in Battle Fleet. Stellar Cross. Headed for the War College, but for the current . . . unpleasantness. And that's only the official record. There's also your crew."

"My—crew?" It popped out involuntarily, and she bit her tongue, cursing her crumbling self-control.

"The survivors have had our visitors' desk under siege ever since your arrival. If I hadn't put my foot down, you'd've been buried under well-wishers—which, since I don't want you plain buried, I'm not about to permit! But my point is simple: amassing that record and winning that loyalty says a lot about your personality." His voice grew suddenly gentle. "You're not used to being helpless, are you?"

Han turned away, horribly embarrassed, but his question demanded an answer. And she owed him one for keeping her alive, she supposed fretfully.

"No," she said shortly.

"I thought not. Which explains exactly why you're reacting this way," he said simply, and Han turned back towards him.

"Perhaps," she said levelly, "but it doesn't help that you haven't told me everything, either, Doctor."

Llewellyn's face stilled at the accusation, and his eyes narrowed.

"Why do you think that, Commodore?" he asked finally, his tone neutral.

"I don't know," she confessed bitterly, "but you haven't, have you?"

"No." His simple response surprised her, for she'd expected him to waffle. But she'd done the little Corporate Worlder an injustice; he was as utterly incapable of evading a direct question as she herself.

"And what haven't you told me?"

"I think you know already," he said quietly. "You just haven't let yourself face it. I'd hoped you *wouldn't* for a while, but you're more bloody-minded than I thought," he added, and a door opened in her mind—a door she had been holding shut with all her strength even as she hammered against it.

He was right, she thought distantly. She did know. Her hand crept over the blankets across her belly, and he nodded.

"Yes," he said gently, and her teeth drew blood from her lip.

"How bad is it?" she asked finally, her hoarse voice level.

"Not good," he said honestly. "A high percentage of your ova are sterile; others are badly damaged. On the other hand, some are perfectly normal, Commodore. You can still bear healthy children."

"At what odds?" she asked bitterly.

"Not good ones," he met her eyes squarely, his voice unflinching, "but you know about the problem. It wouldn't be difficult to check the embryos and abort defectives at a very early stage."

"I see." She looked away, and Llewellyn started to reach out, then stopped as he recognized the nature of her withdrawal. She wasn't dropping deeper into depression; she was merely digesting what she had been told.

He stared down at her helplessly, tasting her anguish and longing with all his heart to comfort her. Yet he sensed something more than anguish under her sick, weakened surface, something pure and almost childlike in its innocent strength, like spring steel at her core. This was a woman who knew herself, however imperfect her self-knowledge seemed to her.

He sank into a chair, knowing she would turn back to him shortly, that his departure would shame her, watching the taut, bony shoulders relax. And as he watched the wasted body unknot, he felt himself in the presence of a great peacefulness, as if she were but the last link in an endless chain, able to draw on the strength of all who had gone before her. He'd already recognized the years of self-discipline behind her serenity, yet now his empathy went deeper, sensing the gift of freedom her parents had given her so long before, and he wished desperately that more of his patients could be so.

Her head moved finally, the delicate skull under the fine, dark fuzz shifting on the pillow, and she spoke quietly.

"Thank you, Doctor. I wish you'd told me sooner—but maybe you were right. Maybe I needed to wait for a little while."

"No, I was wrong," he said humbly.

"Perhaps. At any rate, now I know, don't I? I'll have to think about it."

"Yes." He rose unwillingly, shocked to realize that he wanted to stay within the orbit of her strength, then shook himself and smiled faintly. "Should I send Lieutenant Tinnamou back in? I think she's a bit concerned you might have, er, exhausted your strength."

"Is she?" Han's weary face dimpled. "I hadn't realized I knew so much profanity, but I'd rather be alone for a bit, Doctor. Would you give her my apologies? I'll apologize in person later."

"If you like," he said, relieved to see her smile at last, "but we kindly healers know sick people aren't at their best, Commodore."

"Please, call me Han," she said, touching his wrist with skeletal fingers. "And I *will* apologize to her. But not just now."

"Certainly. I'll tell her—Han." He twinkled sadly at her and touched his nameplate. "And my name is Daffyd."

"Thank you, Daffyd." She smiled again and closed her eyes. He left.

* * *

It took hours to truly accept it. The actual fact was not surprising—not intellectually. Somehow Han had assumed it wouldn't happen to *her*, but she'd always known it could. It was unfair, but then so was biology.

She felt tears on her cheeks, and this time felt no shame. Her life had been so orderly. She'd faced her need to excel in her chosen field, known that pride required proof of her competence. And, as a woman, the pressure for early achievement had been great, for she was not just a Fringer; she was Hangchowese, born to a culture which thought as much in generations as individuals. So her schedule had been set; she would achieve her rank, and then take time for the children she wanted.

She rolled her head on the pillow, agonized by a loss even more poignant because she had never possessed what had been lost. The pain was terrible, but the awful moment of realization was past. All she must do now was face it. All she had to do was cope with the unbearable.

It would have been different if she were an Innerworlder, she thought sadly, for the crowded Innerworlds restricted access to longevity treatments. But Han had been born on a Fringe World blessed with adequate medical technology, one where the antigerone therapies were generally available. At thirty-nine, she looked—and was—the Innerworld equivalent of perhaps twenty, and the differential would grow as time passed. She had expected another fifty years of fertility . . . fifty years which had been snatched away. For a moment, she almost envied the Innerworlders' shorter spans. They would have had fewer lonely years, she thought in a surge of self-pity.

She frowned sadly. Llewellyn was a good man, despite his homeworld, but his every word of comfort only underscored their differences. There were too few people in the Fringe. Alien gravities and environments inhibited fertility —it took generations for the biological processes to readjust fully, and no woman of Hangchow would even consider conceiving a child with a potentially lethal genetic heritage. For them, babies were unutterably precious, the guarantee of the future, not burdens on a crowded world's resources. Intellectually, Han could accept Llewellyn's words; emotionally they were intolerable.

She shook her head slowly, feeling the pain recede as she faced the decision. There was only one she could make and be true to herself and her culture, she thought, and knowing that defeated the pain.

But nothing would ever dispel her sorrow.

Time passed slowly in a hospital. Seeing days slip past without activity to fill them was a new experience for Han, and she felt events leaving her behind. Her battlegroup was disbanded as *Bayonet* and *Sawfly*, the last surviving units, were repaired and transferred to other squadrons, and even her surviving staff was on the binnacle list. Tsing Chang would be returning to duty only shortly before Han herself, and Esther Kane had never cleared *Longbow*. Robert Tomanaga would live, but he would be busy learning to walk with one robotic leg for months to come.

Only David Reznick had survived unhurt. He was the sole visitor she was allowed for two weeks, and meeting him again was perhaps the saddest of her few duties, for if he was physically unscathed, his coltish adolescence was gone. He'd been forced to mature in a particularly nasty fashion, and she was only grateful it had not embittered him. Indeed, she felt a certain subtle strength within him, the strength of a man who has been so afraid that he will never be that frightened again. She hoped she was right, that it was strength and not the final, fragile ice over a glaring weakness. She was in poor shape when he called on her, and the visit was so brief she could scarcely recall it later, yet she felt her judgment was sound.

But her staff's losses reflected her people's casualties as a whole, and she grieved for them. There were over four hundred dead from *Longbow* alone, and it had taken all her will to remind herself that almost five hundred of her people *had* escaped.

Yet no one at all survived from *Bardiche* or *Yellowjacket*, and only twelve from *Falchion*. She supposed historians would call the operation a brilliant success, but twenty-eight hundred of her people had died, and it was hard to feel triumphant as she brooded over her dead in the long, lonely hours.

Yet endless though the days seemed, she *was* improving, and she received concrete proof of that in her third week of convalescence. A chime sounded, her door opened, and her thin face blossomed in an involuntary smile as she looked up from her bookviewer and saw Commodore Magda Petrovna.

"Han!" Magda reached out to grip her hand, and her concerned eyes surveyed the ravages of Han's illness. But they were also calm, and Han recognized a kindred soul in the lack of effusive, meaningless pleasantries.

"Come to view the nearly departed, Magda?"

"Exactly. Mind?"

"Of course not. Sit down and tell me what's happening. It's like pulling teeth to get them to tell me anything in this place!"

Magda scaled her cap onto an empty table and brushed back her hair. The white streaks flashed in the window's sunlight like true silver, and for just a moment Han was bitterly envious of her healthy vitality.

"Not too surprising," Magda grinned. "It's a Rump hospital, and they wouldn't like to talk about a lot of what's happening."

"I think you're doing Captain Llewellyn an injustice," Han said gently from her pillows. "I don't think he worries about his patients' uniforms. He certainly couldn't have been kinder to me."

"Then he's an exception," Magda said tartly. "Most of 'em look like they smell something bad when we walk into a room. Hard to blame them, really. Their defense wasn't anything to be particularly proud of."

"No?" Han's mouth turned down. "They did well enough against me, Magda. They destroyed my entire battlegroup."

"No they didn't, Han. Oh, they hurt you, I don't deny that, but *Bayonet* and *Sawfly* came through practically untouched. And my God, what you did to them! All my group had to do was clean up the wreckage, Han—you and your people won the battle."

Han shook her head stubbornly and said nothing.

"You did," Magda insisted. "The poor Rump pilots were so green they never stood a chance once Kellerman got his fighters launched, and the local population was with us. Some of the planetary garrison tried to hold out, but the ground fighting took less than a day. Thay never had a chance without Fleet support. But if you and your people hadn't smashed those forts up before they came fully on line—" She shivered elaborately.

"They did well enough against me," Han repeated with quiet bitterness.

"No argument. But they were the only vets Skywatch had, and their only Fleet units—one battle-cruiser and a half-dozen tincans—hauled ass as soon as they realized we were in force." She grinned suddenly, her humor so bubbling it reached through even Han's depression. "You should hear what old Pritzcowitski has to say about *them*! They'd better pray *he* never writes an efficiency report on them!"

"I can imagine," Han agreed, and amazed herself by laughing for the first time since the battle. It felt so good she tried it again, feeling Magda's approving eyes upon her. "You're good for me, Magda."

"Fair's fair," Magda said, shaking her head. "If you hadn't done your job, I wouldn't be here. They went for *Snaphaunce* with everything they had as soon as they saw her—fortunately, you hadn't left them much."

"I'm glad."

"So was I. Oh, by the way, I checked on your Captain Tsing on the way up here. He's madder than hell the doctors won't let him come see you, but he's doing fine. In fact, he even kept some hair."

"Thank God!" Han said quietly. "And Lieutenant Kan?"

"A little worse than Tsing, but he'll be fine, Han."

"Thank you for telling me."

"Well, I hope someone would tell *me* if the position were reversed!"

"So the rest of the Fleet got off light," Han mused.

"Yep. In fact, Admiral Ashigara's already headed for Zephrain, and Kellerman's carriers are off to join our monitors and move on Gastenhowe."

"Then why aren't *you* gone?" Han asked.

"I, my dear, am senior officer commanding Cimmaron—at least for now. They added a cruiser and light carrier group to my battle-cruisers, then uncrated those fighters . . . and most of Skywatch surrendered intact when they saw what you did to one detachment."

"I see." Han pursed her lips thoughtfully. "Not bad for a lowly commodore, Magda. I'm glad for you."

"You are?" Magda smiled warmly. "Thanks—but I'm only *your* deputy. You're still senior, so as soon as you're up, the command is yours. So get yourself well and relieve me, Commodore!"

"I'd say the job was in good hands," Han said.

"Thanks, but I'll be glad to turn it over to someone else, believe me. And in the meantime, if you don't mind too much, there's someone out in the hall who'd like to see you. My chief of staff."

"Then invite him in! I haven't been allowed *any* visitors, Magda, and I still haven't thanked him properly for saving my ship at Bigelow."

Magda smiled and stepped back out into the corridor to collect Captain Windrider. Han watched his gaze move over her hairless skull and wasted face and wondered if her appearance shocked him, but he only smiled.

"Good morning, Commodore. You're looking better than I'd expected."

"Better?" Han shook her head. "Were you expecting a corpse, Captain?"

"No, just someone who'd come a little closer to being one."

"Well, I suppose I came close enough, at that," Han agreed, and patted her bed. "There's only one chair, so one of you has to sit here."

She half-expected an awkward pause as Windrider took the chair and Magda perched on the bed, but these were fellow professionals; they knew the risks, and they could speak of them unselfconsciously. But more than that, she realized, she was profiting from how comfortable they were with one another. She knew they'd never met before Windrider became Magda's chief of staff, yet they seemed far closer than the mere professionalism of a smooth command team could account for. It was a personal sort of closeness, one that carried them over any bumps in their conversation without a pause.

The more she listened to them, the more aware she became of the almost telepathic nature of their communication. They used a sort of shorthand, with single words replacing entire sentences, yet seemed totally unaware of it. But they reached out to her, as well, and she found herself opening up to others as she never had before. She wondered later if physical weakness had somehow eroded her normal reserve, but she suspected the answer was far simpler than that: Magda Petrovna.

Han watched Magda, feeling the way she drew both Windrider and herself towards her. Not since she'd been a little girl in the presence of her own mother had Han felt such an aura of peace, and at this moment in her life, she could feel only gratitude, for she well knew how desperately she needed it. She allowed herself to relax completely—so completely that she barely noticed when the conversation turned to her injuries.

She never could recall the exact words in which the information slipped out, but she never forgot Magda's expression. The brown eyes were soft, but they were also warm and supportive. Few people have the gift of offering complete sympathy without undermining the ability to deal with pain. Magda, Han realized, did.

"It's confirmed?" Magda asked gently.

"Yes." Han felt her mouth twist and straightened it, drawing her serenity about her once more. Magda's support offered her strength, and she nodded. "I have about one chance in sixty of conceiving a normal child."

"Shit." Windrider's single, bitter word might have undercut her self control, but she saw the anger in his dark, lean face and eyes. Anger over her loss, utterly unencumbered by self-consciousness. In that moment, he became her brother.

"Have you decided what to do?" Magda's face was serene, and Han felt she would have reached down to smooth her hair, had she still had hair, as she asked the question.

"I've arranged to have my tubes tied." She shook her head wryly. "Daffyd took it worse than I did, though he tried to hide it."

"I imagine," Magda patted Han's sound thigh gently. "Funny how irrational we Fringers are, isn't it?" She smiled and patted her again, then glanced at her watch and rose. "Damn, look at the time! Your 'kindly healer'—" Han grinned at Llewellyn's favorite phrase "—muttered something about firing squads if we wore you out. And you're looking a little peaked to me, so we'd better clear out. But we'll be back, won't we, Jason?"

"Sure thing, Boss." Windrider patted one thin hand, squeezing it as he rose. "Don't worry, Han. We'll mind the store until you come back."

"I'm sure you will." She watched them head for the door and then raised her voice slightly. "Thank you for coming. And—" she found the words surprisingly comfortable for one normally so reserved "—thank you for being you. It . . . helped. It helped a lot."

"Tubewash!" Magda chuckled, tucking her cap under her arm as Windrider opened the door. "Just an excuse to get dirtside, Han!" She sketched a casual salute and stepped through the door, followed by Windrider. It closed behind them, and Han stared at it thoughtfully. Then she let herself settle back into her pillows as the familiar drowsiness returned.

"I'm sure it was, Magda," she whispered softly, lips curving in a smile. "I'm sure it was."

"Courage above all things is the first quality of a warrior."

General Karl von Clausewitz,
On War

Drumbeat

Zephrain, as humans rendered the name bestowed by its Orion discoverers, was a distant binary system. Component B, an orange K8 star, swung ponderously around its yellow G5 companion in an orbit of over fifty percent eccentricity, coming as close as three light-hours at periastron. Both stars had small families of planets, and extensive asteroidal rubble marked the hypothetical orbits of stillborn gas giants which would have formed but for the gravitational havoc wrought by each star on the other's planetary system.

Zephrain A-II was Earthlike—a small, dense world with abundant liquid water and free oxygen. Named Xanadu by a humorously inclined Terran Survey officer, A-II was home to a thriving human population, but Zephrain RDS was on Gehenna, Planet A-III—a lifeless, nearly airless ball of sand not much better than Old Terra's neighbor Mars—precisely because the station must inevitably be the primary target in the system. Since Howard Anderson's day, the TFN had believed that "combat should be kept out in space where it belongs", or, if not in space, at least on worthless planets no one would miss when the planetbusters arrived.

And that, thought Vice Admiral Ian Trevayne, was a very fine policy against aliens who would lose no sleep over the incidental genocide of whole human colonies. But in a war between humans, there were arguments for placing targets like Zephrain RDS next to a city or two. Or would that have given the Terran Republic pause, after all? Certainly the murderous bastards had already shown their willingness to inflict noncombatant casualties, he thought bitterly.

The Terran Republic! Trevayne recalled a cynical query concerning Old Terra's Holy Roman Empire: in what respect was it holy, Roman, or an empire? He almost voiced the thought to the older man beside him, but he knew he would have gotten a look of incomprehension and polite disinterest. Vice Admiral Sergei Ortega was no history buff.

At any rate, there were more urgent matters at hand. Like persuading Ortega to stay aboard this ship.

They stood on the flag bridge of the monitor *Zoroff*, Trevayne's flagship. Accompanying her in orbit around Xanadu were the other ships of the battlegroup he'd brought through the chaos of insurrection to Zephrain. He still couldn't contemplate the journey without a feeling of awe that he had actually gotten away with it.

Battlegroup Thirty-Two had been stunned when news of the first mutinies arrived from the Innerworlds, but Trevayne had foreseen the storm and taken precautions. His personnel, even the Fringers, knew and trusted him, and his captains had been loyal to a man (or woman, as the case might be). The few outbreaks had been quelled with a minimum of bloodshed.

Only then had there been time to come to terms with the *other* news the light cruiser *Blackfoot* had brought. News of the bloody raid on Galloway's World, BG 32's home port, which had gutted the Federation's largest shipyards and destroyed, among other incidental items, Admiral's Row, where Natalya, with seventeen-year-old Courtenay and thirteen-year-old Ludmilla, had awaited his return. . . .

Doctor Yuan, *Zoroff's* chief medical officer, had explained the "denial phase," when tragedy remains merely unacceptable. Luckily for BG 32, Trevayne had still been in that state when a rebel fleet followed *Blackfoot* through the same warp point.

His orders had come with a methodical precision as ship after ship emerged from warp. There were too many to fight—but none had been monitors, and nothing lighter than a monitor really wanted to *catch* a monitor. That natural hesitancy to invite self-immolation had given him the chance to disengage and run, but there were few places to run as the Fringe went mad. He remembered the weary progression of systems: Juarez, Iphigena, Lysander, Baldur—where he'd hoped to break back to the Innerworlds only to meet a rebel carrier group which cost him both scouting cruisers. Baldur had been bad. It was at Baldur that he'd realized he was completely cut off from the Innerworlds, his only choice to stand and fight or head into Orion space.

The Orion commander at Sulzan had been a fool, and Trevayne was grateful for it. The Khan's official policy of neutrality should have meant internment for any TFN refugee, but Small Claw Diharnoud'frilathka had dithered long enough for Trevayne to warp out for the district capital at Rehfrak. The District Governor was no fool, but he, too, had turned a blind eye as BG 32 passed through. Probably, Trevayne suspected, because of the Khan's vested interest in an Innerworld victory . . . though BG 32's firepower might have been a factor, as well. Whatever the reasoning, the governor had allowed him to leave via the one warp point he'd really wanted: the one to Zephrain.

Zephrain, gateway to the region known as the Rim. Zephrain, the largest naval base humanity had ever built. Zephrain, where—to his relieved surprise—the Federation's writ still ran.

The people of Xanadu shared the same political and economic grievances as other Fringe Worlds, and they contemplated the proposed Federation-Khanate amalgamation with equal revulsion. But militant loyalty was bred into them, for their system had borne the brunt of the Fourth Interstellar War. Every man, woman, and child in the Zephrain System had been an expendable frontline soldier against an enemy who saw humans as culinary novelties. Between them and the Arachnids there had been only one shield: the Federation's ships. The Federation was nearly a religion to these people, and they had not been prepared to entertain a schism.

Isolated by rebellion from the rest of the broken Federation, they'd formed a loyalist provisional government. Since Admiral Ortega, commanding the Frontier Fleet elements at Zephrain, had found himself equally isolated from his superiors, he had placed his forces at the disposal of the provisional government. He was neither brilliant nor imaginative, but his integrity was absolute and he had the seniority. Trevayne had placed himself under his command.

But once the desperate race was won, what had happened came crowding back like a slow, dreary drumbeat to which the rest of his life was mere counterpoint. The realization that only Colin was left to him. Colin . . . whom he had last seen as an angrily retreating back.

He remembered the quarrel with merciless clarity. Colin had declared his sympathy for the Fringers, and Trevayne reacted with fury. And that, he thought, was because his son had blurted out things he himself felt but could not say, so that he'd been reduced to sputtering like an idiot about "Your oath . . ."

"My oath," Colin had shot back, glaring at him with Natalya's blue eyes, "is to the Federation, not a bunch of greasy Corporate World political hacks! Can't you *see*, Dad? The Federation you and I swore our oaths to died with Fionna MacTaggart!"

"That's enough!" Trevayne had roared. "D'you think I don't know the Fringe Worlds have grievances? But neither those grievances *nor anything else* can justify shattering over four centuries of human unity!"

So it had gone: the sterile repetition of incompatible positions and the final, angry parting. Now the only anger Trevayne had left was reserved for the fate which had kept him in deep space as a junior officer for most of Colin's boyhood. Only later, with more time in port, had he found that which is given to a parent but once: to rediscover the universe while first watching a child discover it. And he'd found it with Courtenay.

Trevayne made one last try as he and Ortega left the flag bridge.

"Damn it, Sergei, *Zoroff*'s command facilities are far better than *Krait*'s, and incomparably better protected. It doesn't make sense to keep fleet command in something as fragile as a battleship—and you bloody well know it!"

Ortega smiled wearily. He followed Trevayne's advice

on most things, but on this he had his heels dug in and there was no moving him.

"Ian, *Krait*'s been my flagship ever since I've been out here. Most of my people are from the Rim, and we've gotten to know one another, they and I. But if I transfer to *Zoroff*, no matter why, they'll think I don't trust them anymore . . . and they won't trust me. Things are chaotic enough; let's disturb routine as little as possible."

He paused for a moment, then resumed as if reluctantly. "And don't start again on my allegedly indispensable personal acquaintance with the key people in the provisional government. We both know the Rim is still pretty volatile and that we'll probably have to proceed under martial law in one form or another."

"Now *you're* underestimating these people," Trevayne demurred. "They know better than most what war is about, and they put together the provisional government because they're loyal. So you *are* important because of your connections with it. Why, your daughter's one of its founders! There's no need to bypass it. Let's just give it a chief executive who represents the Federation and has extraordinary powers for the emergency. My legal officer and I have come up with a precedent: a captain who assumed emergency powers as temporary military governor of the Danzig System during the Theban War and was upheld afterward. We'll declare you—oh, say Governor-General of the Rim for the duration." He held up a hand against the objections that were halfway out of Ortega's mouth.

"If the Assembly doesn't like it, they can say so when contact is reestablished. But for all we know, Sergei, the Rim is all the Federation that's left. Old Terra could have fallen into a black hole last month, and we'd have no way of knowing it. We're on our own out here, and we'd better start acting accordingly. *That's* why you're so bloody important . . . because you're one of these people's own, at least by adoption!"

Ortega opened his mouth, then closed it. Finally he shook his head.

"For God's sake, Ian, you're moving too fast for me again! Let's at least defer this until the immediate threat is past."

The "immediate threat" was, of course, the rebel attack

that must come, sooner rather than later. Not because of the mammoth building and refitting facilities. Not even because Zephrain held the "Gateway," the warp point which was the Rim's only practicable link with the rest of the Federation. What made Zephrain unique was the R&D Station, where two generations of brilliant minds had happily turned out the blueprints for a whole new order of military technology. They'd been cheerfully oblivious to the fact that none of it was being produced. (Who wanted a new arms race with the Khanate of Orion?) But what they'd never seemed to notice was that their quest for a heavier, longer-ranged missile had brought them innocently to the threshold of a gravitic engineering revolution that would transform more than just warfare. The memory banks of Zephrain RDS were a womb wherein a whole new era gestated—and Trevayne would unflinchingly perform a thermonuclear abortion if he saw the station about to fall into rebel hands.

Zephrain RDS was the key to the Rim. If enough of the new weapons could be put into production—and the Zephrain Fleet base was one of the two or three places in the Federation where it might be done—then the Rim would survive. And, knowing that, Trevayne and Ortega had to assume the rebels *also* knew it and would act to prevent it.

The intraship car reached *Zoroff*'s boatbay, and the two admirals emerged, a study in physical contrast. Ortega was short and slightly overweight, his stocky frame and broad, high-cheekboned face reflecting his Slavic and Mesoamerican ancestry. Trevayne was tall, lean, and very dark, an Englishman with more than a trace of the "coloured" genes that the departing empire had bequeathed to the island's population in the late twentieth century. His hair was beginning to thin on top, but unlike some (including Ortega) he'd made a good job of growing the short, neat beard currently in vogue among male TFN officers. The latter caused him more satisfaction (and the former more annoyance) than he cared to admit.

"After I get back from the exercises, let's both visit Xanadu for a few days," Ortega said. "You've been shipbound too long, Ian—getting a touch of bulkhead fever, I'd say." He grinned toothily. "Besides, I want to introduce you to some of the people in the provisional government—

especially Miriam." His face took on the expression it usually wore when he spoke of his daughter: a mixture of pride and bewilderment. "She's been wanting to meet you."

"I'd be delighted," said Trevayne, not sounding particularly delighted. Ortega noticed the lack of enthusiasm and smiled again.

"You may as well resign yourself, Ian. She's like you—she tends to get her way. It's almost unnatural how much like her mother she is."

They proceeded towards Ortega's cutter, and Ortega paused as the Marine honor guard clicked to attention.

" 'Governor-General'!" he snorted. Then, with a sudden twinkle, "Well, at least it got your mind off trying to keep me aboard *Zoroff*!"

The next day found Trevayne in the small staff briefing room adjacent to *Zoroff's* flag bridge with his chief of staff, Captain Sonja Desai, while his operations officer, Commander Genji Yoshinaka, described the exercises planned for the next few days. Captain Sean F. X. Remko, *Zoroff's* CO, attended via com screen from his command bridge. Part of Trevayne's brain listened to the briefing, but another part considered his three subordinates.

Desai listened to Yoshinaka with her usual thin-lipped lack of expression. Looking at her dark, immobile face, a blend of Europe and India, Trevayne knew she would never be a charismatic leader, but her brilliance was acknowledged even by those—and they were many—who disliked her.

Remko's ruddy, brown-bearded face nodded in the com screen as he followed Yoshinaka's comments. Trevayne could easily visualize the workings of the burly flag captain's mind. Remko was a battle-cruiser man by temperament, but he performed his present duties with aggressive competence. He was a fighter, a man whose sheer guts and ability had carried him from a childhood in the Hellbroth, the worst slum on New Detroit—a planet noted for its slums—to his present rank despite the prejudice his buzz-saw accent engendered.

Yoshinaka was gesturing at the clustered display lights that represented all of Ortega's Frontier Fleet strength, except those units keeping watch over potential trouble spots throughout the Rim, as they floated near the Gateway and its fortresses in preparation for exercises with Zephrain Skywatch. Like Trevayne, the ops officer was that rarity in the TFN, a native Old Terran, and this had always formed a bond between them. It was an unspoken bond—not much ever had to be spelled out for Yoshinaka. He was a deft, subtle man who stayed in the background. No one but Trevayne fully recognized the unobtrusive ops officer's importance to what Yoshinaka himself called BG 32's *wa*, a word inadequately translated into Standard English as "group harmony."

Remko suddenly turned a scowling face to someone outside the screen's pickup. He listened a moment, his scowl fading into tense understanding, then broke in on Yoshinaka.

"Priority signal from Skywatch, Admiral! Missile pods are beginning to transit the Gateway! The minefields are taking some out—but not many!"

Trevayne looked quickly at the display unit. Clearly Ortega had gotten the same message. Some of the yellow and orange lights in the tank—his faster cruisers and destroyers—were already accelerating away from the red lights of his capital ships.

"Captain," Trevayne clipped as he rose from his chair, "sound general quarters. Commodore Desai, we're leaving orbit immediately and proceeding to the Gateway under maximum drive." He strode onto the flag bridge, Desai and Yoshinaka on his heels, as a com rating looked up with a signal from *Krait* that confirmed the orders he had anticipated.

Beneath his decisiveness, Trevayne was amazed that the rebels (he would *not* call them "the Terran Republic") had managed to organize their attack so soon. But then he saw the intelligence center's preliminary analysis of the forces emerging from the Gateway even as the surviving pods launched their clusters of homing missiles to seek out the orbital forts. They were in less strength than he would have anticipated, particularly in carriers. Perhaps they were attacking before they were quite ready. And perhaps they didn't realize BG 32 had arrived? His lips curved wolfishly at the thought.

The fortresses were taking a terrible beating, but their

batteries of primaries were doing their intended job and pulling a lot of the attackers' teeth. Ortega's battleships were launching long-ranged strategic bombardment missiles and would soon be receiving a reply in kind. A high percentage of those missiles were targeting the respective flagships, for both side's fire control could pick out targets on a "first name" basis. It would not, Trevayne thought sourly, be a healthy war for the top brass.

BG 32 was still beyond scanner range of the Gateway. In some commands, the fact that the only hostile warp point into the system was beyond scanner range might have led to a certain laxness in the scan ratings: not in BG 32. Trevayne expected maximum scanner capability whenever the ships were at general quarters, and his captains had learned that his standing orders were best taken seriously. Thus it was that Sonja Desai, her usually immobile hatchet face animated by excitement, exclaimed:

"Admiral, we've picked up a trio of cloaked assault carriers! Now that we've isolated them, we should be able to catch any escorts. . . . Yes, they'e coming in now: two fleet carriers and a light cruiser. The cruiser must be a scout, since she's carrying third-generation ECM. Distance just over eighteen light-seconds, heading . . ." She rattled off the figures, then her head jerked up to dart a startled look at her admiral.

"Admiral, they're on a course about seventy degrees from ours, converging rapidly, and they seem to be coming from somewhere around Zephrain A!"

But Trevayne's mind had already gone to full emergency overload as he assimilated the data and its implications. There was only one possible answer: a defense planner's worst nightmare—a "closed" warp point. The only way to locate a closed warp point was to come through it from the normal warp point at the far end. Obviously the rebels had done just that, undoubtedly with cloaked survey probes, and now that they had the defenders' attention riveted by their great, noisy frontal attack, they'd sent this lot in through the back door neither he nor Ortega had suspected existed.

Yes, it made sense—whether they knew about BG 32 or not. Carriers to get up close undetected and launch a massive fighter attack from the rear, and a scout cruiser's scanners to provide "eyes" without using easily detected recon fighters. And the buggers should have gotten away with it. The chance of long-range scanners picking up a cloaked ship at this distance were minute.

Yet they *had* been caught . . . but long-range scanners were *passive* . . . it'd be some seconds before they tumbled to the fact that they had. . . .

An unholy glee pushed the dull drumbeat from his consciousness. The sods had their ECM set for cloak, and it took time to shift ECM modes. As far as fire confusion was concerned, those ships were mother-naked! Now that they'd been spotted at all, they might as well not even *have* ECM! But they didn't know that yet! If he attacked now—*before* they realized and launched . . . !

The stream of thoughts and conclusions ripped through his mind in so small a fraction of a second that his stream of orders never even hesitated.

"The battlegroup will alter course to intercept the carrier force. Commence firing with SBMs—*now.*" They were still outside normal missile range—but not SBM range. "Implement anti-fighter procedures."

BG 32 reoriented itself. The four Brobdingnagian monitors lumbered into a tight, diamond-shaped formation with their two escort destroyers positioned to cover their blind zones. The attached recon group (a light carrier with two escort destroyers) took up position astern and launched all three of its fighter squadrons. AFHAWK missiles slid into their shipboard launchers. And before the maneuver was even completed, the monitors twitched and shuddered, expelling a cloud of lethal strategic bombardment missiles from their external racks. The deadly swarm of missiles flashed away, closing on the rebel ships.

"We're getting some individual IDs, Admiral," Desai reported as her screen flickered with sudden data. "The CVAs are *Gilgamesh*, *Leminkanien*, and *Basilisk*, sir. CVs *Mastiff* and *Whippet*, and . . ." She sucked in her breath sharply and stopped dead.

Trevayne heard the hiss and turned toward her in concern. Her face was even more frozen than usual, and her eyes were haunted as she looked up at him over the terminal.

"What is it, Sonja?"

"Admiral," she said, very quietly, "the scout cruiser is *Ashanti.*"

Every officer on the flag bridge either personally knew or had heard of Trevayne and his family—and that Lieutenant Commander Colin Trevayne was executive officer of TFNS *Ashanti.* Heads turned and eyes looked at the admiral.

"Thank you, Commodore," Trevayne said levelly. "Carry on, please."

Yoshinaka glanced quickly at the command bridge com screen, seeing the pain in Remko's dark eyes. Years before, struggling upward through the tight, almost hereditary ranks of the peacetime TFN, the flag captain had encountered Innerworld senior officers who'd barely troubled to conceal their snobbery and others who'd displayed their enlightened social attitudes with forced, patronizing tolerance. And then Lieutenant Commander Sean Remko had found himself serving a flag officer who quite simply didn't give a damn about where Sean Remko had been born or how he talked.

And now, watching Remko stare from the com screen at that same officer, Yoshinaka understood the inarticulate flag captain's need to offer Trevayne something.

"Sir, the carriers are what matters. A scout doesn't have enough armament to hurt us much . . . and the missiles are still under shipboard control . . . it ought to be possible to . . ."

Trevayne also understood, but he turned to the screen and calmly cut Remko's stammering short. "Fight your ship, Captain," he said.

Then he settled back in the comfortable admiral's chair. The drumbeat was back, but he ignored it. There were decisions to be made in the next few minutes, and there was no time for anything else. No time to examine the new sensation of being utterly alone in the cosmos but for the cold companions Duty and Self-Discipline. No time for grief, or self-hatred, or nausea. Plenty of time for all of that, later.

ALLIANCE

Xanadu averaged slightly warmer than Old Terra, and its axial tilt was less than fifteen degrees, giving it short and mild seasons. Prescott City, on the seaboard of the continent of Kublai, lay just inside the northern temperate zone and was enjoying a typical winter as Ian Trevayne stepped from his shuttle. The day was blustery but only mildly cool; the chill was in his soul.

He spent a moment acclimating himself. (Weather of any sort was always a little startling to a man who spent most of his working life in artificial environments, and the 0.93 G gravitation was perceptibly different from the TFN's statutory one G.) Then he crossed the ceramacrete to greet Genji Yoshinaka. The dapper ops officer saluted and fell in beside him.

"Good afternoon, Admiral. Your schedule's been arranged for the evening. In the meantime, your skimmer is waiting. The pilot is a Prescott City native; he says Ms. Ortega's address is a good kilometer from the nearest public landing platform, so I've laid on a ground car to take you the rest of the way."

Trevayne looked around him. Low clouds scudded rapidly across a sky of deep blue crystal. For the first time in months, he made a completely impulsive decision.

"Cancel the ground car, Genji. I'll walk."

Yoshinaka, struggling to keep pace with his long-legged boss, was startled. In the week since the engagement people were beginning to call the Battle of the Gateway,

Trevayne's days had been regimented almost to the second. It was inevitable, of course, especially given the new responsibilities which had fallen to him when Sergei Ortega had died with his flagship. But Yoshinaka understood why the admiral had attacked his work with such furious energy. There were too many ghosts, and Trevayne sought to hold them at bay in the only way he knew. Knowledge made his impulsiveness, his willingness to waste time, all the more startling. But, then, Yoshinaka reflected, the admiral had never been a predictable man.

Trevayne had visited Xanadu before, but only for brief conferences at the base itself. Now, for the first time, he looked down from the skimmer and saw the planet's chief city not as an abstraction to be defended, but as a bustling urban sprawl. He couldn't recall what Prescott City had been called when it was founded during the Fourth Interstellar War—probably something else outre from Coleridge. The old name didn't much matter anyway, for it had soon been renamed in honor of Commodore Andrew Prescott, whose statue and column dominated the lawn before Government House. It was a fitting tribute to the survey officer who had provided the Terran/Orion alliance with the information it needed to win that war—and who'd died doing it. Trevayne's mouth twisted with the wry grimace that now served him for a smile. He hoped Winston Churchill had been wrong about the bad luck that attends nations which change the names of their cities.

It was hard to quarrel with Xanadu's choice of the name, though. Time after time, the war had brought large-scale space combat to this system. At the touch of the destructive energies those battles released, a living planet would wither like a leaf in a flame. Thanks to Andrew Prescott, the people of Xanadu had finally awakened one morning and known they could live and bear children without that fear.

Until now, Trevayne thought, and the bile rose in his throat. Now the fear was back, but this time it was fear of the rebellious ships of the TFN itself, the TFN which for centuries had stood between *all* the worlds of Man and that horror! As Sergei had stood. . . .

His controlled face tightened as his vivid imagination

pictured the loathsome mushroom clouds once more. Only the consuming demands of responsibility had kept him functioning under the shocks of the mutinies and the deaths of his wife and daughters. And then Colin. . . . His mind shied away from the thought like a wounded, skittish horse. In the aftermath of battle Trevayne had deliberately filled the little free time he might have had with a hectic round of self-imposed duties. Such as this one: a call on Sergei's daughter to express his condolences. It ought to fill the time between now and tonight's round of appointments and paperwork. And the time wouldn't be totally wasted. She was, after all, politically influential.

The wind gusted as he turned into Miriam Ortega's street, and he cursed as he nearly lost his cap. Then the gust died and he straightened his cap, glancing around at his surroundings.

The street skirted the broad estuary of the Alph, running down to a seawall and the azure, white-capped harbor. This was one of Prescott City's oldest residential districts, and the houses were on the small side but well-built, mostly of stone and wood, as first-wave houses tended to be. High-rises and fused cermacrete came later, as did the premium on space which would have doomed the large old native trees surrounding the houses. The architecture was vaguely neo-Tudor, and he suspected it had developed locally; it certainly fit the materials and the setting.

He drew a deep, lung-filling breath of the salt-tinged air and decided he'd been right to take the time to walk. Sensory deprivation was an ever-present danger in space; it had probably begun to catch up with him. In the midst of artificiality, the mind tended to turn inward on itself. His native Old Terra might be out of reach, but here he could at least touch the soil of a world humans had made their own.

A few children were at play, and at the sight of them a shadow chilled his mind just as the low-flying clouds periodically blocked out the warmth of Zephrain A. A small boy looked up and smiled at him. Trevayne hurried on.

Miriam Ortega's house wasn't far from the seawall. He stepped through the old-fashioned gate in the low, stone wall along the street, noticing the faint rim of salt clinging to the seaward stones. He climbed the steps and rang for admittance, and the door swung open.

The woman in the doorway was in her middle to late thirties, he decided. She was of medium height and rather sturdy build, with thick black hair pulled back in a severe style which accentuated her high cheekbones. Those cheekbones reminded Trevayne of Sergei, but the rest of her features, including the strongly curved nose, seemed to owe more to Sergei's late wife. Ruth Ortega had been from New Sinai, and her genetic heritage was strong in her daughter's face. Miriam Ortega, he thought, was no beauty.

"Ms. Ortega?"

"Yes. You must be Admiral Trevayne. Your yeoman called earlier today. Won't you come in?" Her voice was husky but firm. Though she seemed somber, there was no quaver.

She led him down a short hallway to a sitting room whose large, many-paned window overlooked the street. Though not messy, the room looked very lived-in. It was lined with old-style bookshelves, and an easel with paints and brushes stood near the window. A desk sat to one side, built around a functional data terminal and utilitarian tape and data chip racks.

"Do you paint, Ms. Ortega?" He gestured briefly at the easel.

"Only as an off-and-on hobby. No real talent, I'm afraid." They sat down and she lit a cigarette. "I'm going to give it up this summer—smoking, that is, not painting. Right now, though, I seem to need all the bad habits I've got to see me through."

Trevayne was uncomfortably reminded of his reason for coming. He cleared his throat.

"Ms. Ortega, the last time I talked to your father, he spoke of you. He said he wanted me to meet you. I deeply regret that we're finally meeting under these circumstances. But please accept my condolences for your loss. Believe me, I share it. Your father was, in many ways, one of the finest officers I've ever served under."

God, he thought. I didn't intend to sound so formal; it's

almost stilted. But what can one say? I've never been at my best dealing with human tragedy. Including my own.

Miriam Ortega inhaled smoke and let it trickle out. "You know, Admiral, I think Dad was a bit disappointed to have produced possibly the most unmilitary offspring in the Federation, but I managed to soak up enough of his attitudes to understand him. However easygoing he sometimes seemed, he felt very strongly about certain things. One of them was the Federation, and another was his concept of what TFN service meant. He used to quote some ancient saying about placing your body in harm's way, between the horror of war and those you're sworn to protect. He could imagine no higher calling." Her face had worn an inward look, but now she looked up at Trevayne and he could almost feel the unconquerable vitality she radiated. When she spoke again, her voice was still controlled, but the words were vibrant.

"Dad died the way he would have wanted to. I can't deny I'm grieving for him, but at the risk of seeming callous, I can't honestly say I feel sorrow. Sorrow isn't big enough . . . there's no room for pride in it!"

Trevayne was startled by how closely she'd paralleled his own earlier thoughts. But beyond that, he suddenly wondered how he could have thought this woman unexceptional-looking even for a moment. She wasn't conventionally pretty, no; but her face was a strikingly vivid and expressive one, uniquely her own. She was like no one else.

For an instant he wanted to reach out to her and tell her of his own loss. She was the sort of person who inspired confidences. But no, he had no right to burden her with his problems. And he wasn't sure he was ready to expose his own wounds.

"I know you were close to your father," he said. "I recall him mentioning that you moved out here when he was first posted to Zephrain."

"I suppose my closeness to him was a form of overcompensation. I didn't see much of him when I was young—he was in space a lot, and Mother played a much bigger role in raising me. Whenever he was around, he did his best to turn me into a tomboy." Her mobile features formed a rueful smile. "Some would say it took. Anyway, you're right about my coming out here. It was just after my divorce. I was in the mood for a change of scenery, and Mother had died just before he was out-posted; he was still taking it pretty hard."

She broke off for a moment, drawing on her cigarette. Her face was briefly thoughtful before she shrugged and looked up again.

"I had a law degree from New Athens and reasonably good references, so I was able to establish myself here on Xanadu. I found I liked it here. What started as a 'stay close to Dad' sort of thing turned into something else entirely, in a sense. I landed a position with one of the better firms—Bernbach, de Parma, and Leong—and suddenly I was one of the old hands. That doesn't take long here in the Rim, you know. And our firm's always been heavily into local politics, which is how I ended up involved in the formation of the provisional government." Trevayne nodded, though he suspected that wasn't the half of it. Suddenly she looked self-deprecating and waved her cigarette dismissively.

"Here I am running off at the mouth about myself when I've got the most famous man in the Rim sitting in my living room! Just bringing your battlegroup all the way out here made you a hero to these people, you know. Since the battle, you've become even more of one, if that's possible! I'm probably boring you stiff. . . ."

"No, no," Trevayne denied. "Far from it. In fact, you were just coming to something I need to know more about. I'm still not too clear about the origins of your provisional government."

"No?" She regarded him thoughtfully for a moment. "How much do you know about Xanadu's history, Admiral?"

"Only the bare-bones outline from the handbook, I'm afraid."

"Then you know Xanadu was settled during the Fourth Interstellar War when the Navy built the Fleet base. What you may not realize is just what that meant for the makeup of our population. There was a tremendous amount of military construction going on sixty years ago, and that required a large labor force. People came from all over the Federation, and today's population is about as racially mixed as you'll find anywhere. Which—" a sudden smile

"—is probably one reason I fit in so well! Anyway, the point is that this isn't one of the planets settled by closeknit ethnic or national groups. To govern themselves, this polyglot crew needed a simple pyramidal structure to interact on. Xanadu is divided into prefectures, which are grouped into districts, above which are provinces. Each prefecture elects a representative to the district assembly. The district assemblies each select one representative to the provincial assemblies, which each send one member to the Planetary Council. There's also a popularly elected president, who appoints the judiciary. There's a lot more to it, of course, but that's the basic idea." As democratic systems went, Trevayne reflected, it owed more to the French than to the American model.

"Actually, it's worked pretty well," she said. "The planet has taken on a sort of uniformity in diversity. The Xandies are probably on the way to developing what the anthropologists call a 'planetary ethnicity.' " Seeing his puzzled look, she elaborated. "People from Xanadu are called 'Xandies.' It's not a slur," she added quickly. "We call ourselves that." He noted the shift from third to first person.

"Anyway," she continued, "the pro-rebel party here was extremely small and—partly as a result of being so alienated from the Xandy mainstream, I suppose—extremely militant. Right after word of the mutinies arrived, a gang of fanatics tossed a bomb which killed the president and several high-ranking members of the government . . . not to mention a good number of innocent bystanders." She grimaced. "The chief conspirators fled off-planet and got as far as Aotearoa. I was a member of the delegation sent to arrange their extradition, and, in the course of the discussions, it became clear that we needed some sort of intersystem authority to deal with any further terrorist acts locally, since we were completely isolated from Old Terra. The result was the provisional government, which includes Zephrain and several of the nearer systems—the most populous and highly-developed ones in the Rim. Brilliant improvisation!" She beamed at him in mock self-satisfaction. "Dad's support gave it some teeth, but it's still pretty chaotic."

"Yes. Your father and I talked about this. As I see it, the

problem is that the Rim is on its own indefinitely. We need a Rim-wide provisional government, if only to perform the kind of day-to-day functions that the Federation always provided. But it isn't only day-to-day matters . . . we've handed the rebels a setback, but we haven't heard the last of them. And it's only a matter of time before the Tangri Corsairs take advantage of this civil war to start raiding again." He rose and began pacing as he went on. "I said to your father that we may as well be all the Federation that's left . . . and I wasn't just being dramatic. We're isolated to an extent that no one in the government has ever dreamed of, much less planned for! Thank God we've got a loyalist provisional government to work with." He stopped suddenly in the middle of the room and looked at her and realized that she'd been watching him intently.

"Ms. Ortega, a while back you said something about not wishing to seem callous. Well, neither do I. But I must tell you that what I said earlier about sharing your loss was meant not just on a personal level. The fact is, I'd planned to have your father, as TFN senior officer, declared emergency governor-general of the Rim systems. It's legally defensible, but without support from local leaders, it would probably do more harm than good. With the contacts he'd built up in his years out here. . . ." His voice trailed off.

"Sorry," he said. "Didn't mean to get carried away. And it's all a matter of might-have-been now that he's dead."

Miriam Ortega's expression had become even more intent. Now her eyes flashed.

"No! It still makes sense—beautiful sense, politically as well as militarily. Your idea of a 'governor-general' is perfect. He'd represent the Federation, so he'd provide a focus for loyalist sentiment. And he'd give the provisional government exactly what it lacks: a strong executive. And . . . we've got the perfect man for the position."

Trevayne looked at her levelly. "Me," he said, slightly more as a statement than a question.

"It's got to be you," she said emphatically. "As the ranking TFN officer in the Rim, you're the only possible choice. And remember what I said earlier; your prestige couldn't be higher."

Neither of them had really noticed the courtesy call

turning into a political conference, but that, Trevayne realized, was exactly what it had become. He'd already reached the same conclusions, but he'd needed to hash out the problems and objections with someone. And in the loneliness of supreme command, there had been no one.

"I can't do it alone," he began. "I don't know these people . . ."

"But I do," the woman said flatly.

Two pairs of dark-brown eyes met, and they were allies.

"I can't just make the proclamation out of the blue, though." He resumed his pacing. "That would defeat the whole purpose of involving the Rim leadership. I need to meet the key people in this provisional government and arrange for a statement of solidarity from them to follow the announcement. And we need to set up an interim legislative assembly to handle inter-systemic statutory matters. Just the inflation that's bound to overtake a wartime economy will require a mass of bread-and-butter amendments to practically all Federation statutes that specify monetary amounts. . . ."

"Good point," Miriam interjected. She cocked her head to one side and looked at him. "I must say, for a professional military man you seem to have quite a good grasp of these things."

"I've read a little history." He gave a deprecatory half-smile. "But as I was saying, I need to meet with the loyal leadership unofficially, so it probably wouldn't be a good idea to do it at Government House. . . ."

"Why not here?" she asked.

Trevayne stopped in midpace. "Why not, indeed? Can you contact the people I need to talk to?" She nodded. "As to when . . . my schedule isn't too flexible. I don't know how much longer I'll be able to stay dirtside." No more than a few days, he thought. Maybe after the trip to Gehenna. . . .

"How about the day after tomorrow, at 1000 hours?"

"Day after tomorrow?" he echoed faintly, staring at her.

"Well," she said reasonably, "these people are scattered all around the planet. I may not be able to get them all together by tomorrow."

He nodded slowly. It was a new sensation for him to find himself caught in someone else's slipstream.

"We won't have time to bring in anybody from off-planet," she was saying, "but at least Bryan MacFarland—he's an Aotearoan—is already in Prescott City. And, of course, Barry de Parma—he's a senior partner in my firm and he's got a finger in every political pie on the planet. And . . ."

"Make a list. I'll need a briefing on each of them. It shouldn't take too long to . . ." His voice trailed off as he looked at the clock. "Bloody Goddamned hell!" he exploded. "Er . . . excuse me." She choked down a laugh as he adjusted his wrist communicator. "Genji?"

"Admiral? I was trying to decide whether or not to call you."

"Genji, I'm going to be at Ms. Ortega's a bit longer than I expected. You'd better postpone tonight's appointments. And don't schedule anything for day after tomorrow, at least not in the morning or early afternoon."

Two days later, they were once again alone in her sitting room, this time among a litter of scattered chairs and heaped ashtrays. He waved a hand vaguely before his face, as if to brush away the canopy of tobacco smoke. Aside from the chairs and ashtrays, the room was much as before, except for the cloth that covered the easel.

"Well," Miriam said, "I think you've done it."

"You had as much to do with it as I did," Trevayne demurred.

"No, it was you. You didn't just win them over to the idea, you overwhelmed them with it. When you announce the Rim Provisional Government, they'll come through right on schedule—and they'll do it because they know you're right. We'll reconvene the current provisional government as a sort of committee of the whole to organize the Rim Legislative Assembly, then invite all the Rim systems to send representatives."

"Good. In fact, I'd like you to move ahead on setting that up right now, but the public announcement is going to have to wait a week or so."

"A week?" She cocked her head to one side thoughtfully. "No problem. I'll go ahead and get the messages out—they're going to take a month or so to reach some of the more distant systems—but why wait that long for the initial announcement? The provisional government can be ready to go in two or three days."

"I know. But for now I have to go to the R&D Station, which means a flight to Gehenna, of course. My chief of staff is organizing a project out there—one that's at least as important to the survival of the Rim as what we've started at this end."

"Oh? Ready to start producing new weapons?"

"How the devil did you know that?" Trevayne stared at her, reminding himself once more never to underestimate this woman.

"What else would you be doing on that dust ball?" she asked dryly. Then she shook her head at him. "Don't worry—I won't mention a word to anyone. But every Xandy knows what Zephrain RDS has been up to for the last forty years or so, you know. Not that it matters too much, I suppose; it's hardly likely to get into the rebel news channels, now is it?"

"I suppose not," he admitted with a reluctant smile. "On the other hand, good security is as much a set of mind as anything else, so I'd rather not discuss it just now. And I'd appreciate your keeping mum about it."

"Don't worry, I will," she assured him.

"Thanks." He glanced at the clock and stood, picking up his cap. "I've got to go—my shuttle's waiting at Abu'said—but I'll be in touch directly I get back. I'll want your help on the finishing touches to the proclamation."

"Try and keep me away from it!" She also rose, facing him. "You know, I really believe we're going to pull this off."

"So do I. It's not easy to feel pessimistic around you! Besides, I was impressed by your colleagues. I thought I hit it off particularly well with the MacFarland chap."

"Yes, I was sure you'd like him. He even sounds like you."

Trevayne almost choked. That God-awful Anzac twang?! Then he threw back his head and laughed for the first time in far too long. She blinked at him in momentary startlement, then burst out laughing, too. And then his elbow brushed the easel, and the cloth slipped off.

"Oh, shit," Miriam said quietly.

Trevayne gazed at the charcoal sketch for a long moment, his laughter dying, his face turning thoughtful. Then he eyed her quizzically.

"Do I really look that grim?"

"Yup," she replied, not quite her usual brassy self, but standing her ground. He took a closer look.

"I suppose I've never thought of myself as looking that . . . harsh."

" 'Harsh' isn't the word I'd use. 'Tough' comes closer. You've got the sort of face that shows absolutely no vulnerability. And—" her voice was suddenly both gentle and bold "—that's a pity, because I think you're a very vulnerable man in a lot of ways. One who's been hurt." She stopped abruptly, as if she had surprised herself.

Trevayne looked at the sketch a moment longer, absorbing the closed-off expression her charcoal stick had captured and feeling her words sink under the edge of his armor. Then he turned to face her.

"Yes, I have . . ." he began, then stopped. Once more, he wanted to speak of how badly he'd been hurt. But he had to leave. Besides, he knew now that he would tell her everything when he saw her again . . . and, he realized with dawning surprise, that was enough. What really mattered was knowing there was someone he could talk freely to after so long.

"Ms. Ortega . . ."

"Miriam."

"Miriam. As I said, I'll be in contact when I return. And . . . I'll look forward to talking again."

"So will I, Admiral Trevayne."

"Ian."

"Ian." She smiled her vivid smile. They shook hands.

He left and walked up the street. There was a brisk wind off the harbor once more, but the day was cloudless. Some of the same children were playing along the street, and the same small boy smiled at him.

He smiled back.

SEPARATION OF POWERS

Genji Yoshinaka had never seen Sonja Desai so angry. To be honest, he couldn't swear he'd ever seen her display so much of *any* emotion.

"The Admiral must be out of his mind!" she muttered through clenched teeth. "No," she continued, answering herself before Yoshinaka could get a word in, "of course he's not. But we all know what a strain he's been under. . . ."

"Now, Sonja," Yoshinaka interrupted, all diplomacy, "you know the political rationale for what the Admiral is doing. We've discussed it often enough since arriving in the Rim. And if you feel so strongly about it, why didn't you voice your objections to him when he was on Gehenna?"

"Oh, yes, I've heard all the political arguments, and I'm only to happy to defer to the Admiral's judgment on *that* sort of thing." Her voice held an infinity of exasperation with politics and the other incomprehensible interactions of her fellow humans. "But," she continued, suddenly almost venomous, "I always assumed we were talking about some ceremonial parliamentary talkfest that would give the local political gasbags an outlet for their self-importance while we get on with the important work. I never dreamed that we were going to be expected to take the farce seriously!" She glared across the room at the cluster of civilians . . . and, it seemed to Yoshinaka, at one of them in particular.

The room she glared across was deep in the heavily-shielded core of Government House in Prescott City. The shielding—like the architecture, which was what public buildings had looked like in the days of the Fourth Interstellar War—reflected the structure's origins. Its security aspects had been largely habit, given an enemy from whom nuclear warheads were more to be expected than espionage, but they'd made this particular conference room the natural site for Trevayne's first joint meeting with both his military staff and the leaders of the newly-inaugurated Rim Provisional Government. Both groups now stood awaiting him . . . and, as if by gravitational attraction, had clumped themselves into opposite corners of the large chamber.

The thought of security got Desai off to a fresh start.

"Damn it, Genji," she said, low-voiced and intense, "I don't really mind the idea of setting up a civilian government for the Rim; I suppose I wouldn't even *want* us to have to carry the whole burden of administration, which we would under martial law. But I simply can't believe that the Admiral really plans to grant security clearances to the members of this 'Grand Council' who're directly connected with the war effort. Is that even *legal?*"

"Matter of opinion," Yoshinaka opined. "He's doing it while wearing his Governor-General's hat, which puts it in what might tactfully be called an ill-defined area of the law. As he's fond of saying, the Cabinet can tell him if they don't like it—after contact is reestablished."

Desai waved a hand impatiently. "That's not really the point anyway. You haven't been out to Gehenna, but you know what's at stake here. We're not talking about some kind of minor engineering refinements! We're talking about a whole new order of technology!" She paused and took a breath. "I've got to make him *see* that we don't dare compromise security on this thing . . . not after what's happened on Gehenna."

Yoshinaka nodded soberly. He could understand her feelings, after what she'd been through mere days before. But, as always, he found her intensity oppressive. She had no lightness in her. And this vehemence wasn't like her at all.

"I've got to make him *see!*" she repeated. "Surely it must be clear now that he can't trust these . . . colonials!"

Yoshinaka was shocked. Abrasive Desai might be, but

he'd never heard a remark even remotely like that from her. It didn't even make sense; her own ancestors hadn't exactly evolved from the primordial ooze of Nova Terra! And Sonja Desai *never* talked nonsense. What was her problem?

He drew himself up slightly. (He still had to look upward at her, as he did at most people.) "I think," he began, in his best conversation-closing voice, "that the Admiral is committed to the course he's taken, Sonja. And I think you missed your chance to talk him out of it when you had him to yourself on Gehenna. And I *definitely* think that, in spite of what's happened since then, it would do far more harm than good to raise the point at this time, in this company. I strongly advise against it."

Desai's rejoinder was lost forever as an old-fashioned double door swung open and an usher intoned "The Governor-General!"

Trevayne was wearing an expensively-tailored civilian suit, making clear which of his figurative "hats" he was wearing. The point was not lost on the officers and politicians as they took their places on opposite sides of the large conference table. The glance he shared with Miriam Ortega, on the other hand, went unnoticed by almost everyone.

"Please be seated, ladies and gentlemen," Trevayne invited, all affability. They did so, military crispness opposite civilian casualness, and Miriam absently lit a cigarette.

"Filthy habit," Desai muttered to Yoshinaka, just below the threshold of public audibility. Miriam, almost directly across the table from her, raised a single eloquent eyebrow and blandly put out the cigarette.

Introductions and other preliminaries completed, Trevayne turned to specifics.

"We all know what's occasioned this meeting," he began, "and I know everyone shares my relief that Captain Desai is able to be with us." A murmur of agreement ran around the table. Trevayne resumed, addressing Desai. "Sonja, I apologize for having to bring you here from Gehenna on such short notice, particularly straight from sickbay." He indicated her left arm, still immobilized even though the wound was, by the standards of modern medicine, minor. "But we need your input, as you were closer to the incident than anyone . . . closer than you would have liked, I daresay!"

Desai didn't share in the general chuckle. "Thank you for your concern, Admiral," she replied. "But there is one preliminary point which I feel it is my duty to raise before the discussion enters areas of sensitive military information. I refer to the matter of security . . . especially in light of what has just happened on Gehenna."

Yoshinaka groaned silently.

Everyone at the table—everyone in the Zephrain system, for that matter—knew what had happened, only hours after Trevayne had left Gehenna to return to Xanadu and announce the formation of the Provisional Government. The security advantages of an uninhabitable planet were part of the reason Zephrain RDS was located on Gehenna. But, inevitably, a city had grown up, under domes and burrowed beneath Gehenna's reddish sands, in response to the presence of the Station and a fair number of miners . . . a city whose lower levels had sheltered a surprisingly well-organized rebel underground with carefully-developed plans to sabotage the Station.

Still, the rebels had moved before they were quite ready, unable to resist the temptation of bagging Trevayne during his inspection tour. Desai's media disinformation concerning his departure schedule had prevented that, at least. He'd been in space when the rebels had struck, heavily armed and using access codes obtained by blackmail of certain key personnel.

Of course, they hadn't expected a walkover. The vicious, utterly unexpected boarding actions of the Theban War had cured the TFN of its habit of relegating small arms—and training in their use—to the Dark Ages and to such present-day Dark-Ages types as Marines. Side arms were now part of the service uniform . . . but they were laser side arms, ideal for space but subject to many inherent limitations on the ground, which was why hand-held laser weapons had never entirely supplanted slugthrowers. The rebel attackers had used slugthrowers . . . and antilaser aerosol grenades. Surprise had been nearly total, and the Station's upper levels had, for a time, resembled a scene from Hell. Desai herself had been caught in a surrounded office block, where she'd had good use for the personal combat training she had detested and never expected to use. But Marine quick-response teams had been on standing alert for Trevayne's visit and hadn't quite had time to stand down. Reinforcements had arrived—in combat zoots—before any crucial data or equipment had been destroyed, and no attackers were believed to have escaped. Damage had been extensive, however . . . especially to Desai's temper.

"And so," she concluded her description of the attack, "our schedules have been set back by weeks. I think this incident reveals a *very* serious security problem involving . . . certain elements of the Rim populations." The civilian side of the table was utterly quiet.

"I wonder," Desai finished, looking straight at Miriam, "if the Grand Councilor for Internal Security would perhaps care to comment on the fact that this conspiracy arose among the civilian population of Gehenna . . . without being detected."

At the head of the table, Trevayne frowned. Sonja was obviously in one of her moods . . . but he'd thought she had understood the necessity of tact in dealing with the Provisional Government. And she was being utterly unfair; Miriam hadn't even *held* the internal security portfolio at the time the attack took place, much less while it was being prepared. There hadn't been a Rim Provisional Government to hold it in!

But he couldn't dress Desai down publicly, for any of a number of reasons, not the least of which was that Miriam *had* to handle this on her own if she was to command any sort of respect from the military people. So he held his tongue and let her respond.

"First," she said, slowly and deliberately, to the room at large, "let me say that I share the Governor-General's relief that Captain Desai escaped serious injury, and that I deeply regret the casualties that occurred . . . casualties that might have been avoided if our people had been given a free hand to investigate certain early leads which were duly passed on to Navy security on Gehenna. Correct me if I'm wrong, Captain Desai, but I believe that this information was what led you to take the very sensible precaution of leaking a false itinerary for the Governor-

General's tour." Taking Desai's tight-lipped silence as confirmation, Miriam continued. "Jurisdiction over the civilian population of Gehenna has always been unclear. The Navy considers the entire planet a military reservation, and regards civilian law-enforcement officials as being there more or less in an advisory capacity. This is unfortunate, as local people with an intimate knowledge of local conditions would have access to sources of information beyond the normal compass of Navy security. They would be in a better position to ferret out the small lunatic fringe that I can't deny exists, and whose very powerlessness (as I've mentioned to the Governor-General) makes it more apt to reckless acts of violence. The solution is to give my new organization, representing the loyal mainstream of the Rim, full authority to police our own few renegades."

A confident rumble arose from the civilian side of the table. Miriam sat back and, after a moment's hesitation, lit a cigarette. She didn't—quite—blow the smoke in Desai's direction.

"Well," Trevayne said, stepping in to fill the gap before Desai could speak, "I think Ms. Ortega has raised some valid points. At the very least, we need to address the jurisdictional question posed by the civilian habitats on Gehenna . . . which, of course, didn't exist when the RDS was founded. Comments, anyone?"

Discussion proceeded without anything provocative from Desai. Trevayne, relieved, exchanged a quick smile with Miriam. No one but Yoshinaka noticed that Desai grew even stiffer than was her wont.

"I don't think your Captain Desai likes me very much."

Trevayne waved a negligent hand as he and Miriam walked together down the corridor after the meeting had broken up.

"Oh, don't feel singled out," he said airily. "I'm afraid Sonja's like that with everyone. It's just the way she is. Don't give it another thought."

"Maybe," Miriam replied dubiously.

HONOR

"Begin," the judge said, and Lieutenant Mazarak unleashed a short, straight lunge in sixte.

Han's wrist flicked, brushing the blade to the outside, arm extending in a quick riposte in the same line. But he shortened to parry and fell back, and she followed, her mind almost blank as hand and eye and reflex carried the weight of her actions.

Back and forth, blades grating and slipping, dreamy thought coming in a curiously fleeting pattern. Few Hangchowese bothered with the ancient dueling sword, especially in its Western forms, and Han had never considered it herself until she'd been wounded. Yet it seemed she possessed a natural aptitude, and the elegant converse of steel suited her.

She disengaged and Mazarak pursued, pressing her cautiously, yet Han felt he was more defensive-minded, and she believed she had a better sense of point. She feinted above his hand, dropping her point to go in under his drawn guard, but he parried like lightning and riposted in octave. She put his point aside—barely—with a counterparry, and he tried a quick double disengage in sixte. But she was ready, seizing his blade and carrying it low and outside in a quick bind that flashed instantly into a fleche. Her epee snaked home as she passed to his left, and the scoring light lit.

"*Touché*," the judge intoned, and they drew apart, breathing just a bit more heavily and saluting as they prepared to reengage for the next point.

Han emerged from the salle, mask in hand and épée under her arm, shaking her sweat-damp hair. She hadn't had it back all that long, and she rather enjoyed the feeling.

"Han," Magda Petrovna said, "that's the silliest sport ever invented."

"Come now, Magda! Its origins were anything but silly."

"Maybe." Magda tucked a proprietary arm through Jason Windrider's. "But I'll settle *my* quarrels decently . . . with pistols at twenty meters, thank you!"

"Russians have so little soul," Han mourned. "It's fun, Magda. Not like judo, but I had to get back in shape somehow, and I thought I'd try something new." She shrugged. "I like it."

"Well, it certainly seems to've gotten you back on your feet, Admiral, sir," Jason Windrider teased.

"It does, does it, *Commodore?*" Han asked deflatingly.

Windrider stroked his new insignia and grinned. "Just trying to keep up, Admiral. And you and Magda haven't had your stars all that long."

"No, we haven't," Han said more somberly, glancing at the heavy braid on Magda's cuff.

When she was in uniform, her own sleeves matched Magda's and it made her uneasy. She'd been confident enough when they made her a commodore—but that was before Cimmaron.

Yet the Republic had no choice. It had paid heavily in ships and personnel for its string of victories, and disproportionately so in the flag officers aboard their easily identified command ships.

Nor had all of them died victorious. There were still no formal avenues of communication between the Republic and the Rim Systems, but Vice Admiral Trevayne (and what a shock to discover he was not only alive but in Zephrain!) had supplied a casualty list, and there were few Republican survivors. Neither Analiese Ashigara nor Colin Trevayne was among them, and Han wondered how Trevayne could live with what he'd done. The question held a dread fascination, for he, at least, had demonstrated just how far duty and honor could carry a person.

But the Republic's heavy butcher's bills explained the rapid promotions. Han had been a commodore for less than eighteen months, and ten of them had been spent as Daffyd Llewellyn's patient. What he'd been pleased to call a "fractured" femur had required massive surgical reconstruction, and the antigerone therapies had their disadvantages. To stretch the life span, they slowed the biological clock—including healing speeds. The quick-heal drugs which were part of the doomwhale's pharmaceutical cornucopia could offset that, but not after such rad poisoning as Han had survived, which had made her a semi-permanent fixture at the hospital, though she'd bullied Llewellyn into out-patient status the moment she began therapy.

Magda had been only too glad to turn over the Cimmaron command. And, having experienced the restrictions of a dirtside appointment for the last eleven months, Han didn't blame her at all.

"At least you look healthy enough jumping around with that ridiculous thing." Magda's teasing voice pulled Han back from her thoughts.

"Thanks. BuPers thinks so, too—I got confirmation of my new status yesterday, and I'm back in space next month! I'm going to miss Chang, though."

"I imagine so," Magda agreed, and Han hid a smile as her friends exchanged glances. She knew they both resented the fact that Windrider's promotion made him too senior to remain Magda's chief of staff even while it delighted them both as proof of his professional reputation and future.

"Who's replacing him?" Magda asked after a moment.

"Bob Tomanaga. He's cleared for active duty again, too."

"Tomanaga?" Magda repeated.

"I know—he worried me once, but I was wrong. It's just the way Bob is. He can't seem to be discouraged or even detached no matter what." Han shook her head. "I don't know why he's so round-eyed."

"Certainly not," Windrider agreed, grinning disrespectfully.

"Well," Han paused by her waiting skimmer, "back to the salt mines. You two will join me for supper, won't you?"

"I will," Magda agreed with a slight pout, "and Jason

may. His group's spacing out with Kellerman, you know."

"I'd forgotten." Han frowned, rummaging through her orderly memory. Kellerman was slated to carry out another probe of the rear approaches to the Rim Systems. The lifeless warp lines there were ill-suited to sustained operations, and neither Han—nor anyone else, it seemed—expected much to come of the probes. But there'd be enough skirmishing to satisfy the newsies, and the Fleet was stretched thin at the moment. The Rim had been demoted to secondary status while the frontline systems were stabilized and the new shipyards got into production.

"It's all right, Magda," she said finally. "Anton and the dockyard are squabbling over *Unicorn's* repairs. He's not going anywhere without his flagship, and the yard won't turn her loose for at least another forty hours. You'll both have time for supper."

"And for a little something else, God willing," Windrider murmured as he opened the hatch for Han. His eyes twinkled wickedly, and Magda actually blushed. "But we *will* be there for supper, Admiral. Won't we, Admiral?"

"Unless I brig you for disrespect," Magda growled, and tossed Han a salute. "Bye, Han. See you this evening." And the skimmer swept away.

"Well, Chang, I guess this is goodbye."

"Yes, sir." The bulky captain faced her over her desk, cap under one arm, unreadable as ever, and Han studied him carefully. They liked and respected one another, but there was an inner core to him which she had never cracked. Not that it mattered, she thought with sudden affection. However he ticked, he was the most utterly reliable subordinate a woman could want.

No, not subordinate. Assistant. Better yet, colleague.

"Chang, I won't embarrass you by saying how much I'll miss you," she said slowly, "but I *will* say that *Direhound* couldn't find a better skipper. And—" she looked into his eyes "—that no one ever had a better chief of staff."

"Thank you, sir," he said. "It's been a pleasure, Admiral. I—" He broke off suddenly, and gave a tiny shrug.

Han nodded, surprised less that he'd stopped than that he'd spoken in the first place. It was like him, she thought. So very like him.

"Very well, Captain." She held out her hand with the traditional blessing. "Good fortune and good hunting, Chang."

"Thank you, sir," he said gruffly, gripping her hand hard.

She squeezed once, then stepped back as Tsing turned to leave. But he halted at the door of her office and placed his cap very carefully on his head, then turned and threw her an Academy-sharp salute.

Han was startled. Navy regs prohibited headgear indoors dirtside, and it was officially impossible to salute without it. But her own hand rose equally sharply, and Tsing turned on his heel and vanished.

Good bye, Tsing Chang, she thought wistfully. *You never doubted me during the mutiny. You fought with me at Cimmaron. You saved my life. I suppose that's all I really need to know about you, isn't it . . . my friend?*

"Well, Admiral," Robert Tomanaga crossed Han's office without even a limp to betray his prosthetic leg, "it's a new staff, but it looks good."

"Not entirely new. We've got you and David from the old team. That's a pretty good survival rate, considering."

"I suppose so, sir," he agreed, but his tone was a clear rejection of her implied self-criticism, and she shook her head mentally. Bob Tomanaga's voice and face were as communicative as a printed message and it felt strange to always know precisely what he was thinking, but right now he meant what everyone meant whenever she let her guard down. No one else seemed to think the casualties might have been lighter . . . if only she'd been more clever.

She put the thought aside and leaned back in her chair, considering her new staff. Aside from Reznick, now a lieutenant senior grade, whom she'd been determined to have, she hardly knew any of them, but Bob was right: they looked good.

Her new ops officer, Commander Stravos Kollentai was small, slight, and arrogant—the perfect fighter jock—but his efficiency reports were excellent and he radiated an aura of almost oppressive energy and competence. Her astrogator, Lieutenant Commander Richard Heuss, was a quiet fellow with fair hair and eyes like gray shutters. He said little, but his navigation was beautiful to see. And finally there was the new staff slot filled by Lieutenant Irene Jorgensen: battlegroup intelligence officer. Fleet had decided to remove the intelligence function from the ops officer's jurisdiction, which made sense, Han supposed, given the type of war they were fighting, but it felt strange to have the spooks speaking for themselves on the staff. On the other hand, the tall, scrawny lieutenant hid a lurking humor behind her muddy brown eyes and appeared to have a computer memory bank concealed somewhere about her unprepossessing anatomy.

"Have the official orders come through yet, Admiral?" Tomanaga asked, breaking her train of thought.

"Yes. Admiral Iskan will relieve me tomorrow and we'll move out to *da Silva*." Thank God. She'd been half-afraid the Admiralty would leave her here now that Cimmaron had been upgraded into what was clearly an admiral's billet even for the admiral-starved Republic.

"I see." Tomanaga frowned. "Any word on our destination, sir?"

"Not officially. But Fleet Ops whispered something about Rigel."

"Rigel, sir?" Tomanaga blinked.

"I think Fleet wants to keep an eye on Admiral Trevayne," Han said slowly, swinging her chair gently. "We're still not sure what happened, you know. I think someone's running a little scared over Zephrain RDS."

"Stupid of them, sir, if you'll forgive me," Tomanaga said.

"Oh? And on what do you base that pronouncement, Commander?"

"I don't think any 'mystery weapon' did in Admiral Ashigara, sir. The ops plan relied too much on surprise and ECM, and they screwed up when they tried a pincer. All it gave them was lousy coordination. That's why the diversion got chewed up when the main attack went wrong."

"And how did it go wrong?"

"I'm not certain," Tomanaga admitted, "but the survivors all agree BG 32 wasn't involved in the Gateway fighting till close to the end—so Trevayne must've been busy destroying the carriers. But carriers are faster than monitors, and Admiral Ashigara's fighters had more firepower than BG 32, which means that somehow or other he spotted them despite their ECM and clobbered them before they launched. It's the only answer I can think of, sir."

"So it was bad luck?"

"Maybe," Tomanaga said, "but it was compounded by bad planning. They should've concentrated in Bonaparte and taken everything in through the new warp point to pin the *defenders* against the Gateway. Then we'd've had tactical command exercised in one place over only one force that could've withdrawn down a single warp line. As it was, both COs were out of contact and neither could cut and run as long as that might leave the other unsupported—a classic example of defeat in detail, *triggered* by bad luck, but not caused by it."

"You could be right," Han admitted, for she'd pondered much the same thoughts herself. "But why not new weapons, as well?"

"The time factor, sir. I don't care if Trevayne is a special emissary from God Himself, it takes time to turn research into hardware. That's why we should hit them again now—immediately. Forget the border. We've got the Rump on the run; keep them there with feints and go for Zephrain now, before they really do get new hardware on line."

"I'm inclined to agree, Bob. Unhappily, grand strategy is the First Space Lord's job. And whether you're right or not, it makes sense to picket the old Rigelian and Arachnid systems, whatever the Rim is or isn't up to."

"Agreed, sir, but a monitor battlegroup with carrier support is hardly a 'picket.' It's a vest-pocket task force, and one cut for a mighty big vest. We'd be better employed striking directly at Zephrain rather than worrying about what they may do to us." Tomanaga sounded unwontedly serious, even worried. "If we *don't* hit them pretty quick, we may find ourselves up against exactly what we're afraid of right now. Give Trevayne time to get the new systems on line, and . . ." He shrugged eloquently.

"Consider your point made," Han said softly. "Write up a staff appreciation and we'll sit on it long enough to see where they send us. If we wind up out near Rigel and we still agree you know what you're talking about, we'll update it and fire it off. Fair enough?"

"Yes, sir."

"Good. Meanwhile, tidy up here and we'll transfer out to *Bernardo da Silva.*"

"Yes, sir." Tomanaga left, and Han frowned pensively down at the desk she would delightedly turn over to Jack Iskan in two days, wishing she disagreed with her chief of staff.

"Another day with nothing to report, sir." Tomanaga sounded disgusted. "I don't see why they're so damned mesmerized by the need to picket the Rim. Go in now and smash 'em up fast—take some casualties if we have to, but get it over with—and we won't need to scatter a quarter of our available strength out over the damned approaches."

Han tried and failed to imagine Tsing Chang unburdening himself with equal frankness. It was strange how well she got along with someone so different from Tsing. Just as strange as to remember that she'd once distrusted Tomanaga's enthusiasm.

"Well, Bob, we've sent off your appreciation," she said calmly. "In fact, we've done everything we can short of taking it upon ourselves to attack single-handedly."

"I suppose so, sir," Tomanaga agreed sourly, "but the crews are beginning to go stale."

"I know." Battlegroup 24 had maintained its long, slow patrol of the old Rigelian warp lines, with an occasional foray into dead Arachnid space, for almost five months without a sign of the enemy. They'd encountered a single Tangri battle-cruiser, but the horseheads had shown admirable restraint and declined to match themselves against four monitors, two fleet carriers, two light carriers, and four escort destroyers.

Yet that very boredom had been a godsend for Han, and she would have been the first to admit it. Patrol duty wasn't glamorous, but at least it let someone a bit skittish over reassuming a space command ease back into it. Her worries had faded as she grappled with her new responsibilities, and she could look in her mirror now and recognize herself again.

"Well," she said finally, "let's find something to occupy them, then." She swiveled her chair down and frowned—her equivalent of raging consternation—and tapped her terminal. "You've seen this from *Shokaku*?"

"That freighter, sir?" The light carrier's recon fighters had found the remains of a freighter drifting erratically around the star Orpheus.

"Yes. Does anything about it strike you as odd?"

"You mean aside from what she was doing there to begin with?"

"Exactly. There haven't been any inhabited planets in the Orpheus System since the Alliance dusted the Arachnids out eighty years ago. I suppose her skipper *might've* taken a short cut, but it's hard to believe anyone would try it unescorted this close to Tangri space."

"But she's here, sir, and she *was* looted."

"True," Han nodded. "But did you examine the passenger list *Shokaku* pulled out of her computers?"

"Well, no, sir. Why?"

"They recovered the bodies of all twenty-five crewmen," Han said.

"So? The horseheads don't take prisoners, sir."

"True. But the passenger and crew sections were undamaged. Whoever attacked raked the drive and command sections with primaries and needle beams, then looted the holds and finished off the crew in the process."

"Yes, sir. Typical Tangri work." Tomanaga was puzzled. Clearly his admiral had noticed something he had missed.

"Except this, Bob. According to the passenger manifest, there were fourteen young women aboard that ship. So where are *their* bodies?"

"What?" Tomanaga rose and moved to her desk. "May I, sir?" he asked, laying his hand on the swiveled terminal.

"Certainly."

He turned the screen and peered at it thoughtfully, mind racing.

"It doesn't make sense," he muttered. "Only the women are missing."

"Exactly. And the Tangri have never shown any particular interest in kidnaping young, female Terrans."

"Yes, sir. So it had to be someone with a use for them. . . . What about ransom? Were any of them wealthy?"

"On a tramp freighter?" Han shook her head. "Navy nurses and doctors from Zephrain."

"So whoever hit her didn't hail from the Rim, either." Tomanaga frowned. "I don't like it."

"Neither do I. Nor, I suppose, did those passengers and crewmen."

"Sorry, sir. I meant I don't like the implications. Whoever did it isn't based at Orpheus—we swept the place with a fine-toothed comb. That means inter-system raiding. And that, sir, means there's a joker in the deck. If we spot anyone, we can't know whether it's the Rim or these pirates."

"Perhaps." Han cleared her screen and a warp chart flickered to life. She tapped it with a stylus. "Here's our patrol area. Here's Orpheus." She touched a light dot to one side of their patrol area. "Now, everything Rimward of Orpheus belongs to the Rim, and whoever it is can't operate from there, because both sides watch those warp points like hawks. And he can't operate from here—" her arcing stylus indicated their patrol area "—or *we'd*'ve spotted him. But that leaves this warp network over here, see?" She tapped the screen. "It connects with Orpheus from the back . . . and it also extends all the way to here. . . ."

"My God! Right into our rear areas!"

"Precisely. I don't know who they are or where they came from, but someone is raiding civilian traffic from a base somewhere along this warp network. There's nothing much out here but outposts and mining colonies—no heavy traffic, sparse populations, slow communications. They could be almost anywhere. Take over a mining colony and the nav beacons and you control all communications with the system. Who's to know you've done it?"

"Then we'd better get a drone off immediately, sir."

"Agreed. But what then? It'll take two months just to reach Cimmaron. Then two more months for Admiral Iskan to reply or relay it—four months, minimum, for whoever it is to go on doing whatever they're doing. No, we have to deal with it ourselves."

"But, sir, this area—" he indicated the suspect warp lines "—is outside our patrol area. It'd take us—what, five weeks?—just to get there, and it'd mean abandoning the picket. I don't think the Admiralty would like that."

"The Admiralty isn't out here, Bob: we are. We won't take the entire battlegroup, anyway. We'll take one other monitor, *Shokaku*, and two of the cans and leave the rest here under Commodore Cruett. I suppose I could detach Cruett, but it's my responsibility if decisions have to be made."

"Yes, sir. But—"

"Bob, we're going. We're supposed to prevent things like this, war or no war. Understood?"

"Yes, sir."

"Good. Then get together with Stravos and rough out a set of orders for Cruett. And ask Dick to lay out the best search pattern for us. I don't want to be gone any longer than we have to be."

"Aye, aye, sir." He left and Han cocked her chair back once more, studying the star map and disliking her thoughts.

TRNS *Bernardo da Silva* plowed slowly through space, accompanied by her sister monitor *Franklin P. Eisenhower* and the light carrier *Shokaku*. Two escort destroyers watched the rear while *Shokaku*'s recon fighters swept the detachment's projected track and flanks, and Rear Admiral Li Han sat on her palatial flag bridge, fingers steepled under her clean jaw line, contemplating her empty plot.

A month of cruising the suspect warp lines, and nothing. Was she on the wrong track? Had she made a major error—one that validated her earlier fears over her judgment? Her face was calm as she silently reviewed her discussions with Tomanaga, her endless perusal of dry facts with Irene Jorgensen. The data was there, she decided once more; only her response to it was suspect.

A bell chimed, and she roused, cocking an eyebrow at the com section as David Reznick bent over the battle code printer. He tore off the message flimsy and turned to her.

"Signal from *Shokaku*, sir. One of the fighters is onto something."

"I see." Han scanned the message. "Doesn't say much, does she?"

"No, sir. But her fighter's going in for a closer look. Shall I sound action stations, sir?"

"Not yet, Lieutenant. We're a good three hours behind

those fighters—we'll have time. Excuse me a moment."

Han summoned up the com image of Samuel Schwerin, her flag captain.

"Good morning, Sam," she greeted him. "*Shokaku*'s fighters have picked up something—no telling what yet—on our line of advance. They're going in for a closer look, but it'll take us about three hours to catch up with them, so I thought we might advance lunch to get it out of the way if we have to go to action stations."

"Certainly, sir. I'll see to it immediately."

"Thank you, Sam."

Reznick's printer chimed again as Han signed off, and she waited patiently. If using coded whisker lasers delayed communications, it also eliminated the chance of message interception and greatly reduced the likelihood of long-range detection. Then Reznick handed her the message, and her face tightened almost imperceptibly as she read it. She turned to Lieutenant Jorgensen.

"Irene," she said quietly, "punch up your shipping logs and double-check for me, please. According to *Shokaku*, this is what's left of a *Polaris*-class liner. I'm afraid it may be *Argosy Polaris*."

"Yes, sir," the lieutenant was punching keys, watching the data come up. "*Argosy Polaris*, sir. Two hundred passengers and a priority medical cargo. Reported overdue at Kariphos ten months ago."

"Damn," Han said softly.

"It's the *Polaris*, sir," Commander Tomanaga confirmed grimly, studying the drifting hulk on his screen. "Somebody ripped hell out of her, too. Must've been quick and dirty to keep her from even getting a drone away. Look at that." His finger indicated the relatively small punctures riddling the command section of the big liner.

"Primaries and needles," Han said flatly. "They knew she was armed—not that her popguns would've helped much. So they closed in, tractored her, and blew her command and com sections before she could yell for help."

"But how did they get close enough? And what's she doing way out here? We're six transits off the Stendahl-Kariphos route."

"I don't know how they fooled her master," Han said, "but getting her here wouldn't be hard. There's no damage to her drive pods. They just blasted the command deck and then gave whoever was left his options: surrender or see two hundred passengers vaporized. After that, they used the engine room controls to bring her out here so they could loot her at leisure. Not the approved technique, but workable as long as they were in company with someone with intact nav capabilities."

"Sounds reasonable." Tomanaga's words were calm; his face and tone weren't. "But it was sloppy to leave her intact. They should've blown her fusion plants or dropped her into the primary to hide the evidence."

"No, Bob. This is a lonely spot, and that's a hundred thousand tonnes of ship. Lots of spares and replacements to be scavenged out of her."

"Of course." Tomanaga shook his head. "Shall I send in the examination teams, sir?"

"Yes. And call away my cutter. I'm going too."

Han swam down the passage of the dead liner, her powerful lamp illuminating the splendid furnishing of first class—marred in spots by laser burns and occasional scars of pure vandalism. The raiders must have damped the power before they depressurized the hull, for the blast doors stood open. She'd seen one grisly corpse—a crewman dead of explosive decompression—and she was coldly certain they'd dumped atmosphere intentionally to kill any fugitives.

She turned a corner and spun gracefully, landing on her magnetized boot soles beside the Marine search party which had summoned her. Two troopers were busy sealing a transparent bubble to the bulkhead around a closed hatch.

"Afternoon, Admiral." Major Bryce saluted her, and she returned his salute, then shifted her magsoles to the deckhead, hanging like a weightless bat to watch over the shoulders of the work detail.

"This is the only hatch holding pressure, Major?"

"Yes, sir. We checked out all the others and came up empty"—he seemed unaware of his own grim double entendre—"but there's atmosphere on the other side of this one."

"How much longer, Major?"

"We've just about got her sealed in, sir." He gestured at the plastic airlock. "Soon's we get a little pressure in there, we'll crack the hatch. Not that it's going to make any difference to whoever sealed it."

Han nodded slowly within her helmet. After ten months, no one could possibly survive beyond that hatch.

"Ready, Major," a sergeant said.

"All right, Admiral," Bryce looked at Han, "would you like to go in?"

"Yes, Major. I would."

"Very good, sir." Bryce managed things smoothly, and Han found herself sandwiched between the looming combat zoots of a pair of Marine corporals as one of them fed power to the hatch from her zoot pack. The hatch slid open, and the plastic lock creaked as its over-pressure bled into the cabin. The corporals moved awkwardly to either side to permit Han to enter first, and she pushed off through the hatch.

It was a tomb.

The first things she saw in her helmet lamp were the rags and plastiseal packed into a pair of ragged holes; one of the primaries that took out the command deck had passed through this cabin. Someone had kept his wits about him to patch those holes so quickly, and the angle of the punctures might explain why the cabin hadn't been searched—they just about paralleled the passage outside, and the single beam had probably pierced at least a dozen suites. Much of first class must have died practically unknowing, and the raiders had probably assumed this cabin's occupants had done the same.

Her evaluation of the patches took only seconds; then she saw the bodies, and her lips twisted with rage.

Children. They were *children!*

She counted five of the huddled little shapes, peacefully arranged in the beds as if merely sleeping, and saw the body of a single adult—a young woman—at a desk to one side. A candle stub was glued to the desk with melted wax, and her head was a shattered ruin, wrought by the heavy-caliber needler death-locked in her hand.

Han looked away and felt her belly knot. There was no nausea—only a cold, deadly hatred for the beings who had wreaked this slaughter of the children she would never bear.

She mastered herself and bent over the stiff corpse of the unknown woman. There was an old fashioned memo pad magsealed to the desk, and Han eased it gently loose. Then she turned back to the lock.

"Dump the air, Major," she said, and for the first time she hated herself for sounding serene under pressure. "And transport the bodies to *da Silva*."

"Yes, sir." Bryce sounded wooden, and she realized he'd been watching his minute com screen; he'd seen everything his corporals' pickups had seen. "We'll be taking them back to Cimmaron, sir?"

"No, Major," Han said quietly. "It won't help their loved ones to see *this*. We'll try to identify them and then bury them in space."

"Yes, sir."

"I'm returning to the flagship, Major."

"Yes, sir. Shall I assign an escort?"

"No, Major. I'd rather be alone, thank you."

"Yes, sir."

Han looked up as Tomanaga entered her cabin. He'd seen the pictures of that cabin and knew his admiral well enough to sense the fury behind her calm demeanor, and he took the indicated chair silently, feeling his way through the storm front of her rage.

"You wanted me, sir?"

"Yes," she said calmly. She tapped the memo pad. "I'll want you to drop this off with Irene. It may be useful."

Tomanaga studied her covertly. Her face was as calm as ever, yet she radiated murderous fury. Only belatedly did he realize what it was. Her dark eyes, usually so tranquil, were deadly.

"Yes, sir," he said quietly.

"In the meantime," Han went on carefully. "I'd like to tell you what it is. *This*, Commander, is a record of what that young woman endured."

"Is there any ID on the attackers, sir?"

"There is," she said coldly. "Allow me to summarize.

Her name was Ursula Hauser, and she was a second-year student at New Athens—a philosophy major." Despite her hard-held control, Han's mouth twisted before she could smooth it. "A philosophy major," she repeated softly. "According to her notes, her cabin lost integrity almost immediately, but Ms. Hauser was a quick thinker, and she managed to patch the holes.

"Then, over the intercom, she heard the boarders killing the passengers, Commander Tomanaga." She looked up, her black eyes pits of flame. "They lined them up, sorted out the ones they wanted to keep—the young, pretty women—and slaughtered the rest in number three hold.

"But Ms. Hauser was determined they wouldn't get all the passengers. She knew a little about small craft, so she decided to try to steal a cutter and escape. She was on her way to the boatbay when she came across five terrified children from third class, running for their lives from one of the raiders. She stabbed him to death . . . with a carving knife from the first class galley." She paused, and Tomanaga felt his pulse in his temples. "She took his weapon, but she knew now that they were between her and the boatbay, and while they might let *her* live, they would certainly kill the children. So she did the only thing she could and looked for a hiding place.

"She was certain they knew their primaries had depressurized her whole cabin block, so she took the children back to her cabin, hoping they would be overlooked and she could get them to the boatbay after the raiders left. But then they dumped the air, and there she was: locked into her cabin with five children, no power, no vac suits, no airlock, and no way out."

Han's voice trailed off and she looked away from Tomanaga's pale face, speaking so softly he could barely hear her.

"So she did what she had to do, Commander. She fed each of those children a lethal overdose of barbiturates from her cabin medical stores. And when she was quite certain they were all dead, she sat down at the desk, recorded all of their names, finished her memo . . . and shot herself." Han stroked the pad. "She was nineteen, Bob."

A long silence fell. Robert Tomanaga had never personally hated any enemy in all his years of service, but at that moment he knew exactly what hate was, and he understood the old, hackneyed cliches about "killing rages."

"But, sir," he sought a professional topic, something to push the sick hatred away, "how did they catch the ship? *Argosy Polaris* was fast—nothing but a fighter could have overhauled her if she'd had any sort of start. Surely her master didn't allow an unidentified ship into weapons range in the middle of a civil war!"

"No," Han said coldly. "He allowed a Republican cruiser patrol to close with him."

"Oh my God. No. . . ." Tomanaga whispered.

"Precisely. Obviously somewhat modified; they've replaced at least some of the hetlasers with primaries. But that was how he identified them to his passengers when he hove to. I doubt he ever learned his mistake."

"Sir, what—?"

"What are we going to do, Commander?" Han laid the pad aside almost reverently, and when she looked up, her eyes were carved from the obsidian heart of hell. "We're going to find them, Commander Tomanaga. We're going to find the vermin who did this, the vermin who used the honor of the Fleet to cover themselves. And when we do, Commander, I only hope they live long enough to know who's killing them!"

"Admiral! We're picking up something on the emergency distress channel!"

Han straightened in her command chair. Two weeks had passed with no sign of the pirates, but the possible hiding places had been narrowed methodically. Now there were only a handful of systems it could be, and Siegried, on the far side of the next warp point, was one of them.

"Get a bearing, David," she said with the special serenity her staff had learned to expect in moments of stress. "Bob, send the group to quarters."

"Aye, aye, sir!" Tomanaga snapped, and the high-pitched shrilling of the alert wailed through the massive ship. Han hardly heard it.

"Got it, sir! Oh-one-niner level, two-eight-eight vertical. Looks like a standard shuttle transmission."

"Thank you. Bob, raise Captain Onsbruck. I want one fighter squadron to take a close look; hold the other two back for cover. This could be legitimate or a trap, so tell the pilots to take no chances."

"Aye, aye, sir."

"Thank you." She punched buttons, and Schwerin's face appeared on her com screen. "Captain, until I know exactly what we've got, you will halt the flagship and the battlegroup ten light-seconds short of the signal source."

"Aye, aye, sir."

"Thank you." She cut the connection and turned back to Tomanaga, and the lean chief of staff shivered at the hunger in her normally tranquil eyes.

"And now, Commander," she said softly, "we wait."

". . . know how important it is," Surgeon Commander Lacey told his admiral firmly, "but these are very sick people, sir! Another two days—" He shrugged. "You'll just have to use the statements they've already made."

"Very well. Thank you, Doctor." Han switched off the intercom and looked around the briefing room at the taut, angry faces. The battlegroup's COs attended via com links to their command decks and looked, if possible, even grimmer than her staff.

"Lieutenant Jorgensen," she said, "you've been correlating the survivors' statements. What conclusions have you been able to reach?"

"Everything they've said is consistent, Admiral," Irene Jorgensen twisted a lock of hair around an index finger, "and according to them, the pirate commander is an Arthur Ruyard. Our pre-war data base lists him as CO of the *Kearsarge*, a Frontier Fleet cruiser. Apparently he seized Siegfried by declaring support for the rebellion; once he controlled communications he dropped that pretense, and he's been raiding commerce—ours, the Rim's, even the Orions'—ever since."

"Oh my God!" Captain Janet MacInnes of the *Eisenhower* groaned. "Not the bloody tabbies, too!"

"I'm afraid so, Captain," Jorgensen said, "but they've said nothing about it. I suspect they've chosen to take their losses and deal with the raiders on their own rather than provoking a possible incident because of the Khan's desire for neutrality."

"All right," Han brought the discussion quietly back to immediate problems. "What's your best force estimate, Lieutenant?"

"Sir, they appear to have the heavy cruisers *Kearsarge* and *Thunderer* and the light cruisers *Leipzig*, *Agano*, and *Phaeton*. There are also five or six destroyers and a prewar squadron of system defense fighters operating from Siegfried III."

"But *Leipzig* and *Agano* were destroyed in action against a Rim destroyer flotilla!" Alfred Onsbruck objected. "I saw copies of the Omega drones."

"I don't doubt it," Captain Schwerin said. "Lieutenant—" he turned to the intelligence officer "—I'll bet none of his ships are listed as current members of the Republican Navy, are they?"

"They aren't, sir. *Leipzig* and *Agano* at one time *were* Republican units; none of the others were ever listed as having come over."

"There you are," Stravos Kollentai said crisply. "Ruyard started with only his ship, then picked off the others from either the Rim or us—probably pretending to belong to the same side until he got close enough to spring the trap." He paused and rubbed his nose. "What bothers me is his crews. I hate to think he found that many potential pirates in uniform!"

"He didn't," Jorgensen said. "Two of his first prizes were TFNS *Justicar* and *Hamurabi*—convict ships. According to our survivors, that's where the bulk of his personnel come from."

"I see. And just who are these 'survivors,' Lieutenant?"

"There are seventeen, sir: seven men and ten women. The men worked in Siegfried's mining operations before the war, as did two of the women. The others were aboard ships Ruyard's men captured. I understand—" Jorgensen's plain face twisted with distaste "—that Ruyard intends to found a dynasty. He's been collecting women to 'entertain' his crews, but the prettiest of them are earmarked for his 'nobility.'"

A savage, inarticulate sound came from Han's officers.

"How did they escape?" Kollentai asked after a moment.

"The 'fleet' was out on a raid and they stole an ore shuttle in for repairs—it had a bad drive, but they preferred to take their chances. They made it through the warp point, but then their drive packed in. They drifted for over a month before activating their beacon."

"That," Onsbruck said quietly, "took guts."

"Indeed," Han agreed. "And thanks to them, we know one thing Irene hasn't mentioned yet. This Ruyard doesn't trust any of his prisoners aboard ship for any reason."

"Now isn't that nice of him," Captain MacInnes said softly.

"I see your point, Admiral," Onsbruck said, "but even if we can blast them without worrying about civilian casualties, we have to be in range to do it. And we've got a problem there."

"Agreed." Han nodded with a tight smile. "Commander Kollentai and Commander Tomanaga have given the matter some thought, however. Bob?"

"Thank you, sir." Tomanaga faced Onsbruck, even though he was adressing them all. "Essentially, our problem is that although our monitors outgun them by a factor of five, all of their ships are faster than we are."

"Exactly, Commander. So how do you propose to make them stand still for us?" Onsbruck could have sounded scornful, but he didn't.

"Commander Kollentai thought of the answer, sir. Deception mode ECM. We'll come in openly, but what they'll see will be two battle-cruisers—*da Silva* and *Eisenhower*—and three destroyers—*Shokaku*, *Black Widow*, and *Termite*. Even though the 'battle-cruisers' will outmass anything they have, they won't expect any fighters and their total firepower will be far superior to what they believe we have."

"And if they send scouts out to check from close range?" Schwerin asked.

"According to the escapees, this Ruyard sticks with what works. He closes with his entire force before he drops his mask because his victims are less likely to balk if he gets in close, and, if they do, he's got the close-range firepower to deal with them. The chance to add two 'battle-cruisers' to his force should suck him right in where we want him."

"But if it doesn't?" Schwerin pressed.

"Then we'll just have to do our best, sir. Their fighters can't run; they're restricted to Siegfried III. As for the mobile units, long-range strikes from *Shokaku* should nail at least both heavies before they can warp out. That's better than nothing, sir."

"But not enough." Han's voice drew all eyes back to her, and her face was as cold as her voice.

"We don't talk about it, ladies and gentlemen," she said, "but each of us—even those who only joined up after the mutinies—is here because we believe it is our duty to protect our worlds and our people. That is the *only* acceptable reason for wearing the uniform we wear, and it is also something which, I hope and believe, we continue to share with the TFN."

She looked at them. One or two looked a bit embarrassed—especially David Reznick—but no one disagreed.

"The commanders of these ships have violated that purpose. They are mass murderers and rapists, but they are also outlaws against us. Against *this*." She touched the collar of her uniform. "Against our honor."

She paused once more, and her eyes burned.

"No one—*no one!*—is entitled to do that. The law sets only one penalty for their actions, just as there is only one penalty which can wipe away the dishonor they have brought to our uniform."

She looked at her subordinates once more, seeing her own anger in their faces. Only Tomanaga seemed to fully understand the shame she felt, but all of them shared her fury.

"And that, ladies and gentlemen, is the penalty we will enforce upon them," she finished grimly. She leaned back, her face once more calm, her voice once more serene. "It is my intention to enter Siegfried and attack within the next six hours. Carry on, ladies and gentlemen."

"There, sir," Tomanaga murmured as the enemy light codes crept onto the plot. "Still at extreme range, but they're closing. . . ."

Han nodded, watching the light dots of the piratical cruisers drift slowly closer, the red bands of hostile ships flashing around them. She picked out both heavies and all three of the lights, accompanied by the white dots of four destroyers.

"Data base can't identify the heavies, sir," David Reznick reported. "They've been altered and refitted too much—looks like the missile armament must have been downgraded in favor of primaries, wherever they got them. But I've got good IDs on the lights: *Phaeton*, *Agano*, and *Leipzig*. Two of the tincans are *Pike* and *Bengal*, but we don't know the others. Range is fifty light-seconds and closing."

"Thank you, David. Try to raise them, please."

"Aye, aye, sir."

There was a brief silence in response to *da Silva*'s hail, then the screen lit with the image of a thin-faced, scholarly-looking man who matched the data base pictures of Arthur Ruyard.

"I am Rear Admiral Li Han, Terran Republican Navy, commanding Battlegroup Nineteen," Han told him. "And you are?"

"Commodore Dennis Khulman, commanding the Twentieth Cruiser Squadron," the thin-faced man replied after the inevitable transmission lag, and Han's eyes did not even a flicker at the lie.

"What brings you out here, Commodore?" she asked with just the right trace of curiosity.

"I was about to ask you that, sir." Ruyard-Khulman smiled. "We're on a standing patrol out of Klatzenberger by way of Tomaline, Admiral. And you?"

"Out of Novaya Rodina via Jansen, Schulman, and Kariphos," Han lied equally smoothly. "We didn't expect to see Republican units out this way."

"No, sir. We didn't either," Ruyard-Khulman agreed.

"Well, I suppose we'd better rendezvous and exchange news, Commodore," Han said, watching the other ships creep closer on her plot.

"Of course, sir. But you'll pardon me if I keep my shields up until we do?" Ruyard-Khulman allowed himself a deprecating shrug. "Can't be too careful out here, sir."

"I certainly agree, Commodore," Han smiled, black murder in her heart.

"Thank you, sir. I make our rendezvous in approximately eighteen minutes at our present speeds. Is that acceptable?"

"It is," Han nodded. "I'll expect you for dinner, Commodore."

"Thank you, sir. I'm looking forward to it."

Li Han cut the communication and smiled savagely at the blank screen.

"Fifteen light-seconds, sir," Reznick reported.

"Very well. When we drop to twelve light-seconds, cut the ECM."

"*Cut* the ECM, sir?" Reznick was startled into asking the question.

"That's correct, Lieutenant," Han said calmly. She wanted Ruyard to know what he faced. She punched up *Shokaku*. "Captain Onsbruck?"

"Sir?"

"Prepare to launch fighters when our ECM goes down."

"Aye, aye, sir!"

"Thank you."

Han leaned back and watched the outlaw ships inch closer at their reduced speed. Even now Ruyard/Khulman's pre-planned surrender demand would be ready, but her message would go out first. The last message he would ever have, she thought coldly: the dropping of her deception the instant before she fired.

She remembered her cold-blooded destruction of the *Swiftsure* at Aklumar and recognized the similarity, yet the resemblance was only superficial. *Swiftsure*'s people had been enemies, but they had been honorable foes, worthy of a far better end. These enemies were scum.

"Thirteen light-seconds, sir," Reznick reported softly. "Standing by to disengage ECM. Disengaging . . . *now!*"

The battlegroup's ECM died, and the monitors and carrier stood revealed. Han watched the fighters spitting from *Shokaku's* catapults, but only with a corner of her eye. Her attention was on the dots of the enemy.

"Sir! Message from *Kearsarge*!" Reznick sounded startled. "They want to surrender, sir!"

Ruyard was fast on his mental feet, Han thought grimly. He knew he couldn't outrun her missiles, so he wasn't even trying. He was banking on the fact that the Terran

Navy—Federation or Republican—always gave quarter if it was asked for. It might be another trap or simply another example of his using the Navy's honor against itself. She watched the last of the fighters launch, and her face was bleak and cold.

"Captain Schwerin."

"Yes, sir?" Schwerin responded, his voice neutral.

"Open fire, Captain," Rear Admiral Li Han said softly.

War Warning

Leornak'zilshisdrow, Lord Sofald, Sixteenth Great Fang of the Khan, and District Governor of the Rehfrak Sector by proclamation of *hirikolus*, appeared on the Orion passenger liner's com screen, and Ian Trevayne looked for the first time at the being who had held his life in his hands thirty-one standard months before. Studying the tawny-furred, felinoid face, he noted admiringly that Leornak's whiskers were spectacular even by the standards of well-endowed Orion males. Rumor had it that the Orions approved of the current Terran fashion of growing beards; they felt it lent human faces a certain much-needed character.

Leornak smiled a fang-hidden carnivore's welcome and spoke, producing a series of sounds suggesting cats copulating to bagpipe music, then paused. Like many high-ranking Orions, the governor understood Standard English well, but the Orion vocal apparatus was poorly suited to produce human-like sounds. The problem was mutual, of course, which was one reason humans persisted in calling Orions "Orions." The thoroughly inaccurate label—assigned by ONI when Terrans first learned of the three-star-system, fourteen-warp-point nexus near the Great Nebula in Orion which was the heart of the Khanate—was far easier to pronounce than *Zheeerlikou'valkhannaieee* . . . and even that was but a crude approximation of what the Orions called themselves.

Trevayne shook the inconsequential thoughts aside as

the translator on Leornak's jeweled harness used his ship's sophisticated computers to produce pedantically exact English, complete to properly interpreting Leornak's formal tone and nuance.

"Welcome to Rehfrak, Admiral Trevayne. I am glad for the opportunity to meet you in person—although you will understand that the welcome must be entirely unofficial. I trust you are not in quite so much of a hurry as you were on your last visit?"

Trevayne smiled back, careful to hide his own teeth as good manners demanded. As an Englishman, he could appreciate studied understatement.

"No, Governor, this time I'm not trying to make good an escape—which I managed only as a result of your good offices. But, as you so rightly point out, these proceedings are unofficial—and, in my case at least, clandestine. The sooner I can meet with my government's representative, the better for all concerned."

"Of course, Admiral. He has already arrived and is here aboard my flagship, *Szolkir*." With further exchanges of courtesies, arrangements were made for Trevayne to be picked up by one of *Szolkir*'s cutters.

Trevayne watched Leornak's flagship gleam in the reflected orange light of the gas giant she orbited as the cutter approached her. Like all Khanate officers with sufficient pull, Leornak flew his lights aboard one of the *Itzarin*-class assault carriers. The Orions and the Terran rebels were as one in the prestige they accorded strikefighters and the starships which carried them, he thought dryly. In fact, for all their noisy anti-amalgamation invective, the Fringe Worlders were a lot like the whisker-twisters in many ways. Some twentieth-century wit had observed that the really great hatreds are between peoples that are alike and can't stand to admit it. Apparently that held as true between species as between human groups.

Trevayne gazed at the lovely killing machine and smiled faintly. After the next battle, the Khanate, as well as the "Terran Republic," would have some reassessing to do. He watched the cutter dock, and his mind slid back in time to the day, almost exactly a standard month before, when his journey had truly begun. . . .

* * *

Trevayne sat in a familiar conference room in Prescott City and looked around the table at the Grand Council of the Rim Provisional Government, which people were beginning to call the Rim Federation—though not in Trevayne's presence!

His Councilors were chosen by the Legislative Assembly from among its own members. Their function, in theory, was to advise the Governor-General; in practice, they governed the Rim when Trevayne was in deep space, which was often.

It was all very novel to these Outworlders, but Trevayne had read enough history to know he'd set in motion a reenactment of the birth of parliamentary government in his native England seven centuries before. In fact, this was what cabinet government was *supposed* to be like, for there were no structured parties in the Rim. That, he thought glumly, would come later, along with organized voting blocs, mass-media electioneering, and the rest. And would the people of the Rim, having tasted home rule, be willing to give it up when (the word "if" did not even cross his mind) the Federation won the war?

He looked at each Councilor, and at one in particular. To some extent Miriam Ortega owed her rise to the memory of her father, but that was only a part of it—and, after the early days, a small part, overshadowed by her own intelligence and force of personality.

Her eyes met Trevayne's. They'd been lovers for over a year.

He looked away, sweeping the other Councilors with his gaze once more.

"Ladies and gentlemen," he began, "I've called this meeting to confirm the rumor: we've received, through the Orions, a reply to our message to the Federation!"

He waited for the inevitable hubbub to die down. The Rim's only warp connection with the Innerworlds (other than those in rebel-held space) was the very circuitous one through the Khanate by which Trevayne's command had reached Zephrain. Afterwards, the Khan had closed his frontiers to *all* human entry. Even the raw materials purchased by the Innerworlds traveled only in Orion hulls, and only after a long and frustrating period of indirect negotiation had the Orions agreed to carry one message for Trevayne and to bring back one reply.

"All the Orions will say," he resumed, "is that the Federation is sending a representative to Rehfrak, which is as far as they'll let him come, in one standard month. They'll allow me to go to him—alone, secretly, in one of their own unarmed civilian craft. I'm frankly amazed that they're willing to violate their self-imposed neutrality even to that extent."

"Do I understand, sir, that you intend to accept this, uh, invitation?" Barry de Parma, chairman pro tem of the Grand Council, looked shocked at Trevayne's nod. "But the risk! You're indispensable. . . ."

"The Orions," Miriam Ortega cut in, "favor the Federation. They're neutral only because they know overt help from them would give our side an 'alien' taint." She smiled wryly, knowing that much of the resentment felt by the rebelling Fringe Worlds was shared by the people of the Rim, including some in this room. The Corporate Worlds had been wrong to accuse the Fringers of "xenophobia," but there was no doubting the Outworlders' grim determination to remain independent of the Orions. She hid a sigh of impatience with her fellow Councilors, saying only, "They have no motive for treachery."

"Precisely," Trevayne agreed, "and as for my . . . classified knowledge," he added, knowing they all took his meaning, "I'm not a technician, and no hard information could be got out of me. Besides, we have no reason to think they know there's any to get." He changed the subject before any cautious souls like de Parma could spot the gaping holes in his rationalization.

"Now, about security. Obviously, this jaunt can't be a matter of public knowledge." They all nodded, knowing how their people would react to the news that the Provisional Government was having any dealings whatsoever with the tabbies. "Officially, I'll be on exercises with the Fleet, and all transfer operations will be in the hands of people I can trust."

"What if you're gone an unusually long time?" De Parma looked glum. "What if questions come up for debate in the Assembly?"

"Don't let them," Trevayne replied cheerfully. "You're

here because together you can control the Assembly. As a countryman of mine named Disraeli, who had some small experience in these matters, once said, 'A majority is the best repartee.' "

Miriam gave him a glare beneath which a smile flickered. "You and your quotes! No one out here can ever be sure you're not making them up!"

He smiled at her. "Would that I were so creative!"

Trevayne came back to the present as the cutter's hatch opened. A proudly overconscientious young Cub of the Khan, whiskers almost visibly atwitch with curiosity, led him to what would have been called the wardroom in a human capital ship, but no military courtesies were exchanged. The wardroom was under heavy guard, but when Trevayne entered only two individuals rose to greet him. He recognized Leornak at once, and the human beside him looked vaguely familiar. Trevayne felt he ought to recognize the man, but he couldn't quite place him.

"Welcome to *Szolkir*, Admiral," Leornak greeted him.

"Thank you, Governor." Trevayne watched Leornak's tufted ear twitch as his computer translated the Standard English into Orion. It was an impressive performance, but the Orions had always been exceptionally good with computers and cybernetics—not that they had all the answers. Like the Federation, they'd been persistently thwarted in their efforts to create an artificial intelligence which didn't go promptly insane on them. Still, they made much more use of voice-coded software, even aboard warships, than Terrans did.

Of course, their language and vocal apparatus gave them a considerable advantage there. There were no Orion homonyms, and Orion voice patterns were even more readily identifiable than human patterns, which made computer authentication much simpler. More importantly, perhaps, Orions tended to express strong emotions—like excitement and fear—with visual cues, not voice cues. To date, the Federation had been unable to devise a voice-coded software package which could cope with human stress patterns without requiring a prohibitive amount of storage space. Trevayne himself had been a gunnery officer aboard the superdreadnought *Ranier* the last time BuShips had tried to introduce voice-cuing into Fleet use, and he still shuddered at the memory of *that* fiasco.

Leornak reclaimed his attention with a graceful gesture at his human guest. "Allow me to present an old colleague and sometime opponent, Mister Kevin Sanders, representing the Prime Minister of the Terran Federation."

Of course! Trevayne shook hands with the tallish, slender man, whose sharp features and gray Vandyke gave him a foxy look. He was well over 120, Trevayne remembered; in an age before longevity treatments, he might have been a sprightly and well-preserved sixty. Like Trevayne, he wore conservative civilian clothing.

"Good to see you back on the active list, Admiral Sanders," Trevayne said after the initial greetings. "Last I heard, you were still engaged in ruining the image of retired officers."

Sanders' merry blue eyes twinkled upward into Trevayne's somber dark-brown ones, and he chuckled.

"Strictly speaking, I'm no longer an 'admiral.' True, I was dusted off and brought back to ONI after the insurrection—for some reason, there were quite a lot of early retirements about then. But I resigned my commission last year to become a minister without portfolio in the Dieter Government—a liaison of sorts between the cabinet and the intelligence community."

He noted Trevayne's raised eyebrows at the words *the Dieter Government*, but he said nothing. Privately, he was impressed by how well Trevayne had controlled the surprise he must have felt. "But," he concluded, "that's more than enough about me. It's a privilege to meet you, Admiral, and also a pleasure. For one thing, we're both members of a rare breed out here: I'm also from Old Terra."

"Yes," Trevayne said. "I know."

"Oh?" Sanders' gaze grew a trifle sharper. "How?"

Trevayne indulged himself. "I've always been fascinated by the variations with which we native English-speakers still manage to enliven what's become a universal trade language," he said with a professorial air Miriam would instantly have recognized. "You, sir, are a North American—from either the old Canadian Maritime Provinces or the Tidewater area of the old American states of Virginia and

Maryland, I'd say. The two dialects are almost identical, you know."

Sanders managed to keep his aplomb, saying only, "The latter is correct." He wasn't at his best dealing with people as clever as himself, a deficiency he ascribed to lack of opportunity for practice.

Leornak's grin grew and his whiskers quivered slightly as he regarded the two humans. "Kevin," he said to Sanders, "I had a feeling this meeting would be a salutary experience for you. Unfortunately, I have duties to attend to and I must leave, as much as I am enjoying this. And you gentlemen doubtless need a degree of privacy—but I shall expect you for dinner afterwards."

Trevayne felt a momentary uneasiness at the invitation. Terran and Orion biochemistries were close enough to make such shared social events practical, but humans found some Orion culinary practices . . . disturbing. His queasiness died quickly as Leornak's slit-pupilled eyes laughed at him. Of course—a confirmed old cosmopolite like Leornak could be expected to defer to his quests' sensibilities by avoiding such customs as munching live specimens of that species which had always reminded Trevayne of hairless mice.

After the door closed behind Leornak, the Terrans sat at a low table on the cushions which served Orions in lieu of chairs, and Sanders poured from the bottle he and Leornak had been sampling. Bourbon, Trevayne thought dourly, had become so popular among upper crust Orions that it was one of the Federation's major export items. Why the bloody hell hadn't the tabbies had the common decency to take a liking to fine, malt Scotch?

He raised the glass, returning Sanders' brief salute, and drank. Then, somewhat fortified, he asked the question he had not cared to ask in Leornak's presence.

"Ah . . . correct me if I'm wrong, but did I understand you to refer to the *Dieter* government?"

"Why, yes," Sanders answered with a look of bland innocence. "I noticed you seemed surprised," he added. Damn the man!

"Well," Trevayne said carefully, "my last news from the Innerworlds was just before the mutinies. You must admit, at that time Mister Dieter's political star wasn't exactly in the ascendant." The single time he'd met Dieter, the man had struck him as a typical, blindly avaricious Corporate World political hack. "It's just seems a trifle . . . odd, from my perspective out here."

"Admiral, never underestimate Oskar Dieter," Sanders said. "Simon Taliaferro did, and it cost him."

Trevayne blinked at the other's sudden seriousness. Clearly there had been some changes in the Innerworlds!

"But," Sanders went on more lightly, "the Admiralty's briefing chips will bring you up to date on background events and time is short, so allow me to discharge myself of my instructions and deal with the present and future."

He set his glass aside to open an old-fashioned briefcase with an extremely modern security system.

"And so to business, Admiral . . . all of it pleasant business for you. You're now a Fleet Admiral, and all the field promotions you've made are retroactively confirmed. As is your assumption of the title 'Governor-General.' In fact, I should have greeted you as 'Your Excellency,' which is how the protocol experts have decided a governor-general should be addressed." Trevayne gave the older man what he hoped was a quelling glare, but it was difficult to tune up the full voltage against a man more than twice his age. And he suspected that even at full bore, his expression would have had little effect on Sanders, who only grinned and continued as flippantly as before.

"There was a little more trouble about this Rim Legislative Assembly of yours. No provision for it in the Constitution, after all. . . ."

"There's also nothing in the Constitution about an insurrection that isolates part of the Federation from Old Terra," Trevayne cut in. "These people remained loyal when all the rest of the Fringe revolted—and, I might add, despite their systematic abuse by the Corporate Worlds. Their loyalty is a priceless resource—we'd be wasting it if we hadn't involved them in their own defense!"

"*Pace*, Admiral!" Sanders raised a hand. "All was ratified. Oh, a few politicos are afraid you're setting up as an autonomous warlord out here, but of course they keep quiet about it. They want to stay in office!" He chuckled, then paused at Trevayne's puzzled look, but understanding dawned quickly.

"Of course! How could you know? The fact is, you've become something of a legend, Admiral. The original reports of your flight from Osterman's Star into Orion space captured the public imagination, especially since no one even knew if you'd survived. Then when the news broke that you were not only alive but had rallied the Rim and given the Rebels a bloody nose, to boot—well, I can hardly overstate the reaction. The Federation has produced precious few victories and even fewer victorious commanders. When an authentic hero turned up, there was no shortage of Corporate World money to publicize him."

Sanders' eyes danced. He'd watched happily as Trevayne's embarrassment grew visibly. Now he gently administered the coup de grace.

"You'll be pleased to know, Admiral, that you're the subject of a lavishly financed, hugely successful holodrama mini-series entitled *Escape to Zephrain*. You were played by Lance Manly, only slightly aged for the role." He sat back and listened with pure pleasure while Trevayne swore in six languages for a full minute without repeating himself. He waited until the new fleet admiral had run out of breath, if not obscenities, before he continued with a toothy grin.

"I've brought chips of the entire series, Admiral. The government feels it will enhance civilian morale in the Rim. . . ."

But Trevayne's habitual self-control had reasserted itself. "I'll take personal custody of those chips, if you don't mind." And cycle them through an airlock at the first opportunity! "But don't keep me in suspense any longer, damn you! How is the war going?"

Sanders was suddenly serious. "Not well. The rebels have gained control of all the choke points connecting their systems to the Innerworlds—without, I'm sorry to say, very much hindrance. You may not realize how extraordinary Admiral Ortega's and your success in holding your forces together really was, Admiral. The government put the Navy in an incredibly vulnerable position, and when the shooting started, the Fleet simply disintegrated before our eyes. Before we got the news about Zephrain, we'd estimated that our ninety percent of Frontier Fleet had gone over—now we've revised that to just over eighty percent. But what really hurt was losing over fifty percent of Battle Fleet's active units."

"*Fifty percent!*" Even this man could be rocked by some revelations, Sanders noted. "Sweet mother of God, man!"

"Fifty percent," Sanders confirmed grimly, "but that doesn't mean the rebels got all we lost." His face suddenly looked every day of its age, and Trevayne leaned back against his cushions.

Of course. It had to have been like that, or those Battle Fleet monitors already would have taken Zephrain away from him. He closed his eyes in brief pain as he contemplated the grim scenes that must have occurred within the Federation as scattered, mutinous battle-line units went down under the fire of their own service—and took their share of loyal ships and crews with them.

"So they had both the time and strength to grab their choke points," Sanders went on after a moment. "Not only that, but by now they've had time to set up a few yards of their own. So far we haven't seen any heavy capital ships among their new construction . . . but give them time. They'll get to it. They got too much breathing space, and crushing them is going to be long and bloody. And, of course, there's always someone waiting to step in as soon as there's an opening. Like the Tangri. I noticed in your report that you've had a few brushes with them out along the Rim?"

"One or two," Trevayne agreed calmly. "Not very many, though. I adopted an argument they understood, and they've left us alone since."

"Really? I've had some experience of the Tangri myself, Admiral. I'm afraid I'm not familiar with an 'argument' they pay any attention to."

"Oh, but you are, Mister Sanders." Trevayne chuckled dryly. "As a matter of fact, I believe you were present in the Lyonesse System when the same argument was propounded once before." His better nature triumphed just before he added, "That was before my time," and he ended with a simple, "I estimate three percent of their raiding force got home."

"Ah!" Sanders nodded. "It's a pity the Federation has always been too easygoing to use that argument more often. Still, I suppose the plutocrats have been more concerned with squeezing the Fringers. And they have other worries now. There was even some wild talk about bringing Battle Fleet home to 'stand shoulder-to-shoulder in defense of the homeworld!' But, of course, that was before they really understood the Fringe's objectives. The rebels want to secede, and for that they only have to hold what they've already got, not add more stars to it. Except—" he looked sharply at Trevayne "—for the Rim. They want that. And now they feel they can take it."

He patted the briefcase. "I've brought ONI's analysis for your perusal. The prognosis is: you can expect a really massive attack on Zephrain within sixty standard days. The question is: can you hold?"

Their eyes locked as Sanders silently asked the question that could not be asked aloud aboard an Orion warship. Have your people managed to transmute the theoretical data at Zephrain RDS into the kind of hardware that will even the odds you'll face?

Trevayne understood. And he knew that if Leornak had any conception of what was truly at stake, all the possible "diplomatic repercussions" in the Galaxy would not assure his own safety. Leornak would have to try, even though torture was notoriously unreliable, even though all TFN officers were immunized to truth-extracting drugs, and even though the limitations of hypnosis were still essentially what they had been in Franz Mesmer's day.

So he answered simply, "Yes."

They settled back on their cushions and sipped their bourbon, two men who understood one another perfectly, and Sanders smiled his impish smile again.

"Well, Admiral, I'm confirmed in my view that the government acted wisely in ratifying your actions. That's the one advantage of a plutocracy: it can sometimes be frightened into doing the sensible thing." He caught Trevayne's disapproving look and deliberately misinterpreted it. "Oh, yes, of course the good Leornak is bugging us . . . but only for his private amusement and the edification of his own superiors. And while those superiors would rather do business with *us*, they don't have much emotional investment in this war. Not like those of us who're out to avenge the blood of kith and kin, as it were." He stopped suddenly, looking uncharacteristically uncomfortable.

"Apologies, Admiral. That was an inappropriate thing to say. Of course I know about your family."

But Trevayne hardly heard him, for in the corridors of his memory, a long-shut door swung open.

It had been sixteen years before, with his younger daughter Ludmilla newly born. He'd taken his family to Old Terra for the first time. They'd visited England, of course, and Moscow. And like all human visitors to the birthworld, they'd journeyed to Africa where the Temple of Man exploded up over Olduvai Gorge in arches and spires that soared towards infinity while *homo erectus*, captured forever in the masterpiece of the twenty-second century sculptor Xentos, gazed at the lights in the night sky and wondered. . . .

But the image that haunted him still was from the Mediterranean island of Corfu, whose mountains meet the sea to subdivide beaches into ancient coves where squinting, sun-dazzled eyes can sometimes momentarily glimpse Odysseus' galley rounding a headland. Until the day of his death, he would never be able to think of his older daughter Courtenay without seeing a four-year-old girl on the beach at Corfu, the brilliant sun conjuring reddish glints in her chestnut hair . . . followed swiftly by the dissipating radioactive dust which, for a little while after the missiles struck, must have colored the dawns and sunsets of Galloway's World.

He allowed himself five twenty-nine hour Xandy days in Prescott City after his return from Rehfrak. On the sixth day, he awoke and walked to the open window to gaze out into the high summer of Xanadu's northern hemisphere. Imported elms mingled with native featherleaf and falsepine across a well-tended lawn crystalline with dew, and creatures that weren't quite furry birds flew overhead in the early-morning light of a sun just too yellow to be Sol. He sniffed the cool air, already sensing the heat the day would bring, and there was a strange stillness in his heart.

He heard a stirring behind him as Miriam reached for

him in her sleep and, finding his side of the bed empty, awoke. She smiled sleepily.

"For God's sake, Ian," she murmured. "Put some clothes on if you're going to stand at the window. At least spare what little's left of my reputation."

He smiled. Their affair was the worst-kept secret in the Zephrain System, if not the entire Rim. In fact, he'd been considerably relieved when he viewed the mischievous Sanders' wildly overdone HV chips (which had since mysteriously vanished) and found no mention of Miriam. He sat down on the bed and kissed her forehead gently.

"Go back to sleep," he whispered. "No need for you to get up yet. But I have to leave."

She was fully awake now, and her smile departed. "I suppose it's useless to tell you again that any of your new-minted admirals—Desai, Remko, any of the rest—are competent to act as your in-space commander? Or to remind you of your importance to the Rim?" She caught herself before saying "the Rim Federation."

He thought ruefully of his last conversation with her father. "My 'importance' ends the day the rebels break through," he answered grimly. "The Rim lives or dies with the Fleet. I may as well do the same."

"Ian," she smiled again, "you're full of shit, as usual. I'm a Navy brat, remember? I know the real reason you're going."

Of course they both knew the unwritten (and therefore unbreakable) rule that required any TFN commander who could manage it to be in space with his personnel in battle. Howard Anderson had been aboard one of those twenty-third century battlewagons, now so quaint-seeming, at Aklumar. Ivan Antonov and Raymond Prescott had ridden their flagships into the meat-grinders of Lorelei and Home Hive III. And Sergei Ortega had flown his lights to the end in *Krait* at the Battle of the Gateway. . . .

Miriam looked up at the swarthy, invulnerable face and ran her fingers through the close-trimmed, slightly graying beard. Few who knew him saw any reason to dispute the common judgment that he was "complex" and "inscrutable" —some might even add "sinister." She alone had come to know his face lied, that his complexity, seen whole, resolved itself into concentric rings of defense around the dull hurt at the center of him.

Miriam's lovemaking was no more passive than anything else about her, and she pulled him down to her, kissing him. "You don't have to leave just yet," she said softly, "and God knows how long you'll be gone . . . ." And, for a time, nothing existed for either of them except the other.

Afterwards, she sat on the bed among the tangled sheets, hugging her knees and smoking as she watched him dress and groom himself meticulously. Yes, she thought, even the surprising personal vanity fits the pattern. It was a part of the fortifications.

What she did not know, what she would never know, was that without her he was alone with his hurt.

Then he turned back to her, totally familiar and yet almost a stranger in his uniform. They kissed once more, lingeringly, and it was time for him to go.

"You realize, of course," she said with mock severity, "that while you're gone, in addition to being miserably horny, I'm going to have the Devil of a time keeping the Grand Council in harness."

He paused at the door and grinned innocently. "Well," he began, "in the words of a noted pre-space Chinese philosopher . . ."

He managed to beat the hurled pillow through the door.

CONDUIT

Kevin Sanders hardly noticed the Marines guarding the prime minister's residence. He hadn't been on Old Terra many hours, and he was far more concerned with smelling unrecycled air and seeing more than a handful of faces in one place.

He glanced at his watch as the elevator whisked him to the penthouse. He was running slightly late, but political meetings, he'd learned long ago, were very like social gatherings; it was better to arrive late—even by a large margin—than early by the smallest.

The elevator doors opened, and he stepped out to be met by a tall, fair-haired young man.

"Evening, Heinz. I take it they're awaiting me with bated breath?"

"More or less, Admiral Sanders."

Sanders sighed. Heinz von Rathenau, Dieter's personal security head, was the only member of the New Zurich Delegation to follow him—officially, anyway—into the prime minister's residence, and he seemed incapable of forgetting the titles people had once acquired—or "earned," as he put it. Sanders suspected him of incurable romanticism.

"Shall I go on in, Heinz?"

"Of course, sir. Conference Room Two."

"Thank you."

Four people sat around the polished crystal conference table. Sanders nodded pleasantly to Sky Marshal Witcinski and Chief of Naval Operations Rutgers and bestowed a special smile on Susan Krupskaya, his successor at ONI, then half-bowed to the prime minister.

Dieter was the least impressive of them all, physically speaking, but his was unquestionably the dominant presence. Which was no small trick, given the wealth of experience his military subordinates represented. Either Sanders' first impression of Dieter had been sadly mistaken, or else the man had somehow grown to meet his moment. He suspected the latter, but he was none too sure his suspicion didn't stem from his own dislike of admitting mistakes.

"Mister Sanders." Dieter did not rise, but his courteous greeting gave the impression he had. "I'm glad you were finally able to join us."

"Thank you, sir." Sanders hid a smile. "I'm sorry—I am running a bit late." He didn't mention that he'd walked rather than take a ground car.

"Quite all right," Dieter said. "Man must walk before he can run, I suppose." He smiled pleasantly. "But you're the man of the hour, after all—or, at least, the man who's met him." He leaned back and waved at a chair. "Let us hear your report, Mister Sanders. Please."

"Yes, sir." Sanders laid his briefcase on the table and snapped its security locks. Reinforced titanium sheathing gleamed dully on its inner surfaces as he extracted a folder of holo chips and laid them on the table.

"This is the official report, sir. But I gather you want an . . . ah, off the cuff summation?"

"Precisely, Mister Sanders. Your summations are always so enlivening."

"Thank you, sir. I strive to please."

"I'm sure." Dieter opened an inlaid cigar box and waited while Sanders selected and lit one. Then he cleared his throat gently. "Your summation?"

"Yes, sir. Frankly—" Sanders eyes swept the group, his customary levity absent "—we're damned lucky. I was prepared for a determined man, but not for the one I met. In my considered opinion, the Governor-General will hold the Rim Systems if any living man can do it."

"A strong endorsement, Kevin," Susan Krupskaya said quietly.

"Is it?" Sanders suddenly grinned impishly. "Let's just put it this way, Susan—he puts Lance Manly to shame."

"So you're confident he can hold Zephrain?" Witcinski asked somberly.

"I am. More importantly, *he* is. Mind you, we couldn't talk openly on board an Orion carrier, but when I asked him if he could, he answered with one word: 'Yes.' "

"That sounds like Ian," Rutgers said.

"Yes. The Governor-General *does* seem rather, ah, formidable," Sanders agreed. "And he clearly feels he has the firepower he needs . . . plus the locals' full-blooded support. At least," he chuckled dryly, "he defended them most vehemently against a few carefully dropped aspersions."

"That sounds like him, too," Rutgers said.

"And it brings up another point," Witcinski pressed. "Forgive me, Bill—I certainly don't wish to impugn the honor of an officer who's accomplished what he has—but there *has* to be some temptation towards empire-building in his position."

"I suppose so—for some," Sanders broke in before Rutgers' anger could find expression. "Sky Marshal, you no doubt know that Admiral Trevayne lost his wife and daughters on Galloway's World?"

"Yes," Witcinski agreed guardedly.

"Well, sir," Sanders said quietly, "he's lost his son now, too." He watched the sudden pain in Rutgers' broad face, then eyed Witcinski.

"I'm sorry to hear it, Mister Sanders," the Sky Marshal said gruffly, "but how does that answer my question?"

"His son," Sanders said very softly, "was aboard one of the ships BG 32 destroyed in the Battle of Zephrain." He kept his eyes on Witcinski as Rutgers gasped in dismay. "I submit, sir, that neither you, nor I, nor anyone else has the right to question his loyalty after that."

"No," Witcinski said slowly, "I don't suppose so." There was no apology in his voice, only understanding, but Sanders was content. Witcinski was very like Trevayne—a little harder, perhaps, a little narrower . . . certainly less imaginative. But in one respect they were identical: neither ever apologized for doing what he felt was necessary.

"And your estimate of the military situation, Kevin?" Rutgers' voice was flat, its impersonality covering his own pain.

"The Governor-General provided a force summary, but it's not exhaustive. We were both aware that Fang Leornak was certain to read his report—one way or another." Sanders shrugged and grinned again, dispelling much of the lingering solemnity. "Leornak and I are old friends, so I made his job a little easier by leaving the report on my desk when we went to supper."

"You did *what*?" Witcinski stared at him.

"Of course I did, Sky Marshal," Sanders said cheerfully. "It was only courteous."

"Courteous?!" Witcinski glared at him, and Sanders smiled.

"Please, Sky Marshall!" He waved an airy hand. "The Orions certainly know as much about Zephrain RDS as Admiral Krupskaya and I do about Valkha III. Which is to say each side knows the other has a facility where all that nasty weapons research has carefully not been carried out for the last sixty years. Leornak is a civilized old cat, by his lights, but if he thought he had any chance to discover the contents of Zephrain RDS, he'd have no option but to try—a point, by the way, of which the Governor-General seems well aware. As long as Leornak can tell the Khan there's no evidence of such data's being transmitted, he can avoid the unpleasant and diplomatically catastrophic necessity of . . . acquiring it." He shrugged. "So I made it easier by giving him access to the recorded data, since I felt confident Admiral Trevayne was too wise to record anything incriminating. Now Leornak can assure the Khan that no sensitive data was transmitted . . . which meant, incidentally, that the Governor-General and I could leave his flagship."

"My God!" Witcinski shook his head. "I think you actually enjoyed it!"

"My dear Sky Marshal! Why else would anyone *become* a 'spook'?" Sanders permitted himself another chuckle.

"But you do have a strength estimate?" Rutgers pressed.

"Certainly. The full data is in the report. Fortunately, few capital ships were actually lost at Zephrain. His damaged units have been repaired, and apparently he's undertaken a program of new construction, as well. . . ." Sanders' voice trailed off in deliberately tantalizing fashion.

"New construction?" Rutgers frowned at him. "What sort?"

"A new group of monitors—he says." Sanders' voice was quite neutral.

"Says?" Krupskaya asked sharply. Trust Susan to be the first to pounce, he thought wryly.

"Let's just say I think he finessed some clues past the Orions—which takes some doing with a wily old whisker-twister like Leornak."

"Clues, Mister Sanders? What sort of clues?"

"Just this, Sky Marshal—he's building *only* monitors, each of which is tying up the full capacity of a Terra-class space dock, and he's named the first of them *Horatio Nelson.*"

"What? What sort of name is that for a monitor?"

"Precisely, Sky Marshal. Monitors are named for TFN heroes, yet this ship isn't. The Orions probably won't give it a thought—after all, our nomenclature is as confusing to them as theirs is to us—but a non-standard name suggests a non-standard class, no? Coupled with the building capacity devoted to each of them and the fact that he doesn't seem to feel the need for carriers—" Sanders raised one hand, palm up.

"I see." Witcinski scratched his chin. "I believe you have a point, Mister Sanders."

"So Admiral Trevayne has a sizable conventional force, plus whatever unorthodox vessels and weapons he may be building," Dieter mused. "And on that basis, he feels confident of defeating anything the rebels can throw at him." He nodded slowly. "My friends, I think that may be the best news since this whole sorry disaster began. If he's right—if he *can* hold—it may be time for us to consider Operation Yellowbrick." He glanced at his two senior military commanders. "Comments, gentlemen?"

"Really, Kevin," Susan Krupskaya chided as she poured scotch into his glass, "you should watch the way you talk to the Sky Marshal."

"Why?" Sanders yawned and stretched, looking briefly more cat-like than an Orion. "Has he noticed something?"

"Kevin, you're a clever man, not to mention devious and underhanded, but the Sky Marshal is cleverer than you think. He may not waste time on decadent things like social amenities, but he's quite well aware you enjoy twitting him."

"Nonsense! That man's not 'well aware' of anything that doesn't mount shields, armor, and energy weapons!"

"Oh, no? That's not what his war diary says."

"*War diary?*" Sanders sat up and frowned at her. "You've been tapping the confidential war diary of the military commander-in-chief, Susan?"

"But, Kevin," she batted her eyelids demurely, "you always said that anything someone considers worth keeping a secret is probably worth knowing. Besides, he's a Fringer; it seemed like a good idea to check him."

"But if he catches you at it," Sanders said warningly, "not even Dieter's going to be able to save your shapely ass."

"No?" Krupskaya grinned a trifle crookedly. "Why do you think I warned you he's cleverer than you think? Here's my last intercept from his diary." She tossed him a sheet of facsimile.

"Ah?" Sanders glanced at the transcript and began to chuckle. After a moment, it became full-throated laughter, and he raised his glass ungrudgingly to the absent sky marshal. All it said was: "My Dear Vice Admiral. I trust you and Mister Sanders have enjoyed being on the 'inside.' L. Witcinski."

"And he accused *me* of enjoying it!"

"And he was right, you old reprobate!" Krupskaya shook her head wryly. "I'm still not certain how he caught me, but he thinks you put me up to it."

"Well, I suppose I did, in a sense," Sanders agreed lazily. "After all, I taught you everything you know."

"Not quite everything," she said dryly. "And before you start blowing your ego out your ears, I have something for you. Here." She handed him a sheaf of pages.

"Ah! An excellent job, Susan. Excellent!"

"Sure." She shook her head at him. "Kevin, what are you up to? Here's proof that Captain M'tana and Alistair Nomoruba are feeding information to the rebels, and you won't let me do a thing about it! Damn it, they've been doing it for over two *years* now!"

"So they have." Sanders finished the first sheet, nodded to himself and crumpled the paper, breaking the security coating, then tossed it into the ice-bucket at his elbow.

The sheet touched melted ice-water and vanished as he turned to the second page.

"I've done a lot for you, Kevin," Admiral Krupskaya said sternly, "and I'll probably go right on doing it, but you owe me an explanation. I don't mind putting my career on the line, but sitting on this may violate my sworn oath as an officer."

"Sweet Susan," Sanders said soothingly, "the skill has not yet deserted these palsied old fingers. This old eye has not yet lost its keenness. This old ear has not yet—"

"Spare me a full catalog of decrepit organs that are still more or less functional," she interrupted rudely. "What you're saying—in your thankfully inimitable style—is that *you* know what you're doing?"

"Precisely."

"Kevin," she said with unaccustomed severity, "I'm no longer a wet-nosed snotty in your operation on New Valkha. I have my own duties—and I've run about as far with this as I intend to without an explanation."

"Ah, but your baby fat made you such a charming ensign," he said gently. "Still—" he weighed the angry fondness flashing in her eyes and shrugged "—perhaps it *is* time for the wily old master to enlighten his round-eyed, admiring disciple."

"*Kevin—!*"

"*Pace*, my dear!" His eyes still gleamed, but his voice was serious, and she settled back to listen. "Consider: I first tapped into this conduit less than a month after the POW letter exchanges began, correct?"

"Yes."

"Fine. And at the time, the information passing through it, while undoubtedly useful, wasn't precisely Galaxy-shaking. Correct again?"

"Yes."

"Well, as I taught you in the dim mists of your youth, my love, one *never* tampers with a conduit unless the information passing through it is of deadly importance. Instead, one monitors it, traces it, and, above all, makes certain it carries information in apparent security, thus preventing the ungodly from tinkering up something one *doesn't* know about to replace it. This is spook basic training manual stuff, is it not?"

"Yes, Kevin," she sighed. "But why not tell *anyone* about it?"

"My sweet, a secret is a secret when only one person knows it; anything else is simply more or less compromised information. Dear, toothsome Susan! I wouldn't have told *you* if you hadn't been moving into the worry seat at ONI!"

"And if you hadn't needed my help to stay tapped in!"

"That, too, of course," he admitted graciously.

"All right. I can accept that. But look at some of this stuff, Kevin! Details of the communications with the Orions to set up your trip. Or here—" she pointed at another sheet "—details of cabinet meetings, for God's sake! We're talking heavy duty data, Kevin. This is no longer Assembly gossip!"

"And quite interesting it is, too," Sanders agreed brightly.

"Damn you, Kevin! Don't evade me! Why can't I even tell *Heinz* that someone *inside the cabinet* is passing priceless data to the enemy?"

"Priceless?" Sanders finished the last page of the intercepts and watched it curl into nothingness in the ice-bucket. "Perhaps, and perhaps not." He stirred the clear water and clinking ice with an idle forefinger.

"No 'perhaps' about it!" Krupskaya snorted.

"Actually, you know, there is," he corrected gently. "Consider this, my dear—everything you've picked up from the cabinet is purely political. There hasn't been one scrap of military intelligence."

"That's true," she agreed slowly, her tone suddenly thoughtful.

"Now," Sanders purred, "who has access to all *this*—" he tapped the bland water in the ice-bucket "—but *not* to military data? The same cabinet meeting which discussed sending me to the Orions also discussed our entire naval strategy, yet there's not a word of that in here. Surely that would be worth more to the rebels than, for example, Prime Minister Dieter's requests for opinions on granting the 'Republic' limited belligerent status?"

"Selective information," she said softly, nodding her head. "But why? You're right; it's valuable, but less valuable than military intelligence."

"Ah, but is it?"

"Damn you," she said without rancor. "Don't start your damned double-think on me now!"

"I'm not. But who does it have value for? The recipient . . . or the sender?"

"I don't pretend to understand that one—yet. But I will, I promise you!"

"I'm sure you will," he soothed, his smile taking the offense from his words. "You were always my best student, or you wouldn't be sitting where you are now. But unlike you, my love, I already know our mole's identity."

"And you don't intend to share it with me?" she said resignedly.

"No, Susan, I don't," he said, his suddenly flat tone contrasting sharply with his normal urbanity. Then he smiled again. "But it's a *lovely* game, my dear! I know—but does he know that I know? And if he does, does he know that I know that he knows that I know? *Ad infinitum*, of course."

"Kevin Sanders," she said acidly, "if I didn't trust you more than my own mirror, I'd have you in irons under babble juice therapy this second!"

"And, my dear," he purred, "if I didn't trust you—and *know* that you trust me—I would never have recommended you to run ONI, now would I?"

Susan Krupskaya laughed and shook her head. "Hold out your glass, you rotten old bastard," she said affectionately.

"Here. The latest information for Captain M'tana."

The tall man took the record chip and tucked it inside his tunic beside his holstered needler. He frowned.

"You seem displeased." The observation was made gently, but there was a chuckle in the voice.

"No, sir. It's just . . . just . . ."

"Just that it goes against the grain to pass things to rebels?"

"Well, yes, sir," the courier said unhappily.

"But we don't give them any military data, now do we? Just political information to let them know what's happening in the Cabinet and Assembly."

"Yes, sir, but—"

"But me no buts." The voice hardened slightly. "The 'rebels' are Terrans, too, you know. Possibly better Terrans than we are. It can't hurt to give them this information—and someday it may do a great deal of good for them to know precisely what the government *really* thinks."

"Yes, sir," the tall young man said, and turned away with the priceless—if non-military—intelligence tucked into his tunic. He would see to it Nomoruba got the information without a clue as to its source. Heinz von Rethenau might not understand the motives of the Terran Republic's most highly-placed spy, but he knew he could never question them.

After all, Oskar Dieter *was* the prime minister.

FORTRESS

Ian Trevayne stood on the flag bridge of his new flagship, in orbit around Xanadu, and watched the great curve of the planet on the big screen. That blue, cloud-swirling loveliness woke the home-calling of his blood, and his eyes swung toward the constellation Xandies called the Hexagon. There, the astronomers asserted, lay Sol.

How far was Sol from Zephrain? The question was a fascinating one for the theoretical astronomers (whose current best guess was seven hundred light-years), but of no significance whatsoever to the working spacers who traveled the mad ingeodesics of the warp lines. Yet Trevayne contemplated the sheer distances involved more often of late, deliberately dwelling on the immensity of space and time as a sort of tonic when his spirits flagged. For huge though the universe might be, Man's very presence here, in this system, was the best measure of his own stature. Seven centuries from Earth Trevayne had come, as the lonely radiation of light rode the vacuum. Surely after such a voyage as that he could accomplish what duty demanded.

He shook himself and dismissed that thought to consider the ship he rode. Shortly before the war, the Zephrain Fleet base had laid down a prototype fortress, larger even than a monitor and with far more mobility than the usual OWP's station-keeping capabilities. As far as Trevayne was concerned, anything mobile, however slow and clumsy, was a ship, and after completing it with major modifications, he'd given it a name. It was now TFNS *Sergei Ortega*, and it was the largest self-propelled structure ever wrought by *homo sapiens*—but not for long. The militant energy of the Rim had come together with the scientific wizardry slumbering at Zephrain RDS and birthed the five mammoth constructions that orbited alongside *Ortega* in various stages of incompletion, overshadowing even her bulk. Destroyer-sized construction ships slid between their massive ribs; tractored barges piled high with steel and beryllium and titanium from Zephrain's mammoth smelters shuttled back and forth among them; and fierce, tiny constellations of robotic welders lit their bones. Only one was even partially operational, but he'd at least decided on a name for that one: TFNS *Horatio Nelson*. When Miriam had asked who that was, he'd told her she could bloody well look it up.

He thought of those gargantuan monsters—he would, he supposed, probably call them supermonitors—and of the wholesale refitting of the other Fleet units, and, not for the first time, he was awed and even a little frightened by the Faustian dynamism of the Rim society. He never realized (no one did, except Miriam Ortega, and she only dimly) that it was he who had tempered that unique human metal into the terrible weapon now poised to strike.

It struck on the twenty-third standard day after Trevayne had been piped aboard *Ortega*.

Genji Yoshinaka (a captain, now, and Trevayne's chief of staff) scanned the reports of SBM carrier packs coming in from the closed warp point near the photosphere of Zephrain A—the "Back Door," as it had come to be called—then looked up to meet Trevayne's eyes as they realized they'd won their first gamble. They'd counted on the rebels rejecting another pincer after their earlier disaster and made their own deployment accordingly. Their mobile units—now officially listed by the TFN as Fourth Fleet—covered the Gateway, but the orbital forts which once had protected it did not. They'd been repaired, refitted, and towed across the system to join the handful of new forts protecting the Back Door. There was a reason for that redeployment, and the rebels were about to discover it.

Trevayne spoke a few quiet words, and the orders went

out, setting in motion long-prepared contingency plans, both in space and on Xanadu. The fleet uncoiled itself from the Gateway in response, reaching out on the flag plot like gleaming tendrils of light. And on the planet, sirens screamed and civil defense teams sprang into orderly action. Kevin Sanders' briefing might stress the rebels' promise to avoid further strikes on populated worlds so long as the Federation did likewise, but Ian Trevayne would take no chances. There would be no mass murder on Xanadu.

He watched his secondary plot—the one tied directly into the Back Door fortresses—and his hard smile tightened as a crazy quilt of explosions erupted about the warp point. The hordes of tiny robotic spacecraft with their loads of homing missiles were taking a beating, he thought coldly. SBMHAWK carriers had always been largely immune to minefields, for it was hard for the hunter-killer satellites to target something so small, and harder still for them to catch the agile, wildly evading packs before they stabilized their launchers and fired. That was what made them so deadly against fixed defenses like OWPs . . . until Zephrain RDS had supplied an answer: a new mine with vastly improved tracking systems and a far higher attack speed. Their attack radius was shorter than for conventional mines, and their lighter warheads were largely ineffectual against shielded and armored warships, but they were deadly against the unprotected SBMHAWKs.

Their shorter range required denser patterns and there had been insufficient time to build enough for both warp points. But Trevayne and his staff had reasoned that the rebels would prefer the Back Door to the long-established Gateway defenses, and placed their limited supply accordingly.

"Skywatch says the new mines took out ninety-plus percent of the missile packs before launch, Admiral," Yoshinaka reported crisply. "Operational orders transmitted to mobile units and acknowledged. All ships closed up at action stations and redeploying towards the Back Door. All civil defense procedures implemented on Xanadu."

"Thank you, Commodore," Trevayne acknowledged formally, his eyes on the main battle display. Any moment now, he thought. . . .

* * *

The rebels received the first of several surprises as their lead units emerged to find their attack warp point still covered by heavy OWPs. Vice Admiral Josef Matucek, commanding the Republican van, watched in horror as his superdreadnoughts warped into a holocaust of close-range beam fire. Shields flared like paper in a furnace as the heavy batteries of energy weapons—energy weapons which should have been blasted to rubble by the torrent of SBMHAWKs—ripped his ships apart.

It was incredible! How had they *survived?* And having survived, where was that hurricane of force beams *coming* from? Every Terran fortress designer was imbued with the necessity of balancing force beam and primary beam armaments—the former to batter down shields and armor at close range when the capital ships came through; the latter to lacerate the hangar bays of the carriers in the follow-up waves—but those forts couldn't possibly mount anything *but* force beams! There was no room for anything else, and their heavy fire gutted the leading Republican ships. Fragile datalink systems collapsed in electronic hysteria under the pounding, and the superdreadnoughts had to fight as individuals, surrounded by those demonic fortresses like mastodons besieged by tigers.

But superdreadnoughts were tough. Eight were destroyed outright, and a dozen more were crippled, half-demolished, hulls glowing with the energy bleeding into them from the defenders' force beams, but they struck back hard. Their crews were every bit as courageous, every bit as determined, as the defenders, and they blew a gap in the in-system edge of the defensive ring. Neither Matucek nor many of his people lived to see it, but the follow-on wave of carriers found a hole wide enough to offer escape from the full fury of the distance-attenuated force beams.

They charged through it—only to reel in shock as every surviving fortress cut loose with the same incredible number of *primaries* and taught the Republican Navy the power of the "variable focus" improved force beam refined from the theoretical data at Zephrain RDS. Stressed field lenses allowed the same projector to operate in primary mode, projecting a beam which was tiny in aperture and brief in duration compared to a regular force beam. And while, like all primaries, it lacked the wide area effect of the force beam, it was a weapon to which electromagnetic shields, metal armor, and human flesh all offered equal resistance—that is to say, none at all.

The vicious beams stabbed through the carriers, crippling electromagnetic catapults and, all too often, the readied fighters, as well, and the first carrier wave staggered aside, toothless, their riddled fighter bays useless.

But even the improved force beam required a cooling period between primary-mode shots, and the rebel commander turned the full fury of his fleet upon the remaining fortresses. The Book called for intact forts to be bypassed, for the follow-up waves to flood through the holes opened by SBMHAWKs and the assault waves to draw out of range of the surviving energy weapons, but that was impossible here. Admiral Anton Kellerman threw the surviving ships of the first wave into the teeth of the big forts, and the primaries' slow rate of fire proved decisive. They died hard, but they died . . . and took half a dozen more superdreadnoughts (and six assault carriers which had no business—by The Book—in such an engagement) with them into death.

Trevayne watched grimly as the relayed scanner images recorded the destruction of Zephrain Skywatch. He'd known from the first that this was the probable outcome of a truly determined assault—and so had the Skywatch crews. He wondered how many of his personnel had died with their fortresses. Not so many as would normally have been the case, but far more than he would find it easy to live with. He'd done his best to reduce the death toll by employing as much automation as possible, but there had to be some human brains behind the robotics. There had been, and most of them had been volunteers. He only hoped the specially-designed escape pods built into the fortresses had saved more than a tithe of those extraordinary people.

It might have been different if he'd dared to marshal Fourth Fleet behind Skywatch. The firepower of his mobile units, coupled with that of the forts, would have smashed the rebel attack into dust—but someone had had to cover the Gateway in case he and Yoshinaka had guessed wrong.

He studied his display narrowly, wishing for the thousandth time that even one of his supermonitors was operational, but only the immobile, half-finished *Nelson* was even partly so. Another thirty standard days might have changed that, but he had to fight with what he had, and, as he watched Anton Kellerman gather his shaken units back into some sort of formation amid the drifting rubble of Skywatch, he wondered grimly if it was enough. He'd been confident when he told Sanders he could hold Zephrain, but ONI had underestimated the rebel attack strength by at least a factor of three. Too many of those ships out there weren't listed in his flagship's data base. New ships, the fruit of the shipyards Sanders had warned him about.

But Skywatch had done bloody well, and that had to be a very shaken rebel commander. Virtually all of his superdreadnoughts had been crippled or destroyed outright, and his carriers had suffered heavily. He had to be wondering what fresh disaster awaited him from Zephrain's Pandora's Box, and if he could just be convinced that what awaited him was even worse than it actually was. . . .

He watched a small rebel force line out for Gehenna while a second, larger one headed directly for Xanadu and his own forces, and wondered what the rebel commander would do with his surviving strikefighters? The Book called for a close-in launch to avoid as much AFHAWK attrition as possible, but he might be shaken enough to launch at extreme range. Trevayne hoped not, for that was the one thing he truly feared.

He encouraged the enemy's adherence to The Book by holding back his own fleet—including the monitors of BG 32, commanded now by Sonja Desai and very different from any other monitors in space. There were a few monitors in the rebel fleet. They must have been the rear guard, protected from the first crushing embrace of action because their long building time made them so hard to replace. But his primary interest lay with the surviving carriers as *Ortega* shivered, moving into a slightly wider orbit in company with BG 32. *Ortega* and Desai's monitors were datalinked to the immobile *Nelson*; they couldn't leave Xanadu without dropping the partially-operational supermonitor out of the net, and he needed *Nelson*. He needed her badly, and he had to suck those carriers into range of her weapons before they launched. . . .

Anton Kellerman watched the plot aboard his CVA flagship *Unicorn* and wondered just what Trevayne was playing at. He'd once served under the Rim commander, and the one thing Trevayne had never seemed was hesitant. Yet he wasn't moving forward to engage. True, he was badly outnumbered—by at least three-to-one in fighters, Kellerman judged—but still . . .

It was possible he wanted to engage close to Xanadu for a very simple reason: he could have based hundreds of strikefighters on the planet. Yet those stupendous, half-completed hulls drifting in orbit above the Fleet base seemed to argue that he couldn't have built *too* many fighters. Could it be they'd caught him with his pants down? Was it possible that, despite the long delay, he wasn't ready for them?

Kellerman hoped so. His own people were badly shaken. Few of them had ever imagined an opening phase such as they'd just endured; none had ever actually witnessed its like. He settled deeper into his command chair, watching his plot, wondering, and the gleaming diamonds of his battlegroups crept across it toward the waiting wall of Trevayne's warships.

The fleets were still beyond the range at which combat could even be thought of when the rebels received their next surprise.

As a lieutenant, Ian Trevayne had commanded the corvette *Yang'tze*. That starship had been only a little larger than any one of the launchers which now awoke on *Ortega*, *Nelson*, and Sonja Desai's monitors. *Ortega* and *Nelson* each mounted five of them; *Zoroff* and her sisters mounted only three each, and they'd sacrificed ninety percent of their normal armament to squeeze them in. It was a desperate expedient which deprived Fourth Fleet of the solid, close-in punch monitors normally provided, and Trevayne had hoped to reconvert the standard monitors as the supermonitors came on line. But now those launchers spoke in anger for the first time and hurled missiles forth at velocities heretofore unthinkable.

Those missiles were less physical objects than energy states as they lunged at the rebel ships. Given the relatively innocuous name "heavy bombardment missiles," or HBMs, they were twice the size of any missile ever before used in space combat. And the monstrous housings which launched them weren't mass drivers like other missile launchers; they were something else—something technicians feeling their way through an entirely new technology with no ready-made jargon had dubbed "grav drivers." Nor did those missiles rely upon conventional drives; their initial velocities actually *increased* as their new gravitic drive fields cut in.

Even at their speed, the HBMs' range was such that Kellerman's scanners had time to record their novel drive patterns before the first salvo came close enough for cybernetic brains to decree the moment of self-immolation. Forcefields within the warheads collapsed, and matter met antimatter. If the target was a small ship, the small ship died. A capital ship might absorb more than one hit—but not even the most heavily shielded and armored ship could survive more than a very few.

Admiral Kellerman was not a man to panic, and he did not panic now. At such ranges, a high degree of accuracy was impossible, and nine of the first salvo were clean misses. His point defense ignored them, concentrating on the other thirteen, and his seasoned crews stopped ten of them short of his ships' shields. But three got through, and the assault carrier *Hector* vanished in a brilliant flare of light. He winced inwardly at the prodigious power of the new weapons and ordered his fighters launched to clear the suddenly threatened "safety" of their bays. And then Anton Kellerman got his final surprise.

"Admiral!" A scanner rating stiffened at his console as the second wave of HBMs came in. He was a veteran, but his voice wavered on the edge of hysteria. "Admiral! Those misses from the first salvo are *coming back!*"

Kellerman was still turning towards him in disbelief when he, the rating, and the rest of *Unicorn*'s 180,000-tonne hull ceased to be.

* * *

A ripple of shock ran through the rebel fleet as it realized what had happened. Unlike normal missiles, these new monsters didn't simply self-destruct when they overran their targets and lost their vectors. Instead, they turned, and on-board seeking systems of unheard of power quested with insensate malevolence to reacquire the targets they'd missed and bring the HBMs slashing back around in repeated attack runs.

The Republican Navy's appetite for surprise died with its commander. Too many links in the chain of command had already been ground to powder by Skywatch's savage defiance. No one above the rank of rear admiral survived, and the terror of the Rim's new weapons was upon them. The attack force began shedding battlegroups as carriers and battle-cruisers, destroyers and heavy cruisers—the ships with the speed to run—turned and fled. It didn't happen instantly, but the first desertion was like a tiny hole in a straining dike, and the ugly stench of fear was contagious. It swept the Republican command bridges like pestilence, proving that even the most courageous could be panicked by the unexpected.

The Gehenna-bound flotilla had already turned back, and would make it through the Back Door. So would the fastest ships of the main force—those with skippers ruthless enough to abandon their fellows. But for the battleships and the handful of monitors and surviving superdreadnoughts there was no escape.

Trevayne's force accelerated outwards from Xanadu, and something resembling an orthodox space battle began. *Ortega* moved ponderously with BG 32's monitors, advancing beyond *Nelson*'s datalink range; but it no longer mattered. The one thing Trevayne had feared most—sustained stand-off fighter strikes from beyond even HBM range—had evaporated with the flight of the carriers. Only two of them stood to die with the rebel battle line, and their fighters were hideously outnumbered by the fighter strength Trevayne could bring to bear. Stripped of their supporting elements, the rebel capital ships stood no chance against the firepower he commanded—especially since his every ship had been refitted with an improved force beam armament.

More salvos of HBMs were launched, targeted with cold

logic on the lighter battleships and superdreadnoughts. If any ship was to be retaken for the Federation, it would be those monitors—on that Trevayne was savagely determined. The range fell, and space was ugly with the butchery of ships and humans as whoever was in command over there fought to close to SBM range, matching futile gallantry against the deadly technical superiority slaughtering his ships with machinelike precision.

But Fourth Fleet smelled victory in the blood, and Trevayne slewed his ships away, holding the range five light-seconds beyond SBM range while his deadly salvos went out again and again. Yet another was readying when the surrender signal finally arrived. Yoshinaka's face lit and he turned to Trevayne . . . who sat in the admiral's chair and said nothing.

In default of a cease-fire order, the grav drivers flung the waiting salvo outward.

The surrender signal was repeated frantically. The rebels launched deep-space flares which dazzled visual observers and stabbed the com links with screeching static from radioactive components; there could be no mistake.

His staff officers stared at Trevayne. His face was a mask of dark iron set in an indescribable expression none of them had ever seen as he sat absorbed by the tale his battle plot told, saying nothing.

The HBMs continued to home on the monitor *da Silva*, now the rebel flagship. What, Yoshinaka wondered, must those poor bastards be feeling?

Trevayne continued to stare fixedly at the impending final carnage. And on the other side of his eyes, a little girl with chestnut hair played on a beach beside a sunlit sea, and the world was young.

Yoshinaka felt the almost physical force with which everyone else on the bridge pled silently with him to intercede.

He sighed and reached out towards his admiral, turning over in his mind the appeal he wanted to make . . . Ian, right now you're the hero of the age. Don't ruin it. And don't ruin the Rim Federation, which will always be your lengthened shadow. . . .

But, of course, that wasn't the thing to say. Instead, he

touched his friend's shoulder and said, very firmly: "Admiral, they have surrendered."

Trevayne looked up, and his eyes were suddenly clear.

"Quite," he said conversationally. "Cease firing. Reassume control of the missiles and maneuver them to cover the surviving rebel ships. And have communications raise the rebel commander."

So vast was the range at which the engagement had been fought that there was almost a full minute's delay before the big com screen lit. The face upon it belonged to an officer he had known a lifetime ago, in another era.

"This is Fleet Admiral Ian Trevayne, Provisional Governor-General of the Rim Systems. Am I addressing the rebel commander?"

Fifty long, endless seconds trickled past between question and reply.

"As the senior surviving officer of this force, I can nego—" The face of the small woman in the screen was shocked, her voice dull, but she paused suddenly, realizing exactly how he had addressed her, and a flicker of pride reignited in the olive-dark, almond eyes. "I am Rear Admiral Li Han, of the Terran Republican Navy, sir!" she said sharply.

Trevayne's voice did not rise appreciably in volume, but it left no room for any other sound. "Spare me your comic-opera political pretensions, *Captain.* There will be no negotiations. Your ships will lower their shields and heave to for boarding by officers who will take command of them in the name of the legitimate Federation government. Any resistance to our boarding parties on any ship will be construed as a hostile act, terminating the present cease-fire. Is that understood?"

He stood rigidly, watching the screen, waiting as his words winged across to that other bridge, and when they reached it, it was as if he had slapped the rebel commander across the face. Fury flashed in her eyes as she remembered another time and another commander who had faced her with the same option. Yet far more than a single battle-cruiser's fate hung on her decision this day, and the factors she'd gambled on then weren't present now. Thousands of Republican personnel had died already; the death of her remaining ships would achieve nothing. But Trevayne read her rage and leaned forward with a tight, merciless smile.

"I wish you would, Captain," he said, and his voice was a soft, hungry whisper.

It is not pleasant to see the beaten face of a human who accepts defeat neither easily nor often. Most on *Ortega*'s bridge looked away in something akin to embarrassment as his words burned across the light-seconds. They stared at their consoles, waiting, as Li Han faced their admiral and saved the lives of her crews by forcing herself to say: "Understood."

Trevayne broke the connection and spoke in a drained, almost inaudible voice. "Commodore Yoshinaka, please take charge of the surrender arrangements. I'll be in my quarters." He turned on his heel and strode away.

He had barely stepped off the flag bridge when the cheering began, and spread, and grew until the mobile fortress rang with its echoes. He never heard it.

"War is fought by human beings."
General Karl von Clausewitz,
On War

BOND

De facto capital of the Rim Worlds or no, Prescott City wasn't much of a city by Innerworld standards. But it was the largest one on Xanadu, and it was large enough to have traffic problems. Ground traffic was bad enough, but the aerial traffic patterns were even worse, despite the best efforts of overtaxed controllers, human and robotic.

It might not have been so bad had the Provisional Government not established itself here. Not only had the city's population risen by almost fifty percent, but more and more military skimmers reduced its traffic patterns to chaos as they cut across them, their shrill transponder signals clearing a path through the carefully-nurtured order. To the air traffic authorities, the Peaceforce skimmer approaching Government House was only one more flaw in the jigsaw puzzle of their job.

Government House, located on a hilltop in what had been the outskirts of town two years earlier, was the city's most imposing edifice. Silhouetted against the bustling traffic of Abu'said Field, it took on an even more imposing air when the Fleet was in port. Unlike the newer buildings surrounding it, Government House dated back to the Fourth Interstellar War and the initial settlement of Xanadu. Constructed of natural materials, its facade dominated by the addition of Commodore Prescott's monumental bronze column, Government House had been built to last for centuries—and on a far larger scale than it had needed to be. For it had been more than a mere headquarters for a new planetary government. It had been a grand gesture of defiance, thrown in the faces of the Arachnids, one warp transit away.

Ian Trevayne had once told Miriam Ortega that Government House reminded him of a certain Peter the Great, who'd constructed a new capital city on the territory of a country he was then fighting for possession of that very land. Miriam, to his delight, had responded with a pithy phrase from her late mother's lexicon: Government House, she'd said, had *chutzpah*.

The Peaceforcer skimmer slid down onto the Government House roof just at sunset. (At least, Zephrain A was setting. Zephrain B remained high in the sky, glowing as a very tiny sun or a very bright star, depending on how one chose to view it.) A Marine major in undress dark-green trousers and black tunic stepped onto the roof to meet the brown-uniformed Peaceforcers who emerged from the skimmer. With punctilious formality—the two services wasted little love on one another—he took custody of their prisoner, addressing her with a noncommittal "ma'am." Whether Li Han was a captain or an admiral—or, in fact, whether an admitted rebel and mutineer was entitled to a military rank at all—involved political questions the major preferred to leave to older, wiser, and better-paid heads.

Li Han looked even smaller than usual between her two guards. They towered above her, and their combined body weight outmassed her by a factor of almost five. Her cheeks were slightly sunken (the food at the prison compound was adequate, but not always appetizing), emphasizing her clean facial structure, and she moved with her habitual grace, thanks to a rigidly self-imposed exercise schedule, but she looked like a child in an adult's pajamas in her standard-sized gray prison garb. The major eyed the unprepossessing little figure with a measure of curiosity mingled with contempt—anything less like a Navy flag officer was hard to imagine.

Until she opened her mouth.

"Good evening, Major," she said crisply. "You may escort me to the Governor-General."

The major's hand was halfway into a salute before he caught himself. He managed to maintain his military bearing, but there was a brief pause before he mumbled, "This way, ma'am." He turned on his heel and led the small, ramrod-straight figure to the elevator, glaring at any of his subordinates who looked like they might even be thinking of smiling.

Prisoners were rare in warfare against alien species—the only sort of war the TFN had ever fought. Not only did ship-to-ship combat generally result in the annihilation of the loser's crew, but what prisoners were taken were usually turned over to the xenologists (or their alien equivalents) rather than becoming a charge of the military authorities. Hence, the Federation's Navy's codes, both for treatment of prisoners and conduct when captured, were badly underdeveloped. As senior prisoner, Han had been forced virtually to reinvent the whole concept of a POW doctrine.

She'd been offered parole and freedom of the planet, as befitted her rank, but she'd refused, electing to stay with her fellow prisoners. The shock of defeat and—far worse—the desertion of their fellows had come hard for them. Morale had deteriorated as their sense of betrayal became resentment, directed almost as much at their own officers for surrendering as at those others who had deserted them. For Han, even less accustomed than her crews to the notion of defeat and supremely incapable of dishonoring herself by abandoning her comrades, surrender had held a particularly painful poignancy. And the situation was made still worse because her battlegroup's late transfer to Kellerman's command had left her a virtual unknown to most of her fellow POWs—an unknown who'd surrendered them all to the Rim. But she'd attacked her problems and theirs with all the compassion and ruthlessness which made her what she was. Now, nine months later, the captured Republican personnel were warriors once more.

But once the immediate personnel problems were resolved, Han found herself with nothing to do. The camp was like a well-run ship or squadron, fully capable of humming smoothly along under the direction of her exec as long as she stood aloofly behind him as the distant yet instantly available balance wheel. She'd found that being a "commander-in-chief," even of a prison camp, was even more lonely than battlegroup command.

As fall gave way to the short, mild winter of Xanadu's temperate zones, Han realized the irony of her success. She'd given her subordinates purpose and unity while she herself fretted like a captive bird against the maddening inertia and monotony of her captivity. Only once had there been any excitement to vary the soul-crushing boredom of her life.

Han's experience with governments in general, and particularly with those serving the purposes of the Corporate Worlds, had not been happy. So when she was summoned to meet a Ms. Miriam Ortega, Provisional Grand Councilor for Internal Security of the Rim Systems, she was prepared to confront yet another bored, insensitive bureaucrat.

But Ms. Ortega had begun by gracefully dismissing the camp commandant, effectively placing the entire interview off the record, which was not typical of the red tape-worshiping automatons Han associated with "government" outside the Terran Republic.

It was both a shrewd and a generous gesture, Han had thought, and felt herself warm towards the other woman. She thawed further as they discussed camp conditions and the needs of the prisoners, and it was heaven to talk to someone new after months of the same faces! Especially to someone like this irreverently intelligent woman with her earthy sense of humor. Han had worked hard for the serene devotion to duty which was hers, yet she'd paid a price of loneliness along the way. Now, as she talked with Miriam Ortega, she felt the attraction that opposites often exert, and it was hard to remember they were enemies.

When it was time for her to go, she'd risen with regret. Yet before she left, she'd fumbled to frame an awkward question, despite her fear that it might shatter the precarious rapport she'd found with her "enemy."

"Ms. Ortega, I couldn't help wondering . . . with your last name . . ."

Miriam Ortega, had stopped her, answering the question before she could complete it.

"Admiral Ortega was my father," she'd said simply.

Han had regretted the painful question, under the circumstances, but the woman with the marvelously expressive face had continued.

"He was a man of strong principles and he died acting

on them—a pretty good way to go, I think." Then, with another smile, "I hear you've very nearly done so several times!" and the thawing process was complete, the rapport no longer forced.

Han was stunned, later, to learn through the carefully-cultivated guards' grapevine that Miriam Ortega was Ian Trevayne's lover. To be sure, he *had* been out of contact with his wife for over three standard years. But . . .

Han had never met Natalya Nikolayevna Trevayne, but the woman's flawless beauty had been the subject of frequent comment by envious male officers and ostentatiously indifferent female ones, and there had never been a whisper of a hint of infidelity in all the Fleet gossip. Surely Miriam Ortega, however striking in her own dark, very individual way, couldn't possibly be Trevayne's type! And yet . . . was it her imagination, or had a certain humorous warmth crept into the other's voice whenever she spoke of "the Governor-General"?

Then, with the onset of spring, came the summons which had taken her from the compound for the first time in half a year. Now, walking under guard through the corridors of Government House, she concentrated on looking unconcerned as she wondered why Trevayne had sent for her.

They came to the suite of offices from which Ian Trevayne ruled the Rim Systems. Han and her intelligence officers had spent considerable effort piecing together a schematic of the Provisional Government, and she sometimes thought it might have been designed by the legendary pre-space engineer Goldberg. Most of the day-to-day administration devolved on the departments headed by the members of the Grand Council, who were members of the Rim Legislative Assembly and so responsible to it. But they worked for and in the name of Governor-General Trevayne, who, even though he was the sole member of the executive branch, wasn't even a member of the Assembly, much less responsible to it. *He* was responsible directly to the Federation Legislative Assembly on Old Terra—with which he was only infrequently and circuitously in touch by some means Han had yet to uncover. It was one of those legal tangles which *homo sapiens* secretly and guiltily loves, she'd decided, but it worked . . . as her present captivity demonstrated all too well.

The major ushered her through the bustling outer offices and knocked at the Governor-General's private office doors. A voice from within called admittance, and the major pushed the old-fashioned doors open and stepped back, coming to a sort of half-attention as she passed him. He closed the doors quietly, not without a sigh of regret. Normally he had no strong interest in the meetings of his superiors, but this time he couldn't quite suppress his curiosity. Somehow, he felt, any discussion between those personalities was bound to produce some very interesting by-products.

Trevayne sat behind his desk, wearing the carefully-tailored civilian dress he permitted his Governor-General persona. A broad window behind him overlooked Prescott City, and a cabinet below it held two holo cubes. One showed three women—no, Han decided, a woman and two teen-aged girls. In the other, a dark young man in the black-and-silver of a TFN ensign tried not to look too pleased with himself. She looked away and came to attention before the desk, and a brief silence ensued as she and Trevayne regarded one another and both recalled another meeting in another office.

Trevayne spoke first. "Please be seated," he invited.

"I prefer to stand, sir."

"Just as you like," he nodded, sounding unsurprised. "But please stand easy, Admiral Li."

What he'd said registered as she went into a stiff "at ease," and Trevayne smiled briefly at the minute widening of her eyes—her equivalent, he suspected, of openmouthed astonishment.

"Yes," he continued, "we've received one of our infrequent messages from the Innerworlds. It seems the government has, for legalistic reasons with which I'll not bore you, has chosen to accord limited belligerent status to those worlds styling themselves 'the Terran Republic.' " He sounded as if he'd bitten into something sour. "This entails, among other things, recognition of all commissions bestowed by that . . . entity. I have, of course, no alternative but to conform to this policy." He allowed himself a wry smile. "I console myself with the thought that its purpose is 'not to confer a compliment but to secure a convenience,' in the words of Winston Churchill, with whom you may not be familiar—"

"On the contrary, Admiral," Han interrupted. "Winston Churchill was a politician on Old Terra during the Age of Mao Tse-Tung—a very eloquent spokesman for an imperial system which was already doomed."

Trevayne was momentarily speechless, but he recovered quickly and resumed. "We're also in receipt of one other bit of news which I think you'll find pertinent. The Federation has agreed to a general prisoner exchange to reclaim the loyalist personnel incarcerated by the various Fringe Worlds. You'll be leaving Xanadu within the week."

It was Han's turn to find herself completely at a loss. Trevayne awaited her response with curiosity.

"Admiral," she said finally, "I believe I *will* sit down."

He motioned her to a chair. "You will, I trust, be able to inform your superiors that you've been well treated?"

"Yes," she admitted, still grappling with the stunning news. Then she shook herself. "In particular, I'd like to commend the compound medical staff for their skill and, even more, for their humanity." She thought of Daffyd Llewellyn on another planet, and smiled. "That quality seems to transcend political alignments—at least in the best doctors." Trevayne nodded, declining to mention the considerable care he and Doctor Yuan had given to selecting the prison camp medical staff. "And," she continued, "please convey my respects and gratitude to Grand Councilor Ortega for the interest she has taken in our welfare." She watched curiously for his reaction, but he only nodded again.

"I will. And in return, I'll ask you to convey a message for me." He gazed at her over steepled fingers. "Certain medical personnel from Zephrain, whom we'd thought lost to Tangri corsairs, were repatriated by your government before the negotiations for the present exchange had been formally begun. From them, we've learned that they were in fact captured by humans, of a sort—former TFN personnel indulging in a bit of free-lance piracy." His words could have been light. They weren't.

"Historically—" his eyes grew very hard "—brigandage by renegades purporting to represent one side or another is one of the inevitable consequences of civil wars—one of the many nasty consequences which the initiators of the breakups always seem to overlook, and for which they never accept the slightest responsibility. But I disgress." His expression softened a trifle. "Please express to your superiors my thanks for repatriating our people. And," he added, leaning forward and smiling very slightly, "please accept my personal thanks for ridding the Galaxy of a particularly loathsome excrescence on the human race."

Han nodded, taken slightly aback, for she hadn't even known the doctors and nurses had been returned, though she'd urged the Admiralty to do so. On the other hand, her recommendations might have had more weight if a certain portion of the Republican Navy hadn't disapproved of her handling of the situation. If Ruyard's surrender had been accepted, they pointed out, the Fleet would have gained five cruisers, plus his destroyers.

She and Tomanaga had argued that her actions had been good and prudent tactics, precluding any possibility of further treachery on Ruyard's part and so terrifying the pirates still on the planet as to prevent any last minute atrocities. Nevertheless, Han had been officially censured, though the First Space Lord had told her privately that he approved her handling of the battle.

Personally, Han had never considered the episode a "battle" at all, though it was now officially called the Battle of Siegfried. From her perspective, it had been a case of vermin extermination.

Silence stretched out across the desk as Trevayne toyed with a stylus, and Han sensed an unaccustomed hesitance, even an awkwardness, on his part.

"Admiral," she asked tentatively at last, "may I go?"

"Eh?" He looked up quickly, as if caught off balance while trying to formulate a statement or question. "You may," he said gruffly.

Han stood and walked toward the doors. Then she stopped and turned back to face him.

"Admiral, if I may ask . . . why did you bring me here to tell me this, instead of simply sending word through Commandant Chanet?"

Trevayne glanced back down at his desk for a moment, seeming to gather himself. Then he looked back up at her.

"Admiral Li," he almost blurted, "were you, by any chance, involved in the raid on Galloway's World?"

Han eyed him sharply. Now why, she wondered, did he want to know *that*? There'd been some ugly repercussions over the strike, she recalled, despite the fact that every strategist had always known the Jamieson Archipelago was a primary strategic target. Still, both sides had been horrified by the heavy civilian casualties, and the raid had led to the *de facto* agreement banning nuclear strikes on inhabited planets. But why. . . ?

Understanding struck. Her glance switched quickly to the holos as she remembered a conversation in Admiral Rutgers' office, and her eyes widened in horrified understanding.

And then her gaze met Trevayne's. His eyes were almost beseeching, and he read the shocked compassion in hers. For an instant, there was an intangible bond between them.

Han needed to say something—she knew not what—to reach out to this man who'd lost so much. She opened her mouth to speak . . .

. . . and remembered the Second Battle of Zephrain, when Fourth Fleet hung beyond weapon range and the deadly HBMs kept coming in spite of her desperately repeated surrender signals. As the missiles which had already been fired looped impossibly back, closing through the storm of counter missiles and point defense lasers, joined by fresh salvos from the enemy fleet, Han had sat in her command chair, giving her orders calmly, holding her people together even as she waited to die with them.

And now she looked at the dark, menacingly bearded face across the desk and saw not a man whose family had died but the callous, murderous commander who had been willing to butcher her helpless crews.

"No, Admiral." Her voice rang in the still room. "I had no part in that heroic action!"

She watched Ian Trevayne rise, his dark face expressionless despite the terrible fire that blazed suddenly in his eyes. She watched him walk around his desk, and the furious anger of his anguish came with him. She sensed the murder in his heart, but she held herself stiffly, her own eyes hard and hating as they burned into his, refusing to flinch.

He stopped, fisted hands clenched at his sides, and muscles trembled in his arms as he fought to keep them there—fought to control the furious need to smash them into her suddenly hateful face.

And then he straightened, expelled a long breath, and was no longer a mere vessel of fury. He jabbed the button which summoned the Marine guards.

"Remove the prisoner," he told them, looking over her head. They did. And as they hustled her out of the door, she looked back, and in his face she seemed to see a reflection of herself, like a mirror of the soul. She couldn't explain the sudden surge of empathic understanding, for she herself had never felt what she saw in that face . . . except, possibly . . .

Comprehension came wrenchingly as she remembered *Argosy Polaris* and those child-bodies. And at that moment, she knew exactly how Ian Trevayne saw those to whom he'd almost done what she had done to Arthur Ruyard.

Their eyes met one more time, and for the barest instant the bond was back. But now their tenuous, shared understanding encompassed the unforgivable wrongs they'd done one another, the wrongs that were somehow a microcosm of the whole, colossal tragedy in which they were caught up. The understanding flared up between them, hideous with the deadly, conflicting tides of duty and desperation and hatred which could bring good and decent human beings to such a pass, but for only an instant . . . then it was cut off by the closing office doors.

Trevayne stared at the closed doors for a moment. Then he walked to his office's private washroom and stared into the mirror for a long, long time, as if prolonging the hideous glimpse he'd gotten into his soul.

COUNTERSTRIKE

The prisoners had departed and spring was turning into summer when the Orion courier craft emerged from the Zephrain-Rehfrak warp point. The commander of the picket stationed there had explicit orders covering this rare occurrence, and a brief message was smoothly transferred before the Orions departed as quickly as they'd come. The message was beamed to TFNS *Horatio Nelson* in a high-speed squeal carried by a hair-thin laser, and *Nelson*'s receiving dishes scooped it out of space and beamed it down to Government House with equal security, and Ian Trevayne called an emergency meeting of the Grand Council.

"The Orions are being even more uninformative than usual," he told them. "They say only that an emissary will be arriving here from Rehfrak in less than three standard weeks. Period." He shrugged. "This will be the first time an Orion has come to Zephrain since the war began—more than that; as far as I'm aware, it will be the first time a highly-placed Orion official has paid an official call on *any* section of the Federation during that time. There's no hint as to the purpose of the visit, but I'll wager it's something big. Remember, the Orions don't prize prolixity the way we do. Among them, the more important an announcement is, the more terse it's likely to be." He hoped the implication wouldn't be lost on certain overly-verbal persons, but he suspected it would be. "So," he concluded, "this emissary will probably be quite a high-ranking Orion. Possibly even Leornak himself."

"Or someone even higher?" queried Barry de Parma.

"There *is* no one higher in this part of Orion space," Trevayne said flatly. "Only five Orion military officers outrank Leornak'zilshisdrow, but that's only part of it. Theoretically, the Khanate is an absolute monarchy, but the district governors are practically autonomous as long as they follow the Khan's policy guidelines. You might say Leornak has what we'd consider permanent emergency wartime powers, if only because of the sheer distance between him and the Khan. No, anyone higher than he would have to come all the way from New Valkha itself; and if we rate that kind of attention, God only knows what's afoot!

"At any rate, we have to decide on the nature of our welcome. I propose to greet the envoy aboard *Nelson*. It never hurts to impress the Orions—though, needless to say, I have no intention of inviting as knowledgeable an old cat as Leornak to examine our new weaponry!" They all nodded at that. "And I think we should have a high-powered political presence on board: Mister de Parma, Ms. Ortega, and Mister MacFarland."

Again, there was no demurral. De Parma, as titular head of the Grand Council, was an obvious choice. So was Bryan MacFarland, Grand Councilor for External Affairs. He'd always had little to do, inasmuch as the Provisional Government's only exchanges with other human polities had been restricted to nuclear warheads and the only nonhuman powers with whom the Rim had contact were the Orions (whose official policy was one of non-intercourse for the duration) and the Tangri (whose permanent policy was that humans were simply an exceptionally dangerous species of prey). Now it seemed his hour might have arrived. Besides, Trevayne found him a refreshing personality. His world of Aotearoa, as its name suggested, had been settled initially by New Zealanders, but most of its subsequent immigrants had been from Australia. Now the Aotearoans were more Aussie than the Aussies—just listening to MacFarland reminded Trevayne of his tour at the Navy's strikefighter pilot program at Brisbane on Old Terra.

There was another, unspoken reason for including him, though. So far, the pressure of the war effort had kept the other Rim Worlds from resenting the disproportionate role played by Xandies in the Provisional Government, but it was only a matter of time. Trevayne intended to forestall it by involving as many non-Xandies as possible in high-level functions. Miriam, though a Xandy by adoption, wholeheartedly approved. She herself had no obvious business aboard *Nelson*, but no one questioned his decision to include her.

It was odd, he thought. In most times and places, a relationship like their never-acknowledged but widely-known one would have damaged her politically. But it hadn't done so here. Perhaps, he thought wryly, it was because no matter how tightly allied they were, she never hesitated to disagree (sometimes violently) when she thought he was wrong—and her disagreements weren't always announced in private. No one could ever think Miriam Ortega's politics belonged to anyone but herself, and it showed even more strongly against the virtually unbroken deference her fellow Grand Councilors extended towards his policies.

Miriam looked up and hid a smile as his musing glance slid past her. She knew what he was thinking, just as she knew his habitual blind spot kept him from seeing the answer. Part of her fellows' acceptance came from the fact that she refused to be awed by their governor-general, but at least as much stemmed from the unique status their relationship had conferred upon her. In the eyes of the Rim population, Trevayne's standing was such that he was, quite simply, above resentment, and she, by close association with him, shared in the *mana*. Yet he would never understand the way it worked, she thought. He was too intimately acquainted with what he considered his weaknesses to accept that the Rim could see him—or her—in that light. And she'd be damned before she'd in any way suggest it to him.

The Orion cutter completed its docking sequence in *Nelson*'s boatbay, where Trevayne stood before a group that included Vice Admiral Sonja Desai, Commodore Genji Yoshinaka, and Captain Lewis Mujabi of the *Nelson* in addition to the Grand Councilors. The officers (including Trevayne) wore full dress uniform for the occasion, and each left shoulder bore the distinctive patch which Trevayne had recently authorized for the Rim armed forces: a ring of stars (one for each Rim system) surrounding the planet-and-moon of the Federation. Miriam had suggested that the stars should encircle a human hand with the *digitus impudicus* upraised to express the true spirit of the Rim. Trevayne was privately convinced she was right, but he had—reluctantly—vetoed the suggestion.

The hatch opened, and the emissary emerged.

Trevayne said, simply, "No."

"But yes!" Kevin Sanders beamed, stepping down the short gangway ramp with a spryness that longevity technology alone couldn't explain. He was, as usual, clearly enjoying himself.

Trevayne stepped forward and bent slightly so he could speak softly into Sanders' ear. "You old sod! How the hell did you talk the Orions into letting you through? No, wait, let me guess: I daresay you had your spies dredge up something in Leornak's sex life to hold over him!"

"Admiral! I am cut to the quick! I'll have you know that I've never approved of blackmail. I much prefer bribery; greed is more dependable than fear. The fact is," Sanders grinned hugely, "I brought him a case of Jack Daniels. Been keeping him supplied since the war began."

Then he became, if not serious, at least sincere. "It was necessary for a cabinet-level official to come here, Admiral, and I pulled every string in sight to be the one. May I say that's it's a pleasure to see you again? As a token of my esteem, I've brought you a case of Glen Grant."

Trevayne's face was momentarily transfigured. Then he glared. "At least have the goodness to tell me what *I'm* being bribed to do."

"All in good time, Admiral," Sanders said with another of his disarming chuckles. "For now, let's not keep the reception committee waiting."

Trevayne introduced the Gray Eminence of Terran Intelligence to the officers and politicians. Sanders bowed over Miriam's hand with courtly grace, addressing her as "Madam Ortega" and, incredibly, leaving her almost flustered. The bugger plays the gentleman of the old school to the hilt, Trevayne thought dourly.

Then they all moved towards *Nelson's* wardroom, where Captain Mujabi had prepared to extend his ship's hospitality. Trevayne contrived to maneuver himself and Sanders into an otherwise empty intraship car, intending to grill the unexpected visitor. But as soon as they were alone, Sanders turned to him with an expression that was half-amused and half-abashed.

"Ahem . . . Admiral, do you recall the HV chips I gave you at Rehfrak?"

"Yes," Trevayne replied, caught off balance. "They've unaccountably disappeared, I'm afraid." Please, God, he thought quickly. Don't let the bastard have another set!

"I'd suspected that might happen. However, the series was such a resounding success that they've produced a sequel: *Triumph at Zephrain*. I had intended to arrange direct distribution rather than troubling you with the matter . . . thus minimizing the possibility of the sort of accident which befell the original." He paused, gauging the visible effect of all this on Trevayne. Judging the risk of coronary arrest to be within acceptable limits, he rusumed.

"But I've changed my mind after meeting Ms. Ortega. You see, she figures rather, ah, prominently in the sequel. And I can see now that the unknown actress who, for obscure reasons, was chosen to play her was badly miscast. She isn't endowed with the Grand Councilor's vivid personality and lively intelligence—however well-endowed she may be in certain other respects. So, Admiral, I think I'll let you be the judge of the production's suitability for public display in the Rim systems. Or, for that matter, private viewing by Ms. Ortega." He smiled beatifically.

Trevayne forced himself to recall a bit of folk wisdom from Sanders' part of Old Terra: He may be a son-of-a-bitch, but at least he's *our* son-of-a-bitch. Suddenly he grinned. He might as well, he decided, give over trying to resist the man. It was hopeless, anyway.

"Very handsome of you," he said. "Glen Grant, is it? For God's sake, call me 'Ian,' you sodding Yank!"

* * *

"All right. Talk."

Trevayne and Sanders sat in the former's stateroom. Like all spacecraft living quarters, it was compact, but it was comfortable and laid out so efficiently its efficiency was barely noticeable. Captain Mujabi, who hadn't been expecting an extra passenger for the return to Xanadu, had assigned Sanders a similar compartment. Fortunately, the *Nelson* class was designed to house admirals and their staffs.

Trevayne watched Sanders' eyes twinkle. The evening's socializing (a nearby supernova would have been less of a novelty than a visitor direct from Old Terra) had been so intense that he'd managed to pry Sanders loose only by leaving Miriam to fight a rearguard action. He more than suspected that Sanders had enjoyed every moment of his notoriety—he certainly hadn't made any effort to assist in separating himself from it!

"Talk," Trevayne repeated. "I'll not get a wink of sleep until you tell me the news."

"Well, Ian," Sanders temporized, "there was more truth than poetry to the excuse you used to haul me out of the wardroom: I *am* a bit fatigued. After all, I'm not as young as I once was. . . ."

"You'll bury us all," Trevayne said flatly. "Stop playing games, for once, and tell me exactly what you're doing out here. You may as well face the fact that you're not getting out of this stateroom until I know!"

"Very well." Sanders sighed in mock resignation. "As you've no doubt gathered, your victory at Second Zephrain changed the entire complexion of the war. As I mentioned at Rehfrak, the rebels have been pressing us hard almost from the beginning, and to date, it's always been a matter of their taking choke points away from us, no matter what minor tactical successes we've had." He paused thoughtfully, face very intent. For just a moment, Trevayne realized, his mask was slipping.

"You know, Ian," he said slowly, "I think the Innerworlds were even less well-prepared for this war than they've been thinking."

"How the bloody hell do you 'prepare' for something like this?" Trevayne asked quietly. "It can't be done."

"No, but there are . . . mindsets, call them, which can

make or break your ability to cope when it comes," Sanders countered. "Look at it this way. Anyone who could count knew that the Fringe, with thirty percent of the people, provided sixty percent of the Fleet—but no one really seemed to think about the attitudes which sent so many Fringers into uniform. And not just the sheer numbers of them, either; the composition of the Fringer military should have given us pause."

"You mean all the female personnel?" Trevayne asked softly.

"Exactly." Sanders eyes lit as he realized Trevayne understood precisely what he meant. "Fringe Worlds are chary with the lives of their women, Ian. They have exactly the opposite problem from that of the Innerworlds; too few people and too much planet. So every potential mother is desperately needed, and they've acquired a whole new social status as a result. Fringer women tend to be protected as their planets' investment in the future, yet over forty percent of all Fringer military personnel are women. That bespeaks a culture which places a high premium on military responsibility . . . a higher premium, I'm afraid, than Innerworlders do."

"The old 'rich democracies are soft' argument?" Trevayne could have sounded mocking, but he didn't.

"In a sense. Not so much soft, though, as inexperienced. There haven't been any real penetrations of Innerworld space—except for Timor and the Alpha Centauri raid—in two centuries, Ian. Innerworlders have been insulated from the realities of warfare, and, frankly, they didn't have the initial personal commitment the Fringers had. Then they lost all those Fleet units and, as a result, all the early engagements. It shook them pretty badly. In fact, I'm afraid there was a lot of defeatism—or, no, not *defeatism* so much as fatalism. There was no fire in the Federation's belly, if you'll pardon the purple prose." He grinned, and the serious, analytical thinker vanished once more into the persona of the japester.

"But all that changed when First Zephrain convinced the Innerworlds we can win victories—and they don't even know about the new technology yet. So now the Corporate and Heart Worlds are feeling full of beans for the first time since this war began, and the rebels have been given a shock that puts *them* on the defensive for the first time. So . . ."

The light above the stateroom door flashed in a series of blinks Sanders suspected wasn't as random as it seemed. Trevayne touched the admittance stud, and Miriam Ortega stepped through the door as it slid open.

"Sorry I took so long," she said to Trevayne. There were only two chairs, so she perched on the edge of the bunk. "Barry can be long-winded at times. Hope I haven't missed too much."

Sanders cleared his throat and gave Trevayne a quizzical look, only to be answered with a bland smile.

"Ms. Ortega is cleared for 'Most Secret,' " he said. His smile broadened slightly as he added. "By me, under my emergency powers. I call your attention to the documents you gave me at Rehfrak. . . ."

"No problem with clearance, Ian," Sanders waved that point aside. "But while I don't wish to appear ungracious, Ms. Ortega, it's my duty to question your need to know."

"Ms. Ortega is my closest ally in the Provisional Government. Whatever it is you expect out of the Rim Systems, she's going to be instrumental in mobilizing political support for it. She'll have to know sooner or later." Trevayne's face showed a trace of exasperation. "It's as I told you at Rehfrak. D'you think the Rim puts out the kind of effort that won Second Zephrain because I stand over them with a whip? Not bloody likely!"

Sanders understood. He'd noted, without comment, the patch on Trevayne's left sleeve: hardly a standard TFN shoulder flash! Fleet flashes indicated individual planets, members of the Federation—not whole multi-system political units. He glanced over at Miriam, watching her busy herself lighting a cigarette as if to stand aside from the discussion. She felt his gaze and looked up with a flashing smile.

"Just think of me as part of the furniture, Mister Sanders. My application for a Beautiful Female Spy's license was turned down when I flunked the physical. And," she added, her smile turning into something suspiciously like a grin, "please call me Miriam."

Sanders smiled back. He wanted to play no power games with these people. In theory, he spoke with the voice of the prime minister. But that, he acknowledged wryly, was bullshit. If Trevayne didn't happen to like an order, he had every legal right to demand confirmation from the cabinet—which was impossible. And then they'd be back at square one. So, he concluded happily, to hell with it.

"Believe me, Miriam," he said in his most winning voice, "you'll never be mistaken for part of the furniture. And I'm grateful to Ian for giving me an out for including you in the discussion. Now, where was I?

"Oh, yes, the effect of Second Zephrain on the Innerworlds. You see, the rebels were already on the defensive, but the Innerworlds didn't really realize it. The insiders knew, of course; why should the rebels come to us anymore? They already *had* everything they wanted in Innerworld space. So they reverted to a holding stance and turned their attention in your direction, and there wasn't a lot we could do about it, especially not now that the rebel yards appear to be keeping pace with their losses in everything but heavy battle-line units. Now, however, they've run slap into your new technologies, and it's clear the new developments give the Rim a tremendous combat advantage. But that advantage doesn't apply to the Innerworlds, because there's no way to send us the data through Orion space. Oh, our R&D efforts have been spurred, of course—but so have the rebels', and, for that matter, the Orions'. In engineering matters, knowing for certain that a given thing can be done is half the battle. But even so, R&D takes time.

"So the cabinet and admiralty have decided to make the time lag in development an asset rather than a liability. They've decided on a coordinated attack to open up a corridor between the Rim and the rest of the Federation *now*, while only the Rim has the new weapons. The purposes, of course, are manifold, but one of the obvious ones is to hit the rebels before *they* have time to develop the same weapons and, simultaneously, to get actual samples of the technology into Innerworld hands. Once we can apply Innerworld industrial capacity to turning out the new weapons you've already developed, we'll be able to put an end to this war.

"And that, to answer your question, is why I'm here: to coordinate this end of Operation Yellowbrick, the campaign to reunite the loyal segments of the Federation."

"But . . ." Miriam paused. "Excuse me. I may be a Navy brat, but I'm also about as unmilitary a person as you're ever likely to meet. Still, it occurs to me that there are a dozen rebel-held systems on the most direct warp line between Zephrain and the Innerworlds, aren't there?"

"Thirteen, to be exact," Sanders replied. "Yes, I know that sounds like a lot of systems to blast your way through. But if we attack from both ends simultaneously . . . well, I've lost most of my initial skepticism now that I've seen this ship. I knew about her in a general way, but nothing I'd heard or read quite prepared me for the impact. How many *Nelsons* do you have?"

"Six. Four more in a month or so," Trevayne responded absently. He'd taken on a thoughtful, brooding look while the other man had been speaking.

Sanders' well-schooled features hid his astonishment. Ten of these leviathans, constructed and manned by a thinly-populated region like the Rim?! Trevayne was right: these people were . . . formidable.

The other two, he could tell, were deep in their thoughts. Trevayne was at his most inscrutable. Miriam puffed on her cigarette and looked worried.

Abruptly Trevayne looked up, and the introspective look was gone.

"Yes," he said. "I agree. It can be done. And this damned deadlock is going to continue as long as the Federation is split into two parts, neither strong enough to scotch the rebellion. Every month of delay will only create a greater subliminal acceptance of the *status quo* by everyone involved. So when is our offensive scheduled to begin?"

"The details are in my subconscious, to be retrieved under deep hypnosis by means of . . . a certain trigger word I'll tell you how to obtain later." Cautious habits die hard. "But it's about three standard months from now."

"Three months! Bloody hell, man! D'you realize what's involved? Nobody in history's ever tried to mount a sustained offensive through this many warp connections! The supply problem alone . . . we'll have to commandeer half the bleeding freighters in the Rim just to haul ammunition! And I don't suppose you have detailed information on the defenses we'll encounter along the way, now do you? *I* certainly don't! And no bloody way to get it, either—you can only send probes so far, you know."

"Ah, but think of the incentive you have: getting rid of me!" Sanders beamed innocently at them. "Not wishing to belabor the obvious, I haven't mentioned that I'm your permanent guest until we fight our way back to the Innerworlds. After all, it's out of the question for me to go back through Orion space now that they know approximately what your new weapons can do. I may be a technical near-illiterate, but I *have* seen some of what you've got at first hand. Leornak would hate it, but he'd have to arrange an 'accident' and go back to drinking domestic Orion booze!"

Trevayne laughed. Miriam smoked her cigarette and glanced back and forth between the two men, very thoughtfully.

There was little leisure for anyone after their arrival at Xanadu. The welter of details inundated them so completely that it was several days before Trevayne and Sanders could sit privately in Trevayne's office discussing his plans for a final fleet operational exercise.

"Are you sure you won't come along? I can promise you quite a show."

"Thank you, Ian, but the trip out here was all the spacing I can handle for a while at my age." Trevayne snorted. If Sanders had been much younger he wouldn't have left him on the same planet with Miriam.

"No, seriously," Sanders insisted. "I've been chronically fatigued lately. I think I'm still having trouble with this twenty-nine-hour day. One loses one's adaptability in such things, you know. Still, I wouldn't have missed this for the Galaxy. I was getting bored with Old Terra and the cabinet, not necessarily in that order."

Trevayne was quiet for a moment, regarding his blotter with pursed lips as if the mention of the cabinet had started a new train of thought. When he looked up, he spoke with some hesitancy.

"Kevin, if you don't mind my asking . . . how well do you know Prime Minister Dieter?"

"Personally? Hardly at all. He's not an easy man to know. Why?"

"Oh, I was just wondering what you think of him."

"Or," Sanders grinned, "put another way, how did the man responsible for the mess wind up as prime minister? Actually, it was pretty much a matter of elimination; every other Corporate World delegate was too discredited, and we're just damned lucky he was available. He's had to accept a pretty broad spectrum of ministers—all the way from Amanda Sydon as Treasury Minister to Roger Hadad from Old Terra as Foreign Minister—but he combined Defense with the premiership, and that gave him a leg up. By now, he's firmly in control and shaping up very nicely." Sanders shrugged.

"I'm relieved to hear you think so highly of him," Trevayne said slowly, "but I'm a bit concerned by this policy of what seems to be *de facto* recognition of the Terran Republic. Of course," he added, "this is all entirely off the record. Publicly, I've followed the government line to the letter. But privately . . . well, I can't help thinking that you've lost half the battle when you accept the other side's semantics. It was a mistake your ancestors and mine frequently made in the twentieth century."

"It wasn't an easy decision," Sanders acknowledged. "But there are difficulties in fighting a war when you don't recognize your opponent's legal existence. Some of them are amazing. It reminds me of the American Civil War, six centuries ago. The government of the old 'United States' never officially recognized the secessionist confederation as a separate nation, but in practice it treated it as a belligerent in a number of ways. For example, it declared a blockade, which is by definition something you do to a foreign power. The legally consistent approach would've been to simply declare the seceding states' ports closed to foreign commerce, but the only effect of that would've been to make the United States government a laughingstock."

"I know," Trevayne nodded, "but I never realized you were a history enthusiast, Kevin."

"I leave that to people like yourself," Sanders grinned with an eloquent, seated half-bow. "But there's been a lot of research into the civil wars of Old Terra lately. We don't have much recent experience to go by, so Dieter's had the archives turned upside-down for precedents." He paused thoughtfully.

"That's one of his great strengths, you know: he's a detail man. And his other strength is his ability to face new realities squarely . . . not an easy thing to do, but, then, he's had a lot of experience since the MacTaggart assassination. Now that he's learned how, he's very much in the mainstream tradition of the Federation, of course. You know the Federation has never been a monolithic ideological state. Centralized, yes, but not monolithic; it couldn't have been, even when it was restricted to the Solar System. The rebels recognized that when they opted for such a loose, federalized system, but realists have always known the Federation could only function as a template on which diverse cultures and interests could interact and reach compromise accommodations." He stopped rather abruptly, his mischievous look suddenly returning. "Anyway, whatever else can be said of Dieter, he's unquestionably a superb judge of character. After all, he brought me out of retirement, didn't he?"

Sanders rose from his cluttered desk and stretched. He was the last one left in his offices in Government House—not surprisingly, at this hour of the night. The staff Trevayne had assigned to him had all gone home, leaving him to cope with the effects of Xandau's damned, long day as best he could. Ever since he'd arrived, he'd felt as if he'd stayed up far too late. Which, he decided, he really had in this case. He switched off the light and started to leave, but stopped on seeing the figure silhouetted in the door to the still-lighted outer office.

"Good evening, Kevin," Miriam Ortega said. "May I come in?"

"Certainly." He turned on the desk lamp and waved at a chair, sitting back down himself. They sat on opposite sides of the bright pool of light, and Government House was quiet around them.

"To what do I owe the pleasure?" he asked, thinking this was the first he'd seen of her since Trevayne had departed for the Fleet exercise. She got out a cigarette, and he automatically reached across with an antique desk lighter. The spill of light from the small flame glowed on her bold features as she puffed the tobacco alight. Blue smoke spiraled through the island of light and vanished into the surrounding darkness.

"Well," she said around the cigarette, "I was wondering if you were ready to tell me what you weren't telling us aboard the *Nelson.*"

Sanders almost dropped the lighter.

"Whatever do you mean?" he asked warily. Miriam sat back and blew smoke in his direction with a gently malicious smile uncannily like that he sometimes saw in his mirror.

"When you and Ian discussed this offensive, I couldn't help noticing a slight discrepancy between what he said and what you said," she said. "He took it for granted that reopening contact with the Innerworlds was the first step in a final campaign to force the rebels back into the fold. And you never corrected him. *But*—" she gave him the same smile once more "—you never actually said that, did you? The closest you came was . . . oh, how did you phrase it . . . 'putting an end to this war.' At the time, I thought it might just be the nit-picking lawyer in me, which was one reason I didn't mention it. But now I've gotten to know you better than that, Kevin. No matter how glib and charming you may be, you never say anything—or leave anything out—without a damned good reason."

Sanders savored a number of unaccustomed sensations and stalled while he collected his thoughts.

"Why else have you waited so long to mention this?"

"I've been waiting for a chance to talk to you alone. I have a strong sense that, underneath all your game-playing, you wish Ian well. So I'm giving you a chance to explain your reasons for letting him jump to a false conclusion. And," she finished pointedly, "you're still stalling."

He capitulated. "You know, Miriam, I've see enough since I've been here to realize who the real power in the Provisional Government is. Now I begin to see why. Very well, I'll make a clean breast. What I said aboard *Nelson* was absolutely true, so far as it went. The offensive *will* begin on schedule, and its objective *is* to open up a warp connection between the Innerworlds and the Rim. But once that's done, Prime Minister Dieter plans to offer the rebels a peace settlement based on acceptance of the *status quo*. The result will be a Terran Republic consisting of all the Fringe Worlds—except those we'll have seized to serve as the corridor we need—and a Federation shaped rather like a dumbbell." (He was speaking in terms of the layout of the warp network. If the Federation he described had been charted in actual three-dimensional space, it would have resembled a geometrician's opium dream. But she understood.) "And they'll accept it. What I said about the combined military potential of the two loyal segments of the Federation was also true."

"How do you know all this?"

"I don't—not officially. But I've worked closely enough with the PM to learn how his mind works. Also," he added with his most impish grin, "I have my own sources. Deviousness, my dear, has its uses."

"Of course," she observed dryly.

She was a strong woman, he thought. Despite her suspicions, confirmation of exactly what he'd been holding back must have been quite a shock, yet she was adapting nicely. He folded his hands neatly on his blotter and awaited her response with interest.

Miriam sat back to digest his words. As always with Sanders, it was wheels within wheels. She doubted that she could ever fully understand this sophisticated old man from a sophisticated old planet. But her instincts continued to tell her that he was fundamentally a friend to Ian, which made him at least an ally of hers.

She noticed that her cigarette had burned low and stubbed it out, selecting another one. She glared down at it for a moment. She really ought to cut back on the damned things . . . to hell with it. She lit up.

"Kevin, you must know that Ian and I are . . . close. What makes you think I won't tell him all this?"

Sanders leaned forward into the pool of light. His blue eyes were disconcertingly sharp.

"You won't tell him for the same reasons I haven't. Our mutual friend is an idealist in the truest sense. He also thinks in straight lines, something I've forgotten how to do, if I ever knew how in the first place. He can imagine no conclusion to the war except the triumphant restoration of the Terran Federation, and the truth would be . . . unacceptable to him. It would, I think, be something even you would have to bring him around to seeing only slowly. And we don't have time to do things slowly, Miriam; not if we're going to strike before the rebels find an answer to his new weapons." His eyes grew even sharper. "Since we don't have that time, he's going to be risking his life in this campaign very shortly. You have even better reason than I for not telling him anything that might impair his effectiveness!"

She glared at him. "Don't you ever get tired of manipulating people?"

"Miriam, it would take a far bigger man than me to manipulate either you or Ian. The fact is that you know I'm right. You also knew Dieter is right. The Federation simply won't work on any basis but a consensual one, and that's gone now, as far as the Fringe is concerned. Maybe they're even right to pull away before the hate that's built up curdles us *all* internally. The most we can hope for is an Innerworld/Rim unity with the Corporate World arrogance knocked out of us."

She puffed thoughtfully. "You may have a point. But unless Dieter is prepared to give up the whole idea of an Orion amalgamation, that issue is still going to be with us. I can tell you the idea doesn't sit well with the Rim—and that's just one aspect of a broader issue. You've got to understand that people out here are passionately loyal to the *idea* of the Federation. But they're also passionately attached to self-government, and they see no contradiction between the two."

"Federation member planets have always had local self-government. . . ."

"Maybe so, but it's beyond that, now. The Rim is no longer a gaggle of unrelated planets. We've acquired a sense of identity—almost nationhood—by successfully defending ourselves. And the provisional government Ian's organized has given us a Rim-wide forum. You've probably heard people out here use the phrase 'the Rim Federation.' " She paused thoughtfully.

"Ironic, isn't it?" she went on with an odd half-smile. "Nobody talks about the 'Rim Federation' around Ian! The whole concept is anathema to him. As far as he's concerned, he's simply holding the Rim for the Federation—and he may be the only man in the Galaxy who could have done it." She leaned forward, and her eyes glowed as they caught the light. "But in the process of doing what's necessary—militarily and politically—for that, he's fathered a new nation! The Federation's going to have to take account of the rights, interests, and, yes, prejudices of the Rim. Otherwise, Dieter's policy will fall flat on its ass. And besides . . . I think we've earned it!"

Her voice had become a harsh clang of pride. After its echoes died away, Sanders remembered to breathe.

"I agree," he said quietly. "The postwar astrographical realities will necessitate some form of special autonomy for the Rim within the Federation. I tell you quite frankly—I'm rapidly learning better than to try to bullshit you—that the Amalgamation *will* come. There's been too much public commitment to it and too many Innerworld voters see it as a symbol of victory for Dieter to resist it even if he wanted to. But home rule should shield the Rim from most of the things people out here find repugnant about it. No doubt if our friend were here he'd find all sorts of historical precedents for it—from his own ancestors' commonwealth period, perhaps."

His eyes took on a faraway look.

"You know, this may turn out for the best. Amalgamation opens up fascinating possibilities for interspecies cultural interaction, which probably means it's the wave of the future. But at the same time, human-dominated societies will continue to have something to offer. And the Terran Republic is . . . immature. It may be that your own 'Rim Federation' will incorporate the best of both worlds, especially if it can avoid the mistakes of either."

Miriam realized anew that she would never know quite where she stood with this man. There was something almost inhuman about that long a view. She wanted to ask him if he had any parochial loyalties, any passionate attachments, any fundamental beliefs of any kind. But that wasn't how the question came out.

"Kevin, were you ever young?"

"Miriam," he suddenly flashed his toothiest grin and chuckled, "you wouldn't have *believed* me as a junior officer!"

* * *

"Attention on deck!"

The men and women in *Nelson*'s staff briefing room rose to attention as Trevayne strode in.

"Carry on, ladies and gentlemen," he said briskly, moving towards the head of the U-shaped table, and they immediately resumed their seats. He took his own place and came directly to the point. "I want to congratulate all of you on the results of the exercise. Even Commodore Yoshinaka could find little to criticize." A rueful chuckle went around the table. "I won't ask you to congratulate your personnel for me, because I plan to do so personally on the fleet-wide communication hookup at 2100 hours."

He paused, his eyes sweeping his officers. They were a mixture of his handpicked people from BG 32 and Sergei Ortega's best subordinates, welded into a team in the fires of battle. He allowed himself to consider them one by one, as if in a final testing for weak links in the chain of command.

Sonja Desai, now a vice admiral, commanded his second supermonitor battlegroup. (Trevayne himself commanded the first, in addition to holding overall command, and Vice Admiral Frederick Shespar commanded the third.) Rear Admiral Remko, now commanding the battle-cruisers and their supporting craft, sat beside her. Ever since he'd received his new appointment, Trevayne thought with an inner smile, Sean had worn the look of a man who was once again in his element.

Genji Yoshinaka sat quietly at Trevayne's elbow, as he always did. Their link had grown even stronger since the Second Battle of Zephrain. Neither of them ever mentioned the incident which had caused it, but their shared understanding needed no statement. Trevayne had persuaded him to accept promotion to commodore by agreeing to let him stay on as chief of staff, though a captain might have filled the billet.

Vice Admiral Shespar sat at his other elbow, a dark-visaged, competent man with hard eyes who'd been Sergei's second in command before BG 32's arrival. Beyond him was Commander Joaquin Sandoval y Belhambre, another of Ortega's people, and one of the few actually born in the Rim. A fighter pilot who'd distinguished himself in the Battle of the Gateway and against the Tangri, he'd shown an unexpected gift for operational planning as a carrier group ops officer, in which position he'd caught Genji's eye.

Sandoval had brought along his intelligence officer, Lieutenant Commander Lavrenti Kirilenko, who was widely regarded as a man to be watched. Though young, he had the kind of face which, Trevayne thought, lady novelists used to call "saturnine." He also had a sardonic sense of humor, but there was a kind of purity about his approach to his profession: the amoral fascination of a chessmaster. Trevayne suspected that he had the potential to develop into another Kevin Sanders. If so, the great difference in their ages was just as well; one per century was enough.

Opposite Trevayne sat Flag Captain Lewis Mujabi, an even rarer bird than Sandoval in many respects—a Fringer whose native planet had seceded without him. In an era when more and more of the human race was blending into a nice, even shade of brown, Mujabi was so black he was, in some lights, almost purple. His people, predominantly African to begin with, had settled Kashiji, a planet near the inner edge of the liquid-water zone of a class F2 sun. Natural selection, abetted by some modest genetic engineering, had taken its inevitable course.

BG 32 itself was now commanded by Rear Admiral Maria Kim, originally one of its ship captains. Another, Commodore Khalid Khan, led another battlegroup built around monitors captured at Second Zephrain (two of which had also been added to Shespar's BG 3 to round out its lower supermonitor strength). Rear Admiral Carl Stoner, who'd commanded Ortega's Frontier Fleet carriers, filled the same billet under Trevayne.

Looking around the crowded room at these officers and the others who comprised Fourth Fleet's brain, Trevayne could barely repress a thrill of pride. He abandoned himself to the reverie for just a moment longer before he cleared his throat and continued.

"Turning to the classified folders before you, I would ask you to open them now." There was a crackle of breaking seals. "Commander Sandoval will briefly summarize."

He had stressed the adverb slightly, and there were grins around the table (not least from Sandoval himself), for the ops officer had earned a reputation as a raconteur of hilarious but lengthy anecdotes.

"Yes, sir. I'll keep it brief, sir." There might have been just a suspicion of irony in his voice. It was hard to tell, but Genji Yoshinaka had recommended Sandoval for the job partly because he was a brilliant, irreverent soul who refused to be completely in awe of anyone or anything, including admirals. Now the dark, wiry commander, very young for his job, rose and switched on a holographic star display.

"First, ladies and gentlemen, allow me to point out that although the joint operation we are about to undertake is called 'Operation Yellowbrick,' we are concerned only with that portion of it called 'Operation Reunion.' "

There was a chuckle at that, and Trevayne hid his own smile. Sanders had tended towards a sort of scandalized chagrin when Trevayne had announced the change in operational designations. Sandoval and he had stood to their guns, however. Trevayne had argued that there were innumerable precedents for renaming subsections of campaign plans and that the new name had more positive morale connotations. But what had really floored the Old Terran was Sandoval's irreverently point-blank refusal to lead men and women into battle under an operational code name from a five-hundred-year-old children's story—and, no, Sandoval wasn't impressed by the fact that the story in question had always been one of Admiral Sanders' favorites.

"This operation is relatively straightforward," Sandoval went on, "although it may or may not be simple. Our only really difficult strategic decision was whether to make our breakout through the Gateway or the Back Door. Either would take us to the Purdah System, meeting the bare-bones ops plan the Joint Chiefs sent us via Admiral Sanders, but the Gateway route does so in only three transits. The Back Door takes four, and would almost certainly meet stiffer resistance, since that route leads into the Bonaparte System"—a star blinked on the display—"which contains the major rebel base from which Second Zephrain was launched. Drone probes and raids have given us pretty good intelligence on our home warp points, and based on that data, we decided on the Gateway. It'll be rough, but not as rough as Bonaparte.

"After the breakout, we hope to proceed rapidly. Our axis of advance will be through these systems." A net of warp lines lit in red as he touched a button. "There are two main problems in an offensive like this. One, of course, is supplies, especially of depletable munitions. The fleet train is accordingly of the first importance, and guarding it is going to be essential. This will become especially true as we advance, because we'll open 'sally ports' on our flanks as we bypass warp points to other rebel-held systems. It's also possible, as we all know, for commerce raiders to operate for a time within a single system, even if cut off from outside support. We consider the risk to the fleet train will not become critical, however, until we reach the Zapata System, the first major choke point on our planned route.

"And that brings us to the second major risk to our momentum: lack of intelligence. To be perfectly frank, we have no idea what system defenses we'll face after our initial breakout. Until we control more warp points, we can't even use probes, much less scouting squadrons, so we're going in blind. On the other hand, we know the rebels must have been committing the majority of their industrial capacity to shipbuilding, judging by what they used at Second Zephrain and the enemy deployment data Admiral Sanders brought us. Presumably, that means they can't have built a lot of fortifications out here, at least not behind the immediate 'front line' systems. As for Fleet units—" he shrugged slightly "—we think they were badly hurt at Second Zephrain, and we've demonstrated the efficiency of our weapons. Unless they have a radically higher number of hulls than ONI estimates, they shouldn't be strong enough to stop both us and the forces attacking to meet us."

He stopped and seated himself.

"Thank you, Commander," Trevayne said, rising. "That's about all that can be said at this stage—and it was admirably brief." He allowed himself a slight smile as his staff chuckled. "We'll meet again tomorrow, after you've had a chance to study the plan and formulate questions. In the meantime, remember the com hook-up at 2100. I want every man and woman in the Fleet to hear me."

He strode out. The room seemed to get bigger, as rooms tended to when Trevayne left them. . . .

Neither of them had planned it that way, yet they found themselves alone outside the elevator that would take Trevayne away.

Virtually everyone else who was to be aboard *Nelson* for Operation Reunion, including Sanders, had already left Xanadu. A floater waited on the roof of Government House to take Trevayne to Abu'said Field and his cutter. It was a trip he'd made many times, but they both knew this time was different. This campaign would, one way or another, change their lives. Win or lose, it would never be the same again.

They'd said their farewells the previous night, and they'd both dreaded any last-minute awkwardness. But with the inevitability of gravity, they found themselves facing one another outside the private VIP elevator.

"Well," he said, "I'm off." Brilliant, his superego gibed; too bloody scintillating.

"Send word back whenever you can," she said. And within her: My, how terribly clever!

They stood in silence for a moment, and then gathered each other in. They kissed with utmost gentleness.

"Miriam, I'll be back. I *promise* I'll be back."

She put her hands on his shoulders, holding him at arms' length and grinning wickedly. "Well," she purred, letting her eyes travel suggestively downwards, "I know from experience that in your case talk is *not* cheap."

He broke into a grin of his own. They hugged one another once more, hard. Then the light above the elevator door flashed. The door opened, and closed again, and he was gone.

Miriam sighed. As always, everything that mattered was left unspoken. She even understood why; as long as they were cracking wise, they were on safe ground. She turned, eyes downcast, and walked away.

Out of the corner of her eye, she saw the light flash again. She turned back, curious, as the doors slid open.

"Forget something?" she asked.

"Miriam," he stepped towards her, "I suddenly realized that . . . well, that there were things I'd left unsaid. I . . ."

She raised a hand, almost afraid, and pressed her fingers to his lips. "Hush, darling. We both know that. We've never needed to say much, have we?"

He seized her wrist almost roughly and forced her hand aside. "No! It's different now, and I can't leave without saying . . . that . . ." His throat seemed to constrict. And then, like a dam bursting, "Miriam, I *need* you! I love you!"

And her own dam burst.

"Oh, God, Ian, I love you, too! I love you so much!"

And all the restraint of the past was less than a memory. They kissed, and it was like the first time they'd ever kissed each other.

After a little while, as stars and planets measure time, she spoke.

"What do you suppose we were so afraid of, all this time?"

He didn't answer. Another moment passed before he spoke again, almost lightly.

"You know, if we run down to the Judge Advocate General's office, we might just be able to find someone authorized to perform a marriage."

She sputtered with laughter and looked up at him, eyes shining. "Ian, you're so full of shit your eyes are browner than usual! You know you've got to go. We'll talk about this when you get back. And for God's sake, let it keep till then! Right now, you need more things on your mind like Commodore Prescott needed more Arachnids!"

He laughed, a joyful sound of final release. Then he sobered, gripping her shoulders firmly.

"Miriam, remember what I said: I . . . promise . . . I . . . will be . . . back!"

Miriam Ortega was a Navy brat. She knew, better than most, what could happen when ship met ship in deep space combat. She had already lost a father to exactly that, and she knew no one could predict exactly where the warhead or the beam would strike. And yet, she also knew that Ian Laurens Trevayne always kept his promises.

"Yes, my precious love," she whispered. "I know you will."

* * *

As the cutter left the pale-blue reaches of the upper atmosphere for the velvet-black realm of space, Trevayne gazed out the port. For the first time in years—too many years, filled with columns of numbers on phosphor screens—he really saw the universe in which he moved and worked. His gaze ranged further and further out, sweeping over the unwinking, jewel-hard stars strewn in their myriads down the roaring, mind-numbing reaches of infinity.

God, he thought. How beautiful it is.

THE SHORTEST DISTANCE

Rear Admiral Li flinched as rolling drums assaulted her ears, then straightened her shoulders quickly. Other returning prisoners crowded the shuttle hatch behind her, and not the most jaded of them could hide his reaction to the scene.

The domed spaceport on Bonaparte's second moon was jammed with black and silver uniforms. Thousands of them! Han stared out over the sea of faces through the crashing fanfare of *Ad Astra*, the ancient twenty-first century hymn chosen as the Republic's anthem, and she was stunned.

A rear admiral greeted her with a crisp salute, and only reflex action brought her own hand up in response as she recognized Jason Windrider. His dark eyes glowed, and as the last bar of the anthem crashed out and the music died, his hand came down in a flashing arc. Han's matched it.

"Welcome home, Admiral!" He gripped her hand tightly.

"Thank you." Han swallowed, blinking burning eyes, and smiled. "Thank you, *Admiral*," she said more firmly. "It's good to be back."

"We've been waiting for you," he said warmly, "and you may as well accept the inevitable." His smile was both wicked and warm. "We're proud of you, ma'am, and you're going to have to put up with us while we show it!"

And then he was leading her down the flag-draped landing platform stair, and the roar of cheers split the bright, dome-filtered sunlight around her.

* * *

"Well!" Jason Windrider doffed his braided cap and waved at a chair. "Thank God that's over! Though I must say—" he cocked his head critically "—the Golden Lion looks good on you, Han. Sort of sets off your hair."

"Thank you," she said dryly, trying to hide her own deep emotion as she sat. She touched the Golden Lion of Terra—the highest award for valor of Republic and Federation alike. "If this is what the loser gets, I'd like to see the winner's medals!"

"*You* didn't lose, Han," Windrider said decisively. "You and Bob were right. We should've gone in fast and nasty, before their new forts and beams and those Godawful missiles were on line."

"Maybe," Han said, "but *I* surrendered, so I'm the one who's going to face a Board over it—and maybe a full Court."

"The Court already sat," Windrider said, suddenly grim, "on the admirals who ran out on you. I won't lie to you—some people *were* cashiered, but everyone knows you held the battle-line together in a hopeless situation and then had the good sense not to get thousands of people killed for nothing." He shrugged again. "That's more or less what the Admiralty said, in fancier language, when it recommended you—unanimously—for the Golden Lion."

"I see." Han drew a deep breath and felt the tension flow away at last.

"Do you, now?" Windrider grinned. "Actually, there's an even more tangible proof of their lordships' attitude."

"Oh?" she eyed him suspiciously. "A blindfold and a last cigarette?"

"You have an untrusting nature," Windrider said sorrowfully. Then he became more serious. "I'm afraid it's slightly non-reg, Han, and Magda wanted to give you this, but she can't make it, so I have to deputize. Here."

Han opened the small case and gasped as she saw the double stars nestled in the dark velvet. She stood abruptly, left hand rising to the single star at her collar, and her eyes were shocked.

"Yes, sir," the rear admiral said. "Congratulations, *Vice* Admiral Li!" He reached out and unpinned her rear admiral's star gently, then took a paired star from her and slid its pin through her collar.

"B-but I'm not *ready!*" Han wailed. "I was only a captain four years ago!" Yet she seemed unable to resist as he fastened the badge in place. "I just got back from surrendering an entire battle fleet!"

"Han," Windrider said severely, "sit down and shut up."

She sat obediently, too shaken to notice how brashly a rear admiral was ordering a vice admiral about.

"Better," he said. "Now listen to me. Every senior officer in the Fleet knows you and Bob wanted to attack earlier, and most of 'em know the panic that *really* beat us at Zephrain wouldn't have happened if you'd been senior to the bastards who— Never mind." He shook his head sharply. "But there's not a one of them who questions giving you that star. None. And no doubts will be entertained from you, either, young lady!

"Besides, we need you. Admiral Ashigara is dead, and so are Kellerman, Matucek, Ryder, Nishin, Shukov, Hyde-White, Mombora. . . ." His voice trailed somberly off, and she stared at him.

"That many?"

"And more," he confirmed. "Han, we never did have many admirals, and those we had have taken a terrible pounding; we've *got* to promote. I was a *commander* four years ago, for God's sake! If I can take my medicine and wear one star, you can damned well wear two—got it?"

"Yes, sir," she said meekly, touching her collar badges and smiling at last. "I just hope it isn't a mistake."

"Han, will you *please* get it through your radiation-jellied Oriental brain that you've got those stars—*and* that medal—because you're one of the best we've got?" She eyed him doubtfully, and he grinned. "Besides, if we don't give 'em to you, somebody might try to give 'em to *me*, God help us!"

The skimmer swooped downwards, and Han peered out at the lights blazing against the night. They marked a sprawling mansion, one-time home of the Corporate World manager of Bonaparte's largest *chesht* plantation, taken over by the Republican military when the focus of operations shifted to Zephrain.

Windrider grounded the skimmer and popped the hatches, and Han climbed out, wrinkling her nose as the reek of over-ripe *chesht* mingled with the fresh smell of marshes. It amazed her that something whose flavor had supplanted chocolate and vanilla alike in Terran estimation could smell so horrible in its native habitat.

Strange voices shrilled and clicked in the night, and wings fluttered as Bonaparte's equivalent of a bat flitted past. She glanced upward, but the two larger moons had set and the third, Joseph, was little more than a low-albedo lump of captured asteroidal rock. Its wan illumination barely brought a glow to the mists and hinted at rather than revealed the artificially precise spacing of angular machinery. *Chesht*-pickers rusting in idleness, she thought as the cool breeze off the marsh rustled the *chesht* pods. Bonaparte's F1 primary was hot, but the planet was near the outer edge of the liquid-water belt. Even high summer was cool, which suited Han well, for it produced a climate very like that of her homeworld.

Jason however, came from Topaz—a warm, dusty world with little axial tilt—and he preferred less chilly environs. He rubbed his hands briskly and tried to look patient as she sucked in the crisp air.

"All right, Jason," she smiled finally. "Lead on."

"Good!" he agreed quickly, and guided her through a double-paned door into what had been a palatial foyer before the Republican Navy took charge. A pair of Marine guards came sharply to attention as they stepped inside, and as Han noted their unsealed holsters, she suddenly realized what those angular shapes in the marsh had been: not *chesht*-pickers, but heavy armored vehicles. And the thick glass entry doors weren't glass at all, but armorplast capable of resisting medium artillery fire!

"Good evening, Admiral Li. Admiral Windrider." A Marine major saluted them. "May I see some identification?"

He subjected their ID folios to the most rigorous check Han had seen since the war began. What in God's name was going on here?

"Thank you, sir." The major returned her ID and summoned an armed orderly. "Chief Yeoman Santander will escort you to the planning room."

"Thank you, Major." Han returned his salute, then followed the silent yeoman into the house proper and down a corridor. He stopped and opened a door, raising his voice without entering.

"Admiral Li and Admiral Windrider, sir!" he said crisply, and stepped back as they passed him.

"Thank you, Chief Santander," a warm, easily-recognized voice said.

"Magda! Jason didn't say you were here!"

"I know he didn't." Magda Petrovna smiled from behind her desk in the large, brightly lit room, and the paired stars on her collar mirrored Han's. "Very few people know I'm here, and they aren't talking."

"But why all the secrecy?"

"I'm about to tell you, Han," Magda said with the chuckle Han remembered so well. "After which you'll disappear, too. Where's she off to, Jason?" Brown eyes rose to smile over Han's head at Windrider.

"Vice Admiral Li is returning to Novaya Rodina for debriefing," Windrider said smoothly. "In fact, I escorted her aboard ship myself."

"You see?" Magda asked with a grin.

"No, I don't see at all!"

"It's pretty simple, really. You and I, my dear, are the Republic's last great hope." Magda's voice was humorous; her eyes weren't.

"Meaning what?" Han demanded.

"Meaning that you and I—with the help of a few souls like Jason, Bob Tomanga, and Tsing Chang—are now the Republic's answer to Ian Trevayne."

"We're going back to Zephrain?" Han was stunned by the recklessness of the idea. "Magda, I don't think you understand just what—"

"No, Han," Magda said softly. "Trevayne is coming to us. He's staging a breakout sometime in the next five standard months."

Han sat down heavily. It had all come at her too fast, she thought dazedly. The homecoming, her medal and promotion, all the secrecy and security—now this. She couldn't have understood correctly.

"Five months." She shook her head. "Magda, it isn't possible. He doesn't have enough hulls to mount a sustained offensive—not a decisive one—now that we know what he's got and the panic factor's been eliminated, and there's no point in his taking losses for anything *in*decisive. Besides, those monsters of his take a long time to build—they mass over a half million tonnes *each*, Magda! He won't risk them without a decisive objective in view."

"Correct." Magda tipped back her chair and a half-smile lurked in her eyes. "But he *is* coming out. What could inspire him to do that?"

"Nothing," Han said, but she sounded less certain. She thought furiously for a minute, then looked up again. "Are you saying they're planning a joint operation? A simultaneous attack by the Rump and the Rim?"

"Give the lady the prize," Windrider said softly.

"But that's crazy, too," Han protested quietly. "There's no way they could coordinate. I never figured out how they get messages back and forth, but it seems pretty clumsy, however they do it."

"Right again," Magda nodded, "but let me show you something." She rose, and Han's eyes widened in amazement.

"Damn! I keep forgetting to allow for that." Magda stood back from her desk and patted her stomach with a wry frown. Her new figure, Han thought with a helpless chuckle, was *definitely* non-reg.

"What's so funny?" Magda demanded, then touched her stomach again and laughed. "*This* isn't what I wanted to show you."

"You thought I wouldn't notice?"

"No, you silly slant-eye, I just forgot you didn't know. It's all over the Fleet by now—and that cad in the corner is making insufferably proud noises over every bar on Bonaparte."

"I see." Han managed to stop chuckling, but her voice was a little unsteady. "And you don't think your timing was a bit off?"

"Hell," Magda laughed, "this little stranger is one reason I *got* this job. Everyone knows pregnant women are barred from combat. Ergo, *I'm* barred from combat, which makes my disappearance for planning purposes that much easier to explain. And as for my 'timing'—" she met Han's eyes, suddenly serious "—you're one reason for that."

Only Magda could have said that without opening her own wounds, Han thought affectionately.

"I don't want what happened to you happening to me now that I've found Jason," Magda said quietly. She reached out a hand, and Windrider was there in an instant to take it. "So I'm having at least one child before I go out to be shot at again. Besides," she smiled gently, and for the first time her voice was hesitant, "this child is for you, too, Han."

"Me?" Han was deeply touched as she took Magda's other hand.

"Yes. We'd like—like it very much—to name her Han."

Han's grip tightened, and a seemingly endless silence stretched.

"If you can't think of a better name," she said finally, "I'd be proud. Very proud."

"Done!" Jason's brusque cheerfulness broke the spell, and Han was grateful. She drew a deep breath and blinked twice.

"But I think you were going to show me something besides my future namesake?"

"So I was," Magda said, tucking an arm through Han's and leading her over to a wall panel. She punched buttons busily, and a huge hologram filled the darkened room. Han stared at it raptly; she hadn't seen a warp map quite that large since the Academy.

Magda picked up a luminous pointer and moved to the center of the map.

"This helps with visualization, Han," she said, turning brown eyes spangled with tiny stars to her friend. "Our warp lines are green. The Rump's are red; the Rim's amber. Notice anything?"

"Besides the lack of any red-amber connections?"

"That's certainly the salient point, but I'm thinking about something else: distances. At closest, they're at least a dozen transits apart—over six weeks for a battle-cruiser at max. So whatever they do, they're facing a long, drawn-out campaign before they get back into contact, right?"

"I'd think so, yes."

"So did we. We have, however, certain intelligence assets in the Rump. Not in the Rim, I'm sorry to say, and our very best conduit didn't give us a word of warning about it, but computer analysis of what we *do* have has picked up on something very interesting.

"First," she tucked her pointer under her arm, for all the world like a pregnant schoolteacher in uniform as she ticked off points on her fingers, "Rump construction rates have been low, which confused as until we found out why. The Galloway's World Raid did more than take out a couple of yards, Han; it took out the entire archipelago. They've recovered now, but it explains why the Rump's been so sensitive to combat losses.

"Second," she went on, "despite their desperate need for ships, they're holding them back. We didn't notice that immediately, but our raids, recon probes, and captured or otherwise compromised Rump deployment orders all indicate it. Why?

"Third, they haven't been massing them opposite Cimmaron, as we might expect. They could cut off this whole quarter of the Republic from there," she gestured at a glowing snake's nest of green warp lines "or go straight for Novaya Rodina. But where the analysis teams finally found them is over here, at a totally new Fleet base at Avalon—a system we've never even threatened.

"Fourth, and finally, we *know* how the Rim gets its messages. They come through Orion space, via Rehfrak." Magda waved a hand at Han's sharp glance. "I know, very un-neutral of them. However, we haven't objected because we wanted to see who goes where along that warp line, and it turns out the errand boy is none other than one Kevin Sanders. Does that ring any bells?"

" 'The Fox,' " Han said softly.

"Exactly. The best chief of ONI in two centuries, and currently a cabinet minister without portfolio. Obviously they need a top man for a hot potato like this, but they're sending Sanders— probably the one person in the Galaxy who knows where *all* the Federation's bodies are buried—through *Orion* space whenever he goes to Zephrain. And the Orions only permit him to go as far as Rehfrak; the Governor-General comes to *him*."

"I'm sure all of this is headed somewhere?"

"It is indeed. Six months ago, Sanders was in Avalon. Then they rushed him back to Old Terra so fast they burned out a destroyer's main drive converters. Why?

Because he's already gone again, making another trip . . . and this time he's going all the way to Xanadu—and staying."

"What?" Han stood straighter and frowned.

"Exactly. It took a lot of work—and luck—to piece his itinerary together, but it's solid. Now why would the Rump separate itself from its foremost spook? Unless, of course, the separation isn't permanent?"

"I see your point," Han mused.

"I thought you would," Magda said grimly. "They're sending him because they need someone with his authority, brains, and experience to coordinate their plan to hit us before we can react to the new weaponry. If they can hammer a bridge between the Rump and Rim—if the Rump's industrial plant gets the data and working models it needs—we're in deep, deep trouble."

"I see," Han murmured once more, searching the red and amber warp lines with her eyes. "They're assembling the Rump pincer at Avalon, so they're not going for any finesse beyond their hope for surprise."

"That's what we think," Magda encouraged her.

"It's the only answer," Han muttered, frowning in thought. "From Avalon, hmmmmm . . . ?" Her eyes narrowed suddenly and she nodded once, sharply. "There's their route, Magda—Avalon to Lomax to Hyerdahl to Thor to Thule to Osterman's Star to Thybold to Juarez to Iphigena to Zapata to Sagebrush to Purdah. From there they might go Rousseau to Ney to Bonaparte to Zephrain, or New India to Zvoboda to Zephrain. I'd bet on the New India Route—not even Ian Trevayne wants to tangle with the defenses here."

"What makes you so certain?" Magda asked, not challengingly but as if she merely wanted confirmation of her own thoughts.

"Only a fool tries to be clever when he can't completely orchestrate a complex operation, Magda. We learned that watching the Orions in the first two interstellar wars . . . and relearned it at First Zephrain. So if you can't be fancy, you be direct as possible, and that route—" she nodded at the one she'd traced out "—is the shortest distance between two points: Avalon and Zephrain."

"I think you're right," Magda acknowledged, "and you might like to know that it took the Strategy Board a month to reach your conclusions." She smiled. "But there's still a billion-credit question, Han. We don't have the Fleet units to oppose both forces at once. We have to stop one of them, then turn to deal with the other in detail, using our advantage of the interior position. So which do we oppose?"

Han blinked at her.

"You're asking me? Magda, I've been out of circulation for a year!"

"But you're also the senior commander who's really seen the Rim's weapons in action, so you can give us the best gut reaction on them. Should we worry more about quantity or quality? Because—" Magda grinned crookedly "—for our sins, you and I are going to be the Fleet commanders who do the stopping. So who do we stop, Han? The Rump or the Rim?"

Han dropped into a chair and thought long, hard and furiously.

"The Rump doesn't have any of the new technology? Just numbers?"

Magda nodded.

"And have *we* come through with any of those 'wonder weapons' people were muttering about before Second Zephrain? Do we have any surprises of our own?"

"A few," Windrider said.

"Then we have to block the Rump with secondary forces and go for the Rim with everything we have," Han said, suddenly decisive. "No matter how many hulls the Rump has, we can tangle them up in the frontier forts, mines, and local fighter bases. We can slow them up, at least, but you've never seen *any*thing like Trevayne's new battle-line. We have to stop him, and stop him hard. If at all possible, we have to cut him up badly enough to move in and take Zephrain away from him. Even if we lose a dozen systems—or twice that many!—to the Rump, we've still got a good chance to win this war in the end *if* we can keep them away from Zephrain."

"And where do we stop them?" Magda asked tonelessly.

"Zapata," Han said crisply. "It's a critical choke point, and we can move stuff in from Bonaparte for the big engagement. Use commerce raiders on the flanks as they advance . . . pick at them . . . get them off balance and force them to overextend . . . then meet them head-on at Zapata and thank God building that monster battle-line's cut into their carrier production! It's our only chance, Magda."

"I see." Magda exchanged a nod with Jason, then turned back to Han. The tangled lights of the holo map gilded her silver-streaked brown hair with a crown of jewels, and her eyes glittered with stars. "That's another thing you and the Strategy Board agree on, and I'm glad you see it so clearly . . . sir."

Something in her voice caught Han's attention, and she stared at her friend suspiciously. No! She couldn't mean . . . !

"That's right, Han," Magda said almost compassionately. "One of the reasons I was ordered to have this little chat with you was to be certain you *did* understand the priorities. You got your second star while you were still a POW—the same day I got mine. And that means you're still senior." She held out the luminous pointer.

"Welcome to supreme command of Operation Actium, Admiral Li."

Operation Reunion

Operation Reunion began with an irruption of SBMHAWK carrier pods into the Zvoboda System. One moment the Republican Navy's detection screens were blank: the next a multitude of unmanned pods warped into the teeth of the forts guarding this gateway to the Terran Republic. A few came to grief in the warp point minefields; a few more emerged in overlapping volumes of space and died with the violence the gods of physics reserve for phenomena which violate their laws. But most survived to fling their missiles at the forts, announcing the arrival of the Federation's warriors in fire and death.

Probes of the Zvoboda System had been limited to avoid alarming its defenders, but Ian Trevayne had a fairly good notion of what he would face. The Republic had erected a formidable shell of big type four OWPs around the Zephrain warp point and another around the warp point to New India, but Lavrenti Kirilenko was convinced there would be few mobile units. The forts were typical of the Republic's designs, each incorporating two squadrons of fighters; that fighter strength, coupled with the forts' own weapons, needed no support to decimate any conventional assault.

Trevayne and Genji Yoshinaka agreed with Kirilenko's assessments; hence the lavish SBMHAWK bombardment that preceded their ships through the warp point. Such a heavy employment of SBMs would seriously deplete their stores for the next assault, but there was no point planning for the next battle if they lost this one. Besides, everything seemed to suggest that Zvoboda had been so heavily fortified that the Republic could have spared little for the defense of New India.

Missiles leapt from their carrier pods, but the Republican gunners hadn't been asleep. The Rim's decreased probe traffic hadn't lulled them; rather it had confirmed their suspicions, and they'd gone on round-the-clock alert. Still, no one could be a hundred percent alert at every instant, and if point defense stopped a lot of missiles, nothing could have stopped them all.

Antimatter warheads flared against shields. Tremendous fireballs wracked the space around them. Armor glowed, vaporized, flared away. Atmosphere whuffed outward, water vapor sparkling, as the missiles savaged the forts. Yet for all their savagery, all their violence, they couldn't prevent the Republic from launching the majority of its fighters.

But Trevayne had anticipated that, and he had no intention of offering up his strictly limited carrier strength for target practice, even if The Book did call for fighters as the best defense against fighters. Instead, the ships that followed the carrier pods into Zvoboda used a tactic which was new, one so unorthodox it took the defenders totally by surprise, yet so simple they wondered why no one else had ever thought of it.

TFNS *Nelson* was the first ship out of the warp point, followed by the monitor *da Silva*. As soon as *da Silva* emerged, *Nelson* grabbed her with tractor beams and began to tow her astern. Simultaneously, *da Silva* cut her own propulsion, maintaining just sufficient drive field to interdict missile fire, and rolled on attitude control to place herself stern-to-stern with *Nelson*—an unheard of position. Then another supermonitor/monitor pair emerged, and another. . . .

All strikefighter pilots knew to attack battle-line units by maneuvering into the sternward "blind zone" created by the slow and clumsy ship's drive field, where its tracking systems were useless and its weapons could not be brought to bear. But the rebel pilots, racing to implement their fundamental tactical doctrine, were slaughtered by defensive fire from the supermonitors and monitors while searching for blind zones that were, in effect, not there! They inflicted damage, of course—quite a lot, in fact. But monitors were designed to absorb and survive damage, and supermonitors even more so. The fighters were cut down before their short-ranged weapons could take decisive effect, and the big ships lumbered towards the fortresses, contemptuous alike of the fighters and mines that sought to hinder them.

The fortress crews knew what their fighters' failure meant. They'd seen the reports on Second Zephrain, and they knew all about the improved force beams Trevayne's ships mounted, but they stood to their weapons, pouring in defensive fire against the oncoming ships. Damage control parties aboard the supermonitors and monitors found their services in high demand, but not critically so, and the capital ships riddled the forts with primary-mode fire and then reduced them to tangled wreckage with "wide-angled" fire even as Sean Remko's battle-cruisers savagely hunted down the few mobile rebel units.

Fourth Fleet reformed into a more conventional order of battle, complete with escort destroyers, and lumbered into a hyperbolic course across the system. Ian Trevayne sat in his command chair, listening to the reports as his crews worked frenziedly on the damage. It wasn't quite as bad as he'd anticipated, he thought. Bad enough, certainly—especially in terms of human life—but no internal damage his repair crews couldn't put right in the seventy-eight hour trip across the system. It was a case of slapdash repairs, of course, but aside from the damage to his ships' armor, virtually full combat efficiency had been restored between the first engagement and the moment the New India warp point fortifications hove into range.

Not that he had any intention of exposing those repairs to fresh damage if he could help it. And he could help it, for the Terran Republic still had no counterweight for the HBM.

The rebel commander knew it, too, and he launched his fighters before the supermonitors came into HBM range. That saved them from destruction in their bays but exposed them to extended-range AFHAWK fire from Trevayne's screen and interception by Carl Stoner's fighters. A few broke through both missiles and defending fighters, displaying the skill and determination which were the hallmarks of Republican fighter pilots, but they were a spent force. The escort destroyers and capital ships blasted them apart in return for trifling damage, and shortly thereafter the HBMs began to batter the fortresses.

The Republican commander had no more desire to die uselessly for a point of honor than Trevayne himself. As soon as he'd satisfied himself of all the facts (and fired courier drones out to New India with them), he surrendered.

His surrender was followed four hours later by another, rendered to the cruiser screen as Remko cleaned up the pieces. Occupation of the domed mining colony on the largest satellite of Zvoboda IV, a "brown dwarf" so massive as to be almost self-luminous, completed the conquest, and Trevayne called a halt. It was time to garrison the domes and send prisoners back to Zephrain, in addition to the usual post-battle chores.

He remained on the bridge while his ships carried out the most urgent of these—the replenishment of their magazines from the fleet train beginning to emerge from the warp point—and waited until the repair ships moved alongside to make good his most critical damage. Then he called a meeting of all ship captains aboard *Nelson* and finally left his flag bridge.

Trevayne couldn't help feeling amused by Yoshinaka's morose expression as they rode the intraship car toward the wardroom. The chief of staff was a natural worrier, and he seemed to feel duty bound to compensate for everyone else's euphoria.

"Well," he grumbled, "at least you followed my advice to hold this skippers' meeting after the first battle."

"Why, Genji-san, I always follow your advice," Trevayne said in the bantering tone he affected when Yoshinaka was in one of his moods. "Didn't I give the second *Nelson* the name you wanted?"

Yoshinaka refused to be mollified.

"Right. You named her *Togo* . . . which," he added pointedly, "you would've had to do eventually anyway, having decided to name the class after wet-navy admirals. After all, he was the greatest fighting admiral in the entire history of Old Terra." He waited, but Trevayne declined to rise to the bait. "And you couldn't have ignored him for long, either—not after copping the *first* ship in the class for your precious Nelson! But then you named ships three and four after Raymond Spruance and Yi Sun-Sin, both of whom made their reputations swabbing the decks with the Japanese! Has anyone ever told you you've got a strange sense of humor?"

"The Grand Councilor for Internal Security has mentioned it once or twice," Trevayne admitted airily.

Yoshinaka's scowl dissolved into a grin. Trevayne had been practically whistling as he was piped aboard *Nelson* on the eve of Operation Reunion, when many others had had an understandable case of dry-mouth. Yoshinaka had no idea what had passed between his admiral and Miriam Ortega, but he was grateful for it—and not just because Trevayne's cheerfulness in the face of a frontal assault through a fortified warp point had been a shot in the arm for everyone's morale.

The car hummed to a stop, and they emerged into a crowded wardroom filled with an uproar of shoptalk as the battle was refought. The monitor skippers—already dubbed the "bass-akwards brigade" by their disrespectful fellows—were the butt of the occasion.

"Attention on deck!" Mujabi's basso profundo cut through the hubbub with ease, and all talk subsided as Trevayne and Yoshinaka mounted the improvised dais where Sandoval waited. Standing at the podium, Trevayne looked down at the array of faces, faces of every color and cast of features in which *homo sapiens* came. Outside himself and Yoshinaka, no one in the room wore the broad stripe; he wanted these men and women to be able to speak their minds freely and openly. His own deep baritone filled the room.

"As you were, ladies and gentlemen. First, congratulations are in order. Your performance in battle was exactly what I would have expected of you—and I can think of few higher compliments. In particular," he added with a slight emphasis, "the monitor commanders are to be congratulated for performing superbly under highly unorthodox conditions." That was true of everyone, he thought. Only a superbly trained and motivated fleet could have achieved the organizational flexibility these people had displayed.

"The reason for this captains' meeting," he went on, "is that we've now seen at first hand what we're up against.

You're here because I want to directly answer any questions you may have, and because Commodore Yoshinaka, Commander Sandoval, and I need your feedback. So let's hear any questions or comments."

Numerous hands went up, and Trevayne recognized what looked to have been the first of them. "Captain Waldeck?"

Sean Remko's flag captain rose. He had the Waldeck look—burly, with a jowly, florid face boasting a big nose and massive chin oddly at variance with the small, pursed mouth.

"A comment, Admiral. If what we've encountered here is any indication, this operation should be a walkover. I refer specifically to the cowardice of the rebel commander. He surrendered when he still had the capability to do us some damage or at least force us to expend a lot of our HBMs on his forts. I think the inference is clear: all the rebels ever had going for them was the elan of their initial successes. Now that that's worn off, they're reverting to their natural state—rabble!"

Mujabi's face got, if possible, a bit darker, even though Waldeck had been careful to refer to "rebels" and not to "Fringers." His eyes flashed dangerously, but he was saved from the need to speak by an anonymous voice.

"Sure," it piped up from the back of the wardroom. "Just like the rabble on Novaya Rodina!"

Waldeck flushed, and his massive jaw clenched as a sound swept the wardroom. It wasn't—quite—a chuckle, but rather an inarticulate amusement too great to be entirely suppressed. For a moment he seemed about to snarl a response, but thought better of it at the last moment.

Trevayne himself was torn by several conflicting emotions. The remark was well-taken (if unkind), and he couldn't help sharing the assembled captains' amusement just a bit. Yet at the same time, the whole Novaya Rodina episode left a bad taste in his mouth.

But as far as Waldeck himself was concerned, Trevayne had tried to keep an open mind. He was born of the close-knit world of the TFN's "dynasties," with few illusions about its inhabitants, and he'd never liked Captain Cyrus Waldeck. And that, he thought, was unfortunate in a way, because for all his abrasive arrogance and snobbery, there was no question of Waldeck's competence. It was because of that competence that he'd assigned Waldeck to command the *Arquebus*, Remko's flagship. Yet he couldn't help chortling to himself just a bit whenever he thought of Waldeck, the embodiment of that clan of Corporate World magnates, directly under Sean Remko's command. Could it be that Miriam and Genji were right about his sense of humor?

"Let's not get carried away by our *own* elan, Captain Waldeck," he said calmly. "It would be the height of recklessness to assume on the basis of one battle that the rebels have lost their edge—and I remind you that the first fortress commander we engaged most certainly hadn't lost *his*. That's an attitude we'll have to be particularly wary of in the next few weeks; now that we've broken the rebel frontier, we're likely to be passing through lightly defended systems until we reach Zapata. The rebels will have to offer battle there. I don't want us to arrive for it in a mood of fatuous overconfidence."

A murmur of agreement ran through the wardroom, and Waldeck, his face once more tightly controlled, sat down. Trevayne's voice had been as pleasant as ever, but his remarks stung all the more following that fathead hiding in the rear ranks.

Waldeck surveyed his fellow captains with hidden contempt. These people's attitude towards Ian Trevayne ran the gamut from deep respect through awe all the way to idolatry, he thought. But, of course, he hadn't assigned *them* to be flag captain to a jumped-up prole from the slums of New Detroit—the cesspool of the Corporate Worlds!

He thought bitterly of Trevayne's reputation for being above social prejudice. For Waldeck's money, that only meant he didn't feel any more superior to Fringe Worlders than he did to everyone else!

And yet, he thought, listening to Trevayne responding to questions and comments, not even his resentment made him immune to the admiral's magnetism. The man had the sort of sublime self-assurance that came from being perfectly suited to the role of leadership he'd been born to fill; people followed him because he expected to be followed, expected it with such certainty that he had no need for bombast. Well, Cyrus Waldeck would follow him, too, but with bitterness eating at his heart.

The assault shuttles were on their way once more, carrying garrison troops to the inhabited planet of the Purdah System, when Trevayne called another meeting aboard *Nelson*. It was a small gathering; Sanders, Yoshinaka, Sandoval, and Kirilenko were there, as was Ingrid Lundberg, the supply officer. Sonja Desai had come over from *Togo*, her flagship, but she couldn't stay long, for she was in charge of organizing the temporary military government of this system. Of Trevayne's closest allies, only Remko was absent; he was busy deploying forces to screen the fleet train while it licked its wounds from the latest of the raids which had occasioned this meeting.

At Trevayne's request, Lundberg began with a summary of the supply picture as the stewards poured coffee. (It was late by ships' clocks.)

". . . And that's about the size of it, Admiral." She ran fingers through her auburn hair. "We lost a lot of general stores when *Falkenberg* blew up, and I'm not happy about losing all those medical stores when they crippled *Jolly Merchant*, but we've actually been fairly lucky . . . so far. The munition ships have avoided any serious losses—though I'm not too happy about the missile supply." She glanced at Sandoval from the corner of one eye. "Some people seem to have the idea missiles come straight from God as needed; they don't. If we can't move colliers safely, I can't continue to meet the ammo demands of the Fleet."

"I see." Trevayne nodded and glanced at Kirilenko. "Lavrenti, what do you have for us on these raiders?"

"Less than I'd like, sir. They're using carriers and staying at extreme range. I suspect we're looking at escort carriers rather than light or fleet carriers—the attack patterns suggest small fighter groups—but whatever they are, we haven't been able to run any of them down. They obviously carry cloaking ECM, and they're as fast as anything we've got." He shrugged. "The best I can report right now is that they're losing fighters steadily, but that's not the way to stop determined commerce raiders."

"Anything more on my pet hypothesis, Lavrenti?" Sanders asked.

"I've subjected it to computer analysis and lots of plain, old-fashioned human skepticism, sir," Kirilenko said, "and I'd say you're probably right. They've set up some sort of deep-space basing facilities out there. Maybe just a couple of old freighters hiding somewhere, but *something*—and in more than one system too. They're rearming somewhere, and I'd bet they've got replacement fighters stashed out there, too. All of which supports your theory: this was carefully planned. It's no last-minute improvisation."

Trevayne's officers and advisers exchanged looks and glanced covertly at the admiral, who leaned one elbow on the polished tabletop and thought. Finally he leaned back and rapped the edge of the table with his light pencil, breaking the grip of the silence.

"Very well. Matters have gone pretty much as expected, in the sense that the rebels haven't committed major forces to defend either New India or this system. They've fought token holding actions, forcing us to expend munitions and inflicting maximum losses in a short time before withdrawing.

"We also anticipated that our advance would expose the fleet train to flank attacks through warp points leading to rebel systems off our line of advance. Again, no surprises . . . except possibly for the weight of the attacks and the fact that they're also using these deep-space bases Admiral Sanders and Commander Kirilenko have hypothesized to operate inside the systems we've reoccupied. And, of course, for the number of escort carriers—or whatever—they've committed."

He paused and looked around the table. "Now, what do these facts, taken together, mean? I realize one school of thought holds that our rapid advance means the rebellion is collapsing like a house of cards. That, I'm sure, is Captain Waldeck's view," he added with a crooked smile. "But I don't believe it. These raids show too much forethought, and they're being pressed too aggressively; we're clearly not fighting a beaten enemy. I still think the decisive battle will come at Zapata, whatever anyone else believes, but in the meantime we can expect more of the same at Sagebrush.

"Therefore," he continued, "we need to further reinforce the escort elements for the fleet train. Commander Lundberg is quite correct about the state of our missile supply—we must both restrict our expenditures and safeguard our existing supplies. For this purpose, I intend to detach Admiral Stoner's light carriers."

"Carl won't like it," Sonja Desai foretold.

"He'll ricochet off the bulkheads," Sandoval added, earning a glare from Desai.

"I know. I also know our carriers are already stretched thin, but it can't be helped. Supplies are our Achilles heel, and whoever's orchestrated the rebel strategy has grasped that fact very well." Trevayne had a pretty definite idea who that person was, but he kept it to himself. "We may as well face the fact that whenever the rebels finally decide to offer battle in earnest, they're going to greatly outnumber us in fighters. Our great strength is our battleline." (The finest in the Galaxy, he thought, but silently; he didn't want to add to the general cockiness.) "It's more important to assure ourselves of an abundant supply of missiles—especially HBMs—for the decisive battle than it is to hoard fighters that won't, after all, be able to go toe-to-toe with their opposite numbers on even terms."

Heads nodded around the table. Then Yoshinaka spoke up.

"Admiral, another concern is the relatively heavy losses among our scout cruisers. We're not exactly oversupplied with them to begin with."

"True," Trevayne acknowledged. "Of course, you expect high losses among them due to the nature of their missions." Deep within him an old pain stirred briefly. He sternly suppressed it. "I'm thinking we ought to conserve them for now and rely on drone probes and recon fighters. In fact, we might make the two problems solve each other by temporarily detaching the scouts to help escort the fleet train." He held up a hand. "Yes, I know it's not what they're designed for, but with their missile armaments, they've got a lot of AFHAWK capability. Besides, I don't think the rebels are going to be expecting escorts with third-generation ECM! It could make things interesting the next time their 'vanishing carriers' pull one of their long-range raids if a couple of light cruisers suddenly drop out of cloak into their midst."

Glances were exchanged around the table as people found, to their surprise, that they liked the idea.

"Yes, sir," Sandoval said. "Of course, the scout cruiser types won't like it at first. They're a bunch of hot dogs . . . almost as bad as fighter jocks," the former fighter jock added. "But give them some rebel fighters to chew on, and maybe an escort carrier or two, and they'll come around."

"Also, Ian," Sanders put in, "we don't need them for recon just now anyway. We've already probed Sagebrush, and I gather we shouldn't need scouts there." He looked to Sandoval and Yoshinaka for confirmation. "We should be able to go through that system rather easily and quickly."

Sandoval grinned from ear to ear. "Like beans through a Gringo, sir."

Sanders spluttered into his coffee and nearly choked. Trevayne, pounding the older man on the back amid the general laughter, tried to give Sandoval the full-powered glare that had reduced strong men to jelly. He failed utterly. It was difficult to get mad at the irrepressible ops officer, and impossible to stay that way.

Impossible, that was, for most people. Sonja Desai's lips, always thin, became practically invisible, and they barely moved as she clipped out, "Admiral, if you'll excuse me I think I'd better get back to *Togo*. The shuttles should have landed by now, and the reports will be coming in." She carefully did not glare at Sandoval.

"I think we've about finished anyway," Trevayne said, and turned to Yoshinaka as Desai rose. "I'll be on the flag bridge for a while, Genji. There are still a few loose ends to tie together before I can turn in." He smiled ruefully. "Y'know, we can use robot probes for reconnaissance—don't you think someone would invent a robot admiral, too?"

After he was gone, Sandoval grinned at Desai's retreating narrow back and muttered to Yoshinaka, "I think we've already got one, sir."

"That will do, Commander," Yoshinaka replied, pleasantly but with finality. Opposites, he reflected, don't always attract.

INFERNO

The quiet buzzer seemed raucous in the darkened cabin, and the tiny woman in the bunk opened her eyes instantly, reaching for her com key.

"Yes?"

"Message from *Maori*, sir. Rim units are emerging from Sagebrush."

"Thank you, Bob." Vice Admiral Li sat up and reached for her battle uniform. "Composition?"

"They wasted a lot of SBMHAWKs on the decoys, sir, then the battle-line came through. They're reforming now."

"Good. Ask Admiral Tsing to meet us on Flag Bridge."

"Yes, sir."

Han sealed her vac suit, and lifted her helmet from the bedside table. Her cabin door opened silently, and the Marine sentry snapped to attention. She nodded courteously as she passed him; her conscious mind never even noticed him.

Trevayne studied the big visual display unhappily. Zapata's G2 sun was a distant, unwinking flame, and the flotillas of Fourth Fleet glittered with its feeble reflected glow. Why did the sight fill him with foreboding? Was it the unexpected lack of resistance?

His drone probes had reported two dozen type four OWPs and extensive minefields covering the Sagebrush-Zapata warp nexus. That had been enough to draw the fire of almost all of his remaining SBMHAWKs, but there had been no shock of battle when the battle-line made transit, for the "fortresses" proved to be unmanned satellites armed only with sophisticated ECM gear to masquerade as forts in the eyes of his probes.

He brooded over the display, pondering the system spread out before him in miniature. This warp point lay nearly in the system's plane of the ecliptic, as did his destination—the Iphigena warp point. But they were almost diametrically opposite one another, and between them was the inner system: the local sun, the two small, airless innermost planets, the Earthlike third planet, and an extensive asteroid belt.

Having the sun directly between him and his destination was annoying. That colossal gravity well made any sort of straight line route impossible, even in this day and age. He'd chosen his course long since: a hyperbola at right angles to the plane of the ecliptic, passing "over" the sun and its innermost children. He wanted to avoid the ecliptic anyway; it would distance him from any traps the opposition might consider springing.

But where *was* the opposition?

He knew he would encounter some fortresses, at least, at the Iphigena warp point; there'd been a couple there even before the rebellion, and the rebels must have reinforced them. After all, that warp point was far closer to the sun than most—less than ten light-minutes beyond the asteroid belt, in fact. The rebels couldn't have failed to construct some asteroid fortresses, the cheapest and in many ways best kind. But there *had* to be heavy mobile forces lurking beyond scanner range. He couldn't be that far wrong about rebel strategy. The increasing ferocity of their commerce raiders had managed to suck off a dismayingly high proportion of his light carriers—which had to be what they'd intended, assuming they meant to engage him here. Unless, of course, they'd followed the same line of reasoning and decided to do something else, just to be difficult. . . .

He shook free of his useless speculations and walked a few paces to join Yoshinaka and Mujabi, who were huddled in consultation.

"Problems, gentlemen?"

"No, sir," Yoshinaka replied. "Admiral Remko reports the screen's deployment complete."

Trevayne nodded. Remko's screen massed twelve battle-cruisers and attendant destroyers. With Admiral Steinmeuller's fifteen heavy cruisers attached, he would precede the battle-line by fifteen minutes, sweeping the space before the ten supermonitors, ten monitors, eight superdreadnoughts, and twelve battleships. The battlegroups had the usual allotment of destroyer escorts, except for the supermonitors, which were flanked by the new escort cruisers designed and built in the Rim, and Trevayne had held back three destroyer battlegroups, built around *Goeben*-class command cruisers.

The battle-line was also accompanied by Carl Stoner's six fleet carriers and three remaining light carriers, with over two hundred fighters. The rebels could put far more fighters into space whenever they finally offered battle, but at least they could no longer count on the edge their pilots' experience normally gave them—Stoner's people had been blooded repeatedly against both rebels and Tangri.

"The fleet is ready to proceed," Yoshinaka continued. "No, we were discussing the lack of opposition. It's almost eerie."

"Yes. I suppose it's possible I've been wrong all along about where the rebels will make a stand, but I still don't think so. And yet . . . if they do plan to put up a serious defense, letting us make transit unscathed shows a high degree of *chutzpah*." Mujabi's eyebrows arched in puzzlement, and Trevayne translated. "Outrageous self-confidence."

"Oh." Mujabi nodded. "New one on me, sir." He considered for a moment. "Rigelian word?"

Li Han folded her hands in her lap and watched her display. The data codes were more tentative than usual because the single scout cruiser hidden outside the asteroid belt was at extreme range. Still, the essentials were clear. A powerful screen had moved away from Trevayne's main force, opening the gap between itself and the battle-line to a full ninety light-seconds, and she sat expressionlessly, watching her enemy advance into what—hopefully—would prove an unsuspected trap. She glanced at Reznick.

"Time to asteroid belt?"

"Their screen will cross it headed in-system in about six

hours, sir. Their battle-line will be approximately fifteen minutes behind them."

"Thank you." She turned back to the display, wishing Trevayne hadn't jumped the gun on them. He'd begun his breakout over a month earlier than predicted, and half her carriers had yet to reach her, nor did she have any idea how the defense against the Rump pincer was proceeding. Her ignorance gnawed at her, and she wished she dared communicate with Magda or Jason, but they needed com silence to do their jobs. She felt herself relaxing as she thought of her friends. If anyone could pull it off, they could.

Sean Remko sat in his command chair like a bear. His combat vac suit and grooming were impeccable, but somehow he always struck Cyrus Waldeck as unwashed and slovenly. The flag captain shook his head distastefully and glanced back at his own display as his ship crossed the asteroid belt, moving at a—to them—leisurely pace to allow the battle-line to keep up. He stiffened as a sudden flicker of light abruptly resolved itself into the data codes of enemy vessels.

"Admiral Remko! We've got—"

"I see them, Captain," Remko interrupted. "Brian—" he turned to his chief of staff "—come to a heading of one-one six. Increase to flank speed. Prepare for missile engagement: carriers are primary targets."

"Aye, aye, sir!"

"Captain Waldeck, stand by to engage the enemy."

"Aye, aye, sir!"

Remko glanced at his elegant flag captain from the corner of one eye, then turned to his com officer. "Get me the flagship."

"Aye, aye, sir."

Remko watched the drifting data codes as he waited for the com link to be established. With transmissions limited to light speed, there was a time lag of just over ninety seconds either way, so he wasted no time trying for an integrated conversation when Trevayne's image appeared on his screen.

"Admiral, we've detected seven fleet carriers, seven battleships, and eight battle-cruisers with nine light cruisers maneuvering as regular three-ship squadrons—almost dead ahead at max scanner range. We should be able to engage them on our own terms—the battlewagons will slow them up for us. But we'll need carrier support . . ."

Trevayne nodded as Remko paused to acknowledge a report. He waved a hand at Yoshinaka and pointed at his chief of staff's communications panel.

"Launch them," he said.

"Sir," Remko looked back out of the screen, "the rebel carriers have launched what appears to be their entire fighter complement. ETA twenty-one minutes. Let me repeat my request for carrier support . . . urgently."

"Already granted, Sean," Trevayne replied. He glanced at Yoshinaka once more and received a nod of confirmation. "Admiral Stoner is proceeding to join you, and he'll be launching directly." And he could fight this lot on slightly better than even terms, he thought. "Good luck. Out."

He watched Remko's face as the seconds ticked past. Three minutes after his last word, his burly subordinate nodded with a grin.

"Thank you, sir. One trashed rebel task force coming up. Remko out."

"Well, you were right about the rebels offering battle here." Yoshinaka spoke as the screen blanked, then paused at Trevayne's unaccustomed scowl.

"Bloody hell, Genji, that can't be their entire force! Where're their battle-line and assault carriers? And look." He pointed to his battle plot. "They're backing away now that they've launched their fighers. Why? They can't outrun Sean with battleships to slow them down. Besides, battleships don't run away from battle-cruisers; they try to *close* before a force like ours can come to their opposition's support." He scowled at the plot, as if by sheer concentration he could know the minds commanding those drifting bits of light. "I don't like it at all, Genji." But the blips told him nothing, and his eyes strayed back to the big visual display as *Nelson* neared the asteroid belt. Planet Three was the second brightest object in the heavens.

"Admiral Petrovna's launching, sir."

"Thank you. Time, Bob?"

"Oh-seven-forty Zulu, Admiral."

"Log it." Han leaned back in her chair. The Book said a commander never committed her forces to combat when she couldn't exercise tactical control, but The Book didn't cover this situation. She'd agonized over her command structure before she finally made her call. Magda had proven her mettle too often to question her ability to handle the role thrust upon her, but Han had really wanted her for the other detached force, even if it was smaller. Timing, she told herself. Timing was everything. She could entrust her own force to no one else—it *had* to be under her direct control, with no com lag—and she needed Magda for the job she had, which left Jason for what was actually the most ticklish aspect of Operation Actium. Han didn't question his ability—only his experience.

"Enemy carriers advancing, sir. They're launching. Plotting estimates two hundred plus fighters. Estimated time to our fighters is twelve minutes."

"Thank you, David. Commander Jorgensen?"

"Full decks, sir, or right next to them. They should have two-forty, plus or minus twenty."

"It sounds like they're biting, sir," Tomanaga observed cautiously.

"Perhaps. But don't underestimate Ian Trevayne, Bob." Han tapped her fingertips gently together, then glanced at Tsing Chang. "Admiral, prepare to move out. Bob, same message to the other battlegroups on whiskers."

"Aye, aye, sir."

The needle-thin com lasers woke, murmuring across the emptiness to the tightly grouped capital ships of the Terran Republic. Han looked back at her display, watching as Magda's fighters plunged into the oncoming Rim ships.

Running battle snarled viciously across the Zapata System, and space became leprous with the ugly pockmarks of nuclear warheads and dying humans. Trevayne felt *Nelson* tremble under full drive, but even at her maximum speed, the ponderous supermonitor fell further and further behind as Stoner's carriers raced ahead to cover Remko's cruisers. His pilots had moved in with the wary skill of professionals, but they'd been disconcerted to find that the rebel fighters mounted a new weapon—a kind of flechette missile, short-ranged and useless against starships but dismayingly effective against fighters. They faced a daunting exchange rate, yet they hurtled into action.

Trevayne sat motionless but for the slow drumming of his fingers. The whole unorthodox course of the battle disturbed him. Simple attrition made sense against the flanks of an extending corridor, but not in a set-piece battle to defend a vital system. And the presence of battleships this far from their retreat warp point did not offer advantages commensurate with the risk. To be sure, they were heavy metal for battle-cruisers, but they weren't fast encugh to crush Sean before he could fall back on the battle-line, however far ahead he got. Damn it, what *were* the rebels up to?

His battle-line had drawn almost level with Planet Three when Trevayne thought his questions had been answered.

"Admiral," Yoshinaka announced, "scanners report nine battle-cruisers leaving Zapata III. Evidently they've been hiding behind the planet—now they're on course to intercept our screen from behind." Even as he spoke, the computers dispassionately added the newcomers to the display.

Things clicked in Trevayne's mind. Of course! The rebels had known he was as likely as themselves to deduce that Zapata was the logical place for them to make a stand—so they'd decided to make it elsewhere! Iphigena? Probably. It didn't matter. What mattered was that their objective for *this* battle was to strip him of his screen for the decisive clash . . . just as their false "fortresses" had already stripped him of most of his SBMHAWKs. And, he thought grimly, they were going about it in an all-too-rational fashion. Caught between these new battle-cruisers and the force with which he was already engaged, Remko would be overwhelmed before he could disengage.

But . . . the rebels had forgotten the onward-lumbering battle-line's heavy external ordnance load of SBMs. Yet there was no time to lose, or the battle-cruisers would soon draw out of range. He gave the command, and the capital ships' external ordnance lashed outward, the salvos of SBMs thickened by the supermonitors' internally launched HBMs.

Trevayne sat back, awaiting further reports as the missiles speckled his display. Those battle-cruisers were doomed. Nothing that size could stand up to that hurricane of missiles. Nothing. Yet there remained the unidentified worry nagging at the back of his mind, the sense of something overlooked. He was still scratching at the mental itch when Yoshinaka turned a carefully controlled face to him.

"Admiral, we've lost missile lock. Those 'battle-cruisers' . . . it seems they were scout cruisers with their ECM in deception mode. They've dropped it and gone to evasive action." Their eyes met, and neither needed to speak. The rebels had just stripped the battle-line of its external ordnance.

Somewhere in the back of Trevayne's mind a part of him reflected that perhaps he'd been too worried about his subordinate's cockiness to recognize it in himself. Or had he simply fallen into a belief in the infallibility of his own judgment? It was easy to do, when Miriam wasn't around. . . .

It only remained to learn why the rebels had mousetrapped him into firing off his missiles.

"They've taken the bait, sir!" Tomanaga's voice was exultant. "They just flushed their XO racks at the decoys!"

"Tracking reports at least ninety percent of their external ordnance fired, sir," David Reznick confirmed.

"Sir, their battle-line's flank scouts will clear the planet in eleven minutes," Stravos Kollentai reported.

"Very well." Han drew a deep, unobtrusive breath, remembering another battle aboard another ship. She glanced at Tsing Chang and saw what might have been a shadowy smile of memory on his imperturbable face.

"Commander Reznick, send to all commands: 'Execute Actium Alpha.' "

"Aye, aye, sir."

"Admiral Tsing."

"Yes, Admiral?" There *was* an edge of memory in that voice, Han decided. She felt a surge of warmth for the bulky admiral, and her face lit with one of her rare, serene smiles.

"Yours is the honor, Admiral," she said simply. "Prepare to move out."

"Aye, aye, sir. Immediately."

"Admiral Windrider is launching!" Reznick reported.

"Very well. Admiral Tsing, engage the enemy."

"Aye, aye, sir." The superdreadnought TRNS *Arrarat* rumbled to life, drive field bellowing muted thunder through her iron bones as Battle Group Nine, Terran Republican Navy, moved out to battle.

"Sir! Admiral Trevayne! The scanners—!"

Trevayne's head snapped around, his eyes flashing angrily at the hapless scanner rating whose incoherent report had shattered the silence. But his scathing retort died aborning as his plot altered silently. The disinterested computers updated the data quietly, and the menace of the new data codes flashed starkly on the screen.

A chain of lights crept around the disk of Zapata III in a sullen, crimson line of hostile capital ships. He sat quietly, his brain racing to assimilate the new data, as eight monitors and twenty-four battleships and superdreadnoughts abandoned their hiding place in the planet's shadow. They were too close and fast for his battle-line to avoid.

And even as they emerged from the shadows there came more reports—reports of swarms of strikefighters spewing out of the asteroid belt behind Fourth Fleet. Of course, he thought coldly, filled with an ungrudging respect for his opponent's tactics. Escort carriers. They had one advantage over larger carriers—with their power down and a little luck, they could be mistaken for asteroids by even the best scanner teams.

Not that they'd needed much luck, he thought grimly, remembering the cloaking ECM on the escort carriers raiding his communications. He'd thought it a financially extravagant way to build such cheap carriers—now he understood why it had been done.

He was back on stride by the time the final report came in. He knew what was happening, understood the deadly ambush into which he and his ships had strayed. This was no mere attempt to stop Fourth Fleet; it was a full-blooded bid to destroy it. *That* was why they'd let him into the system unopposed—to catch his slower battle-line between warp points, unable to retreat, while they hit him from all sides. And with Fourth Fleet gone, the rebels could sweep into Zephrain at last. Oh, yes, he understood—and perhaps alone among all the personnel of the Rim's ships, he was unsurprised as the "battleships" Remkó had been pursuing cut their ECM and appeared in their true guise: assault carriers, already launching against Stoner's isolated ships.

Trevayne watched the ruby chips of the outgoing rebel fighters with bitter satisfaction. He'd been right all along . . . the decisive battle would come at Zapata, but it would be such an engagement as none of them had dreamed of in their worst nightmares. On either side, he thought grimly.

"Admiral," Yoshinaka was saying, "should I recall Commander Sandoval?" The ops officer was on his way to *Togo* to confer with his opposite number on Desai's staff. Trevayne shook his head.

"No, Genji. His cutter has time to reach *Togo* before we engage, but not to get back here." He managed a grim smile. "I'm afraid he and Sonja are stuck with each other for the duration—just as you and I are stuck with another young lady."

"Sir?"

"That," Trevayne jutted his jaw at the oncoming rebel battle-line, "can be only one person, Genji. Admiral Li is back for a return engagement, and she's caught me with my trousers well and truly down about my ankles." He allowed himself a brief chuckle. The sound was harsh, but it seemed to banish his last doubts. He began rapping out orders, and the battle-line wheeled ponderously, abandoning its original course to face its foes.

Trevayne remained confident. The rebel battle-line was powerful, but clearly no match for his own. The incoming fighters from the belt were a threat, but not enough to even the balance *if* Remko and Stoner could fend off the rebel carriers long enough. They were in for a nasty series of external ordnance salvos from the rebel's capital ships, but when they closed to energy weapon range his superior weight of metal would tell. And he could still draw first blood with his HBMs before they entered SBM range.

But it wasn't that simple, as his first HBM salvo revealed. The Republic's R&D teams hadn't produced such spectacular results, perhaps, but they had not been idle. For the first time, the Rim encountered a Republican weapon that was as much a breakthrough as the grav driver. The rebels mounted shields which were outwardly identical to those which had been in use for over two hundred years, and so they were, to a point. But conventional shields collapsed as they took damage and their massive fuses blew; *these* reset automatically and virtually instantaneously. They didn't "collapse"—they simply flashed out of existence, then bounced back . . . as good as new!

On the heels of that discovery came more bad news. While the survivors of the rebels' opening fighter strike returned to their hangars to rearm, the equally-strong second strike ignored Remko to converge on Stoner and his decimated fighters. A tidal wave of fighter missiles overpowered the point defense of Stoner's flagship, and a Code Omega message flashed on the plot with sickening suddenness. Trevayne hid a pang of dismay as TFNS *Hellhound* vanished in a brilliant ball of flame. If the rebel's first strike rearmed and joined the clash of battle-lines . . .

Trevayne's communications section raised *Arquebus* quickly as *Nelson* and *Arrarat* lumbered towards one another. Capital ships were slow; even with the time lag, Trevayne had time to speak to Remko once more.

He outlined the situation in a few brief sentences, then looked squarely at the face of his embattled screen commander.

"It's vital that you hit those carriers hard—preferably while their first wave is aboard rearming. That means close engagement. I repeat, *close.*" He paused, then leaned closer to the pickup. "Sean, you're in command of the screen because I happen to think you're the most aggressive combat commander in the Fleet. Now prove it!"

Remko stared back at him unmovingly for long, long seconds as the transmission winged through space. His face reminded Trevayne of one of Kevin's quotes from the American Civil War—a description of General U. S. Grant: "He habitually wears an expression as if he had determined to drive his head through a brick wall and was about to do it." Remko wore that kind of expression as he rumbled "Aye, aye, sir." Then he blurted out, "Admiral, I'm gonna personally shove a force beam projector up the ass of whoever's in command of those carriers and then cut loose!" He stopped, face redder than usual, and broke the connection.

"Well." Trevayne turned to Yoshinaka and smiled. "Whoever said Sean isn't eloquent?" Then he shook himself as the rebels approached SBM range.

"Genji," he said, "run down to the intelligence center and personally impress on Lavrenti the urgency of analyzing this resetting shield the rebels have." Yoshinaka nodded and moved towards the intraship car. As an afterthought, Trevayne rose from the admiral's chair and walked with him.

"See if you can pick Kevin's brains while you're there." The intelligence center was Sanders' battle station. "And hurry back. Things could get a bit tight in the next few minutes."

Yoshinaka nodded again and stepped into the car. The doors closed, and Trevayne turned back toward his command chair and the battle as the first rebel SBM salvos began to launch. Most seemed targeted on *Nelson*. Yes, he thought, they'll try to begin by destroying one supermonitor, to show their people it can be done.

"Message from Admiral Petrovna, sir. The Rim screen isn't breaking off. She's taking heavy missile fire."

"Thank you, Bob." Han said calmly, watching the plot. She'd hoped the screen would fall back, for her ruse had been intended to destroy Trevayne's fighters and get her own battle-line in range of his without being devastated by long-range missile fire—not to match Magda against the screen in a ship-to-ship action. But it wasn't working out that way. The bickering fight had turned suddenly even more vicious, and that screen commander had kept his wits about him. The worst thing he could possibly do, from her viewpoint, was get in among her carriers and wreck those launch bays. Well, it had always been a possibility. That was why Magda held that command. Anyone who went after *her* in close action was reaching into a buzz saw. Han only hoped that Magda wouldn't be among the chips chewed off by the blade.

"Signal to Admiral Windrider," she said suddenly. "Launch reserve strike immediately." The escort carriers and hangar "barges" hidden among the asteroids were supposed to be the final reserve as well as the rear jaw of the trap, but the Rim screen was doing too good a job of closing with Magda; she would need to retain most of her fighter strength to fend off those cruisers, and the diversion had to be made up from Jason's units.

"Aye, aye, sir."

"Coming into SBM range, Admiral," Tsing Chang said calmly. "Captain Parbleu has a good setup."

"Then you may open fire, Admiral."

"Aye, aye, sir. Opening fire now."

And *Arrarat* bucked as BG 9's XO racks emptied in a single massive volley.

The vast majority of the SBMs targeting *Nelson* were stopped by BG 1's awesome array of datalinked point defense stations—but the laws of chance dictated that some would always get through, and the incoming salvos were massive. Nelson's dying shields were centered in a vortex of nuclear flame, and under those torrents of energy, the supermonitor's massive armor boiled.

Her shields went down, and more salvos scorched in, seeking to exploit her weakening defenses. Again, most were stopped. But dozens slid through the lattice-like intricacies of her point defense lasers and immolated themselves against her drive field in fireballs which gouged at her gargantuan hull. Glowing craters pitted her armor, snapped structural members, wiped away weapons . . . and personnel. And one of those craters, guided by the freakish improbability which rules the tides of war, ripped deep into the heavily armored compartments surrounding *Nelson's* flag bridge.

"Many hits on primary target," Tsing Chang's chief of staff reported jubilantly. "Her shields are down and she's streaming air!"

"She won't have much internal damage yet," Tomanaga commented softly, "but every little bit helps."

Concussion, shockwaves, and the terrible sound of buckling, tearing metal were all the universe there was. In an instant of havoc unacceptable to human senses, almost everyone on *Nelson*'s flag bridge died, except those in chairs with shock frames. Chairs like the one Trevayne was not in. The force of the explosion whipsawed the bridge, hurling him down and smashing him into the pedestal of the admiral's chair. His spinal column fractured and a shard of steel ripped his vac suit. Air hissed from the compartment, and his damaged suit began a deadly collapse. And yet he was, all things considered, unreasonably lucky.

Profiting from the confusion caused by the hit, a second missile from the same salvo drew dangerously close before it detonated—not a hit, but a near miss which flooded adjacent space with lethal radiation. The rent armor of the stricken flag bridge couldn't shield the survivors from death, but again, Trevayne was lucky. The chair behind which he lay gave him some protection. The radiation poisoning he received was not fatal . . . instantly.

Genji Yoshinaka gasped as his suit pressurized. He'd been thrown against the wall of the intraship car by the concussion, but he was dazed only briefly and he heaved himself upright and slammed his fist on the override button. The buckled doors were jammed, and his hand went to the laser pistol by his side. He blasted the doors aside, cutting his way back onto the flag bridge the car had only just begun to leave . . . and into a scene from Hell.

Bodies sprawled amid the twisted, blackened metal. Acrid smoke streamed toward the hungry rents through which atmosphere screamed into space, and severed cables lashed the escaping air like bullwhips, crackling and spitting and fountaining fire.

Yoshinaka's body responded before his numbed mind could understand. He snatched the nearest emergency kit and flung himself at the crumpled figure beside the admiral's chair. His hands moved with machine-like efficiency, slapping seals on the partially collapsing vac suit, and even as he worked he spoke calmly to the battlephone microphone in his helmet.

"Doctor Yuan to the flag bride! Damage control to the flag bridge! Use the emergency bypass route. Captain Mujabi, have com raise Admiral Desai. Inform her she's in command . . . details to follow."

And then there was nothing he could do but wait, kneeling at the side of the semi-conscious figure in the fleet admiral's vac suit with the blood-misted faceplate. He was still there when Doctor Yuan arrived.

"More hits on the primary target, sir," Tomanaga reported. "Her drive field is weakening and her fire's almost ceased. Permission to shift target?"

"Granted."

"*Parnassus* reports critical HBM damage, sir. She's withdrawing."

"Acknowledge." Han glanced at the blinking data codes under the crippled superdreadnought's blip. *Parnassus* was done for—if she had time to withdraw before she went Code Omega it would be a miracle.

"BG 14 reports loss of both escort destroyers, sir. Admiral Iskan requests additional fighter support."

"Denied. We don't have it to spare. Tell him to tail in behind BG 16 and use them for cover."

"Aye, aye, sir."

"External ordnance exhausted, sir. Closing to energy range. Force beams and primaries in range in two minutes."

"Very well. Signal Admiral Kanohe: 'Destroyers attack enemy line of battle.' Signal all battle-lines units: 'Stand by to engage with beams.' "

"Standing by, sir."

"Admiral Tsing, your group will engage the enemy's lead battlegroup."

"Aye, aye, sir."

Sonja Desai was speaking to her chief of staff when Joaquin Sandoval almost ran onto *Togo*'s bridge.

". . . yes. Get her inside the globe. Their fighters aren't going to be busy with our escorts forever, and their capital ships are coming to us. They'll want to stay close—inside HBM range. . . ."

Sandoval waited impatiently. His cutter had come through the beginning of the battle on its final approach to *Togo*, and he was still oversupplied with adrenalin. But he had no intention of giving Desai an excuse for dressing him down by violating any aspect of military courtesy. Finally she turned back to him.

"Commander Sandoval," she began without greeting or preliminary, "I'd better bring you up to speed. Admiral

Trevayne is seriously injured and out of action. I've assumed command. *Nelson*'s shields are down and there's not much left of her armor. She's taken significant internal damage, including the virtual destruction of her flag deck; she can still maneuver, but we'll have to get her inside our globe. Captain Mujabi has taken command of BG 1. We've lost *Olympus*, and *Drake* and two more superdreadnoughts have taken heavy damage. At the same time, the rebels have taken considerable HBM damage, but they're still closing. They'll be in beam range shortly."

Sandoval gaped at her. Mother of God, what did the woman use for blood? Formaldehyde? Aloud, he asked, "And Commodore Yoshinaka, sir?"

"Alive and well."

"I'd better get back, rejoin him. . . ."

"Out of the question, Commander. You can't fly a cutter through what's happening out there." Was it possible that there was a very slight ironic twinkle in her eyes? "Welcome aboard, Commander . . . and strap in tight. Things are going to get bumpy."

"Sir, we can't *stop* them! They just keep coming!"

Magda Petrovna regarded her fighter commander levelly. Commodore Huyler was a good man under normal conditions, but these weren't normal. His pilots were doing everything perfectly—but what could you do when your enemy suddenly began to ignore everything your fighters handed out while he concentrated on mauling your flight decks? And those damned improved force beams were just the weapon to do it with, she thought grimly.

"Admiral." It was the rating monitoring Han's com traffic. "*Parnassus* is Code Omega—so is *Copperhead. Shiriken* reports total loss of energy armament."

"Do your best, Commodore," she told Huyler. "If you can't stop them all, try to cripple as many as possible. Go for the heavy cruisers—you've got better odds there. The screen will just have to handle the battle-cruisers."

"Aye, aye, sir."

The screen blanked, and Magda glanced at her battle plot. She hid her fears well, she thought, for that was part of the game. Yet her carriers *had* to remain in support range of the capital ships. If she let herself be driven away, those mammoth monitors and supermonitors would overwhelm Han no matter what. She leaned over and touched a com stud, opening an all-ships channel.

"This is Admiral Petrovna," she said calmly, watching the Rim ships close on her flagship with magnificent courage. "We're done retreating, people. We stop them here, or we don't go home." She looked back at the plot. In one corner the opposing battle-lines were merging into a single sea of light dots. "Admiral Li is depending on us," she said quietly. "We're not going to let her down."

She heard the cheers ripple through her flagship and closed her eyes in pain.

"Well?"

Captain Joseph Yuan, M.D., rose and looked into Genji Yoshinaka's anxious face. Repair parties labored furiously about them, repressurizing the charnel house that had been a flag bridge. Since they and the medics had arrived, Yoshinaka had finally had time to worry. For the first time since Yuan had known him, his control was perceptibly frayed.

"The admiral is suffering from acute anoxia, shock, and concussion," Yuan said in a voice of dispassionate professionalism. "His spinal cord is severed just below the fifth vertebra, and he has severe radiation poisoning. It's a miracle he's alive—and he won't be for very long. I doubt a fully-equipped dirtside hospital could deal with this. I can't."

Yoshinaka fumbled to grasp what he had heard. Yuan had warned him he might have gotten a bit of concussion himself, but that could not fully explain his pain and confusion.

"You're telling me you can't save him?!"

"Not necessarily. . . ."

Two of Yuan's technicians entered, wheeling in a strangely repellent object. Its attached instrumentation and tankage couldn't hide its basic shape; it was a coffin. Yuan pointed at it.

"There's one chance—not a good one, but beggars can't be choosers. If we act fast, we can get him into this cryogenic bath. 'Freeze' him, to use the vulgar term. Now, you realize that this procedure normally involves an extensive workup, but we haven't time for any of that. We won't be able to 'unfreeze' him."

Yoshinaka stared at Yuan as he would have stared at a horrifyingly calm, reasonable lunatic. "What . . . what's the use, then, if . . . ?"

The doctor raised a hand. "We can't unfreeze him *now.* But we can suspend his vital functions indefinitely. And maybe at some time in the future we'll be able to undo the effects of this quickie job *and* repair the other damage. I can't promise that, but . . ." His temper flared, and Yoshinaka realized that this man might feel as strongly about Ian Trevayne as he did. "Damn it, this is our only chance to save him!"

The technicians had been making hurried preparations as he talked. Now one of his medics looked up suddenly.

"Doctor, his vital signs are weakening fast."

"God*damn* it!" Yuan's face twisted in angry grief. "We may be too late already! Get him in there! Move, man! Move!"

On a sunlit beach in Old Terra's Midworld Sea, a little girl with chestnut hair smiled and beckoned, and Lieutenant Commander Ian Trevayne ran to join her.

Sean Remko's eyes swept the officers facing him—his flag captain and staff—and his New Detroit Accent, always harsh, was a saw.

"Ladies and gentlemen, I don't give a flying fuck about damage reports." His hand slapped his plot like a gunshot. "It's our job to keep those rebel fighters off the admiral, and that means forcing close engagement with their carriers. Those are my orders from the admiral. So I don't want to hear about fighters or missiles or any other goddamned thing. All that matters is that *they've* stopped backing away and we can get at them. Admiral Trevayne's orders apply to every ship—including this one. If anybody hangs back, I'm going to tear him a new asshole! Is that understood?"

The staff types shrank before his fury, and it was the flag captain who spoke a heartfelt "Yes, *sir*!" Remko looked at him sharply and motioned him closer as the others returned hastily to their consoles. When everyone else was out of earshot, he spoke softly.

"You've never liked me much, have you, Captain?"

Cyrus Waldeck looked him straight in the eye and spoke just as quietly. "I hate your guts, sir. But for now, let's go kill those rebel bastards!"

Remko extended his hand. Waldeck took it.

"Sir, the enemy screen has forced a close engagement with Admiral Petrovna. She'll need every fighter she's got just to hold them off—she can't send her first strike back into the main engagement."

Rear Admiral Jason Windrider eyed his chief of staff coldly. He didn't know Magda, Jason thought—not if he thought she'd hold back fighters Han needed. He watched her flagship's light flicker as it took hits, and his teeth ground together. Never before had they been in the same battle aboard different ships, and only now did he truly realize how much it could cost two warriors to love.

He stared at his plot bitterly. He had nothing heavier than a destroyer under his own command—just a lot of immobile barges and tiny escort carriers without a single offensive weapon of their own. There was no way he could come to Magda's aid, even if his orders had allowed it.

"Sir! We've intercepted a signal from Admiral Petrovna." Jason's com officer faltered under his bitter eyes. "She . . . she's sending her first strike back to support Admiral Li, sir. . . ."

Jason closed his eyes briefly, staring deep into his soul. Then he nodded once, sharply. When he spoke, his voice was calm.

"Signal to Admiral Petrovna: 'Suggest you recall fighters. Am moving to support battle-line and rearm fighters engaged against enemy main body. Windrider, out.' " He turned to his chief of staff. "Leave the barges and get these buckets moving, Ivan."

"But, sir," his chief of staff said quietly, "the enemy's between us and Admiral Li." There was no fear in his voice, only logic. "If we come close enough to support her, we'll be in missile range of the Rim battle-line. The ships will never stand it, sir."

"They only have to stand it long enough for Admiral

Petrovna to deal with that screen," Jason said bleakly. "Now get us moving."

"Aye, aye, sir."

Drive fields woke in twenty-four escort carriers scattered among the asteroids, stripping away the anonymity which had shielded them. Two dozen carriers—small and frail—abandoned concealment and darted towards the battling Titans while missile-hungry fighters swerved to meet them.

Jason Windrider watched his plot. Was he doing it because it was the logical move? Or in a desperate attempt to save the woman he loved? If logic dictated, his actions were correct; if he'd allowed love to rule him, they were contemptible. He closed his eyes once more and forced himself to reconsider his decision.

No, it was right, he decided finally. If Magda retained her fighters, she could beat off Trevayne's screen. She'd take losses, but she could do it. And only if her big carriers survived could Han win the battle. So he was right . . . even though so many people would die.

"Incoming missiles, sir," his chief of staff said tensely.

"Stand by point defense," Rear Admiral Windrider said.

The battle-lines crunched together, and the space between them became trellised with beamed energy: the tearing x-ray fury of hetlasers and the space-distorting Erlicher-effect weapons—the metal-wrenching force beams and the stiletto-thin, unstoppable primaries. Under those intolerable hammers of energy, shields flashed and overloaded, dying in bursts of deadly radiation.

The Republic's new screens made a superdreadnought effectively equal to a monitor, at least in its ability to absorb punishment. But the battle-line Ian Trevayne had forged still held the advantage—or would have, but for the rebel fighters and formations of hetlaser-armed destroyers that swept through the carnage. The fighters came slashing in, corkscrewing and weaving to penetrate the defenses. Many died, but others survived, pouring their fire into the Rim ships, breaking off and streaming back to the fragile escort carriers to rearm. The destroyer squadrons were less maneuverable and bigger targets, but there were many of them, and they could take far more damage. They rammed their attacks down the Rim's throat, closing until their shields jarred and flashed against their opponents'. At such range, the hetlaser was a deadly weapon, and Sonja Desai was forced to divert more and more of her killer whales' firepower against those lethal minnows.

She watched the devastation mount about her furiously fighting ships. Omega reports began coming in from the lighter spreadreadnoughts and battleships—only a trickle, yet, but a flood would soon follow. No one had ever seen such extravagant slaughter. The worst engagements of the Fourth Interstellar War paled beside this holocaust—and *still* it grew. It was inconceivable.

Almost half the rebels' energy weapons were a new kind of primary, she noted almost absently. Apparently they hadn't cracked the secret of the variable-focus beam, but they seemed to have come up with something almost as good. Desai was a weapons specialist; she didn't need experts to tell her the rebels had stumbled onto a different application of the forcefield lens principle—one which allowed a "burst" longer than that of the standard primary. Long enough for the beam to "swing" slightly. Its slicing action did less damage than a force beam, simply slashing a five-centimeter-wide gash through whatever it hit. But that was more than enough to cripple any installation—and it passed effortlessly through any material object or energy shield in its path. That was what made it so deadly despite its slow rate of fire; it could damage supermonitors without first pounding through their nearly indestructible shields and armor.

The primary has always held an especially nerve-wracking fear for spacers. One can be standing in an undamaged ship and suddenly find a five-centimeter hole through one's stomach. It happens rarely, of course—human bodies are small objects, placed aboard starships in limited numbers. But even improbable things happen occasionally.

Like the primary which suddenly sliced through *Togo*'s flag bridge. Air began howling into space. Two scanner ratings got in the beam's way, and it cut them in two in an explosion of gore. It swung towards Sonja Desai's command chair, but it did not quite reach it . . . it terminated at the midthigh level of Joaquin Sandoval's right leg. He crashed to the deck, the leg suddenly attached only by a thin strip of muscle and skin.

The primary is not a heat weapon; it does not cauterize. The stump spurted blood.

Sandoval began screaming.

Desai's reflexes thought for her as one hand slammed the release on her shock frame and she flung herself free. No one else on the shocked bridge could move as she ripped a severed cable from a shattered panel. She whipped it around his leg, jerking the crude tourniquet tight even as she summoned the medics via battlephone.

"Sir, *Adder*, *Coral Snake*, *Ortler*, *Thera*, and *Anderson* are Code Omega," Tomanaga reported, his voice hoarse as the nightmare tally rose, his face afire with battle and awe at the unprecedented destruction.

Han sat in her command chair, stroking the helmet in her lap as she absorbed the litany of death. Death inflicted by humans upon humans. Death dealt out in the name of duty and honor. Her shoulders were relaxed, her face calm, but a trickle of sweat ran down one cheekbone.

Arrarat shuddered as another missile exploded against her drive field, and Han looked at Tsing's ops officer; he sat motionless before his panel. His datalink was gone. It was very quiet on the flag bridge, despite the dreadful butchery raging within and beyond the hull. She looked up as a shadow fell on the side of her face, and Tsing Chang looked down at her.

"Sir, you must transfer. *Arrarat* can no longer serve as your flagship."

"No," she said softly.

"Admiral," Tsing tried again, "Captain Parbleu is dead. Commander Tomas tells me we have two hetlasers and one primary left—the armament of a light cruiser, sir. Right now, they're not even shooting at us very much, but it's only a matter of time till they finish us off. You *must* transfer."

"No," she said once more. "I've had three flagships, Chang. I've lost two of them." She looked away from the plot where *Bernardo da Silva* had just died at the hands of her own ships. "I won't leave this one."

"It's your duty, Admiral," he said softly. "This task force is your responsibility—not a single ship."

"Oh? And what of you, *Admiral*?"

"I've only got two ships left," he said simply, "and they're both out of the net."

"But you still have your com." *Arrarat* was doomed, but it seemed to her hypersensitive mind that only her presence had deferred that doom this long. She knew it was irrational, yet she couldn't leave. She shook her head doggedly. "And you've still got your drive, Admiral. Instruct *Arrarat* to withdraw. I can still command from here."

"Yes, sir. You're right, of course." Tsing paused, looking down at her, and his lips curved suddenly in a warm smile. "It's been an honor to serve with you, sir."

She looked up, troubled by his gentle voice even through the mental haze of battle. It no longer sounded like the imperturbable Tsing she knew.

"I'm sorry, sir," he said softly—and his fist exploded against her jaw.

Han's head snapped back, her eyes rolling up. She lolled in her shock frame, and Tsing caught up her helmet and jammed it over her head, sealing it while the bridge crew stared in frozen disbelief. He turned to Tomanaga.

"You've got four minutes to clear this ship, Commodore," he said crisply. He punched the release of Han's shock frame, his face fierce, and snatched her up. He threw her limp body at Tomanaga, and the chief of staff caught her numbly. "Get her out of here. *Now*, goddamn it!"

Tomanaga hesitated one instant, then nodded sharply and raced for the intraship car.

"She'll need her staff," Tsing snapped. "The rest of you—out!"

Li Han's staff never hesitated. Something in his voice compelled obedience, and they were halfway to the boatbay before they even realized they'd moved.

Tsing punched a button on the arm of Han's empty chair, and his voice echoed through every battlephone aboard his savagely wounded flagship.

"This is Admiral Tsing. Our weapons are destroyed. I intend to close the enemy and ram while I still have drive power. You have three minutes to abandon ship."

He turned to his staff.

"Commander Howell, message to Admiral Windrider: 'Vice Admiral Li transferring to TRNS *Saburo Yato* via cutter. Urgently request fighter cover.' Send it and get out."

He bent and pressed buttons, slaving drive and helm to

the flag bridge. He looked up a moment later—his staff remained at their stations.

"Ladies and gentlemen, perhaps you misunderstood me," he said calmly.

"No, sir," Frances Howell said softly. "We understood."

Tsing started to speak again, then closed his mouth. He nodded and dropped back into his command chair, glancing at the chronometer.

"Two minutes, Commander Howell," he said. "Then I want maximum power." He touched a brilliant dot on his plot. "That looks like a nice target."

"It does, indeed, sir."

"She's *what?*" Jason Windrider demanded. Only nine of his small carriers remained, but a destroyer flotilla and two light cruiser squadrons had broken through to protect the survivors while their hangar crews broke all speed records rearming fighters.

"The Flag is transferring, sir," his com officer repeated. "Admiral Tsing requests fighter cover for the admiral's cutter."

"What the *hell* is she playing at now?" Jason fumed, fear fraying his voice with anger. He stared at the maelstrom of capital ships and sighed. "All right, Ivan. See if you can sort anyone out of that mess!"

"Yes, sir."

Only a handful of Carl Stoner's fighters survived, and they'd been driven back by Magda's fighters once she was free to retain them for her own defense. Even Sean Remko's ships had been unable to close on her flagship as her fighters slashed away at their drive pods, slowing them, battering them. She'd lost heavily—five of her own battlecruisers were gone, and two assault carriers and three fleet carriers had been gutted or destroyed—but her remaining hangar bays supported enough fighters to make it suicide for Stoner's survivors to engage her.

Remko had realized that. In desperation, he had ordered them into the butchery of the battle-lines, hoping they might make a difference, that they and the capital ships might offer one another some mutual protection. Now three of Stoner's waifs saw an unbelievable sight: a cutter spat out of the boatbay of a rebel superdreadnought and dashed towards an embattled monitor.

"Zulu Leader to Zulu Squadron," their leader said, his voice ugly with hate and despair. "Must be someone pretty important—let's go get him!"

"Zulu Three, roger."

"Zulu Six, roger."

His two remaining wingmen dropped back to cover him, and the Rim squadron leader stooped on the cutter like a hawk.

Lieutenant Anna Holbeck shook her head in disbelief. Find a cutter and escort it through *this?!* Someone had obviously had a shock or two too many, she thought. But hers was not to reason why.

"Basilisk Leader to Basilisk Squadron," she said resignedly. "Let's go find the admiral, boys and girls."

Five agile little strikefighters slashed through vacuum, closing on Han's cutter. Death crashed about them, but so vast are the battlefields of space that even in that cauldron of beams and missiles, no weapon came close to the deadly little quintet.

"Basilisk Leader, Basilisk Two. I've got her on instruments, Skip—but she's got trouble."

"I see it. Green Section, close on the cutter. Red Section, follow me."

The three Rim pilots were so intent on their prey they never even saw the Republican ships that killed them.

"Sir! One of the rebel superdreadnoughts is closing rapidly!"

"What about it?" Vice Admiral Frederick Shespar grunted, tightening his shock frame as TFNS *Suffren*'s evasive action grew more violent.

"Sir, she's on a collision course—at maximum speed!"

"What?" Shespar stabbed one glance at his flag plot and blanched in horror. The ship coming at him could hardly be called a ship. She was a battered, broken wreck, streaming atmosphere and shedding bits of plating and escape pods as she came, but there was clearly nothing wrong with her drive. It took him barely a second to realize her grim purpose—but a second is a long, long time at such speeds.

"Gunnery! New battlegroup target! Burn that ship d—"

He never finished the sentence. Tsing Chang's flagship hurled herself headlong at *Suffren.* Neither supermonitors nor superdreadnoughts are very fast, by Fleet standards—but these were on virtually reciprocal courses. Two-thirds of a million tonnes of mass collided at a closing speed of just under fifty thousand kilometers per second.

It was too intense to call an explosion.

Some events are so cataclysmic the mind cannot comprehend them. The weapons in play in the Zapata System had killed far more people than died with *Arrarat* and *Suffren*—but not so spectacularly, so . . . deliberately. The devastating boil of light and vaporized steel and flesh hung before the eyes of the survivors like the mouth of hell, and they shrank from it.

As two fighting animals will separate momentarily to draw breath, the battle fleets pulled slightly apart. It wasn't really a lull, for weapons still fired, but a reduction of the unprecedented, unendurable intensity of close combat. As a conscious, ashen-faced Li Han turned from the cutter's viewport, something very like a respite closed in on the warring ships.

The Republic needed it. Scores of fighters were rearming aboard Windrider's and Magda's surviving carriers as Han stepped from her cutter aboard *Saburo Yato* and raced for the intraship car. Her brain was like ice over a furnace. The anguish of Tsing's death warred with a sort of horrified pride in the manner of his dying, but she couldn't let herself think of that. Not yet. There were things to do, a battle to win. She would allow herself grief and pride later. Later, when she had time to mourn as Chang deserved.

She stepped onto *Yato*'s flag bridge, and Admiral Stephen Butesky leapt aside to offer her his command chair. She nodded briefly and dropped into it while a shaken Tomanaga quietly displaced Butesky's chief of staff.

"Status report!" she snapped. She didn't really want to know. She didn't want to consider her hideous losses, or even those of her enemies. But she had a job to do. Thank God for this lull! Perhaps she could—

"Admiral Li?" A strange com rating looked up at her,

eyes puzzled, and Han choked back a sob of grief for the people aboard *Arrarat*.

"Yes?" Her voice showed no sign of her sorrow.

"I've just picked up a parley signal—from Vice Admiral Sonja Desai."

Han blinked, then smoothed an incipient scowl from her face and gestured acceptance, her mind racing. Who the devil was Vice Admiral Desai? It was unheard of! An officer didn't simply send a signal to her opponent while missiles and beams were still flying! Why—

She didn't recognize the dark, sharp-featured woman who appeared on the screen. Her vac suit was drenched with blood—not her own, obviously, for she sat upright in a command chair, clearly in complete command of herself.

"Where is Admiral Trevayne?" Han demanded without preamble.

"Admiral Trevayne is in sickbay. I have assumed command." Desai's habitual expressionlessness did not alter, and she resumed after the briefest of pauses. "The position is this, Admiral Li: we can continue this battle and fight it out to a conclusion, and I believe I can win. Quite probably you disagree. But whichever of us is right, 'winning' in this context means being left with the last one or two ships, or at least with a surviving force too weak to follow up its 'victory.' As an alternative to this profitless slaughter, I propose a cease-fire in place, of indefinite duration, while we apprise our respective governments of the situation." The immobile face took on a slightly rueful expression. "We may have to ask you to transport our messenger to the Innerworlds, but we have with us a high-ranking Federation official who will be able to represent our status to the Prime Minister."

Han's face was like a sculpture as she thought furiously. Could she win if the battle resumed? Yes. With her fighters rearmed and the range too short for the Rim's HBMs to be decisive . . . yes, she could win. She felt certain of it—and she suspected this Desai knew it, too. Yet Desai was also right. Her own battle-line had been savaged, the relentless attacks of the Rim screen had hurt Magda far worse than had been allowed for, and Jason's force was devastated. And she had little idea just how much fight those looming supermonitors still had in them—three were gone, others badly damaged. One hadn't fired in minutes. Was it any more than a hulk? She *knew* she could take them, avenge Second Zephrain's blot on the Fleet's honor . . . and yet . . . and yet there was that edge of uncertainty and her ignorance of how matters stood with the Rump pincer. And there was the terrible knowledge that even victory would leave her on her knees, without the strength to follow through against Zephrain. . . .

But still . . .

Damn it, where was Trevayne? Was he really dead? They'd hardly admit it, would they? And, her dogged honestly demanded, why did she care?

Aloud she temporized. "Such an agreement might exceed my authority. At the least, you're asking me to assume a heavy responsibility."

"No heavier than I'm assuming myself."

"On the contrary; you're occupying four planetary systems of the Terran Republic which I'm under orders to recover—"

"And I am under orders to reopen contact between the Innerworlds and the Rim Feder . . . the loyalist systems of the Rim." Desai's stiffness relaxed just a trifle. "Now that we've each recited our position papers, let's turn to reality. You and I are in command on the scene. We both know our orders can't be carried out—not without a degree of slaughter which passes the limits of sanity and decency. Shall we make our governments aware of that reality? Or shall we continue to carry out our orders in spite of it?" Her eyes bored into Han's. "In the end, I suppose it comes down to a question of where our duty really lies. That's a question many of us have had to face over the last few years, isn't it?"

Two pairs of dark eyes locked. I can win, Han told herself. I can win the greatest space battle in history! Or do I think that because I *want* to win so badly? And if I do, why? Out of duty . . . or hatred? Shame that a man who may not even be alive over there once beat me? Or for the glory? And what "glory" is there in being the woman responsible for such slaughter?

And could I kill them all? Her thoughts turned ever inward. Could I wipe them out—because that's what it comes down to; this Desai will no more surrender if I reject her offer than I would. Even after all that's passed, even if I have the capability to treat them like Arthur Ruyard, could I do it? After Ian Trevayne *didn't* do that to me?

And almost before she realized she was speaking, the quiet words came.

"Very well, Admiral Desai. I agree."

Vice Admiral Li Han stood in a strange cabin, hands by her sides. Her eyes were dry, but her face was strained and drawn. She sank into a chair, her lips trembling briefly in a tired smile. She'd lost three sets of quarters now. She was once more down to a single battle-stained vac suit . . . her painfully reassembled possessions drifting atoms.

Her face crumpled as realization hit. *Arrarat* was gone. All those people. Twenty-five hundred friends. Chang.

She buried her face in her hands, feeling her nails press into her temples as she fought the tears. She wouldn't weep. She wouldn't! Chang had chosen the way he died. . . .

But he *had* died, she told herself sadly. Died under her command—with thousands of others aboard the ships she'd commanded. And she hadn't even won! She'd renounced victory, held her hand in the name of 'humanity.' But what of her debt to those who had died, trusting in her to win the battle?

She straightened her spine and stared into a mirror, her cheeks dry, and scarcely recognized the wan face that looked back at her from those brilliant black eyes. No tears, she told herself. No tears for Chang, for the dead, for the lost victory. The past was past, and the future pressed upon her.

She reached for the com panel and began to punch Magda's code, then stopped. Her hand fell into her lap, and she leaned back in the chair, closing her eyes.

Not yet. She must speak to Magda, must plan and confer. But not yet. Please, God, not just yet. . . .

An odd numbness gripped the officers in *Togo*'s briefing room. It went beyond the inevitable aftershock of battle—even of one such as this.

Sonja Desai looked at the faces of the people who had come so far and given so much for the victory which had been denied them. It wasn't defeat. Not really. But it wasn't victory, either, and the price they'd paid was terrible enough to demand victory.

Sean Remko sat staring dully at the deck, his face working with emotion. He'd learned what had happened to Trevayne, and no assurance that he'd done far more than his "duty" could reach him in the darkened chamber to which he had withdrawn and which held but one thought: he had failed the admiral.

Yoshinaka and Kirilenko sat side by side. They'd come from *Nelson* (along with Sanders, who was even now preparing for his departure) and had arrived a few minutes late, after receiving assurances that Sandoval's condition was stable. Mujabi was present in his new capacity as CO of BG 1—what remained of it. So were the other ranking survivors, including Khalid Khan, who was the first to react.

"What you're saying, Admiral, is that we're simply to keep station here in Zapata until we get orders to the contrary?"

"Correct," Desai nodded. "So are the rebels. This is the precondition to the cease-fire. All major Fleet units must remain in place. Of course, noncombatant supply vessels aren't included, nor are light combatants . . . like the rebel destroyer which will take Mister Sanders to the Innerworlds."

They all stared at her as if she had, inexplicably, left out the most obvious point. It was Kirilenko who blurted it out.

"But, sir, what about the admiral . . . er, Admiral Trevayne?"

Desai's face was at its most flinty. "*Nelson* is, of course, covered by the cease-fire terms and must remain here. But I am advised by Doctor Yuan that Admiral Trevayne can be maintained aboard *Nelson* indefinitely in his present condition. So there's really no problem. Any other questions?"

The stares changed subtly, as if these people were looking at a thing they couldn't comprehend, and were fairly sure they did not want to.

Kirilenko stiffened, and his mouth began to open. Under the edge of the table, Yoshinaka gripped his forearm, very tightly. Kirilenko's mouth closed again, and he subsided.

Desai stood. "If there are no further questions, ladies and gentlemen, please carry on." She walked to the door, then paused and looked back. Everyone was still seated.

Desai looked straight into the eyes of Sean Remko, the senior man in the room. For a bare instant, he stared back with an unreadable expression. Then he lumbered to his feet and said, in a voice like a rockslide, "Attention on deck."

They rose slowly to attention. Desai nodded very slightly and stalked through the door.

Her expression and posture remained equally stiff in the intraship car and through the passageway to her quarters. The sentry snapped to attention, and she nodded crisply to him as she pressed the door stud and entered.

The door closed silently behind her. She stood a moment, her face wearing a vague look which slowly turned into one of pained bewilderment. Something happened inside her, something whose possibility would have been flatly denied by those who knew her. Her features collapsed into a mask of inconsolable grief, and a harsh, low cry welled out of her like the plaintive wail of a maimed animal unable to understand its pain. She hurled herself onto her bunk, burying her face in the pillow as she wept convulsively, and the sound of her empty, tearing sorrow filled her cabin.

A moment later, the door slid open with its usual soundlessness to admit Remko and Yoshinaka. They stopped, frozen with amazement, at the sight of the sobbing woman on the bunk. The woman neither of them had ever thought of as a woman at all. Remko turned to Yoshinaka and opened his mouth, but the commodore put a finger to his lips and slowly shook his head.

They departed as silently as they'd come, leaving Sonja Desai alone with her grief for the man she had loved silently and hopelessly for years.

"Thank God I have done my duty."

Vice Admiral Horatio Nelson,
Orlop Deck, HMS *Victory*
Battle of Trafalgar

CONFERENCE

Oskar Dieter studied the strained faces of his cabinet, remembering the day the first mutiny had been reported, and shuddered. This was almost worse. There'd been no treason this time, yet Fourth Fleet had lost more tonnage in two hours of close action than had been taken from Admiral Forsythe, and the shock cut deep. Even Amanda Sydon was gray-faced and stunned.

He sighed and tapped the crystal table with his knuckles. "Ladies and gentlemen, for the record—" he looked at Sky Marshal Witcinski "—I should like to say that I concur entirely with Admiral Desai's actions." A rustling sigh ran around the table. "Even if she had continued the action and won, it would have cost more than we can stand. Admiral Trevayne's—" his voice faltered briefly "—ships are both our most powerful single striking force and our sole technical advantage. Had Admiral Desai won at the expense of crippling damage to Fourth Fleet, we would have been unable to follow up her 'victory.' Had she lost, the Terran Republic must inevitably have captured sufficient examples of the Rim's weaponry to duplicate it."

He felt his listeners' stab of surprise as he deliberately used the term "Terran Republic" instead of "rebels"—and their horror as they considered the consequences of the Republic's acquiring weapons in advance of anything they could produce.

"I would like to ask Sky Marshal Witcinski and Vice Admiral Krupskaya a few questions," Dieter went on quietly. "First the Sky Marshal. With Fourth Fleet halted, whether by a cease-fire or the destruction of its units, what are the chances for Operation Yellowbrick?"

"Nil," Witcinski said. His voice was like a gravel-crusher. "Whoever planned the *rebels'*—" he stressed the word deliberately—"tactics knew what he was doing. I still don't know how they guessed our plans, but they've put up a web of fortresses and fighters that's stopped us cold. I've suspended operations after taking only two of our target systems, Mister Prime Minister. We could still take the other three our ops plan calls for, but not and have anything left at the end.

"As for Fourth Fleet"—he shrugged—"I can only endorse your own estimate. Trevayne's ships are unique. Now that I've examined Vice Admiral Desai's report, I am even more convinced that they represent a qualitative breakthrough of the first magnitude. Trevayne and Admiral Desai managed to destroy almost fifty percent of the force engaged against them, but the rebel admiral knew the sort of action she had to fight. Trevayne's force lost at least as much as she did. As nearly as we can estimate, almost twelve million tonnes of shipping were destroyed—not damaged, *destroyed*. We don't know about the rebels, but Fourth Fleet lost over forty-one thousand dead. I think that's an effective answer as to whether it can carry out its part of the plan. Without the Rim to meet us more than halfway—" He shrugged again.

"I see." Dieter turned to Susan Krupskaya. "Admiral Krupskaya, what are the odds of the Republic recognizing the futility of further operations on our part?"

"Excellent, sir," she said after a very brief glance at Sanders. "Analysis of our losses must tell them Operation Yellowbrick bled us white. They've been hurt, too—badly—but not as badly as we have."

"I see," Dieter repeated. "And how quickly can they duplicate Admiral Trevayne's weapons without actual samples?"

"It's hard to be precise, sir, but my analysts estimate eight months, maximum, before they have working models." Someone gasped, but Krupskaya plowed on. "We've been looking at the data Mister Sanders brought back, and they're very, very close to the variable focus beams, judging from their new primary. With that head start and the data they must have recorded during the Zapata engagement, they can have that weapon in three to five months. The HBM should take considerably longer—we've no evidence that they've begun experimenting with grav drivers—but their new shields offset that. And we," she smiled thinly, "have no way of obtaining hard data on *their* new systems, since they've carefully used them only against the Rim. It will take us much longer to duplicate them. And, Mister Prime Minister—" she paused and drew a breath "—it is my duty to point out that, judging from their order of battle at Zapata, our previous estimates of their construction rates may be as much as fifteen percent low, so even our numerical advantage is in question."

"Thank you, Admiral," Dieter said gravely, and looked back at his shaken colleagues. "Ladies and gentlemen, I already knew what Sky Marshal Witcinski and Admiral Krupskaya were going to say, and I had them plug that data into our computers. According to the new projections, we stand a sixty-five percent chance of losing the war within one year." The room was deathly silent. "If we hold out for another year, we have a seventy percent chance of final victory—but the computers project a war which will continue for another twelve to fifteen years. With losses," he finished quietly, "which will make the Battle of Zapata look like a children's picnic."

The political leaders stared at him in shock. The military leaders weren't surprised, but their expressions were those of people who'd just bitten into something spoiled. No one questioned his statements.

"I think, my friends," he said very, very softly, looking straight at Amanda Sydon and her "war party" adherents, "that under those circumstances, we cannot justify continuing this war if there is the least possibility of any other acceptable resolution. Even victory can cost too much at times."

Sydon glanced at her supporters, but they refused to meet her eyes. The glare she turned on Dieter was fulminating, yet she said nothing. There was nothing she *could* say, and the voice of protest came from another source.

"But, Mister Prime Minister!" Witcinski protested. "Victory *is* the only 'acceptable resolution!' Yellowbrick should have succeeded—*would* have succeeded if the rebels hadn't figured out what was coming and managed to ambush Admiral Trevayne. I'm not faulting him, sir—it was a brilliant ploy, obviously something they spent months arranging. But now that they've stopped us, they'll exploit. No strategist worth his salt would stop now!"

"Indeed, Sky Marshal? What do you think they'll do, then?"

"They'll leave their forces in the Zapata System exactly as they are," Witcinski predicted. "As far as we can tell, they committed less than ten percent of their assault carriers there—the others are still available for offensive strikes, backed up by their surviving Frontier Fleet fleet and light carriers, while we cut our defenses to the bone for Yellowbrick. They can achieve crushing local superiority wherever they choose, and they know it. They'll go on the offensive and chew us up, hoping for a knockout."

"That would certainly be their most logical course," Dieter said softly, "but they're not going to do it."

"Why not?" Witcinski demanded hotly, feeling his professional judgment called in question.

"I think because they don't want to destroy the Federation," Dieter said slowly.

"No?" Amanda Sydon laughed harshly. "They only went to war against it!"

"Agreed—but I think they just wish to be left alone," Dieter replied. Sydon stiffened angrily, and some of the others joined her, but he raised a hand and his voice was stern with hard-earned authority. "No, hear me out—all of you! From the beginning, the Fringers have been reacting to what they considered an intolerable situation. They reacted militarily because all political avenues seemed closed. They—" He shook his head firmly. "Enough. The point is that they never sought to conquer the Innerworlds. Arguably, they lacked the ability to do so, but it would seem that is no longer true—they have the ability to conquer us if they act promptly. The Sky Marshal's arguments are most cogent, but to succeed, they must act at once. Surely none of us is so foolish as to believe that their strategists are less competent than our own? They *must* know that their advantage is fleeting—that they must act before we make good our losses. Yet they are not going to do so.

"Ladies and gentlemen, I have received a communication from Ladislaus Skjorning." The atmosphere in the conference room was so brittle it could have been chipped with a knife. "He offers"—his eyes bored into Sydon's—"an immediate armistice for the purpose of concluding a general peace." Some of the people at the table looked as if he'd just punched them; others suddenly sat straighter, their eyes bright with hope. He didn't try to estimate the numbers which felt either way. "His message is accompanied by an analysis almost identical to that we have just heard. But in pursuit of his armistice, he has ordered a two-month unilateral suspension of all offensive operations, pending our reply. In short, my friends, he has voluntarily given up his best chance for outright victory to prove he desires peace!"

Ladislaus Skjorning sat in the first-class lounge of TRS *Prometheus* and watched the blue and white planet grow. It had been six years since last he saw that world, and the sight stirred something within him.

It had been hard to induce the Republic to send most of its executive branch into Federation space aboard an unarmed passenger liner, but he'd done it. His cabinet had been relatively easy to convince, but not Congress. Only the fact that the Federation had voluntarily offered a quarter of Battle Fleet as hostages for the safe conduct of their guests had outweighed congressional memories of Fionna's assassination.

Now *Prometheus* slipped into orbit around the motherworld, and Ladislaus hid a grin. One of the more ticklish decisions during the past several months had been choosing the site of the conference. But then he'd remembered that one spot on Old Terra herself was neutral; the tiny country of Switzerland, which had maintained its traditional independence for eleven centuries.

Some of the Federation representatives seemed to regard his suggestion as a subtle compliment, but others—like Dieter—recognized the second half of the message. It was possible to be good Terrans without belonging to the Federation.

A muted bell chimed, and Ladislaus rose, offering his arm to Tatiana Illyushina. The shuttle was waiting to carry them to the city of Geneva for the meeting which might end the dying.

A crowd waited beyond the hatch. Ladislaus stared out, feeling Tatiana craning her neck beside him, and smiled despite his tension. She'd never before been off Novaya Rodina with its vast, endless plains, and the mountainous horizon must seem as strange to her as would his own Beaufort. He knew they were under close scrutiny as his vice president gawked at the peaks, and he hoped wistfully that some might mistake her youthful fascination for callow inexperience. He doubted they'd be so stupid, but . . .

A band struck up, but the music was neither the Republic's *Ad Astra* nor the Federation's *Suns of Splendor.* It took a moment of frowning effort to place it, then he smiled and nodded. It was indeed ancient, he thought, but the venerable *Battle Hymn of the Republic* was a fitting selection for both sides.

He recognized Oskar Dieter and David Haley among the waiting officials. The big, solid-looking fellow in all the braid must be Sky Marshal Witcinski, and the fox-faced man beside him looked suspicously like the briefing holos of Kevin Sanders.

Ladislaus squeezed Tatiana's elbow.

"Tatiana, my love, I'm thinking it's best you deal with yon Sky Marshal and leave the sharp-faced fellow to me."

"Yes, Lad," she agreed demurely, "and I promise not to sign away our claim to Novaya Rodina, either."

"Lass, I'm only worried about your inexperience," Ladislaus teased.

The Federation dignitaries halted at the foot of the pad, and Ladislaus started down through an honor guard of the Republic's Marines. He rather wished he'd brought Li Han or Magda Petrovna for the military discussions. Fleet Admiral Holbein was a good man, but he lacked their quick wits. Yet there could be no question of recalling either of them from Zapata until these discussions were concluded. He sighed and stepped off the last step.

"Mister Skjorning." Dieter bowed, carefully observing

the agreed upon protocols and avoiding official titles. "Welcome to Old Terra."

"Thank you, Mister Dieter." Ladislaus gripped the prime minister's hand firmly and looked into the slender New Zuricher's face. "I'm glad to see you again, sir, and only sorry that it must be under such circumstances. I've said some hard things of you in the past. I would like to retract them now."

"Thank you." Dieter looked away for a moment. "That means a great deal to me in a very personal sense." He looked as if he meant to say more, then shook his head. "Allow me to introduce you to my colleagues, sir."

"It would be an honor," Ladislaus agreed, and the long round of introductions and reintroductions began. He watched their faces carefully as they shook hands or bowed to one another, comparing their responses to those predicted in his painstaking briefings. By the time he reached the end of the line, he knew the intelligence people had been right; Dieter's colleagues were almost evenly divided on the question of peace or war.

It remained to be seen whether he could bring them to decide for peace.

". . . quite impossible." Foreign Minister Roger Hadad shook his head firmly. "Even if we were prepared to stipulate that any planet which seceded—*attempted* to secede, rather—" he corrected hastily, remembering that the Federation had steadfastly denied the legality of secession "—is *prima facie* a member of your Terran Republic, we cannot possibly concede that any world taken from the Federation by force of arms is a 'natural' member of your confederation. The simple fact that a planet was considered a 'Fringe World' before the rebelli—before the war, that is, is insufficient reason for us to resign all claim and abandon its citizens."

"Mister Hadad," Ladislaus rumbled semi-patiently, "that may be true. At the same time, it's to be plain there's no cause to be saying a world *isn't* a natural part of the Republic simply because it dared not secede because it was having a garrison dispatched to stop it." He fixed the dapper minister with a gimlet eye. "I'm not to have been getting off the produce shuttle yesterday, Mister Hadad.

I'll not be accepting any argument which sets the ground for denying the legitimacy of *any* secession."

"But we can't simply tell the citizens of a system like Cimmaron that we've abandoned them!" Hadad protested sharply.

"Cimmaron's folk," Ladislaus said implacably, "welcomed us with open arms, sir. In point of fact, they'll have the pitching of three kinds of fits if we offer to be handing them back to you."

"But—"

"Mister Dieter," Ladislaus turned to the prime minister, "this point must be settled. We'll not insist that anyone leave the Federation for the Republic—but it's to be plain we must insist that the Republic is a legitimate government. And if we're to be a government, we're after having the same responsibility to *our* citizens as the Federation to its."

"I agree, Mister Skjorning." Dieter nodded, and Ladislaus could have sworn he saw a half-wink from the eye away from Hadad. "Roger, we must accept that the Terran Republic exists, whether we like it or not. It follows that its Congress has a responsibility to its citizens. Now, we've already accepted in principle that the worlds which seceded are part of the Republic. The question is what to do with those which were added to the originally seceding worlds by force of arms, correct?"

"Well, yes," Hadad said in a tone of barely suppressed anguish. "But it's not that simple. There are matters of precedent, of—"

"There *are* no precedents," Dieter said, and Hadad stared at him as if he'd tried to sell him a skimmer of questionable pedigree. "Under Federation law as presently interpreted, secession is treason, but we're plainly contemplating turning a *de facto* situation into a *de jure* one. Mister Skjorning," he turned to Ladislaus, "I would suggest plebiscites for all non-seceding planets forcibly occupied by the Republic. Any which wish to remain with the Republic, however they came to be included therein, will be free to do so, but any planet which wishes to return to the Federation must be free to do that, as well. You will appreciate, I trust, that we are not in a position to reciprocate on every planet currently occupied by Federation forces? With, of course, the exception of systems captured during the recent offensive?"

"I do, Mister Dieter," Ladislaus agreed gravely, not mentioning that aside from the systems Trevayne had taken, the Federation did not control any world which had shown an interest in joining the Republic.

"Thank you, sir. Roger?" Dieter leaned back in his chair beside Sanders, returning the session to Hadad's control. The foreign minister didn't seem particularly grateful, but strove to conceal his disgruntlement.

"Very well, Mister Skjorning," he said, scribbling on an old-fashinoned pad. "We'll agree—tentatively, of course—to a plebiscite to determine the fates of the planets captured by the Republic. But that brings up another rather delicate point. You see—"

"You're to be worrying over access between the Rump and the Rim—excuse me, between the Innerworlds and the Rim Systems—across Republican space," Ladislaus said genially, and Hadad nodded. "Well, Mister Hadad, we're prepared to be offering free passage to unarmed vessels, with armed merchant vessels to be passing under bond and with our right of examination. Mail packets and courier drones will be having freedom of passage without censorship or examination. Warships are to be another matter, but we're to be being reasonable so long as you're to be consulting us beforehand. I'm hoping that's to be satisfactory?"

"Er . . . yes," Hadad nodded. In fact, it was rather more than he'd been prepared to settle for, and he felt a sudden, unexpected liking for the big Fringer before him. He smiled.

"Well, Mister Skjorning, I must say you're being reasonable." He seemed to regret the admission as soon as he made it and set his face more sternly. "But there remains the matter of repatriation and property losses."

"Yes and no, Mister Hadad," Ladislaus said, and turned to Tatiana, who looked for all the world like an adolescent observer as she sat next to him. She nodded and opened a memo touchpad, bringing the small screen alive.

"Mister Hadad," she began crisply, "you must be aware that there will be considerable dispute over how much is owed or, indeed, whether *anything* is owed, to compensate private citizens for wartime property losses."

Hadad glanced at Dieter, who returned his look expressionlessly, and then back to Tatiana.

"That goes without saying, Ms. Illyushina. However, we must insist that some clear understanding be reached."

"Naturally. We propose a joint offer of repatriation for any who desire it, this offer to include relocation of families and personal property only. The Republic is prepared to guarantee equitable liquidation of investments and real estate if the Federation will do likewise. Repatriation and relocation costs will be shared evenly by the two governments. Is that acceptable?"

"It will certainly do for a first presentation to the Assembly, ma'am. However, there remain the matters of sequestered property and war losses."

"War losses," Tatiana retorted, "are just that: war losses. If not covered by insurance, the injured party will, unfortunately, be unable to recover. On sequestered property—" she allowed herself a sharklike grin that turned Hadad's blood suddenly cold "—the Republic is willing to be reasonable. We are prepared to stipulate that the respective governments shall compensate their own nationals for their losses."

She leaned back cheerfully as a strangled sound came from Dieter's Minister of Finance, and Ladislaus hid a smile as Hadad's face fell, though it was difficult when he saw the toothy grin Sanders directed at Tatiana.

"B-b-b-but you've seized property worth well over two trillion credits!" Amanda Sydon half-screamed. "The property sequestered by the Federation amounts to less than three percent of that figure!"

"In fact," Tatiana agreed sweetly, "the value of property seized by the Federation is approximately sixty-seven billion credits, while that expropriated by the Republic had a pre-war tax value—" Dieter winced; given the sleight-of-hand Corporate World accountants had routinely perpetrated against Fringe World tax assessors, the tax value could be multiplied by at least two "—of two trillion three hundred and seventy-two billion. The Republic, however, stated at its Constitutional Convention that no Federation citizen's property would be expropriated *unless* our nationals' property was seized." She shrugged pleasantly. "Since the Assembly was in possession of that declaration before passing the Sydon-Waldeck Expropriation Act, we can only assume that the Federation wished to embark on a policy of mutual expropriation. Therefore—"

Ladislaus and Sanders leaned back and smiled at one another as Tatiana and Sydon went after each other hammer and tongs, and Dieter sighed. Amanda was outmatched, he thought, watching Tatiana's cheerful face. Odd how capable the distaff half of the Fringe had proven . . . and how fitting for that capability to cost the Corporate Worlds a bundle.

"Well, Lad," Tatiana sighed and leaned back in her lounger, "I think we've done it." She chuckled. "The Corporate Worlds shrieked like a gelded *megaovis* over the economic clauses—they think its immoral to end a war without showing a profit—but they can't carry a majority on them. Dieter's really cut them down to size since the war began."

"Aye." Ladislaus nodded slowly from his own recliner. "It's a mortal long voyage we've had, but it's to seem we've reached port at last."

"Yes." Tatiana rose on an elbow. "Will you go to the vote?"

"No, lass. I swore to myself I'd never stand in that chamber again, and no more will I be doing it. You go; I'll have the watching of it on HV."

"But you're our president! If you don't go, none of us should."

"Tatiana," Ladislaus never opened his eyes, "it's an impertinent young thing you're after being. It's no matter of policy but a personal thing—one I can't have the changing of even for Oskar Dieter, who's to be deserving better of us. Go, lass."

His obvious exhaustion silenced her, and she studied his face, seeing the lines worn there by the past six years, the almost invisible gray creeping into his blond beard and hair. She felt a sudden tenderness for the huge man who'd carried the personal burden of the Fringe World's fight for so long.

"All right, Lad," she said after a moment. "But I wish—" She broke off. "Lad?"

He didn't respond. His massive chest rose and fell slowly, and Tatiana smiled gently as she rose and left silently.

They had matured, David Haley thought, looking out over the quietly restive Chamber of Worlds with almost paternal pride. The delegates who'd stampeded this way and that in the early days of the crisis they'd created had won their adulthood the hard way, but they'd won it. Now they sat almost silently, waiting as the computers tabulated the vote.

The peace terms represented major concessions on almost every point, he reflected. The Republic had been careful not to humble the Federation's pride, except, perhaps—his lips quirked—on that matter of expropriations, but it had been firm, as well. The Fringers had come through fire and worse to reach this moment. They were no longer suppliants, and they would not retreat a centimeter. It only remained to see if the Assembly had been sufficiently tempered to recognize the essential fairness of the settlement before it.

A light flashed on his panel, and a small screen lit with the results of the vote. He studied them briefly, then rapped his ceremonial gavel sharply, and an electric tension filled the chamber.

"Ladies and Gentlemen of the Assembly," Haley said clearly, "it is my duty to announce the result of your vote on the motion to ratify the peace terms presented by the foreign minister." He drew a deep breath. "The vote is 978 in favor; 453 opposed. The motion—" he paused for just an instant, quivering with relief "—is carried."

There was utter silence for a moment, then a soft stir of mounting conversation. There were no cheers, no shouts of victory. Reaching this moment had cost too many too much for that, but the relief was there. Haley felt it in the air about him as he turned to the Vice President of the Republic of Free Terrans and bent over her hand with a gallant flourish.

Only then did the applause begin.

L'ENVOI

Oskar Dieter stretched out on the recliner under the night sky and pondered the vagaries of fate. He, who had never expected to be more than Simon Taliaferro's shadow, was prime minister—of a diminished Federation, perhaps, but one once more at peace—and Simon was gone.

Now he studied the cold stars, trying to find Fionna MacTaggart, but she had left him. Search as he might, she was gone, and it worried him.

A throat cleared itself, and he looked up to see Kevin Sanders.

"Good evening, Mister Sanders."

"Good evening, Mister Prime Minister." Sanders' voice was gently mocking, but his smile was friendly.

"To what do I owe the honor?"

"Curiosity." Sanders' eyes narrowed slightly. "Tell me, Mister Dieter, did you realize I was tapping your conduit to the rebels?"

"Please, Mister Sanders! To the Republic, if you please."

"To be sure. The Republic." Sanders paused. "Did you?"

"Well. . . ." Dieter cocked an eyebrow at his guest, and then, for the first time in Sanders' memory, he laughed out loud. He nodded slowly. "I did. I realized it before I asked you to leave ONI to join my government."

"You did?" Sanders looked briefly crestfallen, but he rallied gamely.

"Of course. Your silence convinced me you were a man of initiative and discretion. I needed you."

"You needed me because your foresaw this outcome from the beginning, didn't you?" Sanders made it a question, but both knew it was a statement.

"More or less."

"I hope you'll pardon my pointing this out, sir," Sanders said dryly, "but that's rather an odd thing for a wartime leader to admit."

"Is it?" Dieter chuckled again, softly. "I suppose so. But if you disagreed, you should have said so at the time, shouldn't you?"

"Agreed. Still, I wish you'd satisfy my curiosity in one more regard. As a return favor, as it were."

"Of course, if I can."

"Why?" Sanders asked, his humor suddenly gone.

"Because someone had to do it," Dieter said slowly, "and I owed a debt."

"To Fionna MacTaggart?" Sanders' voice was soft.

"You are indeed a perceptive man, Mister Sanders," Dieter said quietly. "Yes, to Fionna. To all those people trapped in a war they didn't want but didn't know how to end, but especially to Fionna. I wonder if she approves?"

"Mister Dieter," Sanders looked down at the reclining prime minister, and a smile played around the corners of his mouth, "I'm sure she does. Fionna MacTaggart was a remarkable woman: understanding, intelligent, insightful . . . but that's not the reason I'm sure she approves."

"No, Mister Sanders? Then what is?"

"She also," Sanders said simply, "had a very lively sense of humor."

"Well, Lad," Tatiana raised her glass to Ladislaus as *Prometheus*' drives hurled the liner outward, "God knows how, but you did it. Even when I thought we'd never make it, you always hung on and kicked us in the backside till we made it work."

She shook her head wryly, and Ladislaus smiled at her gently, leaning back in his chair and savoring the sensation of completion. It was not an unalloyed pleasure, but it was a vast relief.

"They're throwing a party in the Captain's Ballroom, Lad," Tatiana said winningly. "Sort of a rehearsal for the victory ball. Why don't you come?"

"No, lass." Ladislaus shook his head. "It's tired I am. I'll be staying here, I'm thinking. Here with my thoughts."

"All right, Lad." She accepted defeat and pecked him lightly on the cheek. "Get some rest—you've earned it." She started for the door then paused, looking back. "Fionna would have been very proud of you, Lad," she said softly, then started to say something more, only to cut herself off with a tiny headshake. The door sighed shut behind her.

Ladislaus waved his hand above the lighting control, dimming the cabin to comfortable twilight, and pulled a battered tri-di from his pocket. The flat representation was less perfect than a holo cube, but there was no mistaking the very young red-haired woman who stood laughing on the deck of a sloop with an equally young Ladislaus. He studied the print for long, silent moments, his smile bittersweet, then shook his head.

"Aye, Tatiana, I did it," he whispered, and lifted the tri-di until the faint light fell on Fionna's smiling face. "I'm sorry, love," he said softly, and a single tear trickled down his bearded cheek. "I know it wasn't what you wanted—but it was all that I could do."

Magda Petrovna adjusted a lustily crying infant on her hip and poured more vodka. Jason sat beside her, beaming at their guest with a smile Magda knew was far more inebriated than he was as the tiny, immaculately-uniformed woman raised the glass in shaky fingers and studied it owlishly.

"I," Fleet Admiral Li Han, Second Space Lord of the Terran Republic's Admiralty, said with great precision, "am drunk. I have never been drunk before."

"I know." Magda watched her drain the glass. As soon as Han set it down, she filled it again.

"I think you planned for me to get drunk," Han said plaintively.

"Hush, Han." Magda said. "Why would I do a thing like that?"

"Because," Han said carefully, "you think it's a good idea." She hiccuped solemnly. "You think I've been holding things inside too long, don't you—" she paused and gripped the edge of the table, eyes widening as her chair moved beneath her "—my round-eyed friend?"

"Maybe, Han."

"Well, it happens," Han said very slowly, "that you're quite perceptive for a round-eye." Her expression remained relaxed, but a large tear welled in each eye, sparkling on her lashes. "Have been holding it in," she went on vaguely. "Been holding it in ever since Cimmaron, I think." She blinked at her friends through her tears, and her face began to crumple at last.

She drew a deep breath. "All those people—dead. But not me. Funny, isn't it?" She laughed, an ugly sound, and pressed her face into her hands. "They're all dead, but *I'm* alive. Me, the silly bitch who got them all killed. All . . . those . . . people . . ." her voice broke in a sob of pain. "Chang. Chung-hui. All of them . . . because I couldn't do my job . . ."

"Han, Han!" Magda hurried around the table and put her free arm around the slim shoulders, cradling the weeping woman against her. "That's not true! You know it isn't!"

"It *is!*" Han wailed, her voice desolate as the deeps between the stars.

"It isn't," Magda repeated gently, "but you had to say it. You had to let it out and face it so you can go on with your life. Remember them, Han, but don't let the past keep you from reaching out to the future."

"What future?" Han demanded bitterly. "There isn't any future!"

"Of course there is!" Magda laughed softly and pushed her daughter into her friend's arms. Han's grip tightened instinctively, and she blinked down into the small face. Dark eyes stared back up at her, and she smiled tremulously. "You see, Han?" Magda asked gently. "There's always a future, isn't there?"

"Yes," Han whispered, hugging her goddaughter tightly. "Yes, there is, Magda. There really is!"

"I'm glad you agree," Jason said dryly, sitting on the other side and hugging her roughly. "And since you do," he went on in the voice of one bestowing a great gift, "this time *you* can change her!"

"I could make faster progress with this prosthetic leg," Joaquin Sandoval told his three visitors, "if the damned doctors would only let me! I'm strong enough by now to spend more time on my feet. . . . Yes, *feet*, plural!"

"Don't rush it," Sean Remko growled. For him and Yoshinaka, this was simply one of the calls they'd paid regularly since returning to Xanadu. For Sonja Desai it was something more—a farewell visit to the only three men in the Rim who knew she had a heart. She was returning to the Federation.

"Yes," she'd confirmed, seeing their thunderstruck faces. "The Federation—and this Terran-Orion 'Pan-Sentient Union'—recognizes all the field promotions conferred out here, and they say they want me." Her expression had turned uncharacteristically gentle. She'd actually smiled slightly. "And I've gotten homesick for Nova Terra. Besides—" she'd broken off and waved one hand in a curiously vulnerable little gesture.

Now her eyes met Sandoval's, and he, for once, knew when no words were needed.

The air in the chamber deep below the Prescott City Medical Center was so cold it seemed brittle. A thin film of frost covered the enclosed, coffin-like tank in the center of the room with its attendant machinery.

The door slid open, and Miriam Ortega entered, heavily cloaked against the chill she did not feel. She walked to the tank, and for a long, long time stood motionless and unspeaking, her breath white puffs of condensation in the air. After a moment, the tears no one had been allowed to see began finding their way down her cheeks, very slowly in the cold. But the silent communion was unbroken.

Finally, she extended a slightly trembling right hand and gently touched the cover of the tank with her fingertips. Only then did she draw a shaken breath and speak in a very quiet, steady voice.

"Ian, this morning I gaveled to order the constitutional convention of the Rim Federation. Forgive me."

She withdrew her hand slowly, leaving five streaks in the rime. Tiny drops trickled slowly down them, glittering like tears in the cold, still air. After a moment, she took another deep breath, squared her shoulders, turned, and left the chamber.

By the time the door closed, silently condensing moisture had already begun to cover the tiny streaks.